Alison Joseph was born in North London and educated at Leeds University. After graduating, she worked as a presenter on a local radio station in West Yorkshire then, moving back to London, for Channel Four. She later became a partner in an independent production company and one of its commissions was a series about women and religion. She has since also worked as a reader and abridger for BBC Radio Drama. Alison, who has three children, now lives in London.

THE NIGHT WATCH

As a nun who has not yet committed to her final vows, Sister Agnes Bourdillon feels ill-qualified to oversee two novices. Meanwhile, through her close friend, Father Julius, Agnes has met three brothers, Patrick, Matthias and Tad. When Matthias is killed while out riding, it looks like an accident — but another rider had survived a similar incident only days before. Slowly, Agnes pieces together connections between the victims and local landowners. Another death is enough to convince her that a murderer is at work, and she finds that faith is no shield against plain, cold fear.

ALISON JOSEPH

THE NIGHT WATCH

Complete and Unabridged

ULVERSCROFT
Leicester

First published in Great Britain in 2000 by
Headline Book Publishing
London

First Large Print Edition
published 2001
by arrangement with
Headline Book Publishing
a division of
Hodder Headline Group
London

British Library CIP Data

Joseph, Alison
    The night watch.—Large print ed.—
    Ulverscroft large print series: mystery
    1. Agnes, Sister (Fictitious character)—Fiction
    2. Nuns—Fiction 3. Detective and mystery stories
    4. Large type books
    I. Title
    823.9'14 [F]

    ISBN 0–7089–4404–3

Published by
F. A. Thorpe (Publishing)
Anstey, Leicestershire

Set by Words & Graphics Ltd.
Anstey, Leicestershire
Printed and bound in Great Britain by
T. J. International Ltd., Padstow, Cornwall

This book is printed on acid-free paper

For Helen, Kate, Christine and Marybeth

For Helen, Kate, Christine and Matthew

Nought is more wretched in the human
  race
Than country's want, and shift from place
  to place.

Odyssey, Homer
(tr. George Chapman)

Acknowledgements

I would like to thank Gilda and John O'Neill, Diana Boon, Fr Patrick Purnell SJ, Simon Singh, Ian Willis, the Fitzwilliam (Milton) Hunt, and David Fowler and all at the Mathematics Institute at the University of Warwick. Also, grateful thanks to Nicola Bracey for the riding accident.

1

Again the corridor, sun-washed, the light filtering through billowing white curtains. Again she was walking down the corridor, barefoot, and the old wooden floors were drifting with sand, clean white sand. And a loud ticking noise, as if from a clock, tick, tock, her feet, right, left, her toes buried in warm sand. At the end of the corridor there was a door, in shadow, but something was preventing her reaching it, something apart from the clock ticking, something louder, shriller . . .

It was the phone, she realised, waking, opening her eyes, as the billowing sunlight receded and she was in London, in her room once more, in the dull grey light of a winter dawn. She reached out her hand.

'Agnes?'

'Julius.'

'Did I wake you?'

'Um . . . '

'It's nearly eight.'

'Is it?' Agnes sat up. 'I've got a meeting in an hour.'

'Anyone interesting?'

1

'Helen. One of our novices.'

'You of all people to be a novice mistress. Your order obviously feel you need a real challenge this time.'

'It's not funny. And anyway I'm not.' She pulled the covers around her against the chill of her room. 'I'm just supervising the two London ones, that's all.'

'I suppose it's not a bad move. Any novice joining your order will take one look at you and think, Well, if she can stick it then anyone can.'

'Thanks very much. I'll try that when I talk to Helen this morning. Now, did you want anything, or is this just my early morning call?'

'I was inviting you for a drink.'

'Oh. Um, thank you.'

'If your grief-stricken state allows.'

'I'm sure I can manage a mineral water.'

'I'm meeting an old friend.'

'Any friend of yours, Julius . . . '

'Patrick Kavanagh. I thought it was time you two met at last, as you're my oldest friends.'

'I'd be delighted.'

'One o'clock? The pub on the corner, the Rising Sun?'

'Fine.'

'See you then.'

2

He'd gone. She got out of bed, yawned and pulled on some clothes. Silly old Father Julius, she thought. Even though he's my best friend, apart from Athena, or at least my oldest friend, he never takes me seriously.

Perhaps that's what it is to be a friend.

Patrick Kavanagh. The name circled in her mind. Julius has known him even longer than he's known me, from the seminary, in Ireland. When Julius was young, she thought. When he was still living in his homeland, before he left Ireland for ever.

She wandered into the kitchen and put on the kettle. She thought about Julius, about how settled he seemed in London, even though his roots were elsewhere. She wondered whether he ever wanted to go back. He's never expressed any desire to return, she thought. But then, he's so accepting of how things are. So content to be wherever he finds himself. Even though he's an exile, like me. Perhaps that's what that dream's about, that dream I had again last night. Perhaps it's about exile.

She recognised the corridor. It was in her parents' house in Provence. The house where she'd spent so many solitary hours, riding her pony, exploring the overgrown gardens, the straggling orchards, in a childhood of affluence mixed with neglect.

She remembered how they felt, those high ceilings, when you were the only person in the room. The sense of space. Of freedom. Of no one knowing where you were. And no one cared, either. She remembered her mother's tendency to retreat into illness, which had worsened after her father left. And her father had long since died.

She came back into her room. She glanced at the mantelpiece, on which she'd put her mother's clock. It was an anniversary clock, with a spinning mechanism at its base, four brass spheres which circled to and fro, counting time. Perhaps that was the clock ticking in the dream. But why the sand at her feet? And the doorway at the end of the corridor?

She found herself counting through the days. A month since her mother's burial. A month today. It's no time at all, she thought.

She recalled the cemetery, where the few straggling mourners had gathered to lay her mother to rest: the curé; the faithful retainers who'd nursed her; some of the elderly women from the village who always turned out for a good funeral. It had been winter, January, a misty day, and the thin sun had freckled the banks of gentle green and the ancient gravestones. Then there'd been the fresh earth, the gaping grave. My mother, Agnes had thought, watching the coffin being lowered into the earth, with a cold feeling, like terror. Like being cast adrift.

And yet, Agnes mused, going out twenty minutes later into the cold morning in search of a bus, it was a resolution. My mother had been receding from me for months. Years, in fact.

She waited for the lights to change on the main road. She could see the spire of Julius's church through the endless scaffolding which had once been the old buildings around Borough Market and which was now promising a brave new world of glass and steel. She suppressed an urge to turn round, to walk quietly into the church and light a candle, yet another candle, for her mother's soul. But the bus pulled up at the bus stop across the road and she only just caught it.

* * *

Agnes sat on one of the sofas in the silence of the lounge of the order's main house in Hackney. The clock on the mantelpiece ticked loudly. She picked up a magazine, glanced at it, put it down again. How times have changed, she thought, looking around at the comfortable cream sofas, the pale green carpet, the heavy curtains in the bay window.

5

She recalled her novice days in her first order; how it felt to be dressed in black from top to toe. The memory was so vivid she found she'd straightened her shoulders, as if to balance the weight of the heavy fabric. She glanced down at her jeans, her old camel cashmere sweater that still looked somehow French and chic after all these years. Her hand went to her head, as if she expected to feel her veil fastened there; she ran her fingers through her short, dark hair.

She remembered dark oak panelling, tiny windows obscuring the day; sitting in full habit on a hard chair, waiting with two other young nuns for the arrival of Sister Mary-David, who'd swept into the room, tall and severe, and proceeded to lecture them for an hour on what was expected of them in their new life. Namely: obedience and humility; guarding against the false demands of the old self; living entirely in the service of the Lord. She'd spoken in a voice that jarred against the unyielding surfaces of the room, and Agnes had felt that her very essence, everything she'd ever been, was being sentenced to death.

She heard footsteps outside, and breathed again. The door opened in a flurry of young woman, chin-length black hair and flowing pale skirts.

'Sorry I'm late.' She sat down opposite Agnes, shy but poised.

'I overslept too,' Agnes said.

'I was working late last night. At the hostel. Busy night.'

'Are you still enjoying it?'

Helen nodded. 'Very much. I'm beginning to get the hang of it. I find myself thinking, This is what I want to do. This is what it was all about, to end up working in a place like this.'

'I'm glad.' Agnes, watching her, wondered why her face seemed shadowed by doubt.

'It's just . . . ' Helen hesitated. 'That's what worries me. I like it for me. Not for God.' Agnes waited. After a moment, Helen went on, 'It's very me, that kind of work. The hostel's great, I've always wanted to work with homeless kids, runaways . . . But I don't — I don't feel . . . ' she tailed off, troubled. 'Louise said the other night — we were talking about our noviciate — she said that these days she really feels as if she's being called. She said she felt the presence of God in her life. And it made me realise that I don't. I just like what I do.'

'Isn't that a good enough starting point?'

Helen looked up at her. 'That's what Father Julius said.'

'Julius is always right.'

Helen smiled.

'When did you see him?' Agnes asked.

'He called in to the hostel last night.'

'Dear Julius.'

'You're — you're old friends?' Helen watched closely.

'Yes. We met in France. When I still lived there. He was a curate there. A long time ago.'

The clock's ticking filled the silence.

'I gather . . . he met you when you were married.' Helen shifted on her seat.

Agnes smiled. 'Did he tell you that?'

Helen blushed. 'No. I asked . . . um, one of the sisters . . . '

'They love gossiping about me. Yes, I married in France, when I was in my teens. My mother was French, you see. My father was English. They found me a suitably rich man to marry, but it turned out they'd sold me into slavery. He was very violent, and Julius rescued me.'

Helen's mouth was open. She closed it. 'My life's been very simple,' she said.

'It's a better start than mine,' Agnes said.

'But your life . . . Such suffering — it must make you really committed to the order.' She stood up.

Agnes stared at her.

'I'd better go,' Helen said.

8

Agnes stood up too. 'I'm afraid I've not been much help.'

Helen shook her head. 'I'm the only one who can settle this one, aren't I?'

Agnes opened the door for her. 'They've lessened my workload, because of what they call my 'new responsibilities'. I suppose they mean you and Louise.' She laughed. 'I used to work full-time at the hostel, in fact, I helped set it up, with Julius. But now I'm part-time there. In fact, I'm there on Sunday, Medeleine's asked me to cover a shift.'

'Oh. Good. There's a very odd person there at the moment; he arrived last night.'

'What's odd about him?'

'He won't speak. Won't even say his name.'

'Where did he come from?'

'He was found at the airport, last week sometime, wandering on the tarmac. He was arrested for illegal entry, but then they found he was ill, so he was in hospital for a few days. He has no papers, no name, no voice.'

'How old is he?'

'I've no idea. He's got a very old face, but he's small. Thin. They brought him to us because they don't know what else to do with him, but the police said he wouldn't be able to stay. He counts as an illegal immigrant; they'll have to send him back.'

'Back where?'

'That's the problem. No one knows. He had hypothermia; they think he stowed away in a plane from somewhere.'

'A refugee?'

'I think so. But he hasn't uttered a word, not a sound. Doesn't smile. Hardly looks at you.' She gathered her cardigan around her. 'I'd better go. See you soon.'

She went out into the large hallway and up the stairs to her room. Agnes watched her poise, her grace, and remembered her own cowed novice years, as if the habit itself had weighed her down.

Do I envy her? she wondered, going to find her coat. There was a letter for her on the noticeboard and she retrieved it, glancing at the French postmark on the official-looking envelope. She put it in her pocket.

I ran away, she thought. I ran away from France, from my violent marriage, rescued by Julius. I became a nun that way. By default. It wasn't a free decision. Not like Helen's or Louise's.

But it has to become one sometime.

The thought rested in her mind.

She recalled her conversation with Sister Christiane, her provincial director, who'd happened to be in London last week, and who'd 'happened' to coincide at the community house with Agnes, and who'd mentioned,

10

in passing, just very lightly, the issue of Agnes taking her final vows.

' . . . After all, you are in your seventh year with us, and in theory your training is considered near completion, although of course it never is . . . and, of course, you're free to renew your vows for some finite period, two years, perhaps, but we do encourage people to consider their long-term commitment at this point . . . '

Final vows.

Agnes sighed, feeling the letter in her pocket.

And now the solicitors have written from France to tell me the fate of my mother's house. I could open that letter and find that I own an estate in Provence. Or, I could find that there were so many debts that I own nothing at all.

She went to the bus stop. The letter in her raincoat pocket brushed against her leg.

* * *

'So what's wrong with being an heiress, then?' Julius placed a glass of white wine on the table in front of her and sat down with his Guinness.

'I haven't dared open the letter yet.'

'A nice house like that.'

11

'You never saw it. You only knew the house I shared with Hugo.'

'But I can imagine it: olive groves, red tiled roof, green shutters.'

'If I was a proper nun, it wouldn't be a problem. I'd just take my final vows as Christiane suggests, and hand the house over to some charity, or to the order or something, and carry on as I am. Why are you smiling?'

'I was just wondering what a proper nun was.'

'But you know what I mean. If I'd made a proper decision, like Helen, or Louise, then things would be easy. But if I open that letter and find that I have a bolt-hole, then what? You know what I'm like about running away.'

The February sun spilled across their table. The pub was beginning to fill up with lunchtime drinkers, and Julius glanced towards the door. 'Yes, I know,' he said, absently.

'You're not supposed to agree.'

'I know you too well not to.'

They smiled at each other over their drinks.

'So,' Agnes said. 'How has Patrick Kavanagh reappeared in your life after all this time?'

'He phoned me while you were away. Out of the blue. His brother's moved into this area. Tad. You remember, I told you, I think,

12

about his brother? He has learning difficulties; they've finally found an accommodation scheme that suits him. It's a kind of sheltered housing, apparently. And it's only down the road.'

Agnes sipped her wine. She looked at Julius over the top of her glass. She saw his soft white hair, his blue eyes. He must have aged, she thought, over all these years that I've known him. Those lines on his face, they can't have been there when I first met him.

'What are you thinking?' Julius broke into her thoughts.

'I was wondering whether you've changed in the time I've known you, or whether you've always been an old man.'

'Thanks.'

'I meant it as a compliment. I just meant that somehow . . . ' She was aware she was blushing. 'That, in a friendship like ours — we know each other so well . . . '

'We only see our inner selves, you mean?'

'Don't tease.'

'I wasn't.' His hand brushed hers, briefly. 'I . . . ' He hesitated. 'I really wanted you to meet Patrick. You're both . . . you're both very important to me.' He took a sip from his glass. They sat in silence for a moment.

'Did it — did it change your relationship

— I mean when he dropped out of the seminary?'

He frowned, remembering. 'Yes,' he said. 'But there were good reasons. His father died — tragically, in a car crash — during Patrick's training. And Tad took it very badly. He was already someone who found life quite difficult. Their mother spent his childhood fighting to keep him out of institutions. And losing their father like that, when he was still in his teens, made it worse. For quite some time Patrick felt he should be there for the family. Their mother relied on him rather. It wasn't a very happy marriage, I gather . . . ' He shrugged, smiled. 'Patrick studied maths instead. He qualified as soon as he could, to keep the others.'

'And that's what he teaches now?'

Julius nodded. 'At some college. East London somewhere, I think it is.'

'Another exile,' Agnes said.

'Exile?'

'Don't you miss Ireland?'

Julius frowned, thinking. 'I miss — I miss an idea of Ireland,' he said at last. 'My village. My past. But if I went back, you see, it wouldn't be there. Not as I remember it. Not any more.'

'So you're happy here?'

He nodded. 'As happy as anywhere.' He

picked up his glass, then put it down again.

A tall, grey-haired man appeared in the doorway. The sun flashed against the glass of the door as it swung shut behind him. He surveyed the room, then saw Julius, and strode over to them. Julius stood up, and they shook hands warmly.

'Ignatius, how grand.' The man looked towards Agnes and smiled.

'This is Sister Agnes,' Julius said.

Patrick Kavanagh held her gaze. 'So you're Sister Agnes. Can I get you two some drinks?'

'We're all right — ' Julius began.

'Another glass of that?' Patrick indicated Agnes's glass.

'Yes, please.'

They watched Patrick as he waited at the bar, tall against the low ceiling. 'There's no call for that,' Julius said.

'For what?'

'For showing off like that,' Julius said.

'It's only a glass of wine,' Agnes replied.

'It's Lent.'

'So?' She turned to look at him.

Julius shrugged, trying not to smile.

'He's got the same accent as you,' Agnes said. 'That soft Irishness. Maybe slightly more Irish than you,' she added.

'You see?' Julius shook his head. 'Exile. Even my voice has lost its old ways.'

Patrick came back to their table with three glasses. He passed Julius a half-pint of Guinness. Julius took it and drank from it.

'It's Lent, Julius,' Agnes said, and they both began to laugh.

'Is there a joke?' Patrick sat down opposite her.

'Not really. Why does he call you Ignatius?' Agnes looked from one to the other, serious again. The two men looked at the table, like children. Julius sipped his beer.

'It goes back a long way,' Patrick said after a moment. 'We were at college together. With the brothers, weren't we, Ignatius — Julius, I mean.' He laughed.

Julius looked up and smiled at him. 'I think it was something to do with St Ignatius, but I can't remember what.'

'Of course, Ign — Julius was much older than me.'

'I just look younger.' Julius laughed.

'And you didn't become a priest?' Agnes asked.

Patrick shook his head. 'The world, you see. It claimed me as its own — unlike Ignatius here, untouched by worldly vanities . . .'

'Annoying, isn't it?' Agnes sipped her drink.

Patrick smiled at her, then looked at his

watch. 'Is that the time? Matt said he'd be here by now.'

'Matt?' Julius's voice seemed oddly loud, and Agnes looked at him.

'Who's Matt?' she asked.

'My brother,' Patrick said.

'I thought . . . ' she began.

'There are three of them,' Julius said. He seemed suddenly ill at ease, and Agnes wondered why.

'Me, then Tad, then baby Matthias. But we always called him Matt.' He glanced towards the door. A severe dark-haired figure in a long black coat stood in the doorway. He raised his hand, then crossed the room.

'I wasn't sure I'd got the right pub.' He had the same grey eyes as Patrick. He turned to Julius and nodded at him in greeting. 'Ignatius. It's been years.' He offered his hand.

Julius took his hand and shook it, but Agnes sensed his hesitation.

'We haven't got long,' Patrick said.

Matthias looked at his watch. 'No.'

'He gets upset if we're not — '

'Have you seen him much?' Matthias sat down next to Patrick.

'Um — Monday.'

'How was he?'

'Not bad, actually.'

'I saw him last weekend. He came to the stables with me.'

'The horses seem to be helping.'

Matthias smiled for the first time. 'We should have thought of it before. It's like seeing our pa again.'

'How long have you got?'

Matthias looked at his watch. 'An hour. At the most. It's not a good time to be away from the office.'

'It never is.'

'No, but Allen's causing trouble again.'

'So what's new?'

'No, this is worse than usual.' Matthias's expression was tense.

'What do you do?' Agnes asked him.

'Um, insurance.'

'Maths,' Patrick corrected. 'He does sums. And other people pay him huge amounts for them.'

'Actuary,' Matthias mumbled into his beer.

'Rich and brilliant, my little brother. Galling, isn't it? As opposed to me. I do sums and no one takes any interest at all. Except my students, maybe. On a good day. When they decide to turn up.' He turned to Matthias. 'So what's Allen doing now?'

Matthias shook his head. He seemed distracted and uneasy. 'Sometimes I think he's made a pact with the devil, that man.'

18

Patrick laughed. 'The devil looks after his own.' He drained his glass. 'We should go.'

They stood up. As Agnes reached for her coat, Matthias took it and helped her on with it, absently, still preoccupied.

The sun had gone in and the air was chilled. They set off together, leaving the river behind them, skirting the building sites of Borough Market.

' . . . but I'm riding tomorrow,' Agnes heard Matthias say to his brother. 'Can it be next weekend?'

'Sure,' Patrick said. 'Hunting, is it?'

'Of course,' Matthias said.

'We have different attitudes to risk,' Patrick said, turning to Julius as they waited at the traffic lights. 'He rides, I gamble.'

'Still?'

Patrick nodded, and a grey look seemed to cross his face. 'It's OK. It's not as dangerous as hunting, anyway.'

'With my new mare I'm safe as houses. She's a dream, Pat, you should come and meet her. Pa would've adored her.'

'Chestnut?'

Matthias nodded. The lights changed and they crossed the road, where their paths diverged.

'See you again, Ignatius,' Patrick said, his

19

hand on Julius's shoulder. 'Pleasure to meet you, Sister.'

'Hope your brother's settling,' Agnes said.

'So do we,' Matthias said. 'Fervently.'

The two brothers set off along the main road. Agnes took Julius's arm, and they turned back towards the church.

'He'd heard of me.'

'Of course.'

'Why of course?'

'Because. Are you going to open your letter?'

'I'd completely forgotten about it.' They stopped on the street corner, and Agnes took the envelope from her pocket and ripped it open. She unfolded a thick foolscap document and scanned it, the wind flicking at its edges. She sighed, and handed it to Julius. 'Typical of them.'

'Bad news?' Julius glanced at the letter in his hands.

'Emotionally, my parents were hopeless. Utterly hopeless. Financially, they're so bloody brilliant that despite all my father's debts, everything's been paid off and the house is mine. And the garden, and the orchard, and the vineyard. It's typical of them. Ruining my life from beyond the bloody grave . . . ' She blinked back tears, perhaps from the cold wind that buffeted

20

them where they stood.

'Agnes, it doesn't have to ruin your life.'

'I don't need choices, Julius. Not now. I'm fragile enough at the moment, without being tempted to . . . '

'Tempted to what?'

She sighed. 'To belong. Somewhere. To have a home. To put down roots.'

'But isn't that what Sister Christiane means?'

Agnes looked up at him. 'I look at Helen, and Louise, and I envy them. They're not running away from anything, they're running towards something. They're free to embrace the life they've chosen. I never chose, you see. You rescued me, bless you. God knows I'd be dead by now if it wasn't for you. And you found my first order for me — '

'It was the only thing I could think of to do. I knew I had to get you away from that marriage, to somewhere where Hugo couldn't find you. An enclosed order, it was the only thing I could think of.'

'It was OK.'

'It wasn't. You were very unhappy. And a very bad novice.'

'I was in shock.'

'That's what I told them.'

'What made you think I should be a nun?'

Julius hesitated. 'I knew you,' he said.

'You knew me?'

'It was the wrong order, I know. But I could see how strong your faith was. I knew you.'

'You knew I should be a nun?'

He smiled at her. 'It sounds so — '

'Arrogant?'

'Forgive me.'

'And when I changed order, you chose that for me too.'

'You were so unhappy.'

'You've always rescued me, Julius.'

'So this crisis you're having now, it's my fault?' He spoke gently.

She shook her head. 'Of course not. You were right. You did know me. It's just, I never chose. And now with all this talk of final vows, I know that at some point I must.' She tried to smile. 'I should be the novice and Helen should be in charge of me.' She took back the letter from him and put it in her pocket.

'What'll you do?'

'Pray,' she said. 'I suppose.'

'Let me know what he says.'

'He'll tell you first, Julius. You know you're always gossiping with That Lot.'

Julius laughed. 'Come for tea. Tomorrow. Saturday. I'll be at the church.' She nodded. 'See you then.'

Agnes woke up on Saturday morning aware that yet again she'd dreamed of her mother. She sat up, still catching at an image that floated across her mind of her mother's frail body, bathed in candlelight. She remembered her hands, thin and papery, the skin like moths' wings in the amber light.

'Lord, now let your servant depart in peace,' she murmured. She got up and went into the kitchen of her tiny flat. Helen had recently asked her how she managed living on her own. The truth was, Agnes thought, making a pot of tea, that she couldn't manage any other way. Her order was Ignatian, an open order, and some of the other nuns lived alone too, although often just temporarily while their work required it. It occurred to her that no one had ever suggested that she return to live in community in one of the houses. She wondered if this was a sign that the order respected her wishes; or whether it was an oversight, and that one day she'd be asked to give up her flat and take up a single room in one of the order's communal houses. She recoiled at the thought.

A sudden buzz of her doorbell made her jump. 'Sweetie?' It was Athena's voice on the intercom. 'It's me.'

'I hope you've brought breakfast,' Agnes said, opening the door as her friend teetered into the room on high heels.

Athena waved a large sticky paper bag at her.

'Croissants. Those new ones they do at my deli, with almonds and stuff.' Athena threw herself into the armchair. 'God, I'm so glad you were in.'

'Why?'

'A long night, last night. Nic came round.'

'I thought you liked each other. I mean, after all these years of being together . . . ' Agnes looked at her friend, at her thick black hair, her heavy silver earrings. She had a flash of memory, of how Athena had looked just the same when they'd met, all those years ago. 'I'm glad you're my friend,' she said suddenly, then went into the kitchen. 'So what's going on with Nic?'

Athena heard Agnes pouring tea. She sighed heavily. 'It's all such hard work at the moment, that's the problem. It's like someone's died — Oops, sorry, sweetie, I didn't mean, I know, with your mother . . . What I mean is, we're tiptoeing around each other, and Nic's trying to be forgiving and understanding about my bad behaviour last year, but it's obvious he's hopping mad with me, and I don't blame him.'

'Your bad behaviour? As in . . . '

'Yes, sweetie, as in having an affair. And I do love him, really I do, but now he thinks we should go for counselling. Well, I mean, really, sweetie, that would be the last straw.'

'Perhaps he's right.' Agnes came into the room with mugs of tea. She put a croissant each on to two plates.

'Counselling? Me?'

'Well — '

'Honestly, sweetie, it's a ludicrous idea. I've told Nic, I said, I don't want some ghastly Hampstead busybody telling me what I feel, when I know what I feel. It's all my fault, that's what I feel, I did a stupid thing last year by having an affair, and I've wrecked things, and Nic's trying to hold it all together and not get angry — and the point is, he *is* angry. So counselling would just be continuing the pretence.'

'Maybe he suggested counselling so that he'd have a safe place to say what he feels.'

'If Nic and I are going to have a row, a proper, full-blown row, the last thing I want is some ghastly earnest woman in shapeless clothes looking on, going on about sensing our negative feelings and offering us tea.'

'I don't think they do tea.'

'Even worse. I was trying to say to Nic last

night: Why don't you get cross? If it was me I'd have a gin or two, or three — '

'Or six.'

'Or six. And I'd scream and shout and throw things, and say I hate him and I'd never see him again and tell him what a bastard he is . . . and it would burn itself out. And then we'd sit in the smouldering wreckage and kind of . . . start again . . . '

'And what did Nic say?'

'He just went all quiet.'

'Perhaps he doesn't like gin.'

'Whisky, then. Don't laugh, I mean it.' She took a large bite of croissant. 'Oh, I don't know. I just want us to be like we were.' She crossed her legs. 'And I've snagged these tights on the way here, and they're my good ones, cost a bloody fortune. I don't know why I bother. Are you busy later? I thought I'd investigate Knightsbridge today. What's so funny?'

'The word 'investigate'. When you mean 'go shopping'.'

'Of course I mean go shopping. I'm looking for the perfect grey suit, actually I thought I'd found it the other day, but the skirt was all wrong. And one of the department stores is having a cosmetics promotion; if you buy something or other you get all these lovely things free, with a bag too,

26

and it's this fab snakeskin thing in pale green.'

'Athena, you always do those and then you chuck all the stuff away.'

'No I don't.' She helped herself to a second croissant.

'Anyway, I promised I'd have tea with Julius. And before that . . . '

'What?'

'I've got to reply to my French lawyers.'

'About what?'

'It turns out . . . ' Agnes sipped her tea. 'It turns out I've inherited my mother's house. Outright.'

'No debts?'

'None at all. My father, before he died, sewed things up better than we thought.'

'Wow. Lucky old you.'

'But it's not, is it? What am I going to do with it?'

Athena giggled. 'It's typical of you, that is. 'Oh, by the way, I've inherited an absolutely beautiful old house in Provence, with orchards and everything, near the sea, worth a fortune, so I'm going to make sure that I feel as miserable as possible about it.' '

'Seriously, though. I have to give it to the order.'

'What?' Athena was wide-eyed with horror. 'You'll do no such thing. A house like that?

27

They'll turn it into a boarding school or something ghastly, you know what they're like.'

Agnes laughed. 'It would be all right if my mother's death hadn't made me feel . . . I don't know. Sort of — exiled.'

Athena was serious again. 'What do you mean?'

'I don't know. Now I'm orphaned, cut adrift. It's really weird. I've been quite happy being English instead of French, being a Londoner . . . but now she's not there any more, and there's no one left, it's as if I need to grasp hold of something, something I've lost. All the time I've been a nun, there's been this other place, this parallel life, in a way, to do with my mother and that house. And the idea of holding on to it is terribly appealing. The thing is . . . ' She looked up at Athena. 'The thing is, I've always thought, I don't have to be a nun. I could be something else. And now I've been offered this chance of escape. But if I sell the house, or hand it over, then that's it. For ever. There's no parallel life, no other, alternative version of my life . . . No escape.' She sipped her tea, which was cold. 'I look at the novices, and I envy them. I never chose this life, the way they're choosing. And now I could. I could give the house away, burn my

28

boats . . . commit myself. Properly.'

Athena looked down at her snagged tights. 'What a terrible dilemma, sweetie. But — um — if you are thinking of giving the house away . . . '

Agnes laughed. 'You're terrible.'

'I'd look after it, really, sweetie. I'm good with orchards — it's in my blood, you know.'

★   ★   ★

Agnes walked into Julius's office as the church bell chimed four. Julius looked up from his desk, then peered at her more closely. 'You're walking funny,' he said.

'I'm not.'

'At a kind of angle. As if you're trying to hide those shopping bags.'

'What shopping bags?' Agnes sat down in one of the shabby red velvet chairs.

'The ones you've just hidden behind the chair.'

'Oh, those. That Athena . . . '

'What's she talked you into this time?'

'Nothing. You know I have no money.'

'Of course. Every impoverished nun should have an Athena in their lives.' Julius picked up his pen and went back to his paperwork. Agnes watched him, smiling. The leaded window behind him was flecked pink with the last of the day. The anglepoise lamp at his desk caught the edge of his spectacles, so that the frames flashed gold.

She got up and went over to the kettle. 'Patrick's nice.'

'Mmm.'

'Ignatius.'

'That's enough of that.'

'How come he'd heard of me?'

'Everyone's heard of you.'

'Don't be silly, Julius.' She rummaged amongst the tins on the little wooden shelf in search of tea. 'And what is it with you and his brother?'

'Matthias? Nothing.'

'Hmmm.'

Julius looked up. 'Nothing,' he repeated. 'There's no point you going 'hmm' like that.'

'Hmmm.'

Julius smiled and went back to his work. Agnes glanced at him, then turned back to the kettle and made some tea. 'And why do you see Patrick so rarely? When you're such great friends?'

Julius put down his pen. He took off his glasses and polished them. 'He was going to be a priest. Like me. We were very close. And . . . ' He frowned. 'The decision to take the final vows . . . it's very difficult.' He looked at her, unseeing, as if he were focusing on something beyond her. He blinked, and when he next spoke his voice was brisk. 'Anyway, Patrick didn't take the vows. In the end. As you know.'

'So that's it. End of story?'

Julius met her eyes. 'Yes. It was difficult for him to see me after that. We went our separate ways a bit. Tad takes up a lot of his time. He's been in some kind of institution, somewhere outside London. But now he's here, Pat's moved back nearer too. And he got back in touch.'

'And you're glad?' Agnes picked up two mugs of tea and carried one over to him.

Julius smiled again and nodded.

As she sat down again, her foot caught one of her shopping bags, which tipped over. A green snakeskin-look cosmetics bag fell out on to Julius's carpet.

'It was free,' Agnes said quickly.

Julius was about to laugh, but the phone rang, loudly. He picked it up. 'Hello? . . . Oh, hello. What? . . . I'm sorry, I don't . . . ' In the silence of his listening, Agnes watched the colour drain from his face. 'Yes,' he said at last. 'Of course.'

He hung up. 'That was Patrick.' He frowned and picked up the phone receiver again, looking at it as if there was something wrong with it.

'Julius?' Agnes's heart seemed to be beating in her ears.

'He just told me Matthias . . . ' Julius swallowed. 'He went riding today. There was an accident. He's — he's dead.' He was still holding the phone receiver and now, very slowly, he replaced it. Agnes noticed how long his fingers were, how pale they seemed against the black of the telephone.

2

On Sunday after mass, Julius and Agnes left the church in silence. Julius turned to lock the door. A distant shouting broke through the quiet of the morning, and they both looked towards the street. Patrick was at the gate of the church, and now he came up the drive towards them. He was walking unevenly, his coat flapping, his hair dishevelled. Julius held out his arms to him.

'Ignatius,' he mumbled, stooping to Julius's embrace.

'Terrible for you,' Julius said.

'Had to go and identify the body.' Patrick straightened up. His face was tear-stained. 'Awful bloody business. Coroners, inquests . . . Looked peaceful, though.'

'How did — ' Agnes began.

'Head injury. And he fell badly. Bloody chestnut mares. Safe as houses?' He shook his head wearily. 'Anyone fancy a drink?'

Julius led them to a new wine bar which was just opening its doors, and ordered three coffees.

Patrick stared at his cup. 'And the worst is, how am I going to tell Tad?'

'He doesn't know?'

'He's usually around the stables, but he didn't go this week. They don't like him being around the hunt, he feels strongly about these things.'

'Was Matthias hunting?'

Patrick shook his head. 'No. He was going to join them later, apparently. He was off on his own. Said something about his horse needing to sort herself out first. He was riding along the path by the golf course, and they think he was hit by a golf ball. Huge bruise to his head, apart from his fall. Deborah, she runs the stables, she said she's been asking the golf people to put up a fence for months . . . And he wasn't wearing a hat, stupid idiot. Deborah's put a load of new notices around the yard now about hats and safety.' He put his hand to his brow and sighed. 'Bloody funeral to organise, only me and Tad left . . . and poor Karen.' He glanced up at Julius, and Julius looked away. 'They found this on the body. Police let me have it.' He waved a crumpled note at Julius. Julius took it, reluctantly. 'What do you make of it? It's certainly Matt's handwriting.'

Julius glanced at it, then handed it to Agnes. *Please wait for me. I might be later than I thought. I miss you.* She stared at it, remembering the dark-haired man in the

34

expensive coat, the life in his eyes, the tension around his mouth. She looked up at Patrick.

'It won't be for Karen.' Patrick addressed Julius, but Julius studied his coffee, stirring the spoon round and round.

'What will you do?' Julius murmured at last.

'Keep it for now. I don't want to upset Karen.'

'Is Karen — um . . . ' Agnes felt her voice was too loud.

'His wife, yes.' Patrick turned to her. 'They have two boys. Dan and Jake. They're in their teens. Poor Karen . . . ' The reality of it seemed to hit him again, and his eyes welled with tears.

Julius reached out his hand to Patrick. 'I'll do the funeral. If you want. We can bury him at the cemetery; it's not far. If that's what you want. Unless — unless you want to take him back to Ireland.'

Patrick shook his head. 'No point. Not now. Who's there now?' He patted Julius's arm. 'Thanks.' He stood up, clumsily. 'I've got to find Tad. Can't bear it. After Dad's death . . . how's he going to cope?'

They went out into the street. 'Shall we come with you?' Julius asked.

'I'm supposed to be at the hostel,' Agnes said.

Patrick shook his head. 'It's going to be bad enough whatever I do. I think I've just got to face it.' He hugged Julius, nodded at Agnes and left them, his hands stuffed into his pockets as he walked down the street.

Julius was silent. He seemed drained of energy as they wandered back to the church.

'Poor Patrick,' Agnes said.

He nodded.

'And poor Matthias.'

Julius stared at the ground.

'That note — ' Agnes began.

'Don't. Please.'

Agnes glanced at him, surprised. 'I was just going to say — '

'Well, don't.'

Agnes looked at him. She didn't know what to say.

They arrived at his church in silence. 'Have a good hostel shift,' he said.

She leaned towards him and touched his arm. 'Thanks,' she said, but she felt his attention was elsewhere.

★　★　★

Helen led her into the hostel kitchen and made some instant coffee. 'You must meet our stranger,' she said. Agnes was glad of the bright kitchen light, the noise of the residents, the bursts of loud music from the bedrooms overhead.

'How is he?' Agnes asked her.

'The same. I'm glad it's the weekend, 'cos next week they'll be after him. And I can't see it'll help his state at all to be interrogated by the forces of law and order.' She looked at Agnes. 'You OK?'

'Um, yes. It's just . . . One of Julius's friends, he's had some bad news, we saw him this morning. His brother died in a riding accident.'

'How terrible. Did Julius know him well, the brother?'

Agnes hesitated. 'I'm not sure,' she said. She frowned, thinking about the odd glances between Julius and Patrick, the strange intense tone of the note. She looked up at Helen. 'Shall we go and meet our new resident?'

The young man was in his room, and he sat bolt upright on the bed when Helen came in. He glanced at Agnes, then at Helen, with a look of sheer terror on his face.

'Hello,' Helen said.

He was of indeterminate age, so thin the T-shirt he was wearing hung in folds. He was olive-skinned, with dark eyes and hair. He was slightly built, but seemed aged beyond his years.

'Hello,' Helen tried again.

Agnes noticed he was hiding something in his fist, clutched behind him. He stared at her, then at Helen, his eyes darting between them.

'This is Sister Agnes,' Helen said. He didn't move, just his eyes, looking from one to the other.

'Did you have breakfast?' Helen tried. 'Food?' She made a gesture to suggest eating. He began to shake, and his eyes were now fixed on her with an expression of abject fear.

Helen glanced at Agnes, then took a step towards him. He flinched. She moved back again, and he seemed to breathe again.

'Goodbye,' she said.

They left him alone. 'He doesn't come out of there at all,' Helen said. 'I've taken to bringing food up to him. The other residents terrify him.'

'They terrify me sometimes.'

Helen laughed. 'But why was he so scared?'

'He was hiding food, I think,' Agnes said. 'I think he thought you were going to punish him. He had some bread or something behind his back.'

'He must have come from something terrible.'

'Desperate,' Agnes agreed. 'To stow away on a plane . . . '

'He had nothing. Hardly any clothes. No papers. He was hypothermic, and near starvation.'

'Is he injured?'

'He's got some marks, yes. I tried to get the doctor to assess him, but he wouldn't let him get near.'

As they went into the office, the phone started to ring. Helen answered it, then handed it to Agnes. 'It's Julius, for you.'

'Agnes?' Julius sounded weary. 'Patrick's here. He can't find Tad. He's vanished from his flat; he seems to have found out about Matthias from someone. It's very dangerous for him. We thought . . . You're the only one with a car — Patrick's won't start, as usual — we wondered . . . But it'll be like needles in haystacks.'

'Sure,' Agnes said. 'If they can spare me here.' She glanced at Helen. Helen nodded.

Agnes hung up. 'I'm sorry,' she began. 'I have to get the car. Um, I have to look for someone.'

Helen smiled. 'We'll manage. And the community car is outside, I drove it over this morning.'

'Are you really sure?'

'Take it. Honest.'

'Thanks.'

Driving over to St Simeon's church, Agnes found herself reflecting once again on Helen. On her directness, her confidence. She lives her life with such ease, Agnes thought.

I hope all that survives her vows.

The thought was there before she could stop it.

Patrick and Julius came outside when they heard the car pull up on the drive. Patrick got in next to Agnes, Julius in the back.

'Where are we going?' Agnes turned to Patrick. He was white with exhaustion, racked with pain. She suppressed an urge to touch him, to comfort him.

'What did the warden say at his flat, Ignatius?' Patrick seemed too tired to think.

'She said he'd gone out in distress. She tried to stop him, but he was beside himself.'

Patrick seemed to be shivering. 'It was just like this in Kent.'

'How did he find out?' Agnes asked.

'The people at his accommodation said some woman came to see him. It was probably Liz from the stables, though why she'd tell him before me, I don't understand. She's a friend. She's the one who drives him to the stables each week.'

'Do you think he went to look for you?'

Agnes asked Patrick.

'We tried there, didn't we, Ignatius, before we phoned you. Went straight to my flat. No sign, no note.'

Agnes started the engine. 'Where would he go? What's the most likely place?'

Patrick shrugged.

'The stables?' Agnes persisted.

'He doesn't know the way. He usually gets a lift from Liz.'

'There's the shrine,' Julius said from the back of the car.

Patrick blinked as if someone had slapped him. 'Of course. God, Ignatius, the shrine. Why didn't I think of that?'

'The shrine?' Agnes put the car into gear.

'Rotherhithe,' Julius said. 'The church of St Mary.'

'We used to go there as children,' Patrick said.

Agnes pulled out on to the main road, then headed east after the lights. She found herself wondering, as they joined the main route towards the docks, how someone so close to Julius's life, so much a part of Julius's past, should have been kept so well hidden. Thirty years — getting on for forty years since Julius embarked on his training for the priesthood in Ireland? All those years of knowing Patrick and his brothers . . . She glanced at her

41

mirror and caught sight of Julius, looking out of the window. He was pensive, frowning, screwing up his eyes against the slanting thin light of the afternoon.

'Turn off here,' Patrick said. 'At these lights. There's a side street. Towards the river . . . '

Agnes followed his directions. They stopped outside a tiny church, dwarfed on either side by warehouses, their dark exteriors showing years of neglect. They got out of the car. A dog barked in the distance. They could hear shouts of children from the nearby tower blocks.

Patrick approached the church door and pushed at it. It opened. They blinked against the darkness. There was silence, then a rustling sound, and a murmuring in the dimness.

'Tad?'

The murmuring grew louder. In the empty shadows they could see a figure kneeling at the altar rail.

Patrick tried again. 'Tad?'

'He's dead,' the figure answered, turning towards Patrick. His face was wet with tears. Patrick stumbled towards him, knelt next to him, took him in his arms.

★　★　★

Some time later they left the church. A chill dusk was settling over the drab estates. Tad leaned heavily on Patrick as they helped him to the car. The brothers sat in the back; Julius sat next to Agnes.

'We'll get you home,' Patrick said to Tad.

'No,' Tad said. 'Can't stay there.'

'There's nowhere else,' Patrick said wearily.

'I'm hungry,' Tad said.

'Let's get some supper,' Agnes said. 'Or lunch. Or whatever time it is.'

★ ★ ★

They went to the shabby old café on Borough High Street. Agnes sat with Tad while the others ordered food at the counter. For the first time, in the fluorescent light, Agnes could see Tad properly. He was large-framed, like both his brothers, and grey-haired like Patrick. He had a broad face which gave him an air of innocence.

'Do you know Patrick?' he asked her, leaning earnestly towards her.

'Yes, a bit. I know Julius.'

He nodded. 'He looks after me,' he said, after a while.

'How do you — I mean, the shrine . . . ?' Agnes began.

'It weeps, the statue,' he said, as if that

explained everything. 'Our dad brought us to see it, from Ireland. Real tears.'

'Which statue?'

'The Virgin.' He spoke patiently, as if she were a child.

'In the church there?'

'Yes. Real tears. Only sometimes,' he added. 'Not today. Not for Matt. I thought perhaps she'd weep for him, but she didn't. Not today. I looked.'

The others reappeared with plates of sandwiches and mugs of tea. Tad stirred two large teaspoons of sugar into his mug.

'This is Sister Agnes,' Patrick said lamely.

'I know.' Tad didn't look up from his tea. 'It was the horse, you see.' His former calm seemed to be deserting him. 'The horse. He should've known.' He began to stir his tea furiously. 'The name. If you count the letters, and the first initial, and if you say each letter is worth its position in the alphabet — look.' He glanced up, dropping his spoon, which clattered on to the stained formica table. He fished in his pocket and drew out a series of folded sheets of paper, which he now unfolded. They were covered with diagrams, letters and numbers. 'You make the letters the value of their position in the alphabet — his horse's name is like this, see — and then his age . . . ' He showed Agnes a chart of

44

letters and numbers: a series of triangles. 'It adds up to a hundred and fifty-three.' He sat back, as if he had proved something.

'Um, I see . . . ' Agnes looked at Patrick, but he was fiddling with his knife against his plate.

'It was the same with Dad, you see,' Tad went on. 'The numbers were all wrong.' He seemed distressed now, chewing his lip, staring at her as if willing her to understand.

'Which numbers?'

Patrick glanced up at her, as if in warning.

'He drove himself into a wall,' Tad said, as if this explained everything. 'He was forty-nine. And now Matt. And how old was Matt about to be? Next birthday?' His voice was shrill and insistent.

'Forty-nine,' Patrick said, wearily.

'When Liz told me — '

'Why did she tell you?' Patrick interrupted.

'I asked her.' Tad looked at him, his gaze distant.

'But — '

'I phoned the stables. About next week. I want to ride Sancho, I needed them to know. And they sounded — odd. I got Deborah on the phone, and I knew that something had happened. So I waited till I knew Liz was back and I phoned her. I asked her. And she — she had to tell me. I asked her. I knew.'

45

'I see.'

'I wrote down the ages too, forty-nine. Seven times seven. Dad. And then Matt.' He unfolded another piece of paper and flapped it at Agnes. His eyes had a brightness about them, and he seemed tense, his face drawn, his lips still working.

Patrick leaned across to him. 'We should go, Tad.'

Tad turned to him and gripped his arm. 'The funeral, Pat. When is it?'

Patrick glanced at Julius. 'I have to speak to the coroner. Depends when they release the body.'

'When you like,' Julius said. 'Whenever you like.'

'Soon,' Tad said. 'Don't make him wait.'

★   ★   ★

Agnes dropped them back at Tad's flat. They sat in the car, watching Patrick lead Tad up the steps of the building, which was a flat-fronted, concrete construction with wide windows. Then Agnes turned the car round and headed towards Julius's church.

'You'll be in time for evening mass,' she said.

'Mmm.'

'Julius?'

'Sorry?'

'You weren't listening.'

'No. Sorry.'

'How did you know about the shrine?'

'I just remembered. Their father had been a sailor when he was young. Knew that church from way back. He brought them over from Ireland to see it, when they were kids. It made an impression on Tad, I remember him talking to me about it.'

'The statue weeps.'

Julius smiled. 'So their father said. I know Father Dominic, he's the priest there. He keeps very quiet about it. I doubt he believes it. Some old sailors' myth, I think, from when the docks were still working.'

They drove in silence. 'Three brothers,' Agnes said, as they waited for the lights to change on London Bridge Road. 'And they all do sums.'

★   ★   ★

That night at home she knelt in prayer. The candles on her mantelpiece threw warm shadows against the white walls, and the brass spheres of the clock flashed with light as they circled. She murmured the psalm: ' 'My tongue sticks to the roof of my mouth; You have laid me in the dust of the grave . . . ' '

She listened to the ticking of the clock. An image came to her, of the stranger at the hostel, and she wondered how long he'd be allowed to stay.

She turned to the reading in her prayer-book. 'Jesus said to them, 'Bring of the fish which you have now caught.' Simon Peter went up, and drew the net to land full of great fishes, a hundred and fifty-three; and though there were so many, yet the net was not broken . . . '

A hundred and fifty-three. Agnes closed the book in haste, wondering why she felt so uneasy. She began the Ave Maria, but the image of the weeping statue came into her mind, and that troubled her too. She finished her prayers in silence, listening to the stillness of her breathing.

She hoped, as she got into bed, that she wouldn't dream of the house again. Perhaps if I give the house away, I won't dream about it any more, she thought, drowsily, before descending into sleep.

★ ★ ★

She woke next morning with a sense of relief that no dreams had troubled her sleep. The letter from her mother's executors lay on her desk, its cream envelope dappled with the sunrise through her curtains.

I should give the house to Athena, she thought, going into the kitchen to make tea. In the crisp winter's morning, with the slate roofs of the estate across the road sparkling with frost, the house didn't seem a burden any more, merely a decision that had to be made.

Louise, today, she thought, scraping the frost from the windscreen of the community car. My other novice.

Julius can laugh, she thought, driving through the thickening traffic to the order's main house. Sister Michaela, the provincial novice mistress, she trusts me. For a change.

Perhaps I am more settled. Perhaps I have become a proper nun. Perhaps it will be easy to take my final vows.

I'll give the house away. Agnes was aware of a lurch of pain at the thought. Or not, she answered herself. Which makes me not a proper nun at all.

* * *

'Of course, I've always wanted to be a nun,' Louise said, smiling at her through the steam of her mug of tea as they sat in the warm community kitchen.

'Mmm,' Agnes replied. Louise had a pretty,

49

round face, and mousy hair which she wore scraped back.

'At first I thought I'd join the sort of order where you wore a habit, you know, a proper nun.'

Agnes suppressed a smile.

'But then I realised it was important to work, you know, out in the world. I didn't want anyone accusing me of running away from my responsibilities.'

'I don't think anyone in an enclosed order could be said to be running away,' Agnes began. 'Far from it.'

'Oh, I know. Anyway, when Sister Michaela said I could do this placement in a hospice, I was really pleased.'

'And how's it going there?'

'Oh, it's wonderful, so fulfilling.'

Agnes found she was frowning, as Louise chatted happily about being at the bedsides of the dying, and how much she learned about faith and love from being with the relatives of those afflicted. Was it supposed to be so easy? Agnes found herself wondering. Was her supervision of the novices simply a matter of allowing these young women to be so happy in their work?

' . . . and I'm so sure it's what God wants of me.' Louise looked up at her, smiling.

'Um, good. Well . . . '

Louise stood up, clumsy in her plain blue skirt and chunky Aran sweater. 'I must go. I'll write you some notes on what I think, if you like. Reflections, you know. The discernment of God's will.'

'Um, yes. Good. Thank you,' Agnes managed to add, as Louise closed the kitchen door behind her.

Agnes washed up their two mugs. And why shouldn't it be so easy? she thought. Just because I found it hard. And I only found it hard because I was running away. I ran from my parents to my husband, and from my husband to a convent. I never chose.

I've never chosen anything in my life. Except not to leave. And that's a choice I make every day.

3

Agnes sat in the back seat of the funeral car,
next to Julius. She looked out at the
afternoon sun. The brick and slate of the
passing streets seemed sharpened by the
crisp, clear light. They drove north through
Hackney and Tottenham, eventually emerging
into the green spaces at the edge of London.
Agnes felt enclosed by the silence of the car,
as if she were back in France. Another death.
Another funeral.

'He should be buried in Ireland, really.'
Julius broke the silence, and she turned away
from the window to look at him. 'If their
mother were still alive . . . ' He was talking
almost to himself. 'Still . . . ' He shrugged,
touching the crucifix that hung at his neck,
and looked away.

'Who'll be there?'

'Sorry?'

'Today, I mean.' Agnes wanted to keep the
silence at bay.

'Oh, I don't know. His wife.' Julius frowned
briefly. 'His kids, I suppose. The boys. I met
them yesterday, with their mother, Karen.' He
turned to her and squeezed her hand.

'Thanks for being here,' he said.

'I feel a bit of an outsider . . . ' she began, but he shook his head.

'You're here for me,' he said. 'And anyway, Patrick really likes you.' He turned to look out of the window, blinking against the sunlight as the car slowed down for the approach to the cemetery.

Patrick was standing on his own, stiffly encased in a thick woollen coat. He smiled as he saw Agnes getting out of the car.

She came to stand next to him. 'Where do we go?'

'I'm not sure, I'm awaiting instructions.' He clasped his gloved hands together against the cold.

'Who are those people?' Agnes indicated a group of men, all tall, upright, clean-shaven, in sharp black clothes, their outlines marked out by the lowering sun behind them.

'From Matt's work. Insurance people.'

Agnes noticed a woman amongst them. Her heavy winter coat swished expensively against the soft leather of her boots. 'Nice clothes,' Agnes said, and Patrick nodded vaguely, his gaze distracted by a woman who was getting out of a car, flanked by two young men. 'Excuse me,' he said, and left Agnes's side.

'That's Matthias's wife.' Julius followed the

53

line of Agnes's gaze. 'And his boys.'

She was wearing a black hat with a veil, a petite figure dwarfed by her long coat. She walked slowly past the groups of mourners towards Patrick, and took his arm. As she passed the group from Matthias's work, she glanced towards the woman. The woman turned to meet her eyes, evenly, deliberately, her lips bright red above the black fur of her collar. Then Karen looked away, tightening her grip on Patrick's arm. They became the head of the procession with Julius next to them. The coffin was carried from the hearse, silence settling in its path. Everyone moved slowly, walking behind the coffin towards the graveside, forming a circle around it in unspoken agreement. The sun was already turning pink. There was the distant hum of traffic; fragments of birdsong; the sound of sobbing as Karen clung to Patrick and the coffin was lowered into the ground.

'Friends, we have gathered together to commit our brother Matthias to the earth, and to God's mercy . . . ' Julius addressed the mourners. Agnes heard another sob, nearby. She glanced to her right and saw a tousled, dark-haired woman, standing with a little girl. The little girl was tugging at her hand, trying to ask something, and as the woman bent down to attend to the child, Agnes saw the woman's face was drenched with tears.

' 'Lord, now let your servant depart in peace . . . ' ' As Julius said the words, Agnes saw Tad stumbling along the drive, a young woman beside him. She had short spiky hair and was wearing a bright yellow padded jacket; they were both hurrying.

' ' . . . my own eyes have seen your salvation . . . ' ' Tad lumbered to a halt at the back of the mourners. ' ' . . . which you have prepared in the sight of every nation . . . ' ' Agnes saw Tad move his lips with the words.

' 'Glory to the Father, and to the Son . . . ' ' The coffin was now in its final resting place. Earth was thrown on to the grave, and Agnes heard in the thudding soil the memory of her mother's burial, and saw in her mind the parched Provençal ground which had opened to allow her mother in, and closed again behind her. She blinked back tears, staring into this new, fresh grave.

A single red rose landed gently on the coffin lid. Agnes glanced up. Karen had already left the graveside, her face buried against Patrick's shoulder. The people from Matthias's work had begun to move away. Julius was conferring with one of the sons. The tousled woman stood at the very edge of the grave, staring down into it, her eyes wide, her face wet, her hand still poised over the grave where she'd let the rose fall. Then she seemed to recover herself, glanced towards Karen who was already near the cars, and went back to the little girl who was waiting patiently on the gravel path. She bent and kissed her head, then took her hand, and they both walked away from the graveside, keeping their distance from the other mourners. Agnes followed. Tad had joined the group which now clustered by the cars, and his friend in the yellow jacket left his side and came towards the dark-haired woman.

'Mary?' The spiky-haired woman hugged her. 'You OK?'

'Not really, no,' the tousled woman said.

'There's a do at some restaurant, Deborah said.'

'Liz, I can't go to that, can I?'

They hugged again. 'Poor baby,' Liz said.

'She's not a baby, is she?' the little girl said.

The young woman smiled down at her. 'I just meant — '

'But she's not. She's my mummy. Mummies can't be babies too, can they? Can they, Mummy?'

Her mother turned to her. 'No. You're right, Charlie.' She smiled at her through her tears. Then she looked towards the clusters of people as they gathered around the cars. 'Wait here, love, wait with Liz for a minute.'

The little girl took Liz's hand, and her mother walked towards the cars. Agnes followed, seeking out Patrick, just as the woman approached him.

'I think you have something that belongs to me,' she said to him.

Patrick was standing talking to Julius, and now looked up, startled. 'Mary — ' he said.

'You have a note. It's mine.'

'Yes.' Patrick blinked and coloured. 'Yes, of course. I was going to — '

'Were you?' Mary faced Patrick, her eyes dark with grief. Her hair fell across her face and she pushed it away, her gaze still on Patrick.

'Yes, I was.' Patrick recovered himself and reached into an inside pocket. He handed her an envelope. 'I should have posted it to you. Forgive me,' he said. 'I was reluctant to part with . . . I have very little that was his, you see.'

'Even less than me?' Mary's voice softened, and a smile lifted her pale face.

'Poor Mary,' Patrick said, and took a step towards her. Impulsively, he took hold of her hands. 'He was too young to die.'

'It was too soon,' Mary echoed, her voice choked with tears. Agnes glanced at Julius. He was standing, his gaze fixed on Mary, and as she let go of Patrick's hands and turned to

57

him he took a step towards her.

'Hello, Julius,' she said.

'Hello.' His voice was barely audible. Agnes stared at him.

Mary hesitated, moved towards him, not taking her eyes from his.

'Here's Karen,' Patrick said suddenly. Julius stepped back, and Mary fled as Karen approached them, her face white and pinched.

'Patrick?' she said.

Patrick tightened the scarf around his neck. Mary seemed to have melted away into the crowd. Agnes glimpsed her at a distance, with her little daughter.

Karen's gaze followed her. Her lips were a thin line. Then she turned back to Patrick. 'You know where to go now?'

'Yes.'

She turned to Agnes. 'And, Sister, you're welcome too.'

'Thank you,' Agnes said.

'I should have introduced you.' Patrick took Karen's hand. 'This is Mrs Karen Kavanagh, my sister-in-law. This is Sister Agnes, she's a friend of Julius's.'

Karen held her gaze for a moment, then turned back to Patrick. 'I'm going in the car with the boys. I'll see you at this place they've organised.' She hesitated a second, glancing in the direction that Mary had taken, then looked up at Patrick. 'You will be there, won't you?'

'Yes. Yes, of course.'

Karen turned and walked towards the cars, her shiny black heels scrunching the gravel underfoot. Her sons appeared and helped her into the car.

'Well, we should be . . . ' Patrick looked at Julius.

'Yes.' Julius was staring at the ground.

'Who was that woman?' Agnes asked.

'Mary,' Patrick said. 'Mary Wells.' He glanced at Julius again. Julius was digging his toes into the stones of the drive.

'Who's Mary Wells?'

'Oh, just someone whom Matthias knew . . . Well, we all knew . . . ' Again his eyes flashed towards Julius, who kept his gaze fixed on the granite chippings at his feet.

'Why didn't you give her the note before?' Agnes was studying Patrick's face, his discomposure.

'Because I didn't know where she was.'

'You knew it was for her?'

'Yes. I also knew . . . The thing is, I didn't want to part with it.' His eyes moistened.

'She's very beautiful.'

Julius cleared his throat. 'We'd better be getting back. I mean, I suppose — this do

59

they're having . . . '

Patrick nodded. 'Those people from Matt's company. They've hired some flash restaurant place in Liverpool Street. It's a nice thought, but Karen . . . ' He sighed. 'Karen's going to need us there.'

The sun had sunk behind a mass of grey cloud. As they set off in their car towards the City, it began to drizzle. Agnes sat in the back again, and watched the windscreen wipers beat a rhythm against the beaded twilight of the rain. Occasionally she looked at Julius, but he was sitting still, his hands in his lap, gazing out of the window.

★　★　★

'Ah, Patrick, do have a drink. And Father — um . . . '

'Julius,' said Julius.

'Allen,' said the man, offering his hand. 'Allen Hutchinson. Colleague of Matt's. Poor chap. Bloody sad affair. And this is?'

'Agnes. Sister Agnes.' She held out her hand, and he took it. His eyes held hers, and she suddenly remembered Matthias's words about him, or were they Patrick's, about his selling his soul to the devil. Beyond him she could see the woman with the red lipstick, who glanced in her direction as Allen let go of her hand.

'Still,' he was saying. 'Bloody good send off. All we can do really. Help yourselves.' He waved in the direction of the party.

It was a large, bright space, with a floor of polished wood. Young women circulated with trays of canapés. Agnes took a tiny pastry with a swirl of smoked salmon at the centre. She was aware of Patrick's voice above the hubbub.

'That Allen always was a bastard,' he said, looking back to where he stood by the glass door, framed by the darkness of the night outside.

'There's Karen,' Julius said.

'Is Tad joining us?' Agnes asked.

Patrick shook his head. 'No. Too much for him, this kind of thing. Liz said she'd drop him off and come on later.' He reached out as a tray of champagne passed by, took two glasses and handed one to Agnes.

'Thanks.' Once again Agnes was aware of the red-lipped woman looking at her. 'And who's that — that woman?'

Patrick glanced across to her. He shrugged. 'I've seen her once or twice. She works — worked — with Matt.' He drained his glass as the tray passed by again, put the empty glass down and picked up a new one.

'Patrick?' Julius touched his arm.

'I'm OK. I'd better see to Karen.' He left them, striding through the crowd to where Karen was sitting at a table in the corner, her sons with her.

'This isn't right,' Julius said suddenly. 'What would Matthias have wanted with this? His family, so close they were, and the village he came from, just a row of houses really, but . . . ' He surveyed the room, and shook his head. 'I think we owe it to the dead to let the earth they loved surround them.'

'But everyone left the village to come to London,' Agnes said.

'That's what's so sad. Everyone was here. No one to claim him. Exile. All of us, exiles, leaving our villages . . . '

'But you said you didn't mind being an exile.'

'Did I?' His expression was distant as he looked beyond her into the crowd.

'You said it was all in the past.'

His eyes met hers, briefly. 'Yes. The past.' He frowned, troubled. 'Um — would you mind if I went home? I find this kind of thing very difficult.' He kissed her cheek and slipped away, passing unnoticed by Allen who still seemed to be on sentry duty at the door.

'It was kind of him to do the service,' someone said. Agnes turned to see the smart woman at her side. She looked even more angular in her deceptively simple dark suit, her hair in a sleek black bob.

'Yes,' Agnes said.

'He knew the family?'

'Yes.'

The woman stretched out a hand. Her nails matched her lipstick. 'Judy,' she said. 'Judy Meyer. I worked with Matthias.'

'Sister Agnes,' Agnes said, taking the hand briefly in her own. She noticed the woman's smooth pale skin.

'It was difficult,' Judy was saying, 'none of us really knew what to do. The funeral, you know . . . ' She shrugged, then smiled.

'Was it up to you?'

'Well, you know, we wanted to contribute. We felt . . . we felt we were like family, you see. In a company like ours . . . Sister, did you say?' Judy's eyes scanned Agnes's clothes. Agnes had chosen to wear her black silk jacket and trousers, and a white shirt. She felt suddenly shabby. 'A nun?' Agnes nodded. 'Well,' Judy said, 'I don't suppose you can know what it's like.' She smiled again. 'We're very close.'

'I'm sure Karen was grateful,' Agnes said.

'Karen?' Judy met her eyes. 'Oh. Yes.'

'If you'll excuse me,' Agnes said, 'I must pursue that large plate of chicken satay that just went past. I haven't eaten all day.'

She found Patrick sitting with Karen, and sat down next to him. Karen looked up at her. 'Still here?'

'Just. Julius couldn't face it, though.'

'I don't blame him.' Karen smiled weakly. 'These are my sons, Daniel and Jake.' They nodded at her and she nodded back.

'Awful people,' Patrick said, rather too loudly, waving his arm towards the room. Agnes noticed he'd moved on to whisky. 'Insurance. Stinks,' he added. 'That woman you were talking to . . .'

'Judy,' Agnes said. Karen's face tightened at the name.

'Judy. Yes. Met her once, remember now. As bad as the others, no doubt,' Patrick said. 'It's the money. It does them all in. Endlessly speculating, endlessly calculating, probabilities, chances, risk . . .'

Karen touched his arm. 'Isn't that what you do?'

He smiled at her. 'No, my dear. The crucial difference is, you see, that I do it for its own sake. These people do it to make themselves richer. That puts me on the side of the angels.' He laughed, red-faced with passing mirth.

'And Matthias?' Karen said, quietly.

Patrick closed his eyes. 'Matthias,' he said, opening them again. 'An angel too.'

64

'But in the wrong place.' Karen's voice was low.

Patrick patted her hand, and tears welled in her eyes. 'No, not wrong for him. Matthias was brilliant. A shining light in this sea of . . . fools,' he said, looking around the room. 'He survived all this, after all. It was a horse that killed him.'

Karen nodded. 'Yes. A horse.' She blinked back the tears. 'Shall we go home?' The boys stood up. Karen offered her hand to Agnes. 'It was nice to meet you. Perhaps we'll see you again?'

'I hope so,' Agnes said.

Patrick looked after them as they negotiated their way to the door, Karen detained here and there by people wanting to speak to her. As they got to the door, the young woman with the big yellow jacket appeared, said a few words to Karen, and then marched across the room to their table.

'Do they have any beer?' she said, sitting down.

Patrick laughed. 'I'll go to the bar for you.' He stood up. 'Liz, Agnes. Agnes, Liz,' he said, then lurched away from the table into the crowd.

'Hi.' Liz took off her jacket and slung it across the back of her chair. Underneath she had on a plain navy sweatshirt.

'You knew Matthias?' Agnes asked her.

'Yeah. I work at the stables.'

'Oh.'

Patrick appeared with a cold beer and two glasses of whisky, one of which he passed to Agnes. 'I thought you needed this.'

'How astute of you,' Agnes said, 'when we hardly know each other.'

Liz picked up the beer and drank from the bottle. 'God, that's better.'

'How was Tad?' Patrick asked.

She frowned. 'OK. I think. Very — um — you know how he gets. Sort of withdrawn. Probably storm clouds gathering.' She took another swig of beer.

'Thanks for being with him,' Patrick said. 'I should have . . . I should have done more really, but today of all days . . . '

'It's OK. I like him.'

'Yes.' Patrick nodded. 'Yes. How's the head, by the way?'

'Getting there.'

'Liz fell off a horse too, didn't you? Bit of a bump.'

Liz laughed. 'You could say that.' She drained the bottle and passed it to Patrick. 'Any more where that came from?'

Patrick stood up clumsily and returned to the bar.

'The problem is,' Agnes said, 'that every

drink he buys for us, he buys yet another for himself.'

'Let him drown his sorrows, that's what I say.'

'Did you know Matthias well?'

'Pretty well. I've been looking after his horse for the last two years.'

'And you know Mary?'

Liz looked at her, then nodded. 'Yes.'

'Does she work at the stables too?'

'No.'

'She rides?'

'She's an old friend.' She twirled her empty bottle between her hands. 'She rides a bit.'

'She knew Matthias?'

Liz met her eyes, opened her mouth to speak, then closed it again as Patrick arrived with the drinks.

'Bloody bastards, all of them.' Patrick sat down heavily, passing Liz her beer and Agnes another whisky. 'Clustered round that bar, drinking like bloody fishes, no bloody cares in the bloody world, who gives a Queen's arse whether my brother's dead or not, laying on this do for him just so they can drink their bloody champagne all bloody night . . . ' He looked up to see Liz laughing. 'What's so funny now?' His voice was loud and cross.

'Queen's arse,' she said, still laughing.

'And my brother not yet cold in his grave.'

Patrick leaned forward and put his head in his hands.

Liz stopped laughing. 'Patrick, I'm sorry.' She squeezed his shoulder.

'It's not you,' he said, his voice muffled. 'It's this lot. Matthias always diced with the devil, and now the devil's won.' A sobbing sound came from behind his hands.

'It was an accident,' Liz said. 'Just one of those things. Poppy's a challenging horse. No one else can ride her, God knows what'll become of her now.'

Patrick lifted his head. 'Agnes rides.' He turned to her, jovial again. 'You could try her.'

Agnes shook her head. 'I'm a novice really.'

'That's not what Julius said. And he was a brilliant horseman in his day too.'

'He knows nothing about it.'

'Danger addict, that's what he said you were.'

'Thanks very much.' Agnes looked at Patrick, who seemed cheerful now. 'When did he say that?'

'In France. That's when he met you, wasn't it? When they'd sent him to France. Years ago now.'

'Yes, that's right.'

'Course, he was in a bad way then. Poor

68

old Julius. Still, turned out all right for him in the end.'

Agnes stared at him. 'When ... What? What bad way?'

'Long time ago now, of course. But I remember him describing you, even then. Very fond of you, isn't he? He said you were the most self-destructive person he'd ever met.'

Liz was staring at Agnes with renewed interest.

Agnes tried to laugh. 'As you say. A long time ago,' she said, then took a large mouthful of whisky. 'I'm old and wise now.'

Patrick smiled at her. He nodded, slowly. 'Aren't we all.' He picked up his empty glass, stared at it in surprise, then put it down again. 'Better be getting on home, I suppose. It's been a long day.' His eyes filled with tears. 'I don't know what I'll do without him.' Liz took his hand, and he squeezed hers, shaking his head. 'I just don't know what I'll do.'

4

'Coffee?' Julius got up to put on the kettle.

Agnes put her hand across her eyes. 'Um — I think tea, maybe.'

'A heavy night?'

'No. Not really. Well, maybe. Patrick did keep buying me whisky.'

Julius laughed. 'I'm glad I left when I did.'

Agnes sat down opposite his desk. A thin sun shone through the leaded windows, dappling the worn old red carpet at her feet. 'Families, eh?' Agnes said.

'What in particular?' Julius handed her a mug of tea.

'That funeral. That sense of shadows everywhere. There always is, isn't there? My mother's funeral was just the same. The way families go back into the past, there are bound to be legacies. I was just thinking about it, that's all. And Patrick said this weird thing about Matthias's workplace: 'dicing with the devil,' he said . . . and then that woman with the red lipstick, something's not right with her and Karen — and by the way, Julius, Patrick gave me a very full and frank account of your first impressions of me when

70

we met in France.'

Julius laughed. 'He didn't, did he? What did I say?'

'Oh, nothing to worry about. Usual stuff, just that I was a danger addict and the most self-destructive person you'd ever met.'

'That's all right then. For a moment I thought perhaps I'd been rude about you.'

'And Patrick said . . . ' She hesitated, sipping her tea. 'Patrick said you were in a bad way when they sent you to France.'

Julius looked up. He frowned. 'Bad way? Me? No, surely not. I can't think what he means.'

'Can't you?'

'It was a long time ago.'

'Yes.' She sipped her tea, still watching him. 'Julius, you knew that woman. That woman at the funeral.'

Julius stared at his desk for a long moment. 'Mary,' he said at last, not looking up.

'Yes.'

He raised his eyes to hers. 'I knew her back home in Ireland.'

'She must have been very young.'

'Yes. She was. A child. She was a child then. I — I knew her mother . . . ' His eyes seemed misted with memory.

Agnes watched him. She wanted to ask more, but something stopped her, perhaps the pleading in his eyes as he glanced at her again.

'Do you have to be at the hostel?' he asked.

She looked at her watch. 'Yes. You're right.'

'How is it there?' He seemed relieved to have changed the subject.

'I've hardly been there. I'm only on half-time as it is. There's a very odd new resident. He doesn't speak.'

'I met him. He was picked up at the airport.'

'Yes.'

'What will they do?'

'They want to send him back. But with no identification, there's nowhere to send him back to. Helen thinks they're hoping we'll make him talk.'

'And will you?'

'It seems very unlikely. He's — There's a very strange quality about him. It's as if he's not really here.' Agnes finished her tea. 'I'm sure he's been tortured.'

'Is he injured?'

'Not visibly, no. But he just seems to be in constant terror, endless nightmares, you know.' She looked at her watch. 'I'd better get to work.' She stood up and put on her coat. 'Are you seeing Patrick today?'

'Not as far as I know. Tomorrow, maybe.'

At the door she paused, her hand on the

handle. Julius had already bent back to his work, and as she left he didn't even look up.

★　★　★

'You don't feel like washing up, do you?' Madeleine greeted her as she walked into the hostel office. 'There were eleven for breakfast.'

'Isn't there a rota?'

'Everyone's new. There's Jo, but she's rather carrying the burden being the only long-term resident. And we can't ask our silent newcomer.'

'No, I don't mind washing up. Just the kind of brainless occupation I could do with today.'

Agnes found herself alone in the kitchen, and set to on the pile of dirty bowls and mugs. After a while she was aware of someone having come in. She turned round to find the silent person staring at her.

'Hello,' she said.

He stood with his back against a wall, watching her.

She picked up a tea-towel and began to dry some plates. He took a step towards her.

'Would you like to help?' she asked him.

He didn't respond, his eyes still fixed on her face.

She held the tea-towel out towards him. He flinched. She took a plate and dried it, as if to show him. He showed no interest. She put the tea-towel down and went back to the washing up. She was aware of the boy approaching the sink. He came and stood next to her. She continued washing the dishes, piling them up on the draining board next to her. He picked up the tea-towel in one hand, and a plate in the other. He stood, staring at his hands as if they didn't belong to him, still clutching the plate and towel. He moved his hands together so that the things touched. He frowned.

Agnes watched him. 'Like this,' she said, making a wiping motion.

He looked at her, then looked at his hands, as if willing them to move. Agnes moved towards him and he recoiled, his eyes wide. Gently she reached out and took the towel and plate from him. 'It doesn't matter,' she said. 'Another time.'

She dried the plate and stacked it with the others. He watched her. She turned to smile at him, and he met her eyes, expressionless. She went back to the sink, and as she picked up the next plate she heard the door click quietly shut. She was alone in the kitchen again.

' ' . . . For there is nothing covered that shall not be revealed; and hid that shall not be known. What I tell you in darkness, that speak ye in light . . . ' ' Agnes, kneeling in her customary pew, glanced up towards the chapel window. The light was fading behind the stained glass, and the colours were becoming dulled.

Madeleine continued to read. ' ' . . . He that loveth father or mother more than me, is not worthy of me . . . ' '

Agnes looked along the pews to see Helen and Louise, side by side. ' ' . . . And he that taketh not his cross, and followeth after me, is not worthy of me . . . ' '

Is that what I'm asking of them, Agnes wondered, looking at the two novices, that they should take up their crosses?

But how can I, if I've never done the same?

To leap into that void, to abandon everything. The most reckless gamble I might ever take.

' ' . . . He that findeth his life shall lose it; and he that loseth his life for my sake shall find it . . . ' '

The stakes are so high, Agnes thought. Too high. Even for me.

She carried a tray of tea things into the lounge, where Helen and Louise were already waiting for her.

Louise eyed the tray. 'Chocolate biscuits, Agnes? And in Lent?'

Agnes smiled at her, but she seemed to be serious. Agnes put the tray down and handed them both mugs of tea.

Without looking at Louise, Helen reached across and took a biscuit.

'Perhaps Lent is about spiritual relinquishment,' Agnes began. 'Speaking personally,' she added, and Helen smiled. 'It's like the reading today,' she went on. 'Losing life to gain life.'

'But' — Helen spoke through the crumbs — 'all that stuff about deserting your family, it's hard, isn't it?'

'Not for me,' Louise said. 'Mine have been very supportive.'

'I didn't mean that,' Helen said. 'So have mine. In their way. I meant, for us. To turn away from the people who love us.'

'It's about attachment,' Agnes said. 'It's about loosening one's ties to this world.'

'It's still difficult,' Helen said. She looked at Agnes. 'Didn't your family feel rejected when you became a nun?'

'Um, I'm not a good example,' Agnes said. 'I ran away. I escaped and, um, sort of became a nun. It wasn't really a choice.'

'Mine are very happy for me,' Louise said, eyeing the biscuit plate but not taking one.

Helen reached across and took another biscuit. 'Lucky old you,' she said.

'Aren't yours pleased?' Louise persisted.

'My sister's just got married,' Helen said, turning her biscuit over in her fingers. 'They're bound to compare us, they can't help it.'

'It doesn't mean she'll be happier than you,' Louise said.

Helen stared at her. 'But I want her to be happy. Of course I do.'

'But if your parents prefer your sister — '

'They don't. My sister and I are really close, we get on brilliantly, my becoming a nun doesn't change that. We're a close family, we discuss things. My parents have been honest about how they feel, that's all.'

Louise picked up her mug. 'Oh,' she said.

'Didn't you discuss your decision with your family?' Helen asked her.

Louise frowned, turning her mug in her hands. 'Um, they just — they just accepted it, I suppose. I know I'm right, you see. They can't argue with that, can they?'

There was a small silence. Helen turned to

Agnes. 'But do you feel you've lost your life?'

Agnes looked at her open, honest face. 'You see, sometimes I think it's like an arranged marriage,' she said. 'I just mean the idea that you start at the bottom of the mountain and climb it together, rather than the romantic western model, where you meet at the top of the mountain and fall in love, and then you've got nowhere else to go but down.' For some reason the image of Julius and Mary staring at each other came into her mind. 'I think it's been like that for me, that the choice, the real decision to be here, is something that's grown over time.' Absently she reached out and took a biscuit. 'And you see, Lent, it's not about chocolate, for God's sake, it's — it's the time in the wilderness, isn't it? The forty days in the desert, when the devil tempts you to commit to the world, he offers you things that will entrap you to this life, this temporary life, rather than freeing you to proceed to the next, to eternal life. Like he offers Jesus land, a place of belonging instead of a place of exile, which if you come to think of it, had enormous significance to the Jewish people.' Agnes was aware she'd nibbled away at the whole biscuit while she'd been talking. 'And come to think of it, that's what's happening to me, the devil is offering me a place of my own, a house in

Provence, property, an end to exile . . . and it is very tempting. Instead of taking up your cross, the idea that you might leave your cross lying by the road, just walk away from it. Just refuse to take that chance, that last gamble . . . To decide not to throw in your lot, but to hang on to it, cling to some idea of your self that's separate from God . . . '

She'd run out of words, and now she looked up to find both Helen and Louise clutching their mugs of tea, staring at her. 'Separate from God,' she said, meeting their bewildered gaze. 'That's the problem.' She tried to smile. 'I'm — I've got rather a lot on my mind. Look, there's some books here, Pascal, *Pensées*, I'd recommend, *de Mello*; help yourselves. Maybe write down some thoughts for next time.' She stood up. 'Yes. Good. Lent. Interesting time.' She walked to the door, opened it, and went out without looking back.

★　★　★

'Perhaps you're having a nervous breakdown, sweetie.' Athena poured them both a large gin and tonic and handed her a glass.

'Nothing that this won't cure,' Agnes said.

Athena eyed her. 'Then again, perhaps you're not.'

'It was funny, really. They must think I'm barking mad. It's just they're so different from me. They've made this informed, thoughtful, conscious choice. What did I do? I escaped, fled for my life. Thanks to Julius. If it hadn't been for Julius . . . ' She sat down in a huge armchair in the corner of Athena's lounge.

'What's wrong?' Athena sat on the sofa.

'Wrong?'

'It's Julius. When you said his name, just then, you sort of clouded over.'

Agnes took a large swig of her drink. 'Yes. He's — um — Something's happened.'

'What? Not with him, surely not, sweetie?'

'At the funeral. He met this woman. Young woman. They looked at each other, and it was as if they'd known each other for ever. Yes, that's what it was like. And he won't talk about her. I mentioned it today and he kind of warned me off.'

Athena was wide-eyed. 'Julius, eh? Fancy that.'

Agnes smiled. 'What do you mean?'

'Well, sweetie, Julius, he's been kind of — immutable, hasn't he? Like a rock. He never changes. The thought that he might have something shocking, like — like a past, or something . . . ' She shook her head. 'How fascinating.'

80

Agnes laughed. 'Well, whatever it is, we'll never find out.'

'Not from him maybe. But from this mysterious girl . . . '

'Don't you start, Athena.'

'It's just like silly old Nic. Some old flame of his has turned up in his life, apparently. Came to one of his workshops, quite by chance, ho ho ho.'

'Who is she?'

'She's called Linda. I've never met her; he's mentioned her occasionally.'

'Do you mind?'

Athena laughed. 'Oh, no, sweetie. Why should I mind? Nic and I, we're — we're fine, aren't we? And anyway . . . ' Her face shadowed, suddenly serious. 'If we're not, it's entirely my own fault, isn't it? He's been working so hard to forgive me, but these things leave cracks, don't they?'

They sat in silence, sipping their drinks. After a while Athena got up and drew the curtains against the darkness of the windows. 'And were your novices helpful about your house in Provence, sweetie?' she said, sitting down again.

Agnes laughed. 'Barking mad, they'll think. I went on about the devil tempting those of us in exile, in the wilderness, tempting us with a place to belong. Offering me a lovely house, eight bedrooms, en-suite bathrooms, extensive grounds, needs some attention, as if Satan were some kind of up-market estate agent.'

'But of course, sweetie. That would explain everything. It would certainly explain house prices round here.'

★ ★ ★

Agnes got home late. As she let herself into her flat and hung up her coat, she wondered if she was hungry. Athena had been more generous with drink than with food. She wandered into her kitchen, opened some cupboards, closed them again. Her door buzzed; she jumped. She went over to the intercom, looking at her watch.

'It's Patrick. Are you there?'

'Of course I'm here.'

'Sorry to disturb you.' His voice sounded uneven.

'Push the door when it buzzes.'

He stumbled into her flat, his coat oddly buttoned, his hair over his face.

'Patrick, what is it?'

'Have you got a drink?'

'Haven't you had enough?'

'Just a small one?' His indistinct speech made him sound pleading, like a child.

She poured them both a whisky and took his coat.

He sat down awkwardly in a chair. 'I've worked it out, you see.'

'Worked what out?'

'About Matt.'

'What about him?'

Patrick downed the whisky in one mouthful. 'He was murdered.'

5

Patrick took a coin out of his pocket. 'Look,' he said. He threw the coin up into the air. 'Heads he was murdered,' he said.

The coin came up heads.

'Best of three,' Patrick said, slurring the words. He threw the coin again. He caught it, slapped it against his hand, revealed it. It was heads.

'One for luck.' For a third time, the coin came up heads.

'He was murdered,' Patrick said. 'I've been a fool.' He slumped down heavily into her armchair. 'I gave that bloody note away. The one bit of evidence I've got, and Mary Wells takes it away from under my bloody nose.' He held out his glass to her.

'Tea?' Agnes said, taking the glass.

He looked up at her, and started to laugh. 'Tea?' he echoed.

'Do you want some tea? Coffee?'

Something about her tone made him stop laughing. He nodded, as if in defeat. 'Tea. Please.'

She went into the kitchen.

'I shouldn't have buried him,' Patrick said.

'I wasn't thinking clearly. I let the inquest go by, I let the verdict stand — 'accidental death' — but if I'd thought about what he was saying, about Allen, and his work, and Karen agreed, she said he'd been tense for weeks . . . '

Agnes came back into the room, waiting for the kettle to boil. She looked at him; his eyes were hollow, his glance darting from side to side. He drummed his fingers on the arm of his chair. 'And then,' he went on, not looking up at her, but staring instead at his fingers as if they weren't his own, 'the place he fell. Exactly the same place as Liz, only a month or so before. And in both cases, they were felled by a golf ball. They found a ball in the undergrowth, next to where he fell, did I tell you? Only with Liz, it hit the horse and not her, so she survived. But what are the odds on that, d'you see? That's what I keep thinking. And every time I do the sums, it comes up that he must have been . . . must have been . . . ' He collapsed in his chair and covered his face with his hands.

Agnes heard the kettle boiling and went back into the kitchen. When she reappeared, carrying two mugs of tea, he was tossing his coin again. 'See?' he said, showing her the coin as if somehow it proved something. 'Heads.'

'Sugar?'

'Um — what? Oh, um, yes. One please. I think.'

She stirred sugar into his mug and handed it to him.

'It was Allen,' Patrick said, taking the mug. 'It was what he said, at the funeral.'

'What did he say?'

Patrick shook his head. 'Bastard.'

'What did he say?'

'Didn't you hear him?'

'No. Tell me.'

Patrick drank from his mug. 'Is there sugar in this?'

'Yes. Go on.' She sat down on the chair at her desk.

'It was at the restaurant,' Patrick said. 'Quite late on. He and I were by the bar at one point, and he turns to me, kind of jeering. You met the man, didn't you?'

'Yes.'

'Then you'll know what I mean.' He drank thirstily, then said, 'Allen turned to me, there by the bar, and said, 'He always did play for high stakes, your brother.' ' Patrick looked at her, and his gaze was sharp. 'Those were his words.'

'Yes. He said something about not speaking ill of the dead, and then he wandered off and started chatting up one of

Liz's friends from the stables.'

'Yes, I remember him doing that.'

They sipped their tea. After a while, Agnes said, 'But it doesn't mean he was murdered.'

'But then there's the note, isn't there? The tone of that note, Mary's note.'

'But — '

'And I gave it away.'

'It didn't say anything particularly — '

'He expected to get it to her. Via someone else. That's what I mean. He obviously intended to see someone who'd convey the note to Mary.' He was sitting straight now, his gaze direct. 'The hunt went without him. He went off towards the golf course instead; he told the hunt he'd meet them later.'

'He said he was calming his horse down.'

'That's what Deborah thought.' Patrick frowned. 'Maybe . . . ' He slumped a little in his chair. 'Maybe I haven't been thinking straight. I don't know. I was at the casino earlier, and the same numbers kept coming up. Against all the odds.' He drained his cup. 'I shouldn't have let her have that note. Not yet.'

'Patrick.' Agnes looked at him; his skin was papery with exhaustion, his eyes glassy. 'Sleep on it. Grief does funny things. Drinking maybe isn't the — I mean, I don't want to lecture you . . . Julius really cares about you,' she ended, lamely.

Patrick smiled. 'I really care about him.'

'Yes.'

Patrick got up to go. In the doorway he hesitated, huge and clumsy, leaning against the frame of the door. 'Agnes, who do you go to? If you think someone's — if it doesn't seem right?'

'The police, I suppose. But really, Patrick, they've done their work. There's a procedure . . .'

He nodded. 'Yes. You're right.' He yawned. 'Sorry to disturb you. Wasn't quite thinking straight.'

'It's OK. Really. I don't mind at all,' Agnes said, realising that it was true.

★ ★ ★

Julius stood in the church doorway, seeing off the last of his parishioners as they left the church after morning mass. Agnes came up to him and waited with him. As he turned to go back into the church, she caught his arm. 'Patrick came round. Last night.'

'Oh?' He seemed not to be meeting her eyes.

'He was in a state.'

'I'm not surprised.'

'But he thinks his brother was murdered.'

At last he looked at her. 'Had he come from some gaming table?'

'Yes. He said so.'

'I do care about him,' Julius said. He stared into the distance, at the traffic beyond the drive of the church, the passing cars flecked with gold in the morning sun. 'He's an old friend.'

'He said he wished he hadn't given Matthias's note away. To Mary Wells.' Agnes watched him.

'Why?' Julius's blue eyes met hers.

'Don't know. He said it was evidence.'

'How can it be evidence?' Julius sounded irritated.

'Well, of course, it isn't. It's just one of the few things left of Matt, and I suppose it's acquired a meaning because of that. But he was insisting it was a clue of some kind. And he said where Matthias fell, that's where their friend Liz fell, exactly the same place.'

'Maybe it's a dangerous spot.'

'Yes. Maybe.'

'Perhaps he's just like you,' Julius said suddenly.

'In what way?'

'Seeing meaning in things, in random events. Seeing patterns.'

'Is that what I do?'

'All the time. And then you set off and investigate them.'

'But not this.'

'No?' He smiled.

'No.'

'You mean you don't agree with Patrick?'

'Why should it be murder? An accident, that's what everyone said. A bump on the head, fell from his horse, broke his neck. Patrick's just in a state, that's all.'

'Mmm.' Julius was now looking at her sideways. 'It's just not like you, that's all.'

'Perhaps I've changed,' Agnes said.

They walked back towards the church door.

'Perhaps you have.'

'I think it comes from being orphaned, you see,' she went on. 'In a way, I've clung on to a version of my past for much too long. My parents being so unhappily married, my own lonely childhood, all the lies they told me and each other. And then my escape, and marrying Hugo, and being rescued from that terrible marriage by you . . . ' She hesitated, glanced at him, then carried on. 'It's like a story I've told myself to explain how I got to be here. But now I can get rid of all that. For the first time, I can be free of it. I'm free to choose. To choose to be a nun. I can ditch the house in Provence, give it to a charity. I can actually, for the first time in my life as a nun, make the decision that Helen and Louise are making.'

Julius turned to lock the church door. Agnes was just about to speak when someone started shouting from the street, a masculine yelling that made both Agnes and Julius turn. A large, dishevelled figure was coming through the gate to the church towards them.

'Tad,' Julius said.

Tad stumbled along the drive, calling out to them incoherently.

'Tad!' Julius took a step towards him. Hearing his name made him stop short.

'He didn't come,' Tad said, looking from Julius to Agnes, his eyes darting with distress. 'He said he would, but I've waited and waited . . . '

'Who, Tad?'

'Patrick.' He began to wring his hands, kicking at the drive with his heavy feet. 'It's one of us next. It makes me scared when I don't see him, it might be him next and I can't stand it, you see.' He looked up at Agnes, his eyes searching hers for understanding.

'Would you like us to phone him?' Julius spoke quietly.

'They tried. Tom, the warden at my flat, he tried, couldn't get any answer. I went out

91

then, I went to look for him, I thought I saw him in the street but it wasn't him . . . ' His fingers twisted around each other.

'Let's try again, shall we?' Julius took him gently by the arm and led him into the church, Agnes following. Julius went to the phone and dialled Patrick's number. Tad paced the room, flapping his arms by his sides, staring at the floor.

'I've got Tad here,' Agnes heard Julius say. He listened, then said, 'Yes, I thought it was something like that . . . Of course. We'll wait.'

Julius hung up and turned to Tad. 'He was late. He'd gone to your flat, but you'd already left. He's coming over here now.'

Tad stood and looked at him, breathing with relief. He allowed Agnes to sit him down in a chair, and accepted the mug of tea that she handed him. 'You spoke to him?' he said, his eyes wide, turning to Julius for reassurance.

'Yes.' Julius nodded. 'He'll be here in a minute.'

Tad rolled up his sleeve and looked at his watch. He traced the hands with his finger.

'Well, maybe five minutes,' Julius said.

Tad rolled his sleeve down again and drank noisily from his mug. 'I worry, you see,' he said, putting the mug down carefully on Julius's desk. 'They tell me not to, but I can't help it, can I? Not now, not with Matt gone too. You see, after Dad went the way he did, and now Matt . . . I went to the church, I asked Our Lady to promise that it would be me next, not Patrick. Don't let it be Patrick, I said to her, please . . . ' His voice tailed off and he stared out of the window into the distance. He blinked, then turned back to Julius. He nodded. 'Me next,' he said. 'I told her.' He picked up his mug again and drank in silence as a knock at the door announced Patrick's arrival.

'I'm so sorry,' Patrick said, coming into the room. 'I thought I'd said eleven.'

Tad fixed his eyes on him. 'Ten, you said.'

'I think it was eleven.'

'I worry so, you know I worry, you shouldn't make me . . . '

'No. I know. I'm sorry. Shall we go?' Patrick turned to Julius and Agnes. 'Thanks for looking after him.'

'They gave me tea. She did.' Tad pointed at Agnes, rising clumsily out of his chair to leave.

As Agnes opened the door for them, Patrick touched her arm. 'Um, about last night. I was a bit overwrought. I said some things that probably aren't . . . I mean, you know, overdoing it a bit . . . '

Agnes smiled at him. 'That's OK.'

'I was wondering whether . . .' He glanced at Julius. Julius busied himself tidying some papers on his desk. 'I wondered whether you'd like to come riding with me some day.'

'Yes.' Agnes glanced at Julius too.

'In fact, I was thinking of going, um, tomorrow. First time since he died, you see, I just wanted to get out there for some reason.' He looked at her, his eyes pleading.

'Sure.' Agnes nodded. 'OK. I'm not very good.'

Julius looked up at them both. 'She always says that.'

'I'll pick you up, then.'

'Fine.'

'Nineish?'

'Sure.'

'Right. Um, OK.' Patrick hesitated a moment. He glanced at Julius, who had returned to sorting out his desk. Tad was fiddling with the door handle, opening and shutting it. 'Good.' Patrick took his brother's arm. 'We'll go then.' The door closed behind them, and a second later their footsteps could be heard crunching the gravel of the drive.

Agnes glanced at Julius. 'Nice of you to give me permission.'

'I don't know what you mean.'

★ ★ ★

94

'How funny that Julius should surprise you after all these years.' Athena peered into a shop window. 'Oh, these clothes this winter, they're so dull, sweetie. It's all very well looking for a grey suit, but do I have to look like an air hostess?'

Agnes stood next to her. 'That one's quite elegant.'

'It's only five hundred quid.'

'Hmm.'

'You should get it.'

Agnes laughed. 'One day, when nuns are allowed a clothing allowance.'

'I'm sure God wants his girls looking good.'

'But not like air hostesses.'

'Although it's strangely appropriate, don't you think? Do you know, I really fancy some cake right now.'

'Cake would be fine.'

'And how handy that Fortnum's is just down the road.'

★   ★   ★

'You see,' Agnes said, pouring tea into two cups, 'he's just completely evasive. There's definitely something going on that he's not telling me. What's so funny?'

'I've always thought of you and Julius like

some old married couple. And now here you are having secrets from each other. Actually, that makes you even more like an old married couple.'

'It's not about secrets. Not really. But Patrick's known him longer than I have and — '

'See? That's just what I mean. There's a sense in which Julius has always belonged to you, and now you feel that he doesn't, that maybe he never has. Ooh, goody, cucumber sandwiches.' Athena reached across to take some.

'I've never thought Julius belongs to me.'

'You're jealous. You're jealous of this past that happened before you came into his life.'

'Nonsense.'

'Sweetie, I know just how you feel. At lunchtime, today, I went out with Nic; we were at this restaurant, his friend Vince, you know, the chef, he's just gone into partnership with someone. Dead fancy place it is, Brompton Road, very nice. Anyway, this woman comes flouncing up to our table and greets Nic like an old friend.'

'Not — ?'

'Yes. Linda. Exactly. He said it was a coincidence, she knows Vince too, they were all at college together. I think she knew he'd be there, he must have mentioned it to her.'

'What was she like?'

'Oh, blonde, pretty, about size eight.'

'Much too thin, then.'

'I know, sweetie, very unsexy when you're as old as she obviously is.'

'Well, that's some consolation. Have some more fruit cake.'

★ ★ ★

Agnes woke on Saturday to a bright, bracing morning. She dug out her old jodhpurs, marvelling that they still fitted her. She got her riding boots out of the back of her cupboard. They were beautifully made, in dark brown leather. She found some shoe polish and began to clean them, remembering when she'd first been given them — by Hugo, she thought, as if it was in another world, another lifetime, that she'd ever had a husband who might have given her riding boots. I must have had these since I was twenty, she thought. Trust Hugo to buy the best.

Her doorbell buzzed, and she let Patrick in.

'I'm going to have to borrow a hat,' she said. 'This one's too old.'

'Deborah'll have something to fit you,' Patrick said. 'Shall we go?'

As he opened the car door for her he

noticed her boots. 'They must have cost a bob or two.'

'They were made for me.'

'One day you must tell me about your past as a kept woman.'

'Kept in many senses,' she said, getting into the car. 'I paid the price.'

He looked at her sideways as he got into the driver's seat. 'You know, for a nun, you're very — um . . . '

'I'm very what?'

'I'm sure people are always saying things like that, though.'

'I'm sure they are.' she smiled, but he was concentrating on starting the car.

'I thought I'd go north of here on that motorway thing to the North Circular.'

'You know best.'

'If only that were true,' he said.

* * *

They left London behind them and drove through a glittering, frosty morning of bare trees and open fields. He talked to her about the stables; about the horse he'd chosen for her — 'a gelding, nice-natured, but with a lot of spirit'; about Tad, his concerns for him, how pleased he was with his progress — 'it's working with the horses, it's really calmed

98

him down a lot, you should see him with them, it's uncanny'; about Matthias — 'I miss him, Agnes. I can't believe he's gone. I was in his office this week; one of my graduate students is working with his team at work and I kept looking round for him.' He went quiet. They spent the rest of the drive in silence. Agnes looked out of the window at the ploughed earth of the winter fields. She felt suddenly light-hearted.

* * *

'Patrick, there you are. I've given you Mister Blue this morning, because silly old Penelope's gone lame.'

'Agnes, this is Deborah.'

The woman strode towards them, her arm outstretched, her hair roughly tied back, her legs in muddy jodhpurs.

'Pleased to meet you. And you're on dear Basil, you lucky girl.'

Agnes smiled at her, recognising her as one of the stable crowd who were at the funeral.

'I think Liz is coming with you, if that's OK. There's a livery she's working on, needs some exercise.'

'That's fine,' Patrick said. 'Isn't it?'

'Fine by me,' Agnes said.

Dear Basil, Agnes thought, flying through the Essex countryside behind the others, wondering whether he'd stop when they did. Liz seemed to be leaning over her horse's neck, a streak of yellow jacket, mud flying up behind her from the hooves. Patrick was ahead of her, disappearing along a track lined with trees. Liz turned down the track, then Agnes. Dear dear Basil, she thought, ducking under low branches. She brought him back to a canter as she saw the horses ahead slow, and caught up with them in a steady trot.

Patrick was red-faced and grinning. 'You should see your face. It's covered with mud.'

'Good,' she said.

They walked along the track, the horses blowing.

'This is where I fell,' Liz said suddenly.

'Mmm.' Patrick looked around him, distracted.

Agnes checked her horse alongside Liz's. 'What happened?'

'Well, that's what is so stupid. I got concussed. I can't remember. It's not as if I was doing anything wild. It's always the way, isn't it?' She laughed. 'I can jump the highest fences on the craziest horses and I'm fine. And then here I am, walking along in the woods here, and my horse keels over for some reason and I'm left with headaches for a week and a patch of my life I can't remember. But they found a golf ball, so they think it came over the fence there and hit my horse. She's fine now, though.'

Patrick was ahead of them, and now he turned in his saddle. 'Shall we do the hedges?'

'Sure. You OK?' Liz turned to Agnes.

'Um . . . I'm a bit out of practice.'

'They're only little. Look, those three along there.'

Agnes allowed her horse to follow the others as they sped into a fast canter. She remembered other times on horseback as a child in Provence, with her own pony, in the wealth and indolence of a neglected but privileged childhood. And later, when she was married, riding became an escape from the boredom of being Hugo's wife. Boredom. And terror. She leaned over her horse's neck as they flew over the jumps, one, then a second, a third, slowing to a trot as they circled the field.

'You looked great,' Patrick said. 'Not a novice at all.'

'Maybe my youth wasn't so misspent after all,' Agnes laughed, flushed and triumphant.

Liz's horse was tossing and rearing, and

now threatened to throw her altogether as a male voice shouted out from behind the hedge.

'What?' Liz shouted back.

'Liz!' the voice called. A young man appeared, wearing a scruffy anorak and a woollen hat.

'Wez, you bastard, this lady nearly threw me. Bloody chestnut mares.'

'I'm sorry.' He hung his head, grinning.

'Frightening the horses like that — what are you doing, lurking behind a hedge?' Liz was smiling now. Her horse stepped nervously, but no longer seemed determined to oust her from her seat.

'Oh, um, you know. Nothing,' he said. He lifted one edge of his hat and scratched his head.

'I know what you're doing.' Liz laughed. 'Casing the route?'

'Shush.'

'I won't tell.' She was coaxing, cajoling, as if to a child.

'There's a den in the copse over there. Your bastard friends are bound to sniff it out.' He looked up to her, appealing. 'Don't tell, Liz, promise.'

'You shouldn't tell me, then. It puts me in a difficult position.' Her horse pawed the ground, impatient.

'We'd better get going,' Patrick called to her.

'Still,' Wez was saying, 'one less this weekend, eh?'

'What did you say?' Liz was taking up her reins as her horse moved to join Patrick. Agnes followed.

'I said' — he was shouting now — 'I said, at least there's one less now.'

The three riders broke into a trot, leaving him behind. Agnes glanced back to see him trudging away towards the road, his hands in his pockets.

'I didn't hear what he said,' Liz said.

'It was something about Matthias, I think.' Agnes shortened her reins.

'He hated Matthias. He hates them all.'

'The hunt, I assume.'

Liz nodded. 'I'm not supposed to know about Wez and his friends, and their activities, because I'm so in with the riding crowd.'

'But you're friends with Wez too?'

'Not really.' She was quiet. 'He's a friend of a friend.'

'Do you hunt?' Agnes asked her.

'I — um — yes. Sometimes. Less than I used to.'

Patrick's horse broke into a canter as they left the woods and the others followed, quickening their pace as they came out on to a long, open track. Liz's horse started to race Patrick's; Agnes kept behind. Then there was just the speed and grace of her horse, the flickering sunlight on the stubble of crops, the cold air sharp across her face.

They arrived back at the stables, mud-spattered, flushed and happy. Deborah came to greet them.

'All in one piece, then?' She seemed surprised.

Behind her stood a young woman in green wellingtons, holding a small child by the hand.

'Mary Wells,' Patrick said. 'How nice to see you again.'

6

They dismounted from their horses. Two teenage girls appeared from nowhere to lead Patrick's and Agnes's horses away. Liz took hers further up the yard.

Mary smiled as Patrick approached her. 'What are you doing here?' he asked her.

'My daughter rides here. Liz got her interested and now nothing will keep her away.'

'It's in her blood,' Patrick said. Mary glanced up at him. Her eyes seemed liquid with feeling. She looked away.

'Your mother, I meant.' He shifted on his feet.

'I know what you meant.'

They stared at the ground for a moment. 'I — um — I just didn't expect to see you . . . ' Patrick began.

'Well, here I am.'

'How are you?' The words seemed to take him by surprise as he spoke them. He looked up at her.

'As well as can be expected.' Her eyes were piercing blue as she met his gaze.

He reached out and touched her hand. 'I

know . . . I mean . . . ' he began. 'I'm not supposed to know . . . '

'There's nothing to know. Nothing at all. Is there?' Her eyes blazed with the sudden challenge, then became blank again. She looked round for her daughter, who had wandered off and was chatting to Liz by a stable door. 'I'm going now. It's time for Charlie's lesson.' She spoke deliberately, turning away from Patrick without a backward glance.

Patrick joined Agnes as they walked back to his car. He shook his head, began to speak, then shook his head again.

'It must be terrible. If you're someone's mistress and then he dies.' Agnes spoke calmly, watching Patrick. 'The silence must be the worst thing. Not being the widow. Not having the rightful place.'

Patrick got into the car next to her. 'How did you know?' he said.

'Just the way she is, I suppose. And that note.'

Patrick glanced at her, giving nothing away. He turned away and started the car. They pulled out of the drive and on to the road. 'As she said' — he changed gear clumsily — 'there's nothing to know. Not now.'

'How does Julius know her?' Her voice seemed too loud.

He shrugged. 'Just from way back. You know, when we were at St Joseph's together. We were all close. Her mother . . . she'd have been fifty-odd now. Funny to think of it.'

'She died?'

He nodded. 'A few years ago now. Eight, maybe? Ten?'

'She must have been quite young when she died.'

'In her forties. Cancer.'

'How terrible.'

'It was very sad. We were all very fond of her.'

A silence settled on the car. 'Poor Julius,' Patrick said suddenly.

He was staring out at the road ahead, his face blank. Agnes opened her mouth to speak, to ask — to ask what, she wondered. To ask, Why? Why poor Julius? Perhaps it's none of my business, she thought.

★ ★ ★

'Perhaps it's none of my business,' she said, raising her wine glass, surveying Athena's black wool dress and thinking how it suited her. Outside the wide curved windows of the restaurant people passed in groups, their breath making clouds in the evening air.

'Nonsense. How long have you known

Julius? For ever, sweetie. Of course it's your business. Do you think that waitress is ever going to notice us?' Athena picked up the menu. 'How hungry are you?'

'Starving. I spent most of this morning on horseback.'

'Oh, sweetie, how I wish I liked doing things like that. So rejuvenating, isn't it, taking risks?'

'Well, I'm not sure — '

'I'd look ten years younger for it, I'm sure. The outdoor life. Horses are out, of course, too hairy. And all that manure . . . Wind-surfing maybe — no, I hate getting wet. Maybe parachuting, sweetie, what do you think?'

'Hmmm.'

'Gliding? Bungee-jumping?'

'Athena!'

'Oh, good, at last, here she comes. What are you having?'

'Grilled turbot, I think.'

'Mmmm. And the pheasant for me.'

They watched the waitress depart. Athena sighed heavily. 'It's not going to work, sweetie.'

'What isn't?'

'Dangerous sports. For me, I mean.'

Agnes nodded. 'No. You're right.'

'The nearest I get to taking a risk these

days is trying on a size twelve instead of a size fourteen.'

Agnes nodded again. Athena sipped her wine. 'Still,' she said, 'life seems to have acquired an edge, what with Nic behaving like a teenager all of a sudden.'

'What's happened?'

'Oh, an odd phone call, when I was there last night. He wouldn't say who. And him all pink-cheeked and awkward, like a sixteen-year-old. I'd find it endearing in some men, but when your hair's as thin as his, it just doesn't work, sweetie, does it?'

'What will you do?'

'Do? What can I do? If there are fault lines in my relationship with Nic, I put them there. He says there's nothing to talk about. Nagging him will just make it worse. No, sweetie, I've just got to concentrate on being drop-dead gorgeous and hope for the best.'

'More shopping then?'

Athena nodded. 'Frankly, it's the only answer.'

★ ★ ★

They left the restaurant, wandering out into the street arm in arm.

'And are you seeing this Patrick again?'

'I expect so. I mean, only that he keeps on

meeting up with Julius.'

'Is he nice?'

'Um — yes. Yes, he is. A bit — he's a bit distracted. Grief, and drinking, and gambling.'

'Sounds just your type.'

'Thanks.'

'Has he asked you to go riding again?'

'Well, he did. He's riding again tomorrow.'

'And?'

'He thought they might be hunting. It's not the sort of thing you can just tag along for.'

'Oh dear, no, not hunting, sweetie. Aren't we supposed to disapprove of it these days?'

'He's driving his brother over to the stables. He works there at weekends.'

'And you're not going?'

'It's Sunday, Athena.'

'Oh, of course. I forgot.'

Agnes laughed.

'Why are you laughing?'

'It's a funny thing to forget about me. You know, that Sundays might be important.'

'I'm just so secular, sweetie. All I know about Sundays is that some shops are annoyingly shut.' Athena leaned on her heavily as they reached her flat.

'Never mind,' Agnes said as Athena kissed her goodnight, 'there's always Monday.'

' 'And the son said to him, 'Father, I have sinned against heaven, and in thy sight, and am no more worthy to be called thy son . . . ' ' ' Agnes looked across at Louise, who was listening intently, and Helen, who had her eyes tight shut in concentration. The chapel was full, as all the sisters gathered for Sunday morning mass.

' 'But the father said, 'Bring hither the fatted calf, and kill it . . . for this my son was dead, and is alive again; he was lost and is found . . . ' ' '

How easy to be Louise, Agnes thought. Like the older son, who just stays put with his father, sure of his place.

* * *

'I don't think I should be novice mistress,' Agnes said, settling down in the chair next to Julius's desk. The daylight had long since faded from the room, and Julius's anglepoise lamp threw a pool of light that left the outer edges of the room in shadow.

He smiled. 'Why not?'

'I envy them. They're both so sure, particularly Louise. If one of them started saying she wanted to leave, I'd probably support her. She'd become my parallel self who managed to escape.'

'It's this inheritance, isn't it?'

'I don't know what to do. I know what I ought to do, which is just accept. Accept that this life is all there is. It's like Athena and her clothes, she should just accept that there's no such thing as the perfect suit.'

'You'd hate it if she did that, you'd have no one to go shopping with.'

Agnes laughed. 'All right, bad example. Oh, I don't know, Julius. It's like the prodigal son. Some of us just have to learn the hard way, I suppose, that our place is with God.'

'And God is forgiving of that,' Julius said. 'That's the point of that story, that even for those of us who squander all God's blessings, and then have to tread a difficult path back to him' — he spoke with sudden feeling — 'even for us, God is in a way more pleased, because we've learned it for ourselves, rather than just accepting, with blind faith, like the other brother.' He stopped, breathing heavily.

'But Julius,' Agnes said, watching him, 'for you, it hasn't been difficult. Has it?'

He looked up at her, then away. He shook his head.

'I saw Mary yesterday,' Agnes said.

'Where?'

'At the stables.'

'Oh. Yes, of course. Did you have a nice ride?'

'Fantastic.' She watched him still. 'Patrick said — Patrick said it was in Mary's blood. Riding.'

Julius's eyes had a distant look. 'Yes. Her — her family. Horse people, all of them. Connemara ponies.' He nodded. 'In the blood.' He looked at Agnes. 'Does she ride? Mary?'

'A bit. I think.' Agnes met his eyes. 'It was her daughter, yesterday, Charlie, having a lesson.'

'Yes. Um . . . yes.' He stood up, distracted. 'I — um — I have to go now. Get the church ready, you know. Some paperwork still. I'll see you soon.'

She got up and kissed him briefly on the cheek. She hesitated at the door, then opened it and went out of the church. The night was cold. She thought of Julius, sitting in the warm glow of his anglepoise lamp. He told me to go, she thought. He never does that. Something has changed, she thought. Patrick has brought something into Julius's life. And I don't like it, she added to herself, trying to dismiss such a thought as childish. It is childish, she thought, going out on to the main road, waiting by the traffic lights. But I don't.

Late that night she lit her candle and settled in prayer.

'As the night watch looks for the morning . . . '

She thought about Julius, dismissing her from his church. What was it Athena had said? That he was immutable, like a rock. But what if he isn't? she thought. What if I don't know him at all?

'For thus says our God: as a mother comforts her children, so I will comfort you . . . '

Cast adrift, Agnes thought. No mother. No roots. No place to call my own. To throw in my lot with the order. To say, this is how my life has turned out.

But no Julius?

Agnes felt tears prick her eyes at the thought of his distance from her.

* * *

'I went down to the land beneath the earth, yet you brought up my life from the depths, O God . . . ' The words seemed to be spoken, but as she woke, Agnes realised they were from her dream. Something to do with light and darkness. And choosing. It was that door again, the one at the end of the corridor.

The phone rang suddenly. She snatched it up.

'It's Patrick. Um — is that you?'

'What is it?'

'I can't find Julius, you see, I didn't want to bother you — '

'What's happened?'

'It's Tad. He's gone missing. Last night. He didn't come back from the stables. Something happened there, about Matt, it really upset him. We've been waiting up . . . I need to look for him.'

'I'll be right there.'

7

'So what happened?'

Patrick walked slightly in front of her, hunched against the cold. The outlines of the city were softened by the mist. 'There was a row,' Patrick said. 'At the stables, yesterday. Tad got very upset. Liz blames herself, but it's really not her fault. At least she got him back to London.'

'Did he go home?'

'She dropped him off outside the hostel. Yesterday evening. She always does that, he's usually reliable. But it seems he pretended to go in, and then left again.'

'No one saw him?'

Patrick shook his head.

'Where are we going?' They were walking towards the river, dodging the rush-hour traffic that edged its way slowly through the choked streets.

'I thought we should start at the shrine.'

'Of course.'

They walked in silence, until Patrick said, 'Thank you for this. I'd have asked Julius, but I couldn't find him.'

'It's fine.'

The river was a bleak ribbon of grey, stretching away from them into the mist. Agnes wanted to talk, to ask about what had upset Tad, what was the row about, was he violent? Did he often go missing? Why was Patrick so keen not to be alone? But something silenced her, as if her very thoughts were muffled by the grey chill of the day.

The church of St Mary Rotherhithe was unlocked. They went in, blinking in the sudden darkness. There was a solitary clergyman removing altar cloths at the east end of the church. He turned round, surprised to see visitors, then nodded at them and went about his business. At the far end of the Lady chapel, Agnes glimpsed the statue of the Virgin. She was made in porcelain, with a white face and blue garments. It seemed unlikely that she'd ever really weep.

Patrick sat down heavily in a pew.

'Shall we wait for him?' Agnes sat next to him. The heavy wooden door behind the choir stalls swung on its hinges as the clergyman went out into the vestry.

Patrick sighed. 'He kept doing this in Kent. I thought maybe he'd settle down a bit in London.'

'What upset him?'

'I don't know the whole story. Liz tried to

tell me.' Patrick touched the old wood of the pew end; Agnes noticed how long and pale his fingers were. 'I wasn't there. It happened in the yard, I was still out in the fields. Liz tried to explain but it all seemed rather muddled. Someone said something, about the way Matt died apparently, which upset him. But you see' — he raised his head to look at her — 'with Tad, he takes things the wrong way. A quite harmless remark, in his mind, can be taken quite differently.'

The door creaked again as the priest reappeared. He nodded at them again, a candlestick in each hand. 'Father Dominic,' he said, waving a candlestick towards himself in a vague gesture of introduction. 'Can I be of any assistance?'

'No, um . . . ' Patrick stood up clumsily. 'My brother . . . He's — um . . . We were looking for him, that's all.' He took a few steps towards the priest. 'He comes here sometimes, but obviously, today . . . ' He shrugged, defeated.

'I can tell him you were looking for him, if I see anyone who resembles a lost brother.' The priest smiled.

'Thank you.' Patrick smiled back. He rejoined Agnes by the door, and they left the church, blinking once more in the pale light of the misty day.

They walked aimlessly, skirting the edge of the river. The crisp glass of redevelopments gave way to dereliction, to old warehouses that rose up from the river mud in muted shades of brown and charcoal.

'I don't think he'd have strayed this far,' Patrick said after a while. They stopped for a moment, the clouds of their breath merging with the fog.

'We should turn back.' Agnes sounded uncertain, but Patrick nodded. They retraced their steps, staring at strangers. Once Agnes thought she heard his voice, a distant shouting from the muddy banks beneath them, but there was no one there. They passed the church, which now was locked.

'Perhaps he's gone home on his own.' Agnes looked at Patrick. He seemed strained and tired.

'Perhaps.'

'Good dog, there's a good dog.' The voice rose, loud and distinct, from the river bank beneath the church.

'It's him,' Agnes whispered.

'You'll look after me, won't you?' They heard the same voice.

'Tad!' Patrick darted to the wall and peered over.

'They killed my brother, you see, and they tried to kill Liz too.'

'Tad, it's me.' Patrick ran to the steps and descended them fast. Agnes followed.

Tad was staring out at the silted, churning water. Next to him was a dog, sitting at his feet in a bedraggled way. Tad turned and saw Patrick, and smiled at him.

'Tad.' Patrick took his hand and led him gently away from the river, up the steps. 'You must be hungry,' he said when they'd reached the top.

Tad shifted from one foot to the other. 'He was killed, you see. Liz said. She said they'd tried to kill her too.'

'We can go back to our café on the High Street,' Agnes said. 'If everyone can face walking a bit further.'

They walked in silence. The dog accompanied them, but no one felt like arguing about it. They reached the café and, following some instinct, the dog wandered away.

Inside, Agnes was glad of the warmth. They ordered platefuls of fried food and large mugs of tea. When Tad's was put before him, he left it untouched.

'Tad . . . ' Patrick's tone was coaxing. 'What happened? At the stables?'

Tad met Agnes's eyes. 'Liz said . . . Liz said she'd remembered something. She thinks they did it on purpose. Her accident. And Wez was arguing with her, he's such a — such a stupid git.' He emphasised the words. 'He doesn't know anything. And he was saying you couldn't kill someone like that, aiming a golf ball at them, you just couldn't, and I got upset then, because Liz was sure she was right, and I couldn't think straight, I started thinking about what would happen if you tried to hit a moving target with a golf ball, it would be like this, you see, a bit like this . . . ' He indicated an arc with his hands.

'And is that why you ran away from your home last night?'

'Last night?' He screwed up his face, trying to remember. 'No,' he said. 'I left the flats last night because of George.'

'George?' Patrick looked wearily at him. 'Who's George?'

'My dog, of course. He followed me in the street yesterday, he was waiting when I got back, then the stupid people at the flats said I couldn't keep him. So I thought I'd go somewhere where I could.'

'Tad, not another row, please.' Patrick picked at the food on his plate.

'But George — he's mine.'

'If they say no dogs — '

'Then they're wrong.' Tad picked up his knife and fork and began to eat.

They dropped him at the hostel, and he waved them off cheerfully.

'Well, what was all that about?' Agnes said to Patrick as they walked back to St Simeon's.

'I know what it was. And it could have been much worse.'

'What was it?'

'There was our father,' Patrick said. 'It was suicide, you see. We all carry it with us. And now there's Matthias. It's not surprising Tad's feeling the pressure.'

'But — '

'Grief,' Patrick said. 'Like a burden.' At the church gates he grasped Agnes's hand. 'Thanks,' he said.

'And Liz thinks something happened on purpose.' She met his eyes, but they were pale and distant like the mist.

'I've thought about it,' Patrick said, his voice tired. 'You know I have. And now Liz is thinking about it too. But who would want them both dead? Liz and Matt? And if someone did, would you choose something as inaccurate as a golf ball, when the whole bloody sport is built around the fact that you can't predict what the buggers are going to do?'

Agnes smiled. 'No,' she agreed.

'Anyway . . . ' His gaze was distant again. 'Thanks.'

She watched him as he walked away, tall and thin and fragile against the rush of traffic on the main road. She turned towards the church. Julius would be in his office, sitting at his desk in the warmth of his old gas fire. She took a step towards the gate, then stopped.

Perhaps . . . she thought. Perhaps I wouldn't be welcome.

I'm always welcome, she thought. She looked at her watch. She'd promised Madeleine to do an afternoon shift. Might as well be early, she thought, turning away from the gate and heading away up the main road to the hostel.

★ ★ ★

'Someone to see you, Sister.' Agnes raised her eyes from the desk, relieved to be called away from trying to make sense of Madeleine's chaotic paperwork and extrovert handwriting. She went out to the hallway.

Liz stood in the doorway, shifting uncertainly on her feet, the fading daylight behind her. 'They said it would be OK to find you here.'

'Sure,' Agnes said. 'Who's 'they'?'

123

'Um, Julius. Mary's friend.'

Agnes took in these words. Then she said, 'Come in. We might get the kitchen to ourselves for a while.'

Agnes put the kettle on while Liz settled down at the table. 'You see,' Liz began, 'it's about Tad.' She took off her jacket and flung it down on the bench beside her. 'And about Matthias, really. And — I talked to Patrick about it, a bit, but I didn't want to burden him with it; Mary said he's got enough to deal with and she's right, isn't she? And then I thought about telling Julius, but Mary said she thought that wouldn't be such a good idea, and so in the end I thought of you, and I asked Patrick where to find you, and he sent me to Julius's place, at the church, you know, and then Julius sent me here.'

Agnes searched the cupboards for some leaf tea, then settled for teabags. She poured boiling water into the pot. 'And what did Julius say?'

'Oh, not much.' Liz smiled. 'He's a nice man, isn't he? Mary said — ' She stopped, and ran her fingers through her short hair.

'What did Mary say?' Agnes turned to face her, milk bottle in one hand.

'Oh, nothing.' She smiled, more nervously this time.

Agnes turned back to pouring two mugs of tea.

'It was about yesterday, you see, at the stables,' Liz began again. 'Tad was so upset, I'm really worried about him. Patrick said you'd had to go and look for him.'

'Yes.' Agnes handed her a mug of tea and sat down opposite her.

'It was Wez, you see, he provokes him on purpose, even though he knows that Tad's — well, you know, fragile. Wez never liked Matthias, it was the hunting; it was all coming to a head, and Matthias was so certain about the hunt, so kind of insistent in defending it, I knew it would cause him trouble in the end, and so Wez's making some joke about good riddance or something, out in the pony field — he shouldn't even have been there — and then Tad was nearby, and I was trying to shut Wez up, but he wouldn't shut up, and then I said something about my accident, and Wez just laughed and said, 'What were the chances?' And I said, what did he mean, and I realised I'd upset Tad talking about my accident the way I did, and Wez said, 'Golf ball frightening his horse — what are the chances of that happening?' Like it was a joke.' She stopped for breath, shaking her head.

'And Tad heard?'

'Yes.' Liz sipped her tea. 'And it was guaranteed to upset Tad, 'cos things like odds and chances, it's kind of Tad's thing, he does calculations all the time, numbers and stuff, seeing patterns . . . And so when I'd said this thing about my accident, and then Wez went on about chances, Tad went all quiet, and Wez's watching him — '

'Why would Wez provoke Tad?'

''Cos he's a stupid bastard, that's why.'

'Does he dislike Tad?'

'No. But he hates the stables. And he likes a fight.' She drank some more tea. 'You see, round there, that part of Essex, it's a very odd part of the world. There's all that money, and horses, and hunting and stuff — and then you've got people like Wez, who claim to love animals but don't like people, really. And you've got people on the dole who can't afford to buy anywhere to live, and people from the City moving in, pushing up house prices, buying up land. And if they don't move in they commute from their penthouse flats on the edge of the City and use it like a playground, for riding and golf and stuff. There's a lot of bad feeling.'

'You live there?'

'Yes. I'm a local girl.'

'But you drive to London, for Tad.'

Liz smiled at her. 'What is this? Yes, I spend

126

some of the week in London. For the night life. A friend lets me sleep in her spare room. If I'm doing the drive, I take Tad with me.'

'How do you know Wez?'

'He's just part of the crowd. I was at school with his brother. And he goes around with some of my friends.'

'But why attack Tad?'

'I don't think he meant to. But Matthias's death — it's shocked a lot of people. And having Wez making stupid jokes about it — I think it was too much for Tad. All the way home he was drawing his things on bits of paper; he has a notebook, and he was writing numbers and shapes in it, and muttering to himself. I couldn't get through to him. I should've seen him into the hostel myself, but I saw the door open, and I thought that was enough.'

'Don't blame yourself. He was OK when we found him. Just hungry.'

'S'pose so.' She sighed and drained her mug. 'I just wanted to talk to someone about it.'

'That's fine. Any time.'

'Really?'

'Yes. Really.'

Liz reached for her jacket.

'Your accident,' Agnes said, 'what do you mean about it being on purpose?'

Liz sat quietly for a moment. 'I've started to get these flashback things. Only I don't know if it's my memory returning, or just some kind of hallucination.'

'What are they like, these flashbacks?'

'Strange. Dreamlike.'

'Can you remember the accident itself?'

Liz shook her head. 'But it's afterwards. I remember lying on my back. Or maybe I'm imagining it. It's all a bit like a dream, and I'm seeing the branches of the trees and the sun shining through them. But the main thing is . . . ' She hesitated again. 'The main thing is that there's this man. Looking down at me.'

'What's he like?'

'He's got kind of dark eyes, and he's looking at me, and I'm asking him to help, but he doesn't. He just walks away.' She tried to smile. 'It's probably just some kind of imagined thing. Post-traumatic stress or whatever they call it.'

'He might have been a passer-by.'

'But he'd have helped.'

'Perhaps he went to get help.'

'Perhaps. But when I have this memory thing, there's this feeling with it. Kind of menacing. I sense that this man doesn't care . . . doesn't care about how I am. It's weird, and it's quite scary.'

'Was there any reason to be scared at the time? Apart from the fact that you'd fallen off?'

'No. And falling off isn't scary. Not once you're on the ground.'

'No. I suppose not.' Agnes smiled at her.

'Better go. Thanks for listening.' She picked up her jacket. In the hallway she hesitated. 'Me and Matt, you see,' she said.

'But why you two? Who is there who'd want you both out of the way?'

She frowned. 'There's this dispute. About the land. There's a friend of Matt's, he's a bit odd, quite elderly, ex-army, he's taken over his brother's farm. And there's a border dispute, and various people are taking sides. Matt was helping him, and then I got involved, because my father knew the family of this army chap — he's called Stewart Lode. Dad was Master of Hounds for a while, years ago, and so he'd noted when they built the ditches that everyone's arguing about now. And as my dad's dead, I've been the signatory on the documents that go to the solicitors.'

'Supporting this person in the dispute?'

She nodded. 'But you see . . . ' She shook her head. 'It's not just me and Matt, there's other people involved. I don't see they'd single us out, and anyway, it's only a few

129

yards of land, it's hardly worth . . . ' She went quiet. 'It's hardly worth — you know,' she finished.

'No,' Agnes agreed.

'Anyway, thanks for listening. We all liked Matt, we're all a bit upset, that's probably all it is. Thanks.'

'Any time. Really.' Agnes watched her go out into the twilight, her jacket bobbing bright in the yellow of the streetlamps.

At home Agnes made some thin slices of toast and opened some expensive liver pâté from the delicatessen. What did Mary say about Julius? she wondered, spreading the pâté thickly. What was Liz about to say? And these flashbacks, she thought. She pictured Liz, fallen from her horse, her head injured, lying on her back. And some man looking at her.

But it was an accident, she thought. Like Matthias. Wasn't it? Or was Liz right to think there was more to it? What were the chances? she thought. What are the odds of anyone doing such a thing by design? On purpose?

Perhaps Patrick's right. Perhaps there's some kind of pattern in all this. And perhaps Tad's right, and all these diagrams he's been drawing will reveal a great and terrible truth about Matthias's death.

Or perhaps it's all random. All just a string of random events, thrown together with no meaning to connect them. Liz's accident, and Matthias's accident. And only God can know the meaning of them.

And maybe, she thought, maybe even God —

What was I about to think? she thought. That even with God, these events might be meaningless?

Where does that leave my faith?

And what do I tell Helen? And Louise? That, for all we know, the universe may be quite meaningless, a collection of particles, gas and dust, and all the events we experience may have no meaning, not only to us, but in some kind of absolute sense.

She glanced at her mantelpiece, at the icon of St Francis that she kept there, at the clock with its rhythmic, spinning spheres.

A picture of order, she thought. Like the universe, she thought. Everything working according to its laws.

Not meaningless at all, she thought. Not random chaotic particles colliding, but neat, orderly laws. Like clockwork.

She watched the brass spheres spinning, back and forth. Particles colliding. The words stayed in her mind. Collisions, she thought. Like golf balls.

Oh Julius, she thought. I'm becoming an atheist. Help.

She rested her hand on the phone receiver, about to dial his number.

And I can't even talk to you, she thought. Here I am, losing my faith, heading for eternal damnation. And it'll be all your fault, Julius.

The phone rang and made her jump. She picked up the receiver. 'Julius?'

'No, it's Patrick.'

'Oh.'

'I've been thinking about what you said. About what Liz said. Two accidents, two *similar* accidents — the chances, you see. The odds . . . ' His voice was uneven. 'I know I was drunk last time I said this, but — but my suspicions haven't gone away. About Matt's death. And then today, I was at the office, Matt's place, one of my graduate students is doing a placement there. And Allen was talking in his usual way, shooting his mouth off . . . Listen, are you free tomorrow? I'll tell you then.'

'Sure.'

'One o'clock OK? There's a place just behind Blackfriars Bridge, I used to go there with Matt . . . ' His voice faltered. 'Um, got a pen? I'll give you directions.'

After he'd hung up, Agnes stared at the

restaurant's address. What if he's right? What if there's some terrible order in all this after all?

And then what? Does that make my faith stronger, if God shows me some kind of divine pattern? Or shouldn't I have faith regardless of any pattern, any meaning? Shouldn't it just be enough to believe?

She went to bed, thinking she'd dream of the house in France again. But instead she dozed uneasily, trying to shake off an image of lying under a tree in the mud, with the sun shining darkly through branches that shook in a menacing way.

★ ★ ★

Agnes was shown to a table by the window. She was aware of snow-white linen and white plates bright with silvery winter sun.

'I invited Julius.' Patrick's voice came from behind her. 'But he said no. Sorry I'm late.'

'That's OK.'

'Wine? Have you ordered?' He picked up the wine list, handed Agnes a menu, waved at the waiter. 'Red? White? They have a very nice Petit-Chablis here. How hungry are you? The halibut's always good, if they've got it.'

Ice buckets and bottles and glasses arrived, and wine was poured.

'I'm really glad you came,' Patrick said. 'There's really no one else . . . I can't burden Karen with it.'

'What is it?'

'Allen's bought this land. Out in Essex. He's a real East-End barrow boy at heart, but he's got pretensions, I suppose. And he's been developing it, got some local business-man involved out there. And the whole thing's stalled because of a boundary dispute; apparently he might not have the right to the whole piece of land, something about ditches — and he was bragging on about fixing the dispute, and it turns out this neighbour he's been arguing with is a friend of Matt's.'

'Liz told me. I didn't know it was Allen.'

'Some retired army fellow who's taken over his brother's farm.'

'And Liz said . . . ' Agnes took a deep breath. 'She's involved in the dispute too. Her father knew this army chap, apparently. She's been giving evidence.'

Patrick looked at Agnes. He frowned. 'And what's even odder' — he leaned over and refilled her glass — 'is that yesterday we were in Matt's office looking at some basic paperwork, just statistics, pension fund stuff, and Allen comes into the room and insists he needs the papers we were working with, scoops them all up and goes.'

'Perhaps he did need them,' Agnes said.

Patrick shook his head. 'They were old, they were only relevant for my student's analysis. Anyway, it was the way he did it.'

'What do you do?' Agnes asked suddenly. 'I mean, in your work?'

'Maths.' Patrick sounded weary.

'But what kind of maths?'

He smiled at her. 'Whatever they want me to teach.'

'But what do you *do*?'

'Do?' He met her eyes. 'I do sums.'

'What kind of sums?'

'Well . . . ' He fiddled with his knife, crossing it over his fork. 'My own work is in dynamical systems.'

'And what's that?'

'You really want to know? Well, I suppose it's about probability. Predicting the behaviour of things, the likelihood of some things to cluster together and others to diverge.'

'What kind of things?'

He looked at her, and shook his head. 'Not real things. Abstractions of real things. Numbers. Points in space. In a periodic system, points recur precisely. In a random system, points scatter around.'

'So it has no use in this world, then?'

'On the contrary. It's a way of proving things that couldn't otherwise be proved.

When your common sense tells you one thing, the maths might tell you something different.'

'And will the maths be truer than my common sense?'

'Always.' He laughed.

'And you enjoy it?'

'Yes. Well . . . I enjoy my own work. I like teaching. But,' he sighed, 'I can't see I'll be there much longer. Either I'll leave, or they'll get rid of me. They're already talking about early retirement — in fact, at my age, it's not that early, you know. I forget to turn up to these interminable meetings we're all supposed to go to; I don't publish enough for all their assessment exercises . . . I should just crawl away and go and write my definitive publication for my retirement.'

'Which is?'

He laughed, and shook his head. 'No,' he said. 'Not me. I'll go as late as I can, I can't afford to go any earlier.' He sipped his wine. 'That's what makes me sick about the Allens of this world, all that money generating itself out of the fears of ordinary people.'

'You don't like him,' Agnes said.

'With good reason,' Patrick said, as their food arrived. He began to eat hungrily, then stopped. 'Isn't that . . . ?' He was staring across the restaurant.

Agnes followed his line of vision. 'Judy,' she said.

'Yes. Judy.' Patrick returned to his plate. 'How's your fish?'

'Lovely, thanks. So where does this leave you?'

Patrick put down his fork. 'I can't get rid of the feeling that Matt's death wasn't — wasn't straightforward. They said — the pathologist — he had a head injury consistent with being hit hard by a golf ball. And in falling from his horse, as a result of that, he broke his neck.'

'And he wasn't wearing a hat.'

Patrick shook his head. 'He was only hacking, he didn't bother sometimes.'

'He's mad. I mean — I'm capable of behaving dangerously, but I'd wear a hat.'

Patrick laughed. 'The modern risk-taker. We choose our danger carefully — and we always wear a hat.'

Agnes laughed too.

'But you see,' Patrick went on, serious again. 'A golf ball seems to have hit him — they found a ball nearby — and he fell. And exactly the same thing happened to Liz, in the same place.'

'She remembered . . . ' Agnes hesitated.

Patrick looked up sharply. 'Remembered what?'

'She has this flashback of seeing a man

137

staring down at her, after her fall. And then he walked away. She said he was menacing.'

Patrick leaned towards her. 'What did he look like?'

'Dark eyes, she said.'

'Did she recognise him?'

'No.'

'You see?' Patrick's eyes seemed bright in his thin face. 'Something was going on.'

'But Patrick, surely, no one's going to choose that method — '

'How do we know that? For all we know — ' He broke off suddenly, watching someone come towards them.

'Hi there.' Judy was standing by their table.

'Hello.'

'Didn't I see you in the office earlier?'

'That's right.'

Judy looked down at him, but he was staring at the tablecloth. She glanced at Agnes. 'Hello,' she said.

'Hello.'

'We met, at the funeral.'

'Yes.' Agnes looked at Patrick, but he was busy lining up the spare cutlery into neat rows. 'Yes, we did,' Agnes repeated, looking up into Judy's dark eyes.

'Oh, well . . . ' Judy glanced across the room to her table. 'I'd better be going.' She smiled, a charming, generous smile, and then

138

merged with the clatter of the room to join her colleagues.

'I never liked her, either.' Patrick had finished his cutlery arrangement.

'Did Matthias like her?' Agnes watched him.

He looked up. 'I think — the problem is, I think she thought he did.'

'Meaning?'

Patrick sighed. 'Matt was charming. Particularly with women. He didn't know he was doing it, which made him all the more appealing to them. It happened quite often that some lady would misconstrue his customary good nature and assume something — something more.'

'At the funeral, Karen looked at her. At Judy. In a — in a certain way.'

Patrick shook his head. 'Poor Karen. You see, with Matt, you could never be sure. Matthias was lucky, you see.' He smiled at her. 'You know, the classic lucky man. Luck followed him around.'

'But — '

'Two devoted women. More, probably. And his career. Brilliant.'

'But his death . . . '

'Luck too. His kind of luck. We're long-lived, our family. Hang on to life by a thread for decades, withering on the branch.

139

Better to go as he did than fade away in a home for the elderly somewhere. More wine?' He refilled her glass.

Agnes sat silent for a while. She gazed out of the window at the ribbon of the river, sparkling in the sun. She sipped her wine. 'And you,' she said. 'Are you lucky too?'

He smiled at her. 'Not like Matt. Raffles. Tombolas. That's my luck. Silly things. I always get the giant teddy.' He laughed.

'And the casinos?'

'Yes.'

'And the horses?'

'Yes. The horses. But it's all about what you stake. I'll put in twenty quid, and get forty back.'

'You still win.'

'But Matt — Matt played to win. High stakes. He earned a fortune. He had Karen and the boys. He had Mary . . . ' His voice tailed off. 'That's luck. My luck' — he fished in his pocket and pulled out a betting slip — 'Dawn Mist. Two-fifteen at Newmarket.'

'Will it have won?'

'I've no idea. It's an each-way bet. Outsider, twenty-eight to one.' He unfolded the slip and handed it to her. 'You have it.'

'But I'm not allowed to — '

'Just this once. It might not win anyway.'

'But if it does?'

140

'Donate the money. Do what you like.'

Agnes stared at it. She held it between her fingers, then slipped it into her pocket. She smiled at him. 'So you're both lucky. You and Matt.'

'And Tad.'

'But — '

'You don't know Tad. He's the luckiest of us all.'

'But how can he be?'

'With me it's just games. Cards. Horses.'

'And with him?'

He began to undo his cutlery arrangement, reordering the neat lines. 'With Tad . . . Things happen with Tad. It's a kind of gift.' He met her eyes, and saw her incomprehension. He smiled. 'Things happen around him. Kind of miracles, really. Yes. Miracles. He allows things to happen . . . ' His voice tailed off, and he drained his glass. He picked up the bottle, which was empty, and frowned at it.

They left together, and Patrick directed her to the betting shop, before ambling off to catch a bus back to the university.

Agnes went into the shop, blinking against the smoke and dim light after the brightness of the afternoon outside. She presented the betting slip to the clerk at the counter. He nodded. 'Came in second. Good odds.' He counted out a series of notes, rather a lot, it seemed to Agnes. She pocketed them, wondering how to explain her sudden wealth to her fellow sisters. She glanced up at the television screens, fingering the notes in her pocket. I could put a tenner down on the next race, she thought. She gathered her coat around her and went out into the afternoon sun. She realised she was free for the rest of the day, unaccountable to hostel or novices or community. She walked along the embankment, feeling light-headed from the wine and the sun, the winnings in her pocket and the fresh breeze that stirred the water's surface.

★ ★ ★

At home there was a message on her answering machine.

'Agnes, it's Liz. Can you phone me?' The voice sounded nervous and urgent.

Agnes dialled the number Liz had left her. 'Hello?'

'Agnes, hi. Are you free? Now?'

'Um — yes. Suppose so. Why?'

'Do you fancy a trip to the stables?'

'Why?'

There was a brief silence. Then Liz said, 'I can't sleep. These last few nights, they've been awful, I'm so troubled by these

142

memories returning. Annelise — she's my friend — she said maybe I should go back. Walk the path again. See what happens. And then I thought perhaps you'd come with me.'

Agnes looked out of her window at the perfect afternoon, the crisp golden light. 'OK,' she said.

'You see . . . ' Liz hesitated. 'I've remembered some more. The man who was standing looking down at me. He was holding something. It was a gun.'

8

The light was fading as Agnes and Liz walked along the bridle path. They walked in silence. After a while Liz stopped. 'Here,' she said. 'It was here.' Her face looked white in the deepening twilight. Agnes saw bushes, a broad track with horseshoes stamped in it, and beyond the trees the open expanse of the golf course. At the top of the gentle slope of the golf range was the clubhouse, a tiny sparkle of light against the sky.

'So, this man in your memories, what did you remember about him?'

'Dark eyes. Sort of empty smile. And greying hair.'

'And a gun.'

'Yes.' Liz shivered.

'Are you sure?'

'The memories — as they return, you see — have more detail to them. He's holding something, this metal thing with a barrel, like a gun.'

They walked on slowly. The woods around them seemed to quieten in the gathering dusk.

'It turns out,' Agnes said, breaking the

silence, 'that the man in dispute with your friend the farmer worked with Matt.'

'Did he? Is he the one who rides at the stables too?'

'He's called Allen.'

Liz nodded. 'That awful one from the funeral. Then there's another one, a local businessman, Paul Gough. He runs garden centres. Trying to branch out, obviously.' They both glanced towards the golf course, then resumed their walking pace again.

'And,' Liz went on, 'last night, I was talking to my friend Annelise about it. She knows Wez, and, you see, there was all this problem about the hunt. This friend of my dad's, the one who's disputing the land, Stewart Lode — he's a Brigadier or something — anyway, he's banned the hunt from his land. So there's lots of bad feeling about that as well.'

'But why should it be you who gets hit by a golf ball?'

Liz walked in silence for a moment. 'It was my horse, you see. She was hit, they think. Bruise on one side of her head. And they found the ball nearby. And she fell, and me with her. If I hadn't been wearing a hat . . . '

'And Matthias's horse?'

'She fell worse.'

'And he wasn't wearing a hat?'

'No. And he fell at speed.'

'And there was a golf ball?'

'One was found in the bushes, yes.'

The daylight had all but gone. They turned back towards the stables. 'But how do you know . . . ' Agnes began. 'This man you remember, how do you know he wasn't trying to help you?'

'I remembered last night. I was just going off to sleep, and I had the memory again.' She looked around her. The shadowy branches rustled in the evening breeze. She shivered. 'It's his face — it's the expression on it. He's just kind of staring, as if — as if he's studying me. I think I must have tried to ask for help, but he did nothing. And then he ran off. I must have passed out again then, 'cos the next memory is the girls from the yard all gathered around me. Can we go?'

It was dark when they got back to the stables. Liz had cheered up as they left the bridle way. The yard was still busy, as the last few riders came in from the indoor school. People dismounted, grooms scurried around with buckets of hay, horses whinnied in anticipation of their evening feed.

Deborah called to them, 'Nice walk?'

'Sort of,' Liz called back.

Behind Deborah, two people emerged from the shadows, smartly dressed in jodhpurs and boots.

'Hi, Liz.' It was the woman of the couple speaking, and Agnes realised she recognised her.

'Judy?'

'Good heavens, Agnes! What are you doing here?'

'Do you ride?' Agnes kept her voice even.

'Yes. I have lessons. Matthias introduced me here. And this is Charles.' She turned to the man at her side.

'Hi there.' The man greeted them both with a certain reserve. 'I'll be in the car,' he said to Judy, and retreated into the darkness of the yard.

'And Allen,' Judy was saying. 'He rides here too. Matt says — Matt used to say,' she corrected herself, glancing at Liz, 'that he didn't want all us City folk using his patch as a playground. But he was just as bad.'

'Well, yes.' Agnes couldn't think of anything to say.

'Anyway, see you around,' Judy said.

'Sure.' Agnes turned away from them as they drifted back into the darkness beyond the floodlights of the yard.

Liz was standing, rooted to the spot. 'That man,' she whispered. 'Who . . . ?'

'Charles, she said.'

'I know the woman, Judy, she's been

147

coming here a while now. But him?'

'I don't know him either,' Agnes said.

Liz was pale in the artificial light, and her hands were clenched together.

'What is it?' Agnes asked.

'It's him. The man from — the man I remember. From my fall.'

Agnes stared into the darkness, in the direction that Judy and her friend had gone. 'Are you sure?'

'Positive. Absolutely positive.'

Agnes thought she saw a movement beyond the light, but the blackness was intense. Then Liz grabbed her arm. 'Come on. Let's go back to London.'

Liz drove them back. The journey passed mostly in silence, each reflecting on her thoughts. They drew up outside Agnes's block.

'Are you really sure?' Agnes turned to her.

'I've been shaking ever since I set eyes on him.'

'I don't know who he is.'

Liz shook her head. 'I remember him: those eyes, that thin face, looking at me, walking away.'

'What shall we do?'

Liz shrugged. 'Dunno. Find out who he is, I suppose.'

'Yes,' Agnes said. Outside two boys whizzed

past on skateboards, their faces yellow in the lamplight. 'Yes,' she said. 'I suppose so.'

★　★　★

That evening, Agnes lit her gas fire and her candles and knelt in prayer.

Find out who he is, she thought. She had a mental image of a large net descending on her, catching her up in its tangle of rope. She could hear her mother's clock ticking from its shelf.

Do I want to do this? she thought.

Two accidents. If they were accidents.

Perhaps they were just bad luck.

But what is luck, O Lord? If everything's all your doing, how can any outcome be luck, good or bad? If I put my tenner on a horse, are you rewarding me by letting it win? Rewarding me for my faith?

So, if it loses, what then?

The spheres on her mother's clock caught the edge of the candlelight.

Agnes felt the tendrils of the net clutching at her, drawing her into Liz's world, where someone can plan something so — strange, so random. So evil. Drawing her into Liz's world, and Patrick's world, and Matthias's world. And their world is — is Mary's world. And Julius's. Or at least, Julius's past.

Thy will be done.

Was it your will that Matthias die? And if so, was it by accident, or by design? Despite the warm glow of the fire, Agnes shivered.

★ ★ ★

'But it's banal, that's all.' Louise thumped a book down on Agnes's table.

'I enjoyed it,' Helen said, quietly.

'You can't bet on your faith.' Louise was pink with indignation.

'I think when Pascal talks about gambling — ' Agnes began, but Louise interrupted.

'He really seems to think that you might choose to believe in the Lord just because as a gamble the outcome is bound to be better for you.'

'He's writing from a viewpoint of someone who might see no reason to believe in God.' Agnes picked up the book and flicked through the pages.

'Why do you choose to believe, then?' Helen had turned to Louise to ask the question, and her quiet words hung in the air.

'I don't choose.' Louise shifted in her chair.

'But what made you believe?'

'Well . . . firstly I was baptised as a child so

I already belonged to the Lord. And then Jesus spoke to me, and called me to be a nun.'

'Oh.'

In the silence, Agnes said, 'You have to remember, Pascal was a mathematician as well. He was used to seeing life in terms of odds. All he's saying is that in choosing to believe or not believe, we're playing for high stakes.'

'But faith isn't a game,' Louise said.

'He didn't mean it was.' Agnes glanced at Helen.

'It's about taking the plunge, isn't it?' Helen returned Agnes's look. 'It's about just saying, whatever the evidence, whatever my intellect tells me, the important thing is just to go for it. Just to say, Yes. I believe. It's the heart of faith, really, isn't it, not to look for evidence, or even for rewards, just to have faith. That's what it means.'

Louise fiddled with a loose thread on her skirt. 'But God gives us evidence. All the time. I'm not sure I'd have continued to believe without God showing me examples of his love. That's why I don't see why it should be a gamble.'

'How does he show you?' Helen faced her directly.

'By countless blessings. By bringing me

151

here, into this order, for example. Or by making it a sunny day. Or by making me well again when I've been ill.'

'But if you don't get well, what then?'

'But I would. I'd have faith.'

'So if someone dies, does that just mean they haven't believed enough?'

'No, of course not.' Louise sounded uncertain. 'I just mean that God shows his workings in all sorts of ways, so it's obvious we should believe in him. People who don't just aren't using their senses properly.'

Agnes was looking at her watch. 'Sisters, I'm afraid it's time to go. You both have work to get to this afternoon.'

They got to their feet, thanked her for her time, and left in silence. Agnes found herself wondering whether novices usually got on better with each other. They had so much in common, two young women at the start of a new life, having made such a huge step, a huge commitment.

She tidied away mugs, books and papers, remembering her own time as a novice. But that had been in an enclosed order, and she'd spent her time mostly in silence, mostly engaged in endless household drudgery, in a state of dazed relief at having escaped from her marriage. It was hardly a positive decision, she thought. It was a decision by default, organised by Julius, and I just went along with it.

Dear Julius. She remembered him then, young, still with dark hair, but with the same energy, the same light in his bright eyes that he had now.

And yet . . . And yet there's another story, Agnes found herself thinking. Julius's own story of that time. What Patrick said, about why they'd sent him to France. Poor Julius, he'd said. All that time Julius had some kind of grief of his own, and he never let on. Never even said. Never confided in me.

I was in no state to listen. I am now, though. And Julius is pretending that there's nothing to say.

She made herself some coffee and sat in her armchair, gazing out of the window. She thought about Liz's flashes of memory; her recognition of that man Charles, her memory of him, if it was him, staring down at her, in such a way as to frighten her, holding a gun of some kind. And from this, Liz had concluded that it wasn't an accident at all. And neither was Matthias's fall.

Of course, it *was* a coincidence that they should both fall at the same place on the track. But Liz's horse simply got hit by a golf ball, and Matthias wasn't wearing a hat. And there was a golf ball there.

It was hardly the same. It must just have been coincidence. Because, Agnes thought, why would anyone do that on purpose?

A coincidence.

Agnes sighed, finished her coffee and went to wash up her mug. A coincidence. Or divine intervention.

If we think that God created the world and continues to intervene in it, then there's no such thing as coincidence. There's simply what the Lord wills, and sometimes it seems normal and sometimes it seems strange. And sometimes, if the Lord intervenes directly, it seems miraculous.

She remembered what Patrick had said about Tad's particular kind of luck. That he made miracles happen around him.

But if it's all just random, and there's no divine will, and no one winding up the clock, and no order at all . . . then what is there left to believe?

Agnes put on her coat and went out, slamming the door behind her.

★ ★ ★

She knocked on the side door of Julius's church. Eventually it opened and he was standing there, his glasses on his nose. He looked tired, his eyes shadowed.

'Oh. Agnes.'

'The problem is' — she walked past him into the dim passageway — 'I'm turning into an atheist.'

He didn't smile, but led her down the stairs into his office.

'I keep thinking that there may be no divine pattern in anything, and that the whole universe is just meaningless.'

Julius went over to the kettle and switched it on.

'And the worst thing is' — Agnes flung herself into a chair — 'I'm responsible for these novices, and here I am thinking maybe there's nothing to believe, not ultimately anyway, and there's Patrick seeing patterns in numbers, and Tad sees even more than patterns, he sees whole meaning, and I think that must be what drives him mad, and I keep thinking about when I was a novice, you remember, and I was just in a daze, I wasn't thinking about anything, you were doing all the thinking for me, even though you were in a state yourself . . . ' She looked up at him and saw him blink at her words as he handed her a mug of coffee.

'Was I?' He managed a smile as he sat down at his desk.

Outside a blast of police siren cut through the traffic's rumble and then passed by.

Agnes sipped her coffee. It tasted stale.

'Too much milk?' Julius looked at her in concern.

'It's fine,' she lied.

'Sorry. I forget you like it stronger.'

'Julius . . . '

'What?' He was looking at her with the same old gentleness in his eyes.

She shook her head. 'Nothing,' she said. She got up, put the mug of coffee down on his desk and left.

She walked fast down the street, blinking back tears. She thought of Patrick and found that she was engulfed with anger. How dare he come into Julius's life and ruin everything, stir up all this past that they share? And why can't I just ask Julius, why can't I just say, What happened with this woman, this mother of that Mary woman? Why were you in a state when they sent you to France?

I know why I can't ask, she thought, standing by the lights, waiting for them to change. Because I'm scared of what he'll say.

She went home and dialled Athena's number at the art gallery.

'Sweetie, how lovely of you to liven up the day. I haven't seen a soul since about ten this morning. No one buys art in February, for some reason. Are you all right?'

'Sort of.'

'What's that supposed to mean?'

'I'm wondering why I became a nun.'

'Oh, no. Sweetie, I'm not the person to ask.'

'Firstly it was to escape. But then, after a few years it became what I was. My life. And it was all about rejecting my previous life, my childhood, my family, my husband. About having nothing more to do with them. And now my mother's not there, and I've severed all those connections, and all I'm left with is this kind of fragment of a self, which seems to be a nun, but I no longer know why. It's like I told myself a story which was all about why I was a nun, and now those bits don't make sense any more.'

There was a silence at the other end of the line.

'Athena?'

'Sweetie, if I knew why you were a nun I'd try to help, really . . . I mean, poppet, surely Julius is the person to ask about that one? Agnes? Are you there?'

'Yes. Julius.' She fought back tears.

'Have I said something wrong?'

'No. Nothing at all. But the universe doesn't quite make sense at the moment.'

'I know the feeling, sweetie. A drink, maybe? Dinner? Later on? I'll be in.'

Agnes rang off and stared at the phone. Then she dialled Patrick's number and was surprised when he answered.

'It's Agnes.'

'Hello.'

'I saw Liz. We saw Judy at the stables, with some friend called Charles, and she thinks it was the man involved in her accident. Her memory's come back and she remembers seeing him.'

She could hear Patrick breathing. Then he said, 'Are you free, now?'

'Um, yes.'

'I'll be in the Three Horseshoes. You know it? Right by Julius's church.'

'Yes.'

'Ten minutes.'

* * *

It had clouded over, and the stern Victorian lines of the High Street seemed faded in the dull grey light. Agnes heard the bells of Julius's church chime three.

Patrick was perched on a high stool. He looked up as she came and ordered a white wine.

'Bit early for this, isn't it?' Agnes sat down next to him.

He was pushing some coins around in front

158

of him, his fingers moving nervously, endlessly. 'I saw Judy too. At the office. Today.'

'And?' Agnes leaned forward to hear him.

He pushed his hair back from his face. 'She's very cheerful. Even though everyone said she had a bit of a thing about Matt. You'd think she'd have the decency to be even a tiny bit grief-stricken.'

'Did she have a thing about Matt?'

'Everyone thought so. But she's looking for a husband, everyone knows that about her too. Even Allen's been named as a suitor in the past. Now there's this man you saw at the stables, and there's an American boy at the office too; they seem pretty close, he was teasing her. Nice kid, though, friend of Matt's, offered me condolences in a formal way. Touching, I thought.'

'You should have asked her about this Charles person.'

'I will, next time. Local, was he?'

'I've no idea. No one seemed to know him. And there's another thing: Stewart Lode, the person who's in dispute with Allen and his friend, he also wants to ban the hunt from his land,' Agnes said.

Patrick picked up a coin, threw it, caught it. 'Must have made things difficult for Matt, if it was a friend banning the hunt. Heads,' he

159

said, looking at the coin. 'And Allen wants to hunt as well. That's why he's having riding lessons. Obviously aspiring to be a country squire, once he's built his little empire out there.' He met her eyes. 'I've felt so alone with it, Agnes, you can't know. Last night Tad raised it again, after what Liz said to him at the stables at the weekend. But Tad's not in a good state. I shouldn't have discussed it with him, not Tad. Not him.' He put his hand to his brow. 'Since our dad, you see,' he went on, 'the way he died, that just about did for Tad. The chaos of it. But it's better that, you see, than something ordered. Something with a reason behind it. And now because of all this, the idea's been planted in his mind of an event emerging from the chaos into some kind of provable order. For him, it's unbearable. I think that's why he was angry with me. I think the dog was just an excuse.' He tossed the coin. 'Tails,' he said, to no one in particular.

'Dog?'

'George. Won't let it go. Smuggled it into his room. He's insisting he be allowed to keep the dog, though he knows it's against the rules. Just when we'd got him settled in the right kind of place. Typical. He's bound to blow it. This stupid mongrel is now, of course, the most important thing in his life, more important than having a place to live . . . ' He passed his hand across his forehead again. 'If only I wasn't dealing with him on my own. If only Matt was here.'

'Can someone else keep the dog for him?' Agnes asked.

'He won't hear of it. It's the only answer, but he won't see it. He got really angry with me last night.' He tossed the coin again, looked at the face, threw it back with the other coins.

They sipped their drinks.

'This friend with the land dispute, and the ban on the hunt . . . ' Agnes glanced at him, and then went on, 'Brigadier or whatever he is — is it worth talking to him?'

Patrick shrugged. 'Maybe. Karen will know who he is.'

'Is it worth talking to her too?'

'If you like.'

'And Mary,' Agnes said. 'That note Matt wrote her. She must know why he thought he'd be delayed.'

'She won't discuss it. I asked her.'

'And Judy, I'd better talk to her about this friend of hers at the stables.'

'If you can pin her down. She's a very busy woman. High flier.'

'Where might I find her?'

'Judy is generally at the wine bar from

161

about six. You know, the one where they had the funeral do? She drinks there before going back to the office and working till midnight. That's what the others say about her, anyway.' He met her eyes. 'You're serious, aren't you?'

She nodded, slowly. 'It seems I am.'

★ ★ ★

The streets were painted mauve in the gathering dusk. She went back to her flat and sat at her desk, staring at the phone. When it rang, she wasn't surprised.

'Agnes, it's Julius.'

'Yes.'

'Helen, your novice, she's concerned about this boy, this one at the hostel.'

'The silent one.'

'Yes. They've had a letter from the Home Office, Immigration people, something like that. It's all rather urgent, they might deport him. She was trying to get hold of you.'

'Right.'

'Will you phone her?'

'Yes, I will.'

'Good.' There was a silence. 'Where were you?' he asked.

'Earlier? I was out with Patrick.'

'Oh.'

'Julius' — Agnes took a deep breath — 'I don't like what this is doing to us.'

'What what is doing to us?'

'Your past. Patrick walking into our lives like this, stirring things up.'

'I'll be all right.'

'But you're not. Are you?'

Again a silence, before he answered, 'No. Not really.'

'What is it?'

'What did Patrick want?' he asked, suddenly.

'Oh, you know. About Matthias. About whether it was an accident or not. We decided we should talk to a few people.'

'Oh.' She could hear him breathing. 'Agnes?'

'Yes?'

'It was an accident. Surely.'

'But — '

'Why get involved? Why you? Now?'

'Liz thinks someone felled her horse on purpose.'

'Oh.'

'Don't you see? Two similar accidents.'

'They're just random events, Agnes, surely you can see that?'

'Is that God's creation then, Julius? Just random events?'

'I don't look for God's order in that way, Agnes. Do you?'

'At the moment . . . ' She wanted to cry. 'At the moment, even if I looked for signs of God's order, I wouldn't find any.'

After a moment he said, 'I'm not sure I can help.'

'Julius . . . ' She was holding the phone with both hands.

'What?'

'I want . . . ' The words failed her. I want us to be as we were, she tried to say. I want us to be friends again, like we were before Patrick appeared, before Matthias died. 'Julius, I don't want us to change,' she managed to say, her voice choked with tears.

'We haven't changed. I must go. I'm — I'm sorry.'

'Julius?' The phone line was dead. He'd hung up.

She replaced the receiver, her face wet with tears.

9

She washed her face, chose some smart clothes and set out for the bus stop. It had begun to rain, and the pavements were splashed with yellow under the streetlights. She caught the bus across the river, then the tube to Liverpool Street. She moved through the rush-hour crowds, all the time aware of an odd, urgent nervousness. The conversation with Julius replayed itself in her mind, but she pushed it away.

She walked into the wine bar and descended the wide central staircase. Smart young men jostled at the bar. Giggling young women gathered together. In the corner two people sat at a table, deep in conversation. One was a man, with short blond hair and a pale grey suit. The other was Judy.

Agnes took a deep breath and approached them. 'Hello,' she said.

Judy looked up. 'What are you doing here?'

Agnes smiled at her. 'Looking for you.'

She didn't smile back. 'You seem to be good at that.'

'Can I get you a drink?'

'She turned up at the stables last night,'

Judy said to her companion.

'Oh, when you were having your lesson with Allen.' A smile played around his lips. He had neat, even features.

'It's not funny,' Judy countered.

'That man on a horse? Of course it's funny.'

'A beer perhaps?' Agnes's voice cut through their conversation.

He turned to her. 'Forgive me, we were being very rude.' He held out his hand. 'Jed,' he said. 'Jed Ericsson.' Agnes shook his hand. He smiled at her. 'Let me get you a drink. What'll you have?'

Agnes glanced at the empty beer bottles on their table. 'One of those, please.' She sat down opposite Judy, while Jed queued at the bar. 'Patrick said I'd find you here,' she said to Judy.

Judy blinked, then smiled. 'And how is Patrick?'

'Much the same as when you last saw him.'

'Hmmm.' Judy smoothed her hair against her cheek. 'He's quite attractive isn't he?'

'Patrick?'

'That kind of Irish charm.'

'I wouldn't know.'

'Of course. You being a nun. Agnes is a nun, you know,' Judy said as Jed reappeared with their drinks.

Jed surveyed her with new interest. 'Really? A nun?' He had a slight American accent. 'What kind of nun?'

'Ignatian,' Agnes said. 'An open order.'

'Ah,' he said, nodding.

'He doesn't know anything about it,' Judy said.

He turned to her. 'How do you know?'

'Oh, of course you don't.' She turned back to Agnes. 'So, Patrick sent you to find me?'

'Not exactly,' Agnes said.

'Patrick?' Jed asked. 'How is he? I felt so bad missing the funeral.'

'Urgent business in America,' Judy said, mockingly.

'It was. We have important customers there. But I liked Matt, we were good friends.'

'So,' Judy said brightly, 'what else did Patrick say about me? How gratifying to think I've made an impression.'

'Oh, um . . .' Agnes wondered what to say.

'It's your great aim in life,' Jed said to Judy, 'to make an impression.'

Judy met Agnes's eyes. 'Poor Patrick. There's something very appealing about grief, isn't there?'

'I wouldn't know,' Agnes said again.

'No. Silly me.'

'Another drink?' Jed looked towards the

bar. 'Mind you, look at the crush there. Don't these people have homes to go to?'

Judy turned to him. 'Speaking personally, I have at least three hours' work ahead of me.' She smiled at him, charmingly, her hair caressing her cheek.

He turned back to Agnes. 'Patrick must be very cut up.'

'Yes.'

'There's a counsellor at work, he could see her. It might help. Grief, you know, particularly a shock like that . . . ' Jed picked up his beer, put it down again. 'It needs talking out.'

Judy sighed heavily. 'Jed's Californian,' she said. 'It explains everything.' She pursed her lips.

'Not Californian, Jude.'

'Where then?' she asked.

He glanced at her, then at Agnes. 'An exile,' he said. 'From everywhere and nowhere.'

'But your spiritual home is California, you said.' Judy sounded petulant now.

He frowned. 'I did. What I meant was, you have to belong somewhere. It's like Odysseus, the warrior-stranger. The homeless wanderer in the wilderness. *Xenos* . . . '

'Oh, 'Xenos',' Judy echoed. 'As we say in Latin.'

'Greek, actually. It means stranger.' Jed's

168

voice was flat. 'Homeless person, stateless person.'

'He did classics,' Judy said to Agnes. 'He needs to show off sometimes. Balliol, Oxford. Not bad for a homeless wanderer.'

'It's not a joke.' Jed spoke sharply.

'You've done pretty well out of it,' Judy said. 'Brilliant high school career in the States, then English boarding school, Oxford, then back to Harvard — bet Odysseus's CV wasn't nearly so glamorous.'

Jed's eyes narrowed as he looked at her. He spoke quietly. 'There comes a time when you need to go home. Like Odysseus. When I went to Ireland, with Matt — '

'When was that?' Judy asked.

'You know, in January. We were talking to that Dublin company about their merger. And to see Matt in Ireland, on his home soil . . . ' He turned to Agnes. 'I realised how it completes a person, somehow, when they're back home. It was lovely to see it; Matt kind of came to life, although there's hardly anyone left there that he knows now, and I kind of envied him.'

'Do you not have a home?' Agnes asked him.

He shrugged. 'I did. A long time ago. My parents lived in Minnesota. I don't belong there now. Exile, you see.' He took a long

169

draught from his glass. 'You wanted to talk to us — to Jude?'

Agnes felt slightly foolish. 'Um, well, it was just that Patrick was wondering . . . '

'Wondering what?' Judy asked.

'That friend you were riding with the other day — '

'Allen?'

'No, the other one. The man.'

Judy smiled. 'Oh, Charles. He doesn't ride. He's an old friend of Allen's, we were meeting him for a drink. He lives near the stables. He and Allen were at school together, would you believe, though he looks much older than Allen. He used to work with Allen in our company.'

'Did he?' Jed turned to her. 'Charles what?'

'Fielding. Before your time.' Judy smiled at him. 'He took early retirement to concentrate on his clocks.'

'Clocks?' Agnes picked up a beer bottle, but found it was empty.

'He deals in them or something. Antiques, you know. It's all rather a bore, actually, he won't shut up about them. He's a dull man. Lives on his own. Quite nice house. I think Allen wants a house like that.'

'We all know about Allen and his country pretensions,' Jed said.

'He might want to settle down.' Judy eyed

him from behind her curtain of hair.

'Might he, indeed?' Jed returned her gaze. 'Well, I can't see you joining him in the country. When would you get to the gym, for a start? Or is that why Allen's going on about building one out there?'

Judy smiled at him. 'Maybe.'

'Do you train?' Jed turned to Agnes. 'I suppose for you people it's all spiritual training.'

'Train? Well, I — '

'She rides, don't you?'

'Sometimes.'

'You might enjoy the gym,' Jed said. 'Why don't you take her along with you, Jude?'

Judy glanced at him, frowning. 'Um, well . . . '

'Really, you don't have to . . . ' Agnes began, then collected herself. 'I would quite like to try it, though.' She hoped her voice had conveyed the right amount of enthusiasm.

Judy looked at her doubtfully. 'You are — you are allowed, are you? You people, I mean. Gyms?'

Agnes smiled. 'You mean, being a nun? Yes, I'm allowed.'

'The body is a temple of the holy spirit,' Jed said. 'I guess gyms are doctrinally acceptable.'

'False gods, though.' Agnes met his eyes, his gentle smile. 'You have to be wary.'

Judy had taken out an electronic notebook and was consulting it. 'Tomorrow, if you like.' She sounded reluctant. 'I'll tell my trainer that I won't be needing him.' She looked across at Jed, then turned to Agnes. 'Bring some kit, won't you? You do have kit? There's a pool and stuff if you're not up to the machines.'

Jed smiled at Agnes. 'Watch out for those false gods.'

★ ★ ★

'I mean, kit, Athena. Machines. What have I got myself into?'

'Just because you think something's going on and you need to talk to this woman?'

'It's stupid really. And it was his idea, this young American man. She didn't seem keen at all.'

'I suppose your investigations have led you into worse places. Though I can't quite call any to mind at the moment.'

'And what on earth does one wear?'

'Well, sweetie, let's think.' Athena crossed her legs under her on her sofa. 'If it was me, not that I go near these places of course, but clothes-wise, I'd say a Calvin Klein crop top,

172

to show one's abs to best effect.'

'Athena, I don't have abs.'

'Tight lycra shorts, maybe? One of those weird things with holes down your back that you see in those adverts?'

'You're no help.'

'I've got some old leggings you can borrow. From my brief attempt at doing an aerobics class before I realised that I simply did not need to prance about a room with a load of extras from a Fellini film. And you can dig out a T-shirt from somewhere, can't you?'

Agnes nodded.

'What's she like, this woman?'

'Judy. I don't know.'

'Would I like her?'

'You'd like her clothes.'

'It's a start, I suppose. Are you hungry?'

'Yes, actually. Are you cooking?'

'There's no need to look so worried. It's pasta. With a ready-made sauce. And some salad, in a nice plastic bag.'

⋆ ⋆ ⋆

Athena ladled linguini on to two plates. 'You seem tired, sweetie.'

'Not tired, exactly.'

'What, then?'

'Julius and I had a row. At least, I think it

was a row. It's a bit difficult to tell.'

Athena stared at her, the ladle in mid-air. 'How can you have a row and not know about it? When Nic and I have a row, last night, for example, most of Fulham must have heard, not to mention Battersea and all points between here and the South Coast.'

'Last night?'

Athena spooned sauce on to both plates. 'It was terrible, sweetie. It's this bloody woman, this so-called old friend, ho ho ho. God knows what he sees in her. They had lunch together, apparently.'

'But — '

'There's lunch, and there's lunch, sweetie. And this was lunch.'

Agnes nodded. 'Right.'

'And, of course, as he so rightly says, and it's so annoying, after the way I behaved last year, I can hardly begrudge him a bit of space to spend time with a friend. I mean, hark at that, sweetie, a friend . . . ' She passed Agnes her plate.

'But if that's all it is — '

'If, sweetie. It's a big if. And whatever he thinks he's doing, and let's just assume it's innocent, there's what she thinks *she's* doing, which is something altogether different. And don't argue, 'cos I saw the way she looked at him. You can always tell.'

Agnes sprinkled dressing on her salad. 'Takes one to know one.'

'Exactly. The expert eye. She's out to get him, sweetie.'

'She has to reckon with you.'

Athena sipped her wine. She sighed. 'I mean, normally, of course, I'd be confident that I'd win. But I have weakened my position, by being a bit stupid last year.'

'But Nic said he didn't mind, he said it was a learning curve, I seem to remember, enriching your relationship.'

'Oh, he always talks nonsense like that. Comes of working in therapy circles. Of course he minded. Everyone always does. I was unfaithful, sweetie. Let's not pretend otherwise. Infidelity . . . ' She picked up her wine glass, turning it round in her fingers. 'I'd mind. I'd mind terribly.'

Agnes twiddled her fork around in her plate. 'It's loss. That's what's so hard about Julius and me.'

'What was it about, your non-row?'

Agnes frowned. 'We've changed. This guy Patrick, he has a very old, deep bond with Julius. He knows stuff about him that I don't know — '

'I can see that would be annoying.'

'No, it's not that. It's — it's awakened something in Julius. Something dormant.

Something I'd never noticed before. And I feel I've lost him. There's a Julius there that I don't know. Julius's past. Julius as a young man, with all the drive and — and passion of a young man.'

'Passion? Julius?'

'You see? It's just as you said, I've relied on him to be something, something quite specific, a friend and rock — and parent, in a way. And now my mother's died, and I've been feeling quite adrift, and there's this issue with the house and what I do with it, and I need him even more to be that rock — and he's distracted. He's been really stirred up by seeing Patrick again, they're very close, and that girl at the funeral . . . '

'Oh yes. That girl.'

'She's called Mary. She knows Julius, and he knows her. He said he knew her years ago, when she was a child, he knew her mother. But he won't speak about her. Seeing her, he was quite evidently very moved . . . but he won't tell me anything. And Patrick keeps saying things as if I knew what he meant, about Julius having to be sent to France all those years ago: 'Poor Julius,' he said, as if I'd know . . . ' She shook her head. 'And Julius thinks I shouldn't help Patrick investigate Matthias's death, and I'm sure it's just because he doesn't want me getting too close, and I always thought I was the most important person in his life, I always thought he was there for me, and now . . . ' Tears welled in her eyes.

'Surely the reason he doesn't think you should investigate this death is because it was an accident?' Athena spoke quietly.

Agnes looked up at her. 'But . . . ' She sighed. 'It's all so confusing.'

Athena pushed a lettuce leaf around her plate. After a while she said, 'You've made up a particular version of Julius, haven't you? You've needed him to be the version of himself that you've made for him.' Agnes stared at her. 'That's what Nic said,' Athena went on. 'About him and me. And it's true. I've told myself a story about Nic being a kind of immovable point in my life, around which I can . . . ' She sighed. ' 'Play around', is how he put it. And he's right. At least, he was right. Although it's all changed now with these lunches of his. And of course I was so cross when he said all this. I told him he was talking nonsense; you have to, sweetie, don't you, when they start on like that . . . particularly if they're right.' She refilled their glasses, nodding. 'But hearing you now, it's sort of the same.'

'The idea of him not being there for me . . . ' Agnes's voice was almost a whisper.

She gulped some wine.

'He'll be back.'

'But you see, Athena, I simply must know.'

'But Matthias's death isn't the same as Julius's past.'

Agnes met her gaze. 'No. I suppose not.' She sipped her wine. 'Mary — and Julius ... '

'What about them?'

'They've got the same eyes. That blue — that kind of deep blue. The same.'

★ ★ ★

It was late when Agnes returned to her flat. She felt disorientated — because of the wine? she wondered — and muddled images of Julius and Athena drifted in and out of her mind; Tad and Patrick; Judy and Jed, with their strange sparring complicity.

She went over to the window, still in her coat, the room still in darkness. She stared out at the glistening street. Passing cars rippled the puddles with yellow light.

Nothing seemed sure any more. She was an orphan now. She'd spent her life running away: from her parents; from her husband; from her first order; and now she was free. Free to be where she was now, to commit herself to where she was now. Free to accept

178

things as they are.

She flung herself into her armchair. So why is it so difficult? she thought. All my words of wisdom to Helen and Louise about the freedom of relinquishment — God knows, I believe all that stuff. And I know it isn't easy. But you'd think now, now I've come to this stage of my life, now I'm an adult . . . Oh Julius, she thought. Where are you when I most need you?

She took off her coat, lit her candles, knelt in prayer. She immersed herself in the familiar words, clearing her mind. An image came to her, of the silent boy in the hostel. He stood by the sink, watching her wash up.

* * *

It was still dark when her alarm clock woke her. She tumbled out of bed into the nearest clothes, stumbled out of the flat to the bus stop, arriving at the community house for mass as a steely dawn touched the edge of the sky with grey.

' 'I cried to you, O Lord, I pleaded with you . . . ' ' The sisters' voices murmured the psalm. Agnes glanced along the pew. Helen and Louise sat side by side, their eyes closed, their lips moving with the words.

' 'You have turned my wailing into

dancing; you have put off my sackcloth and clothed me with joy. Therefore my heart sings to you without ceasing; O Lord my God, I will give thanks to you for ever . . . ' '

They seem so young, Agnes thought. And for ever is such a long time.

Afterwards Madeleine came and joined her in the kitchen. Agnes sat down heavily at the table.

'Trouble?' Madeleine passed her a mug of tea.

Agnes sighed. 'I'm the wrong person to be novice mistress.'

'It's a spiritual challenge.'

Agnes smiled. 'It certainly is. I keep wanting to tell them to leave now, while they've still got the chance.'

Madeleine laughed. 'Perhaps you are the wrong person.'

'I mean, how can I tell them that this is right for them? It may not be, for all I know.'

'They'll find that out for themselves.'

'But my role is to take on their doubt, isn't it? To allow them to see a way through it.'

'There's nothing wrong with that.'

'But my doubt . . . my own doubt . . . ' Agnes stared at the steam rising up from her mug.

'Is it the prospect of final vows?' Madeleine was looking at her.

Agnes met her gaze. 'I seem to have lost the ropes that bound me here.'

'So it's up to you now. You have to keep yourself here by your own free will.'

'It's frightening. It's like staring into an abyss.'

Madeleine nodded. 'I'm sure Sister Christiane knows how you feel.'

Agnes smiled. 'Maybe. But I shouldn't be in charge of the novices' souls.'

'It's just as well you're not, then.' Madeleine got up, patted Agnes's shoulder and left the kitchen.

Agnes was left alone, turning her mug around between her fingers. After a moment she got up, found her coat, and left.

Back at the flat she dialled Patrick's number. He answered, sleepily.

'I need to talk to Karen,' she said.

'Agnes?'

'You sound terrible.'

'Late night,' he mumbled. 'Why Karen?'

'I had a drink with Judy yesterday. And some American person. Jed.'

'Jed. I know him.'

'I found out who that man was. Charles Fielding. An old friend of Allen's; they were at school together. He lives out near the stables. He used to work with Allen before he retired.'

'Charles? Doesn't ring a bell.'

'He doesn't ride. He collects clocks.'

'Well, if he's cast in the same mould as Allen, the less I know of him the better. Now, Karen's number . . . ' There was a pause, a few loud noises as if he'd dropped the phone, and then he came back on the line. 'Karen's number. Got a pen?'

She wrote down the number. 'Do you think she'd mind if I visited her?'

'I doubt it. She liked you. But don't go planting those thoughts in her head — about the accident, I mean. Please.' He seemed to have woken up. 'It's bad enough me being obsessed. I can't stop thinking about it, but trying to discuss it with Tad was a terrible mistake, I've got to keep it to myself until I've worked it out.'

'I thought she might shed some light about the land dispute.'

'Oh. Yes. That.'

'And this man trying to ban the hunt.'

'Yes. Yes. Well, it's up to you.' There was silence for a moment, then Patrick said, 'Thanks.'

'For what?'

'For joining me. In this.'

'That's OK.'

'I don't feel so alone. It's a dark place, where I am now.'

'Yes.'

'No doubt you have reasons of your own. Good luck with Karen. She'll be glad to see you.' He rang off.

Reasons of my own. Agnes sat, staring at the phone. What a strange thing to say, reasons of my own. And the stupid thing is, she thought, he's absolutely right.

10

Agnes got out of the community car and looked around her. There was a village green, and beyond it the severe stone spire of the parish church. A row of graceful houses flanked the green, their pale walls washed by the thin winter sun. Number 4, Agnes thought, approaching their wrought-iron railings. They looked out of place, as if someone had uprooted part of a fashionable London street and set it down here in this Essex village.

Agnes rang the bell. It seemed to take some time before the door opened and Karen stood there. She looked thinner, although perhaps it was just the line of her clothes: black polo neck and long charcoal trousers. She smiled. 'I was surprised when you phoned.' She ushered Agnes into the hallway, which was carpeted in shabby brown.

'Yes. It must have seemed odd.'

'Did Patrick put you up to it?'

Agnes blinked. 'Um, no. Not exactly.'

Karen smiled a thin smile. 'I thought he might. He knows I'm finding things . . . rather difficult.' She brushed a stray wisp of hair away from her face. 'Would you like some tea? Coffee?'

'Tea, please.'

Agnes followed her into her kitchen. There were clean white work surfaces, pale cream cupboards. Everything seemed to have been tidied away. 'The boys will be back later.' She looked at her watch.

'Are they at school?'

'Danny's at college now, doing A-levels. Jake is at school still.'

'How have they taken it?'

She paused, her hand on the kettle. 'Dan's main response is anger at the moment. Stupid Dad for taking risks.' She picked up the kettle, then put it down again. 'Jake's just like his dad.'

'What do you mean?'

'It's just an accident, he keeps saying. He's kind of philosophical about it. But you see, risk is part of his life too. He and Matthias, two of a kind.' She looked out of the window, gazing beyond the garden to the row of poplar trees in the distance, then blinked and turned back to Agnes. 'Do go and sit down.'

Agnes went into the lounge. It seemed empty, despite the wide sofa and the old armchairs. An antique clock stood alone on the mantelpiece. She sat down.

Just an accident, she thought, the words

ringing in her ears. But is it? And can anything be? Doesn't everything happen by the design of God?

But what was it Madeleine said? That I have to stay in the order by my own free will?

Agnes got up and browsed along the bookshelves. A copy of Pascal's *Reflections* caught her eye, and she drew it out.

'Ah. That.' Karen came into the room carrying a tray. Agnes replaced the book and sat down again as Karen poured two cups of tea and handed her one. 'Pascal,' she said. Agnes nodded. 'He was always reading that,' Karen went on. 'Still,' she said suddenly, leaning back in her chair, her cup and saucer balanced neatly on her knees, 'I suppose you want to talk about Mary Wells.' Agnes stared at her. 'What with you being so close to Julius,' Karen added. 'I expect he was glad to see her again.'

'He's hardly mentioned it.' Agnes replaced her cup clumsily on the saucer.

'Oh.'

The two women looked at each other. The tick of the clock counted time. Outside the shadows lengthened in the fading daylight.

'I'm sorry,' Karen said at last.

'Don't apologise.'

Karen glanced up again at Agnes. 'The past, you see,' she said, 'I mean, their shared past, Matthias and Patrick and — and Mary, it's cast a long shadow. Right across my life.'

Agnes nodded.

Karen poured more tea for them both. 'I was angry with her.' She handed Agnes her cup. 'At the funeral. I thought she had no place there, Patrick asked her not to come but she wouldn't listen. And anyway, he felt sorry for her.' Her lips narrowed. She turned her cup round and round on its saucer in her lap. 'I saw her at the graveside there' — she looked up at Agnes, and her face was pinched and white — 'I looked across and saw she was there, weeping as if . . . as if she had the right . . . ' Her words stopped, choked with tears.

'It must have been awful.'

Karen shook her head. 'At first, yes. But . . . it was strange. I looked at her then, and it was like I was seeing her for the first time. I looked at her for a long time. You see, before, I'd never look at her, because she was — she was his other life, she had no part in mine. I had no interest in her. And anyway, I used to wonder how it was all going to turn out.' She spoke fast, now, the words tumbling out. 'I used to think about all the different ways the story would end. Perhaps he'd leave. Perhaps she'd get fed up with it and leave him. Perhaps I'd leave. Perhaps nothing . . . And then, at the burial, I looked at her and I thought, So this is how it turned out. You and me, here, at the side of his grave. Who'd have thought?' She looked up at Agnes. 'And so, you see, she'd become part of my life. Part of the story. The story that ended at the graveside. And since then I've thought about it a lot, and I've realised that that was what Matthias was doing. He didn't want the story to end, his story. He didn't want to wake up one day and find out that it was all sewn up, that it had all turned out this way: a wife he loved, two sons, a nice house, a nice job . . . He didn't want to wake up and think, So that's it then, that's how the story turned out. It would have bored him. So he kept other stories, other possible lives, a life with her . . . ' The smile had faded again.

'And . . . ' Agnes hesitated. 'Mary's daughter?'

Karen smiled. 'Charlie? No.' She shook her head. 'Not Charlie. Charlie dates from a time when they weren't together. A kind of in-between time. Charlie's another story.' She settled in her chair, weary with speaking.

Agnes sipped her tea. 'Perhaps we all do it.'

'Do what?'

'This business of keeping other options open, parallel lives . . . ' She thought about the letter from the French lawyers, lying

188

unanswered on her desk. 'It's like me, being a nun, but never quite being sure that that's how it'll all end. And anyway' — she looked up at Karen, who was still smiling at her — 'you can never tell, can you? About the final chapter. Look at Matthias, trying to put it off, trying to postpone it indefinitely . . . but despite all his efforts, his story did end.'

'Yes, but he'd won. There was nothing certain. It could have turned out lots of ways. He never knew the ending. He'd won. Again.' She sighed. 'And that's why I could look at her, for the first time, at his grave. Because she didn't know that about him. She didn't know him like I did. She had to fight to keep him with her. I didn't have to fight. Because I knew him.' She seemed to be talking to herself. 'I allowed him to be — I let him be the person that he was. Whereas she . . . ' She looked up. 'She thinks he loved her most of all. But I know it wasn't like that.'

'But she was his mistress.'

Karen nodded. 'She had to tell herself a story, didn't she? That if it wasn't for his family responsibilities, they'd be together. That it was only his duty keeping him here, keeping him away from the woman he loved. But she didn't know him. He had no sense of duty. Only of what he wanted. He was greedy, you see, greedy for life. He wanted more than his fair share.' Her hand went to her hair, a lock of brown threaded with grey, turning it around her fingers. 'He was here because he wanted to be here. If he didn't want to be with me, he'd have left. That's why I felt sorry for her when I saw her. Because I knew the truth of it. A truth she couldn't know.' There was the sound of keys in a door and a loud slam. 'The boys are back.' Young male voices filled the hallway, then went into the kitchen.

Karen stood up. 'Come and see his office.'

They went upstairs. Karen opened a door. The room was a mess, piled with paper and files and clutter, stacked with cardboard boxes. Karen's gaze scanned the room. 'He needed me,' she said. 'He needed us.' She picked up a file, looked at it vaguely, put it down again. 'I thought of leaving,' she said suddenly. 'There were times — once in particular, I was angry with him, with her — I thought I'd go, take the boys . . . ' She bit her lips together. 'And then I'd look at him, and he'd seem . . . so dependent. So hopeless without me.' She bent and picked up a paper from the floor and replaced it on a heap in front of her. 'So I stayed.'

'You loved him,' Agnes said.

'Perhaps. Yes.' She turned away. 'Perhaps it was beyond love.' She went back out on to

190

the landing, closing the door behind them. Agnes followed her down the stairs. From the kitchen came loud clattering.

'The boys always make themselves a snack after school,' Karen said. The kitchen door opened, and Dan and Jake trooped solemnly out, carrying plates piled high with thick slices of bread, biscuits and bananas. They grunted at Karen and went into the front room, and Agnes heard the television being switched on.

'I ought to go,' she said.

'Don't feel you have to,' Karen said.

'I wanted to ask you . . . ' Agnes hesitated. 'About this land dispute. Between Allen and Stewart Lode.'

'Oh. What about it?'

'Matthias was, um, helping Lode?'

She smiled briefly. 'Nice man, Stewart. They got friendly recently, although they're on different sides of the fence about nearly everything. Lode won't even have the hunt on his land. But, yes, he's trying to prove that some of Allen's land is his, and Matt got involved in helping him. Why do you ask?'

Agnes was about to speak, but glanced at Karen and changed her mind. 'Oh, Patrick was talking about it for some reason,' she said lightly.

'Patrick doesn't like Allen either.'

'No.'

'We were beginning to see too much of Allen,' Karen said. She leaned against the banisters. 'He's rather involved in things out here. The stupid leisure centre.'

'And riding lessons,' Agnes agreed.

'I didn't know he was doing that too.'

'With Judy.'

'Oh, Judy.' Karen smiled. 'She's obviously read some new self-help book about how to get your man, and she's on the Sharing Interests chapter.'

Agnes laughed.

'Although,' Karen added, 'if it's Allen she's after, she should take up golf.'

They stood in silence for a moment. A last burst of afternoon sun filtered through the stained glass of the front door, casting blue and gold light across the hallway.

'I'd better be going,' Agnes said. Karen opened the door for her.

'Do you ride?' Agnes asked, on the doorstep.

Karen shook her head. 'Not my thing.' She smiled weakly. 'I don't take chances.' Agnes turned to go, but Karen spoke again. 'Do you — will you see Mary Wells?'

'I don't know.'

'I have some of his things, and they're more . . . more to her taste.' She shook her head.

'Books and things. I'm tired, that's all. Perhaps one day.' She ran her hand down the door frame. 'One day,' she repeated. She looked at Agnes, and her face was pale in the deepening light. 'He loved her, you see. He loved us both.' She raised her hand to say goodbye. 'Come back another time. You're always welcome. Bring Patrick with you.'

'I will,' Agnes promised. She got into the car, started the engine and drove off. In her mirror she could see Karen standing on the step, absolutely still, staring into the distance.

Mary Wells, Agnes thought, who are you? To be loved by Matthias. And forgiven, almost, by Karen. And to have some kind of connection with Julius that everyone but me seems to know about.

I should have asked her, she thought, turning out of the village on to the A road. I should have asked Karen: What is Mary Wells to Julius? She headed for the M25. The oncoming headlamps cut through the settling dusk. I didn't want to know, she thought. I didn't want to hear the answer.

She approached the City as night fell. Its towers of glass glittered with tiny squares of light, lighting up the sky in a celebration of wealth and good fortune.

For those who are prepared to take the risk.

It was ten past six. Agnes glanced at her watch. She'd arranged to meet Judy at seven.

* ★ ★

'Oh, there you are.' Judy was sitting in the foyer of her gym. A large glass partition gave on to the pool, which was bathed in rippling light. 'I've signed you in,' she said, getting up. 'Come on.' She glanced at Agnes's plastic carrier bag, slung her designer sports bag over her shoulder and led the way to the changing rooms.

They got changed next to each other. Judy wore a black lycra crop top and matching shorts. She glanced at Agnes's faded blue baggy T-shirt and leggings, and a shadow of a pout passed across her red lips.

'You can pretend you're not with me,' Agnes said, tying the laces of her trainers.

'It's all right, some people here don't bother about how they look either.' She slung a towel around her neck and headed out of the changing room. Agnes followed her into the gym.

'Do you think you'll manage?' Judy was looking at her doubtfully.

Agnes stared at the lines of machines, at the people running, pedalling, rowing, dripping sweat, getting nowhere.

194

'I do have my routine,' Judy was saying. 'I can't really slow up on it.'

'Let's just start, shall we?'

They began with exercise bikes. Judy pedalled furiously, her eyes glued to the display in front of her. Agnes cycled gently, wondering if her knees would hold.

'Patrick was in again today,' Judy said.

'Oh.'

'He's an odd man, isn't he? And he must be at least fifty-five. Maybe older.'

Agnes concentrated on her pedalling.

'Actually, I'm glad you decided to join me here,' Judy said conversationally. She didn't seem to be at all short of breath.

'Really?'

'Yes. I tried to talk to Patrick about it, but it didn't seem tactful to pursue the subject.'

'Oh.' Agnes, going at half Judy's pace, wondered how she had breath to speak as well.

'This leisure centre of Allen's. Matthias had money tied up in it, and now he's — now he's gone, no one seems to know what's going to happen. I mean . . . ' She peered at the display panel on her machine, and punched a button. 'It could ruin Allen, if the money's just not there after all. On the other hand, if Matthias had sorted out his will, Allen could do very well out of it.'

'Oh.' Agnes stopped cycling to catch her breath.

'Of course, the whole thing's bloody risky, if you ask me. When I found out that Allen had persuaded Matthias to gamble on it too, I knew it was high risk; Matthias always did need the adrenalin rush that comes with crazy odds.'

'Yes.'

'But you can see why I couldn't ask Patrick directly.'

'No. I mean, yes.'

'It's just, with Allen wanting to marry me, I can't afford to take a risk. Financially, I mean.' She stopped pedalling. 'That's enough warm-up, let's do some stretches.' She was glowing with exertion, and dabbed at her face with her towel. Agnes followed her across to the floor mats. Judy took up an odd position with her legs apart.

'Marry you?' Agnes said weakly, trying to make her legs copy Judy's.

'I mean, I've always thought this leisure centre idea was a bad one. There's old Allen with his fancy flat in Spitalfields, and now here he is trying to invest in land in the country, but he's an East-End barrow boy through and through. I'm sure that's why he agreed to come riding with me, just so he can start playing squire of the Manor when he moves out to Essex.'

'But if you married him . . . '

'That's what he keeps saying. We'd have to live somewhere. Much better for the children to live in the country, they could have ponies.' She paused in her stretches. 'And it's a growth industry, leisure, gyms and stuff — he's right, of course. It's just . . . ' She twisted her body round at an angle. 'Now that Jed's showing an interest . . . '

'In you?'

'Yes. And Allen seems to have got keener. He's so competitive, he's jealous of Jed anyway — Jed works for him, but he's a bit of a whizz-kid and keeps earning huge bonuses, and it's quite clear they're thinking of promoting him over Allen, and now here's Allen proposing to me. You see what I mean, it's a terrible risk I'd be taking.'

'What risk?'

Judy relaxed, sitting cross-legged on the mat. 'Of marrying the wrong man. Let's go on the treadmills.'

Agnes found herself running on a conveyor belt. Judy was doing the same, twice as fast. 'You can put it on to walk,' Judy said, breathing fast.

Agnes found a button with an arrow pointing downwards. Her conveyor belt slowed to a comfortable stroll. 'Perhaps you don't have to get married,' she said.

Judy kept up the same even pace. 'Of course I do. I'm thirty, it was always part of my life plan to get married around now.'

'And has Jed proposed too?'

'Well, that's just the problem. He hasn't yet. There's all this uncertainty about whether he moves to the States, to our Seattle office. And also . . . ' She slowed her treadmill, wiping her face with her towel. 'Also I'm not sure either of them are the right man. I keep lying awake at night weighing up their pros and cons, and I just can't quite commit myself to either of them. I mean, obviously money's important, and they're both pretty good prospects on that front, at least. But they're both obsessives. I can't imagine either of them leading quiet domestic lives. Allen's obsessed with making money. And Jed's obsessed with his training.'

'Training?'

'He runs,' Judy said, vaguely. 'Marathon thingies, long distances. At least he'd be fit. I mean, as a long-term risk, he'd probably be quite a good bet. But . . . ' Her treadmill slowed to a halt, and she turned to Agnes. 'How do you know, that's what I keep wondering. How do you know when you've met the right man?' She laughed, breathless, sweat glistening on her brow. 'I don't know why I'm asking you.'

Agnes pressed Stop on her treadmill. 'Surely it's about desire,' she said.

'Desire?'

'Yes. There's no point marrying a man unless he makes you feel . . . I mean, you know. Desire. Physical, visceral . . . '

Judy looked blank.

'Which one of them do you most want to go to bed with?'

Judy frowned. 'I — I hadn't thought of it like that.'

Agnes stared at her.

'Perhaps you nuns are different,' Judy said. 'I'm going to do some weights now. I'll meet you in the steam room if you like.'

Agnes passed the weights room and looked at the bizarre pulley-like contraptions. The steam room suddenly seemed very appealing.

She changed into her swimming costume and did a few lengths of the pool, then went into the steam room. She allowed the heat to soothe her, breathing the warmth. She was aware of other bodies, each one isolated in its private space, hidden by the clouds of steam. A kind of worship, she thought. Thy body is a temple of the holy spirit. Jed said that, she thought. How odd.

She thought about Jed, about the way he was, sitting next to Judy. It didn't seem quite

right, she mused. Nothing between them. No
. . . chemistry, that was the word. He was
quite good-looking, Agnes supposed. But sort
of sexless. Asexual. Perhaps Judy's wrong
about him being a prospect. Agnes smiled in
the privacy of the thick mist of steam. She felt
the sweat dripping from her. It's a kind of
relinquishment, she thought, sitting here, just
being. Or does this worship of the body count
as idolatry?

Beware false gods. Jed again. Perhaps
there's room for a new theology, she thought.
The worship of the body. The theology of the
work-out. Very millennial, she thought. Julius
will laugh.

Julius would laugh.

She stood up, suddenly too hot, and went
to find a cold shower. Judy was swimming
and waved to her. Agnes cooled herself down,
wrapped herself in a towel and settled on a
reclining chair by the pool. Judy came and sat
down next to her. 'I'm ready to go, if you are.'

'Sure.'

They showered and dressed and dried their
hair. Agnes went outside to the foyer.
Eventually Judy emerged, her hair faultless,
her make-up perfect.

'Shall we have a drink?' Agnes asked her.

Judy looked at her watch, frowning. 'Um,
maybe. I ought to go back to the office.

Twenty minutes? We can get something in the bar across the road.'

They sat at the bar with a mineral water each. Judy seemed worn out and pale, in spite of her make-up. She looked at her glass, put it down on the table. 'You see,' she said suddenly, 'none of it is quite right. Allen thinks he wants me, but I'm not so sure, I think maybe it's just because he sees me and Jed together and wants to compete. And Jed is kind of . . . I dunno, flattered, by my being interested, I suppose, but he always seems so vague about his future. And then there's what you said about desire, I was thinking about it in the pool, and I . . . I don't know . . . ' She took a sip from her glass, put it down on the table, stared at it. 'It's very important for my life plan I get married quite soon,' she said, her eyes still on the table. She reached for her bag, took out her mobile phone, checked for messages, and put it back in her bag. 'Patrick's in the office a lot at the moment,' she said suddenly. 'It must be so tough for him.' She drained her glass. For the first time she turned and looked at Agnes. 'I'd better go, I've got some customers to phone in the States.' Her face was flushed, and she seemed hurried as she picked up her coat and bag.

'Thanks for taking me to the gym,' Agnes said, standing up too.

'That's OK.' She put on her coat and belted it hastily.

'You must be very fit.'

'Sorry?' They headed for the door. 'Oh, yes. I am.'

Out in the street Agnes thanked her again. 'Maybe another time,' she said.

Judy's face shadowed with confusion. 'What? Oh, um . . . yes. Sure. Any time. See you.' She crossed the road as the traffic lights beeped and disappeared into the crowds and the darkness. Agnes watched her go, imagining her returning to her office, to its sleek luxury. She imagined her at her desk, calculating risks and odds and probabilities, far into the night.

All this time, Agnes thought, Judy has been trying to work out which is the safer bet, the best option between Allen and Jed, trying to calculate which of the two will fit in best with her life plan. And now she's met Patrick, a hopeless risk altogether. And the one thing she has failed to factor into her calculations is desire.

Agnes turned back towards the Underground station. She breathed in the warm, familiar smell of the tube, glad to become part of the anonymous humanity of the jostling crowds.

11

Agnes arrived at the hostel next morning with a large bag of bacon sandwiches, which she distributed to the morning shift. 'You nuns don't half eat well,' someone said, before the phone rang, the doorbell went, a fight broke out in the lounge, and a new resident arrived with a policewoman. Agnes and Helen were left alone in the kitchen.

Helen went over to the kettle. 'Coffee?'

'It's all instant,' Agnes said.

'Beggars can't be choosers.' Helen handed her a mug.

They sat at the kitchen table.

'How are you, then?' Agnes frowned at her coffee.

'OK. I think.'

'You think?' Agnes looked up.

Helen tried to smile. 'I wish I hadn't read Pascal.'

'Why?'

'It's all so difficult, isn't it? Faith, I mean.'

'Well, yes. It is.'

'I mean, all these last few weeks, I've been looking at you, and thinking, There's someone who's really made a decision, really

203

made a commitment — really knows that being a nun is where she belongs. And I keep thinking, for me — I mean, this work, for example, which I love — I keep thinking, I could do this without being a nun.'

Agnes concentrated on sipping her coffee. 'What do you mean?' she said.

'Well, this work, it's obviously worth while, isn't it, but lots of people do it without it being — being some kind of calling, don't they? That lot who work here, Brendan and Alex and Rosie, they don't need to pretend that God's telling them to — '

'Pretend?'

'That's just what I mean.' She stared at the table, tracing an old coffee ring with her finger. 'I know this is what I want. I just don't know if it's what God wants. Julius said it was about discernment. I went to his mass yesterday and we had a chat. He said you just have to sit with things, to listen, to see what God's asking you to do. He's so helpful, isn't he? I thought, No wonder you're so certain about being a nun if you've had him as your support all these years.' She drained her mug.

Agnes opened her mouth to speak, but closed it again.

Helen glanced up at the clock. 'I ought to go. I've been working with our silent friend. He'll be waiting for me.'

'What's happened with that now?'

'We've got him a lawyer: Colin. Have you met him? We're trying to file a claim for asylum. The voluntary bodies have been really helpful, the Refugee Information people. We're saying he's been tortured. But without knowing anything about him, it's all stone-walling, really. They'll come for him at some point. On the form, it said Name of Applicant. We had to write, 'Unknown'.'

'Xenos,' Agnes said.

'What?'

'It's ancient Greek. For wanderer, exile. Like Odysseus, someone who has to throw themselves on the mercy of strangers.'

'Xenos,' Helen repeated.

'What do you do with him? When you work with him?'

'I just sit with him. Yesterday I had a breakthrough, I went out and bought some picture books, you know, baby books. We sat and looked at them together.'

'Did he tell you anything?'

Helen shook her head. 'He just watched me. I went through every book. I pointed at things, said the word. 'Spade. Duck. Orange.' He watched.' She stood up. 'Still. It feels OK. Just to sit with him. I'd better go.'

She put her mug on the draining board and left the kitchen. Agnes washed up the mugs, dried them and put them away.

So here we are, she thought. Helen and me. Envying each other. Each one thinking the other is certain and clear and sure of her path.

She went into the empty office and sat down with some paperwork, glad of the silence, aware of a sense of fear. Life without Julius, she thought. I can't bear it.

At about eleven, Helen put her head round the door. 'Agnes?' She was flushed and breathless. 'Come and see.'

Agnes followed her into the lounge. The boy was there, absorbed in a brightly coloured cardboard book. He was pointing at a picture. He looked up and saw Agnes, and immediately closed the book and tucked it under a cushion. Helen went to him, retrieved the book and found the page. She put her arm around him, and Agnes noticed he no longer cringed at being touched. 'Look,' Helen said to him. He glanced at Agnes, his face tense.

'It's all right,' Helen said. 'Here we are. Horse.'

The young man took his eyes from Agnes. He made no sound, but stared at the page.

'Horse,' Helen said again.

Slowly he lifted his finger towards the page. He looked at Agnes and snatched his finger away, his eyes dark with distress.

'No one will hurt you,' Helen said to him. 'Horse,' she repeated.

His finger went to the page. It was a photograph of a pony in a field, bright sun, lush green grass. He began to stroke the page, shaking his head, his lips moving. Helen glanced at Agnes, and Agnes realised that he had tears in his eyes.

Silently she went to the door, leaving them both absorbed in their task. She sat at her desk in the empty office. Yes, she thought. I do envy her. I wish I had the time, the stillness, the inspiration, the compassion to have reached out to him.

Whereas I . . . I'm distracted, she thought. Distracted by my mother's death; by Julius's absence from me. By the house in Provence. By all this business with Matthias and Mary and Tad and —

The phone rang and she snatched it up. 'Hello?'

It was Patrick's voice. 'I just wondered how your researches had gone yesterday.'

'They went very well. Karen and Judy. Both spoke very highly of you.'

'Don't tease me.'

'I wasn't.'

'When do you finish your shift?'

'Why?'

'I did rather well last night. Fancy an expensive drink?'

'Sure. I'll be free about three.'

'I'll meet you for tea. There's a nice hotel by Tower Bridge, is that too far? Cucumber sandwiches and champagne.'

'How well you know me.'

'Hardly at all.' He laughed, and then was gone.

Some time later, Agnes was interrupted from her paperwork by the click of the office door. Helen was standing there.

'Horse,' she said. Her face was flushed. 'I can't bear it. Something terrible must have happened to him. When I look into his eyes, there's such suffering there. It makes me angry.' She flung herself into a chair. 'Angry with people. And angry with God. I was reading something about Christ as the suffering God, as the archetype of human suffering . . . but when I look at him, I don't see God, I don't see redemption, I just see human pain. Human evil. He's been destroyed, tortured, traumatised. Where's the redemption in that? He's just a normal kid, from some village somewhere, a Kurd or an Albanian or something, and he's been so badly hurt that he's a shadow of himself . . . and why should I see God in that? What sort of God is that?' She stopped, breathing

208

fast, near to tears.

Agnes reached out and touched her hand. 'I can't really help,' she said, after a while.

'No.' Helen shook her head. 'This is for me.' She stood up. 'It's so hard. To believe. It's all right for — '

'Don't say it.' Agnes held up her hand. 'Don't say it's all right for me. It isn't.' To her surprise she felt tears welling in her eyes. 'Every day — every day I think what you're thinking. I look at the other sisters and I see their certainties, whereas for me — for me, there's only doubt. And struggle. And a sense of falling short.'

Helen was staring at her. 'But what's kept you here, then?'

Agnes met her eyes. 'What's kept me here, all these years, is that I am here. That's all.'

Helen clasped her hands in her lap. Outside the office there was running, shouting, laughter, fading away towards the kitchen. Helen looked at Agnes. 'It really is hard, then, isn't it?'

'Maybe not for you. I'm not really — I mean, you shouldn't take my example as . . . '

'Why not? It's as good as any other.' Helen's gaze was clear and serious. 'So you've found it difficult. So what? I'm going to learn more talking to you about your doubts than I am talking to Louise about her certainties.'

She stood up. 'And I get chocolate biscuits with you. Even in Lent.'

Agnes laughed.

Helen looked at her watch. 'It's the end of our shift, isn't it?'

'Yes.'

'I left Xenos dozing on his bed. He doesn't really sleep. I might come back tonight and sleep here. His nightmares have got worse.'

Agnes nodded.

'Well, then.' Helen hesitated. 'I said I'd meet Louise for tea. Before she sees you.' Their eyes met. 'And don't say anything about biscuits.'

'I wasn't going to. I've been invited to drink champagne, so that's even worse.'

Helen smiled. A shadow of a question crossed her face, but she said nothing. They left the hostel together, and Agnes went to find a bus to take her across the river.

★　★　★

Agnes settled back in her armchair, a glass of champagne in her hand. She watched Patrick as he topped up his own glass. 'You look tired,' she said.

'No, on the contrary.' He shook his head emphatically. 'I'm on good form. Great form. Lucky streak now. Last night, at the

210

tables, I was on a roll.'

'Blackjack?'

He nodded. 'People were coming to watch. It was dramatic, Agnes, really quite something.'

Agnes sipped her champagne. 'What makes it a streak, then? Why isn't it just random good luck?'

'All sorts of things. Coming here, I needed a number six bus, followed by a fifteen. They both came instantly, and they both add up to twenty-one. It's not just the tables, you see.'

'Couldn't you afford a cab?'

He laughed. 'I wanted to test my luck. And I won again.'

'And what happens when this luck runs out?'

'Ah, but you can't tell when. I might have a week of it. Or a month. I've put thirty pounds on the three-fifteen at Cheltenham.' His eyes had a false brightness.

'Patrick . . . '

He picked up the change he'd left as a tip and began to toss a coin. 'Call,' he said. 'Best of three.'

'Heads.'

'Tails.' He revealed the face. 'Again.' He threw the coin up in the air.

'Heads.'

'Heads. Once more.'

211

'Tails.'

'It's Heads. I win again.'

Agnes reached across for a sandwich. 'And where's God in that, then?'

Patrick laughed, but a shadow passed across his face. 'What should I say? That it's not luck at all, but the good Lord smiling upon me? I gave up that one a long time ago, Agnes. Luck doesn't disappoint, you see. Luck doesn't promise anything.'

'Does God?'

'Does he?' Patrick countered.

Agnes frowned. 'Ultimate redemption, I suppose.'

'As I said: I'd rather win on the tables than wait for that.' He looked up as Agnes took another sandwich. 'Save some for Tad, won't you? He said he'd join us.' He raised his glass to her. 'To luck, then.'

She smiled, and raised her glass back.

'So,' he went on. 'What did Judy say?'

'She said that Matthias had invested some money in Allen's leisure centre scheme. And that it was a risky venture.'

Patrick stared at her. 'Matthias?'

'That's what she said.'

'What money?'

Agnes shrugged. 'I've no idea. But . . . ' She hesitated. 'She said she couldn't ask you about it, because it depended on the will.

Matthias's will.' Patrick was turning his glass around in his hands. 'It seems no one knows the fate of the money.'

Patrick looked up from his glass. 'But I know the will. I've read it. I'm one of the executors. There's a trust for Tad, I have to administer it. It's only a small sum — doesn't solve all our problems, despite Matt's promises.'

'What promises?'

He smiled. 'Oh, he'd taken to saying if anything happened to him, Tad would be set up for life. It was always our wish, you see, these accommodation schemes just don't work for Tad . . . Anyway, it didn't quite turn out as he said.' He leaned over and topped up both their glasses. 'So that idiot Allen thought that his piddling gymnasium would be rescued by Matt's will? He's even more of a fool than I took him for.'

Agnes sipped her drink, frowning. 'So if Matthias promised Allen some backing for his venture, and then died — Allen's just lost that money?'

'Perhaps he'd already given him the money.' Patrick frowned. 'But it's not like Matt to back something as dodgy as that.'

'But Judy seemed to think Allen was waiting to hear.'

'For probate, you mean?' Patrick shook his

head. 'Why should Matt mention Allen in his will? It's a crazy idea. No, it seems to me' — he reached across for another sandwich — 'that Allen has got his hopes up about Matthias's promise of some kind of capital, and then Matt dies, and so Allen's left high and dry, with his business going down the tubes . . . and I can't say I can find it within me to feel sorry for him.'

Outside the sun broke through the clouds with the last of the day. The wall behind Patrick rippled with reflected light. 'Did she say anything else?' he asked.

'No, that's about it, really. Except she can't decide who to marry, between Allen and Jed.'

Patrick opened his eyes wide. 'Between those two?' His face creased in disbelief. 'Neither, I'd have thought.'

'That's what I said.' Agnes looked at Patrick, at his lined, lived-in face, his bright, gentle eyes. She decided not to betray Judy's confidences any further.

He leaned back in his chair. 'And how was Karen?'

Agnes sighed. 'As you'd expect.'

He shook his head. 'I don't know how she gets through the days. Every time I see her, she seems worse.' He raised his eyes to Agnes. 'She understood Matt, she did.'

'Yes.'

Patrick picked up the empty champagne bottle, tilted it, frowned at it. 'It's all bloody suspicious. And what you reported about Allen, that makes it even worse. If Allen was counting on money from Matt, and now — now it's gone . . . ' He leaned forward and lowered his voice. 'That's why I think Allen is doing something at work, 'borrowing' from a fund, something like that. Trying to bail himself out. The way he snatched the papers off me . . . ' He shook his head. 'And what with Liz recognising this friend of Allen's . . . '

'Whom do we talk to next then?'

'Stewart Lode? Or Charles Fielding?' Patrick seemed fired up, his eyes sparkling in the pallor of his face.

'But Patrick — '

'Don't tell me.' He held up his hand as if to silence her. 'Don't start on your random bloody universe, or God's own universe or what-have-you. My brother's dead, damn it, and no one can stop me trying to make sense of it, even if there isn't any sense about it. And there's poor Karen too, and Mary, poor Mary . . . '

'Have you seen her?'

'She's in a terrible state. A passion. A life-long passion, that was.'

'You didn't say you'd seen her.'

He glanced at her. 'No. I didn't want to . . . with Julius, you see.'

'Why not?'

Patrick met her eyes. His gaze had lost its brilliance, and now he just looked tired. 'Ask Julius. Please. I can't . . . it's not for me to tell you.'

'He won't tell me.'

'Have you tried?'

Agnes looked at him, then shook her head.

'It's my fault.' Patrick picked up his glass and drained the dregs from it. 'I hadn't seen him in such a long time, dear old Ignatius.'

Agnes suddenly felt like crying. 'Everything's changed, you see. We're not — we used to be close. And now we're not.'

'But a friendship like yours . . .'

Agnes glanced at him. He was about to say something else, but then someone shouted his name.

'Patrick!' Tad was waving wildly, striding through the quiet lounge. He came to a halt at their table, and nodded at Agnes. 'Hello.'

'Hello.' Agnes nodded back.

Tad flung himself into an armchair and took two sandwiches.

A waiter appeared. 'May I get you anything?'

'No — ' Patrick began, but Tad indicated the half-empty plates before them with a wild

216

sweep of his arm. 'The same again,' he said, smiling up at the waiter. 'Please.'

'But not the champagne,' Patrick added.

'Tea,' Tad said. 'Lots of tea. Please.'

'For three, sir?'

'Yes.' Tad smiled benevolently at Agnes and Patrick. 'Tea for three.'

'How's it going, Tad?' Patrick patted his shoulder.

'Not good. No. It's looking bad for George. I told them, if it's between them and George, I'll choose George, and they took it badly.'

Patrick sighed. 'Of course. Good old George.'

'And at the stables, it's not good either. Liz is frightened, she told me she wasn't but I can tell.'

'Frightened? What of?'

Tad took two more sandwiches and chewed, silently. Eventually he said, 'If you fall off a horse, you have a chance, don't you?'

Patrick glanced at Agnes.

'Matthias,' Tad went on, 'he had a chance. Lots of people fall, don't they?' He seemed to expect an answer.

'From horses?' Agnes frowned. 'Yes. Um, they do. I've fallen off loads of times.'

'See?' Tad's gaze was intense. 'He had a chance.'

The tea arrived, with three delicate teacups and saucers. Tad filled a cup, drained it in one gulp, refilled it.

'Why is Liz frightened?' Patrick's tone was patient.

'She won't tell me.'

'Is it the conflicts around the hunt?'

Tad pulled a face. 'They're all stupid, the people who hunt and the people who try and stop them. It's all just fighting. And on Wednesday, she didn't go hunting, and the sabs were out, and now everyone thinks they'd tipped her off and that she's part of them, just 'cos her friend Annelise is friends with Wez.'

'What happened?' Patrick had a coin between his fingers, turning it round and round.

'I don't know, I wasn't there.'

'But they got back safely?'

'S'pose so. Liz said if Matthias was still there, it wouldn't be getting so bad. Maybe that's why she's frightened.' He turned to Patrick. 'I wish he'd come back . . . ' His lips trembled. 'I just want him to be here again. We should be three, not two.' He stopped as the waiter brought another plate of sandwiches. Patrick fiddled with the coin in his fingers. He nodded, glanced at Tad, looked away again.

'It's like when Dad went,' Tad went on. 'It's all wrong. People should be here — ' His voice cracked. He sat, breathing. 'A brick wall,' he said, turning to Agnes. 'That's what did it for our dad.' Patrick tossed the coin. Tad watched him, then went on, 'A brick wall. No chance, you see, not at fifty-five miles an hour. He had no chance.' Patrick turned the coin over in his fingers. Tad sat down, poured tea for himself and then for the others, balancing the tea strainer clumsily on the cups. He drank from his, and the cup clattered as he replaced it in the saucer. 'He had a chance, Matthias. Even without a hat. It's not as if he did it on purpose, not like Dad . . . And he was lucky, everyone said so. But that's not luck, is it?' Again, the dark eyes were fixed to hers.

'No.' Agnes shook her head. 'No, it's not luck.'

'That's why I'm counting,' Tad said. 'If you count, then you can work it out. You can work out whether you have a chance or not.'

Patrick looked up. 'What do you mean?'

'It's in the Bible. 'Were I to count them, they would be more in number than the sand . . . ' '

' 'How deep I find your thoughts, O Lord,' ' Agnes echoed. ' 'How great is the sum of them. Were I to count them, they would be

219

more in number than the sand . . . ' '

Tad had turned to her. ' 'To count them all, my life span would need to be like yours . . . ' You see?' He turned to Patrick, pointing at Agnes. 'She knows.'

'She's a nun,' Patrick said. 'More tea?'

'I ought to be going,' Agnes said.

'So soon?' Patrick smiled at her.

'I have to meet a novice.' She reached for her coat.

Patrick picked up the coin and tossed it.

'No!' Tad lunged to grab the coin. People turned to stare. 'Not chances,' Tad said. 'No more chances. No odds.' He sat, biting his lip, breathing hard.

Patrick patted his hand. 'Sorry,' he said.

Tad quietened. People turned away again, resumed their conversations. Patrick sat, his hand still on his brother's.

Agnes left them there, sitting side by side, lost in silence.

★ ★ ★

Back at her flat she switched on her bar fire and her desk lamp, still in her coat, and turned to the Psalms.

'If I climb up to Heaven, you are there; If I make the grave my bed, you are there also. If I take the wings of the morning, and dwell in the uttermost part of the sea, Even there your hand will lead me, your right hand hold me fast . . . '

She sat, staring at the words, blinking against the tears that pricked her eyes . . . *your right hand hold me fast.*

A promise of love, she thought, wondering why she was crying. Or a promise that wherever you go, there is no escape. Even if it's to a bolt-hole in Provence.

She picked up the letter from her mother's executors. *Please reply at your earliest convenience . . . expressing your wishes for the disposal of the property . . .*

Even there your hand will lead me . . .

If there's no escape, she thought, does it matter where you go?

She jumped as the buzzer on her door sounded. She dabbed at her face, switched on another lamp, took off her coat, smoothed her hair. She greeted Louise with a calm smile.

Louise settled in the armchair while Agnes made some tea. 'How's work?' Agnes asked, waiting for the tea to brew.

'Brilliant.' Louise smiled at her.

'How's Sister Mary-Teresa?'

'Lovely. She works very hard. I want to be like her.' Agnes went to pour the tea. 'That old lady died today,' Louise announced. 'Mrs

Goodison. The one I told you about. It was fantastic.'

'Oh. Good,' Agnes called from the kitchen.

'It was so dignified, and all her family were there, two daughters and a granddaughter, about my age, and she just left us, sailed away. Someone said it was like watching someone drift out to sea, and that was just what it was like. It was brilliant. I hope I go like that.'

Agnes handed her a mug and sat down opposite her.

'There's a new patient,' Louise went on. 'He's quite ill. He's in his twenties, about my age. I talk to him a lot. He says he can't die yet, he's engaged to this girl, they're going to get married, Sarah, she's called, he loves her more than anything, he said. I didn't say anything, I just listened.'

Agnes nodded. 'Go on.'

'It made me think, Agnes. About love. This boy thinks that everything is going to be perfect if he marries this Sarah. But it isn't, is it? The only perfect love is God's, isn't it? I think people these days have a real problem, that the only way we can talk about love is, you know, romantic love. So we invest all this meaning in relationships, and they can never measure up. Because human relationships are never perfect, only God's love is perfect.'

Agnes shifted in her chair. Louise went on, 'Of course, I didn't say all this to him. He needs a reason to live. Although . . . ' A shadow crossed her face. 'He's very ill.' She sipped her tea, then brightened. 'It makes me so glad to have chosen this way. Or rather, to have listened to Jesus when he told me to choose this way. Because this way, I can never be disappointed, can I?' She handed Agnes a sheaf of papers. 'I've written lots of reflections about it. About love and how we mustn't look to illusions here on earth.'

'Thank you.' Agnes took the papers and placed them carefully on her desk.

'I ought to be going,' Louise said. 'I was out for tea with Helen, and I said I'd be back at the house quite soon.'

Agnes showed her out. She came back into the silence of her room. She glanced down at the papers, picked up the first sheet, read a few words: *God, Perfection, Love* . . .

She could hear the church bells of the City striking eight, muted by the cold night air. Julius would be just finishing vespers. She put on her coat and went out.

He was standing by the gate, seeing off the last of the congregation. He looked up and saw her.

'Julius,' Agnes said.

They stood side by side in the chill, their

hands in their pockets.

'Well,' he said.

Agnes took a deep breath. 'Patrick said I should see you. I asked him about Mary Wells, and he said he couldn't say anything and I must ask you.'

Julius frowned. He scuffed the gravel of the drive with his toe. 'There's nothing to say.'

'I was thinking about love today.' She looked at him, willing him to meet her eyes, but he stared steadfastly downwards. 'Louise says, that's my novice, one of them' — she was aware her voice was growing louder — 'Louise says that only God's love is perfect and that it's a human failing to yearn for completion in another human being, when only God can make us whole.'

Julius looked up. 'What does she know about it?' His voice was sharp with anger.

Agnes blinked, stared at him.

'I'm sorry, Agnes, I'm getting cold standing out here. I'd — um — you'd better go now.' He turned and walked away from her up the drive.

Agnes stood and watched him. Her face felt ice cold and she realised she was crying.

There's only one person left to ask, she thought.

12

'Hi, Liz, yes, it's Agnes. Yes, I did find out
about that man you saw. He's an old friend
of Allen's, from school. Used to work with
him. Local . . . Yes, that's right. Bit of a
recluse, I gather, that's why you'd never
seen him before . . . No, I know it doesn't
explain why he should be on the path the
day you fell . . . Riding? Tomorrow? Yes, I'd
love to. That would be wonderful. Are you
sure? That's very kind of you. OK, eight
tomorrow morning. I'll be here. Thanks.
And Liz? Do you have a phone number for
Mary? Mary Wells?' Agnes tucked the phone
under her chin. 'Thanks.' She wrote the
number down. 'Thanks. See you in the
morning.'

Agnes sat at her desk, still in her coat. In
the distance the church bells chimed nine
o'clock. She realised she was very hungry.
One more phone call, she thought. And then
supper. And I can read Louise's notes while I
eat.

★   ★   ★

Saturday morning sparkled with frost and sunlight. Agnes woke early, knelt in prayer, showered, found her riding kit, made some tea and waited for Liz.

They set off in Liz's car, leaving the City behind them. The roads seemed to widen out, empty of traffic. They sat in companionable silence, apart from the hum of the engine.

Liz broke the silence. 'Have you seen Tad recently?'

'Yes. With Patrick, yesterday.'

'How was he?'

'Quite upset. About odds and chances. And Matthias. And accidents. And — um — and you.'

'Me?'

'He says you're frightened.'

Liz tried to smile. 'Oh, he mustn't worry about me.' She changed gear as they joined the dual carriageway.

'He said that the hunt got ugly on Wednesday.'

'It's true. It does all feel a lot more dangerous. Wez's lot are just fools. It really annoys me. I might have some sympathy for them if they weren't such bloody idiots.'

'Tad said you didn't go.'

'No, I didn't.'

'Why?'

Liz was silent. After a while she said, 'I lost my nerve.'

'From the accident?'

'Sort of.'

'But you still ride?'

'Oh yes. And I'll probably hunt again. When I've sorted out my feelings about it. But on Wednesday, from what I heard, it was so ugly, all these grown men on horseback shouting abuse, and these people on the ground, like some medieval battle ... All about a fox. I don't know what to think any more. I used to love hunting ... ' She seemed lost in thought. They left the motorway and turned off towards the stables. 'We were hunting the day Matt died,' she said. 'He was going to come to the meet, but he didn't. Something about his horse. But Mary said he had a note for her, in his pocket. And you see ... I don't know how he expected it to get to her. No one knew about him and her, except for me. So then, I thought, maybe he was expecting to see me, to give me the note.'

'Didn't you see him that day?'

'No. Someone said he'd meet us at second horses. I'd already set off to the meet by then.' She glanced at Agnes, her face tense. 'None of it is right,' she said. 'When I think about it all, it makes me feel cold.' They approached the entrance to the stables.

'Don't mention any of this to the others, will you? It all sounds so mad.'

Deborah came to greet them, gruff and cheery. Agnes saw Mary appear from the yard, with Charlie behind her. She left Deborah in conversation with Liz.

Mary approached her. 'You wanted to speak to me.'

'Yes. I'm sorry about the phone call.'

'That's OK. You wanted to talk.'

'Yes.'

'Are you riding?'

'Just for an hour, now, with Liz.'

'Charlie's having her lesson at eleven. During that, maybe?'

'Sure.'

★   ★   ★

Liz seemed miles ahead, streaking across the open field. Agnes pushed her horse to go faster, catching up with Liz as they reached the woods and slowed to a walk.

Liz laughed. 'Beat you.'

'I wasn't racing.' Agnes blinked in the slanting sunlight, looking back across the field. On the horizon there was a lone jogger, a speck of movement against the shimmering sky.

They ambled back to the stables on a long

rein, the horses puffing and blowing their breathy mist.

'Thank you for this,' Liz said suddenly. 'It's cheered me up.'

'It's cheered me up too.'

'I was thinking dark thoughts. Everything seemed to be making some kind of horrible sense. A kind of sinister pattern, to do with Matthias, and golf balls, and the violence at the meet, and my accident . . . ' She laughed. 'And now it just seems normal again, just, you know, just life. Stuff. Things happen. Annelise says that.'

'Annelise?'

'My girlfriend. She says, 'Stuff happens.' It's her catchphrase. She thinks everything's just random.'

Agnes breathed in the crisp air. She smiled.

At the yard they were met by the stable girls, who offered to sort out their horses for them. Agnes went to find Mary.

Charlie was in the paddock, trotting across some poles on a grey pony. Mary was leaning on the fence watching her. She waved at Agnes. 'Shall we go for a walk? Charlie won't even notice I've gone.'

They took the path into the woods, skirting the bridle way.

'She rides well, Charlie.'

'Yes.' Mary smiled. 'She loves it.'

In her blood, Agnes thought, remembering what Julius had said.

'What did you want to see me about? It sounded urgent.' Mary kept up a steady pace on the soft mud track.

'Um . . . ' Agnes sighed. 'It was about Julius.'

'Oh.' Mary's step faltered.

'I'm sorry to burden you with it.'

'No, that's OK.' She hesitated, then said, 'I need to talk about the past. God knows, I seem to be living in it at the moment.'

Agnes breathed deeply. 'No one will tell me, you see, since Patrick came back into his life, and — and you . . . Since he saw you at the funeral, he's been a changed person; he's not the Julius I know, and Patrick won't tell me, and Karen, I went to see her, and finally I asked Julius what it was about the past returning like this that has entangled him in this way, and he won't . . . he won't talk to me . . . ' Agnes felt her voice crack. She stopped, out of breath.

Mary was looking at her. 'You and Julius must be very close.'

'We were.' She blinked back the tears.

'The past is a powerful thing.' The breeze flicked her hair across her face. 'Julius knew my mother,' she said. 'What I mean is, Julius — Julius loved my mother.

230

And she loved him.'

'When?'

'When he was young. He was a novice priest. In the seminary, in Ireland.'

'Did your mother tell you?'

'Most of what I know, I know from her. But she hardly mentioned it. Hardly ever. I don't suppose my father would have liked it.'

'How did you find out?'

Mary turned and began to walk, following the path between the trees, the ground flecked with gold. Agnes walked beside her.

'Matthias told me some of it,' Mary said. 'He was much younger, you see. There's ten years between him and Julius. He was still young when my mother died.'

'Yes.'

'They all — Patrick and Matthias, and Mum, and Tad, and some of the other families, they all grew up together in the same village. They were like cousins, like brothers and sisters. And then Patrick went to St Joseph's, and he and Julius became best friends, and that was how Julius met Mum. Matthias said it was love at first sight, but it turned out he wasn't even there, so how could he know?' She laughed.

'What happened?'

'I don't know. No one knows. Maybe

Patrick.' She shrugged. 'All I know is it stopped. And Julius went away, abroad somewhere.'

'To France.'

Mary glanced at her. 'Yes, that was it. To France.'

'That's when I met him. He was a young curate there.'

'Was he heartbroken?' Mary spoke lightly.

'I was in no state to notice, I'm afraid. I was in despair of my own. Julius rescued me from my husband, who would otherwise have killed me.' Mary stopped and stared at her. Agnes smiled. 'Just routine domestic violence.'

'But you're a — '

'Yes. Julius pulled some rather high-up strings to get me to England.'

They resumed their gentle pace. 'He's nice, Julius, isn't he?' Mary said, after a while.

'Yes,' Agnes said. She struggled to find the right words. 'When you were born . . . ' she began.

'Yes?'

'I mean, was he still — did he and your mother still . . . '

'My mother was married to my dad by then.'

'Oh.'

'We didn't see Julius any more.'

'Oh. But — but you seem to know him now.'

Mary frowned. 'Yes. He was — he was important, I suppose. I've always known who he is. I think perhaps there were photographs, at home. I knew I'd recognise him.'

'And you and Matthias?'

There was a silence. Then Mary said, 'Yes. Me and Matthias. But not any more.' She walked a few more paces, then said, 'I don't think I can bear it, Agnes.' She stopped to wipe the tears from her cheeks. 'I keep trying to hold it all together, for Charlie's sake; I keep telling myself I knew it would end like this, I knew I'd never have him for ever . . . but it makes no difference. I just miss him. I just want him back. I can't stand it.' She dissolved into tears. Agnes hesitated, then held her in her arms.

'How did you meet him?' Agnes asked after a while.

Mary wiped her face, blew her nose. She went and sat on a log and Agnes sat next to her.

'I was only a child. My mum and Patrick were friends, and later my dad. But Matthias I didn't really know. We'd moved away from the village, me and my mum and dad. I met Matthias again when I was sixteen. We'd moved again, nearer . . . ' She sighed. 'We had this mad summer. He was thirty-five, working in Dublin. A blissful, wonderful summer. But he felt the years between us, he felt burdened by the guilt ... He was already with Karen, then. Me, what did I know?' She laughed. 'I was a kid.' She dabbed at her face. 'And then his company wanted to send him to London, and he agreed. He wrote to me a bit from London, but I didn't reply. I knew it was over. I hung around in Ireland; I met this boy called Gary. I married him, had Charlie. I knew it wasn't going to work, but I tried to make it work for Charlie's sake, for a while. When I left Gary, I decided to start a new life. Liz got me the job here in the stables to start with, we had friends in common in Ireland.'

'But you don't work here now.'

'I liked it, but I wanted to make more of my life, give Charlie more than I had. I did some training through the job centre, I do word-processing now, for a solicitors'. I'm thinking I might do law eventually.' Her face looked clear and happy again.

'And Matthias?'

'I bumped into him. Really. It was chance. I was in the City, I hardly go there, running an errand or something, and he was standing in the street, trying to get a taxi, in a hurry . . . ' She smiled at the memory. 'I said, Hello. And he just stared at me, like I was a ghost. Then his face lit up. Really, I know it sounds stupid, but it was so fantastic to see him.'

'What happened?'

'Well, nothing. It was — it was very difficult.' Her face clouded. 'Very difficult. Nothing happened, you see, because it couldn't.' She fell silent. Agnes was aware of the chill of the log through her jodhpurs. 'We saw each other from time to time,' Mary went on. 'We were astonished. Amazed, I think, to find out that — it was all just the same.'

'So you didn't — I mean, you weren't . . . '

'We went on for years, just being friends. It was him who took the chance. In the end. I didn't want to break up his marriage. But . . . sometimes, the wrong thing to do is actually the right thing.' She smiled. 'What I mean is, sometimes, you can't tell.'

Agnes looked at her hands clasped in her lap.

'I told him,' Mary went on, 'he had everything to lose. And he said, Maybe. But he loved me, you see. He was prepared to risk it for me. And anyway . . . ' She laughed. 'In the end, he won. He died before it could all go wrong.'

'That's what Karen said.'

Mary looked up at her. 'Did she?'

'I'm — sorry . . . '

'No, it's OK.' Mary was silent for a while. 'They had something special,' she said at last. 'Not just the kids, something deeper, that kind of grows if you share the same bed day after day, do the shopping, washing up, that kind of stuff . . . I never had that.' Her eyes welled with tears again. 'I shouldn't have gone to the funeral, but I couldn't bear it, I knew I'd never be able to grieve if I didn't . . . This must sound odd.'

'No. My mother died at the end of last year. I had to be there. Even though we were never — I mean, my early life with her wasn't what you'd call . . . but at the end . . . ' A sparrow hopped at their feet, eyeing them.

Mary spoke quietly. 'It's about resolution. I never wanted him to leave his family. I don't know if Karen understands that.' She watched the sparrow pecking at the mud. 'We should be getting back,' Mary said.

They stood up. Agnes rubbed the chill from her legs. They turned back towards the stables, walking in silence. The sunlight sharpened towards noon, shortening the shadows.

'I do remember Julius,' Mary said suddenly. 'I remember a visit. I must have been about five. He came to tea. I remember it was odd because we sat in the front room, and my mother got out the best tea things. White china, with little flowers. I loved them.' She laughed. 'My mother sort of glowed. He sat in our front room, and he was all twinkly. I liked him too.' She stared straight ahead of her as they approached the stable yard. 'He never came again. Not that I remember. Oh, look at Charlie's canter.' In the paddock the grey pony was cantering a perfect circle. 'She's a natural,' Mary said. 'It's in the blood.' She ran to the fence.

Charlie brought the pony to a halt, and waved to her mother, flushed and smiling. Mary waved back, half turned towards Agnes. She looks just like him, Agnes thought. Just like Julius.

Agnes wandered up to the yard. Two people, a man and a woman, were standing talking to Deborah. Agnes noted the woman's riding boots, in soft brown leather up to the knee, the expensive jacket, and the long riding crop which she tapped rhythmically against her knee, before she realised it was Judy. And Allen, she noticed, recognising the man with her.

Judy's loud, high-spirited laugh rang out across the yard. 'Oh, nonsense,' she was saying as Agnes approached, 'he was just sweet enough to drive me here.'

'He doesn't do it for you.' Allen seemed to be sulking.

'Of course he does. Why else would the poor boy drag himself out of London. He's just very kind, that's all.'

'You're completely taken in by him. He came out here to run. To train for his stupid marathon.'

'You're just jealous.'

'Jed doesn't do anything unless there's something in it for him.'

'Nonsense. You don't know him like I do.'

'If I may interrupt?' Deborah tapped Allen on the chest. 'The golf club. Will you promise to put in a word for me? Can't have their lethal weapons flying across that path any more. It's just a matter of them raising their fence along that path. You will ask, won't you?'

Allen smiled down at her. 'Yes,' he said. 'Yes, I'll ask.'

'Otherwise I might just sue them.' Deborah nodded in emphasis.

'Hello,' Agnes said as Judy turned and saw her.

'What are you doing here?' Allen's surprise was genuine, she thought.

'I've just been riding.'

'How was lazy old Blue, then?' Deborah seemed glad to be distracted from Allen.

'Not lazy at all,' Agnes laughed. 'We

had a lovely time.'

'You must be good for him,' Deborah said. 'In the school he plods around like a brute.'

'Jed will be sad to have missed you.' Judy glanced at Allen as she spoke.

'Is he here?'

'He's around somewhere. He gave me a lift. All the way from London. Isn't that sweet of him?'

Allen was refusing to rise to the bait. 'She thinks it was all for her benefit,' he said.

'And wasn't it?' Judy smiled up at him.

'Oh, I'm sure it was. Shall we have our lesson? Advanced dressage,' he added with a wink, turning to Agnes. 'Madam here looks so stylish on a horse.'

They went to find their horses. Deborah watched them go. 'Bloody townies,' she said, under her breath. 'I'd like to see her do some proper riding. But that would muddy that lovely jacket, wouldn't it?' She smiled briefly. 'Oh, look at those girls, trying to get Lucky out of his stall, they'll just get kicked if they try it that way.' She hurried away, muttering.

Mary and Charlie were walking into the yard with Liz. Charlie was talking animatedly to her mother. 'And then I did some cross-poles, only little, but she said I did them really well and I can do something higher next time . . . '

Liz joined Agnes. 'Do you want a lift back to London? I'll be leaving soon, there's just a livery I've got to exercise.'

'I should get back, thanks all the same.'

'You can ask our charming friends . . . ' Liz indicated Judy and Allen, who were trotting around the indoor school.

'I think I'd rather take the train.'

'I can see your point.' Liz glanced back at Allen, still uneasy.

'I'll get a cab to the station. It's very quick into Liverpool Street.'

They paused a moment, and watched Judy execute a transition from trot to halt.

'She is so glamorous,' Agnes said.

'She gives me the creeps,' Liz said.

'Why?'

'There's something about them . . . like they've all got secrets amongst themselves.' Liz shrugged. 'Stuff 'em, anyway. They're nothing to do with me. Even that Charles, lurking around when I had my fall. I don't care any more.'

★ ★ ★

Agnes arrived back to a damp, misty afternoon, emerging from the station into the drizzling City streets. She let herself into her flat, stripped off all her muddy clothes and

240

had a hot, soapy shower. She made some soup and toast and sat at her desk. She stared at the phone as she ate, wanting to talk to Patrick about Mary, wanting to talk to Helen about their silent resident, wanting to talk to Julius about . . . about everything, she thought. Sometimes the wrong thing to do is the right thing, Mary had said. She and Matthias had been the right thing. And Julius . . . and Mary's mother.

But Julius is a priest. He knows what he's doing. He's always right. It's me who gets distracted, who makes stupid mistakes.

Julius was a brilliant rider. The memory of Patrick's words flashed through her mind. She remembered little Charlie in the paddock today, her horse under perfect control. It's in the blood. Mary said that today. And Julius . . . Julius said —

The phone rang. 'Julius?' Agnes couldn't keep the hope out of her voice.

'No, it's Mary.' Mary's voice was strangely flat.

'Oh.'

'It's bad news. Very bad news. Liz, today. On her way home . . . ' Her words tailed off.

'What?'

'An accident. Her car left the road. Some bastard kids threw a rock through the windscreen. She's — she's dead.'

13

Mary had gone. Agnes held the phone receiver in her hand. After a while she stared at it, then slowly replaced it.

Liz dead. It didn't make sense. Driving home . . . Agnes closed her eyes, then opened them again.

I refused a lift. I took the train.

It might have been me.

She stood up, feeling dizzy. She put her hand to her head, went into the kitchen, looked about as if surprised to be there, went back into her room and opened the window. She breathed in the cold air.

Liz is dead.

An accident.

Another bloody accident.

How many accidents do there have to be before they cease to be accidents? How many random events, before they cease to be random and start to be some awful, terrible chain of related events?

She flung herself into her armchair. What kind of world is this, O Lord, where chaos and randomness are our consolation, but where order is terrifying?

'If I make the grave my bed, you are there also . . . '

Where are you, O Lord? Is this your will? This emerging pattern, where after a series of accidents, two people are dead? Is this your design?

She stood up and paced the room, suddenly angry. Is this your creation, Lord, a chain of random events set in motion, as if you were some mischievous clockmaker? Do we matter so little to you, we mere mortals, that we can be crushed by the inevitable, infinitely turning wheels of your orderly machine?

The phone rang again and she snatched it up.

'Agnes, it's Patrick.'

'Oh God.' She sat down by the desk. 'You've heard?'

'Mary just phoned.' Agnes heard Patrick breathing. After a moment he said, 'An accident. A brick through a windscreen.'

'Yes.'

'I just keep thinking, another bloody accident.'

'Me too.'

'Yes. I thought so. Can you . . . are you . . . What I want to say is, are you free? Now?'

'Yes.' Agnes felt a wave of relief.

'There's a bar, not far from you, on the

river front, near the Globe Theatre. The Newton's Cradle.'

'I know it.'

'Twenty minutes?'

'See you there.'

★ ★ ★

Patrick was already sitting in a corner of the bar, a pint of beer in front of him. As Agnes approached the table he got up and hugged her, holding her for some moments. Eventually he said, 'What'll you drink?'

'Whisky, please. A large one.'

She sat and watched him at the bar, tall and angular, his face lined with anxiety. He came back with the drinks, a whisky for her, another pint for him.

'I'm so scared,' he said, sitting down, 'I'm so scared about Tad. This'll send him completely off the bloody rails.'

'Does he know?'

He shook his head. 'I've told his warden, told them not to tell him, not to put calls through to him, to keep it from him until I'm in a position to tell him myself. No one else can do it. I'm not sure even I can.' He drank from his glass. 'Tomorrow . . . ' He sighed heavily. 'I mean, what sense do you bloody make of it, eh?'

Agnes met his eyes, which were veiled with pain. 'None at all,' she said. She sipped her whisky. 'Either, none at all . . . or that it's all part of God's plan.'

'God's plan?' Patrick seemed angry. 'What kind of plan is that, then? Accidents that make some kind of pattern? But a meaningless pattern? Does your God speak in code, then? Or, even worse, not accidents? Orderly events, caused by careful skill and planning on the part of murderers — '

'Patrick, shush.'

He lowered his voice. 'Do you see what I mean, though? It's unbearable. The chances of it being Matthias, and then Liz . . . the odds on that are so low, so microscopic . . . ' He drained his first pint and started on his second. 'It was the same with Matt,' he said, suddenly. 'It was mathematical, the way he lived. He'd never accept the limits of life, you see. He was always risking losing everything on the chance of grabbing hold of more.'

'That's what Karen said. Well, sort of.'

'She understood him.' He blinked at Agnes. 'Same again?'

'Yes, please. Lots of ice.'

I ought to have said no, Agnes thought, watching Patrick leaning unsteadily on the bar. I ought to get him away from here, take him safely back home — wherever home is, she thought, surprised that she didn't know.

'Cheers,' Patrick said, returning to the table.

'We should go after this,' Agnes said.

'Go where?'

'Home.'

He shook his head. 'Not me. I can't be on my own. Not tonight.'

'Where do you live?'

He looked at her. 'Not far. I have a flat in Spitalfields. Well, the edge of Spitalfields, not the fashionable bit. Rented.'

'Is it nice?'

'What are you, an estate agent? It's OK. It'll do.'

'You need looking after.' It must be the whisky talking, Agnes thought.

He laughed. 'I can look after myself.'

'You're a mathematician. And a gambler.'

'So?'

'Hmmm.' Agnes met his gaze.

He laughed, shortly. 'Anyway,' he said, 'no one would want to look after me.'

'No, that's true.'

'You're not supposed to say that.'

'What am I supposed to say?'

'You're supposed to say, surely there are lots of beautiful young women queuing up to have the privilege of looking after me.'

Agnes looked at him. 'You wouldn't want a

beautiful young woman. You need someone older, wiser, someone difficult and eccentric. You need to meet your match.' It really must be the whisky talking, she thought.

He was staring at her. After a while he nodded. 'Yes. You're right.' He drank some more beer.

'Mary said . . . ' Agnes began.

'What did she say?'

'Nothing.' She sipped her whisky. 'It's just, at the stables today, I asked her about Julius. She said Julius was in love with her mother.'

'That's an understatement. She was his life.'

'And still is?'

Patrick looked at her. He sighed, then drained his glass. 'You see, what Matthias was trying to do . . . ' He scratched his head. 'What he was trying to do was hang on to everything. He'd find himself at a crossroads, and he'd take both directions. It was never either a) or b) with Matt, it was always both. An each-way bet. And the only reason it worked is that he died when he died. He died still having more than one life. Whereas Julius . . . Julius, like the rest of us, chose a path. The right path, instead of the wrong path.'

'Except, like the rest of us, sometimes the right path starts to seem like the wrong one?'

Patrick nodded. 'He's a man in crisis.

That's why he can't talk to you. You remind him of the person he ought to be. You remind him of his failings.'

'What do you mean?'

He frowned at his glass in his hands. 'What I mean is, you knew him since. Since Ireland. You've only ever known him as a priest. With you, he can be that version of himself. But now that version's cracking up, falling apart, and what I guess is, when he looks at you, he's reminded of a time when he could live life as if everything was clear, as if he'd chosen the right path. And now — now that time is over.'

'Has he said anything?'

'No, but that's what I guess. He doesn't mention you at all.'

'Oh.' She watched Patrick turning his empty glass around in his hands. She felt chilled. 'We ought to go,' she said.

'Sure.' Patrick got to his feet, leaning heavily on the table.

'Will you go home?' She put on her coat.

'No. I'll go to the casino, probably. You should come with me.' He held the door open for her.

'One day.'

The air was fresh and cold. Patrick took her arm and they walked along the waterfront. The lights of the opposite bank glittered in the black swirls of the river.

'I turn off here,' Agnes said as they reached the road.

'If you're sure.'

She looked up at him. 'Patrick . . . '

'What?'

'Liz might have had more to say. If she was still here.'

He nodded. 'Yes. Getting her memory back.'

They looked at each other. A car passed, sweeping their faces with white light, and then was gone. Patrick began to speak, then stopped.

'The odds, you mean,' Agnes said.

'Yes. These two deaths — if they're not accidents, if your God really does have some grand design . . . '

'It's terrifying.'

'Staring into a bloody abyss. And you ask me why I can't go home tonight?'

They stood, side by side. They could hear the soft splashing of the river, the water lapping at the stonework.

'Patrick, if Matthias was killed — on purpose, I mean — '

'And Liz.'

'But — golf balls. And horses. And bricks thrown from bridges . . . '

Patrick shook his head. 'Is it that we'd

rather see an order in it, a pattern? Or is the pattern more frightening than the random chaos?'

'Patrick, I don't know. I've been talking to the novices about discerning the will of God in things, and here I am, completely blind.'

He took her in his arms and held her. She felt the warmth of his coat against her face, and her eyes filled with tears.

'You must go home,' he said.

She nodded, allowing him to let her go. 'I'm going this way, to Southwark Bridge,' he said.

'Right.'

'Tomorrow, when I tell Tad, will you come too?'

'OK.'

'I'll phone you. It'll be around lunchtime.'

'Fine.'

He was already across the road. 'Bye, then,' he called to her.

She raised her hand in a farewell, then set off southwards towards the main road. The buzz of late-night traffic calmed her. She wiped her face with her gloved fingers.

To be held, like that. To be comforted. Not to be alone. She felt more tears coming.

So Julius thinks I remind him of the person he ought to be. How dare he? she thought. If he's having a crisis, he could at least share it with me, instead of making me his conscience. How dare he make me his conscience? When he knows I rely on him to be mine?

She crossed at the traffic lights. A car trying to jump the red light hooted loudly, screeching its brakes. She crossed to the other side and found she was smiling.

Oh Julius. What irony is this, she thought. Just when, for once, I've cast myself adrift, just when at last I'm no longer dependent on being rescued by you, just when I find that I don't need you to be my conscience — and now it's my turn to be yours.

* * *

The phone woke her. She reached out an arm and answered it.

'Sweetie, did I wake you? I thought you lot got up at dawn, especially on a Sunday.'

'Is it Sunday?'

'Hard night, was it?'

'Just quite a lot of whisky with Patrick, the lovely Irishman.'

'Fatal, darling. That accent, I melt every time. I just wondered if you were free for dinner this evening, there's a super new bistro that's opened on the Broadway, sort of French-Thai fusion.'

'Um, Athena, hang on, I can't concentrate.'

'Are you all right?'

Agnes sat up. 'Not really. This woman I know, Liz, I've been riding with her a few times. She was killed yesterday, in her car; some kids threw a rock from a bridge. She was on her way back from the stables. She'd offered me a lift, but I went by train.'

'Bloody hell, sweetie, it could've been you.' They sat in silence at the thought of this. 'Bloody hell,' Athena said again. 'And then who would I have had supper with this evening?'

'Athena!'

'I'll see you later. Eightish?'

'Yes. Fine.'

'God, what a horrible story. These kids, they're out of control, aren't they? Bet they never catch them. See you later.'

Agnes hung up. She got out of bed and put on the kettle, yawning. She was due at the community house at eleven.

Bet they never catch them. The words rang in her head. Staring into the abyss, Patrick had said. Random, murderous, chaotic events.

She made some tea, poured a mug and sat by her window. The March sunlight was a pale, primrose yellow.

She thought of Patrick, probably asleep

now. She thought of Julius, lost in his own doubt. She thought of Tad, and Mary, and Karen . . . Do we owe it to them, Lord? And do we owe it to you?

She finished her tea, got up, went to find some clean clothes. She thought about Matthias's office, and wondered what Patrick could find out there. She pulled on some jeans, thinking that she could ask Karen some more questions about Matthias's work, maybe have a look at some of those papers in his study. And Judy — perhaps another trip to the gym? I could ask her about her idea that Allen was expecting some money from Matt. And it was certainly time to visit this neighbour with the land dispute. Lode, Stewart Lode. She put on a jumper, pulled on her coat, and went to find a bus to Hackney.

★   ★   ★

' 'Yet I said in my alarm, I have been cut off from the sight of your eyes; Nevertheless, you heard the sound of my entreaty, when I cried out to you . . . ' ' Agnes knelt in her pew, joining her voice to that of her fellow sisters.

Code, that was what Patrick had called it. God's code. It's just a matter of finding the key.

' 'Be strong and let your heart take

courage, all you who wait for the Lord . . . ' '

So, if I refuse to accept this ugly, random version of the universe, does that mean I believe in you, O Lord? Your order?

She looked up as a sister began a reading from Isaiah.

' 'For the earth shall be full of the knowledge of the Lord, as the waters cover the sea . . . ' '

Agnes glanced along the pews at Helen. She remembered what she'd said, about looking into Xenos's eyes and seeing only suffering.

You ask a lot of us, O Lord. To believe that any of this makes sense.

' 'This is the word of the Lord,' ' the reader finished.

'Thanks be to God,' Agnes echoed with the others as the service ended.

She went to get her coat, hoping to get home before Patrick tried to phone her about Tad. Louise was waiting in the hallway.

'I wanted to see you, Agnes. Are you free, later, maybe?'

'Yes. Yes, I think so.'

'Tea-time?' She seemed nervous, shifting from one foot to the other.

'Yes. I'll come back here — fourish?'

'Thanks. See you then.' She fled up the stairs.

At home, Patrick had left a message on her answering machine, asking her to meet him at Tad's flat at one o'clock, if she was still free. He sounded tired. She went straight out, arriving outside the block just as he approached the front door.

'Patrick!'

He turned and saw her. 'I'd given up on you.'

'I wasn't late.'

'No. I was early.' He smiled. 'Come on.'

Tad was sitting in the lounge, reading a book. He looked up and greeted them with a nod of his head.

'How are you, Tad?' Patrick sat down next to him.

'Fine. At least, I would be, if only they'd stop arguing about the bloody dog.'

'You know the rules, Tad.'

'Rules are made to be broken.'

Patrick looked at him wearily. 'Where is the dog?'

'I'm keeping him outside. There's a garage at the back.' Tad lowered his voice, even though the room was empty. 'I'm stealing food for him. But it's not really stealing.'

'No. Tad . . . '

'What?' Tad looked up sharply.

'Um, Tad — '

'What? Why are you talking in that way?'

'There's some bad news. Very bad news.'

'What?'

Patrick's eyes were ringed with exhaustion. 'Liz. It's Liz.'

'What? Won't she drive me any more? Has she gone off with that bastard Wez?'

'It's worse.' Patrick took a deep breath. 'Tad, she's dead.'

Tad's eyes widened. He stared at his brother, unblinking. After a long moment he shook his head. 'No,' he murmured. 'No, she isn't.'

Patrick nodded. He looked ashen-faced, helpless.

Tad stood up. He began to walk around the room in rhythmic circles. 'Dead,' he said.

Patrick steeled himself. 'She had a car accident. On the way back from the stables yesterday.'

Tad quickened his pace, walking round and round, his arms flapping at his sides. 'Car accident,' he repeated. 'Car . . . ' he said, talking as if to himself.

'Yes,' Patrick said. He covered his face with his hands. Agnes reached out and touched him, her fingertips brushing his sleeve. 'It's too like our dad,' Patrick murmured to her.

'Like our dad,' Tad repeated. 'I saw, you

see. I was there. Was it a wall?'

Patrick uncovered his face. 'A brick or something.' He hesitated. 'Someone threw it. From a bridge. It hit the windscreen. No one else was hurt,' he added, helplessly.

Tad didn't falter in his walking. 'Someone threw it,' he said. 'From a bridge.' He was clenching his fists at his sides. 'Someone threw it — ' He lunged for an ashtray that was sitting on a table and, before either of them could stop him, he threw it hard at the window. It missed the glass, bounced harmlessly from the frame and landed on the floor. He stared at it. 'Threw it from a bridge,' he murmured. 'But they can't, you see.' He stopped, staring at Agnes and Patrick, his eyes wide. 'They couldn't have done it. They'd have missed. The chances of it hitting . . . ' He raised his arm slowly, making an arc in the air. 'They'd have missed,' he repeated. 'A brick wall is different, you see, you have no chance. Liz would've had — she'd have had . . . ' He stood, shaking his head, staring at the ashtray on the floor.

Silence settled in the room. 'I — I just thought I should tell you,' Patrick said, after a while. Tad didn't move. 'Well . . . ' Patrick looked at Tad, helplessly.

'You go,' Tad said. 'You have things to do.' His eyes were still fixed on the ashtray.

Patrick stood up and took a step towards him. 'Tad . . . ' He touched his arm. 'You'll — um — you'll be all right, won't you?'

Tad raised his head and smiled, an odd, empty smile. 'I'm not all right, am I? You know that.'

'No.' Patrick looked lost. 'Well . . . ' He sighed. 'Phone me. Whenever you want. Night or day. I'll be there.'

'Yes.' Tad met his eyes. 'Yes. You'll be there.'

★ ★ ★

They left in silence, blinking in the bright, cold light of the afternoon. Patrick took her arm, absently, as if she were someone else.

'Will he be all right?' Agnes asked as they walked slowly along the street towards the main road.

He turned, as if surprised to see her. He let go of her arm. 'I don't know. It's a terrible thing. He sees patterns in it all, you see, connections . . . Liz's death, in a car and everything, it's so like our father's. Only Dad's was intentional. He wasn't going to take any chances in death, he'd taken too many in life.'

'Why did he — ?'

Patrick shrugged. 'Debts, mostly. His parents had a bit of land, farming land, but they were poor. He left; he tried to set up a chain of stores, grocery stores. Never really got it to work. There was a rumour he had cash stashed away under the floorboards, but we knew better. Gambler, you see. Like Matt. Only without the luck. I believe you turn off here.'

'Actually, I'm going to the bus stop. I'm due back at the community house.'

'Oh. Yes. Of course.' He looked at her, his gaze distanced by fatigue. 'Well, thank you. For being there.'

'It's fine.'

'It's not over, of course.'

'No. It isn't.' She looked up into his face. 'Patrick, what you said about the code, I know it's not the time . . . ' She found she'd grabbed hold of his sleeve. 'It's just, I've been thinking, why shouldn't there be a pattern in it? I was thinking about it, and I thought we might be missing something huge and obvious and true, by saying it's all accidents, even though it's most likely to be accidents, but I've been aware that God's plan for us — I mean, when you said it was a code, I thought, perhaps that's it. Perhaps we should actually believe — I mean just stop doubting it, just have faith that we really can find out what happened. I'm going to arrange to see this Lode man, and I think you should go back to the office and find out what Allen's up to, and — ' She stopped for breath, glanced down at the tweed of his coat that was grasped between her fingers, and relinquished her grip.

He looked down at her. 'Agnes, I'm so tired.' He shook his head. 'Even if what you're saying were true . . . I'm in no state to think about it. It was a late night. And a bad night. Winning streak seems to be over. And now, with Tad . . . ' He tried to smile at her. 'I'm not good for you.' He patted her shoulder. 'Make it up with Julius, eh? He's a good man.' He turned and began to walk away, before she could think of the words to call him back. She watched him disappear, his long coat blurring with the greyness of the street. In the distance she saw her bus approach the stop. She ran to catch it.

14

Louise put her head round the door of the kitchen. 'Oh, Sister, you're there.' Agnes was sitting at the kitchen table, alone, with a large mug of tea. Louise came and sat next to her.

Agnes turned to her. 'What did you want to see me about?'

'Did you read my reflections?'

'Yes.' Agnes tried to hide her weariness, tried to think of something to say about them.

'Did you read the bit about love and relationships?'

'Yes.'

Louise got up and poured herself some tea. 'Only I've changed my mind.'

'Oh.' Agnes stared at her blankly.

'About love, I mean. This young man, the one who's dying, he's twenty-five, he's the same age as me it turns out. And I've been watching him with Sarah, and they're very much in love, and I thought, I was wrong about it being a compromise. Human love, I mean. Because that's why he's going to live, because we — I mean, because Sarah loves him.' She'd coloured slightly, and now turned away to sip her tea. 'He's called Richard,' she added.

'Oh.'

'He's getting better,' Louise said. 'He will get better.' She turned to Agnes and smiled. 'I lent him some books to read, and then he sent for some books from home and he's lent me some of those. It's nice of him, isn't it?'

'Yes.' Agnes looked at her, aware that she suddenly seemed terribly young.

'Anyway.' Louise stood up. She seemed awkward, pink-cheeked, her mug of tea left half-full on the table. 'I'd better go. I'll write some more reflections about love, about human love.'

'Yes. That would be nice. Thank you.'

Agnes stared after her as the kitchen door closed behind her.

When I was her age I'd been a nun for three years.

Perhaps I was too young, too.

★ ★ ★

At five to eight, Agnes flopped down on Athena's sofa. 'Expect nothing of me, Athena. I'm drained. Worn out.'

Athena handed her a glass of clear fizzy liquid that looked like gin and tonic.

'How did you guess?' Agnes smiled and sipped it.

'Expect nothing of me either, sweetie. Finish that and we'll go to the restaurant, I've booked for quarter past.'

★ ★ ★

'So.' Athena waited while the waitress poured them two glasses of white wine. 'Bad day?'

'You could say that. How about you?'

'Not so good. Shall we just forgo any conversation and concentrate on drinking?'

Agnes laughed. 'It's tempting. Except it's Lent.'

'You can have mineral water.'

'Must I? The problem is, you see, that I've always considered the odd glass of wine to be an act of celebration, of sharing in the material world, giving thanks for God's creation.'

'And there's me just thinking it was about having a drink. Cheers, by the way.' Athena raised her glass.

Agnes turned her glass around in her fingers, watching the light from the candle at their table refracting into gold. 'If God made all this, it seems churlish to turn one's back on it.'

'Absolutely, sweetie.'

'On the other hand, I can see that we shouldn't attach to these things, these illusory consolations.'

'Illusory? This wine seems pretty real to me.' Athena drank some more.

'It should be possible to turn away from this as an act of celebration too, to offer this moment to God.'

'Look, do you want that or not? I'll quite happily have the whole bottle to myself, the way I'm feeling at the moment.'

'Athena, I'm sorry. Completely self-indulgent of me.' She put her glass down. 'Is it Nic?'

Athena drank some wine and looked at Agnes. 'I think so.'

'You think so?'

'How can you tell? We seem OK, we're trundling along as usual, we're good friends . . . but he's just not there. He can be in the same room as me, but he just isn't there. Do you know what I mean?'

'Yes. Yes, I do.'

'Of course, it's all about Linda. She's helping him with publicity, did I tell you, sweetie? So helpful of her, don't you think? It seems to involve them leafleting nice cafés in fashionable parts of London.'

'How very noble of her.'

'Absolutely.' Athena shrugged. 'I mean,

life's just a mess, isn't it, sweetie? No sense in it at all. Just when I'd got to the point in my life where I was ready to commit to Nic, really commit. I don't mean live with him or anything silly like that, but you know — be serious and grown-up and let him borrow my washing machine when his breaks down. That sort of thing. And it turns out I'm too late.'

'But he must still care about you.'

Athena poured herself some more wine. 'Maybe. Maybe not. Maybe I shouldn't expect perfection. It's not as if we were ever like you and Julius.'

'Me and Julius?' Agnes stared at her.

'I mean, in the way Julius cares about you.'

'Does he?'

'Sweetie, you should've seen him this morning.'

'This morning?'

'Yes, I bumped into him; I was buying croissants up at Butler's Wharf. I meant to tell you, it was such a funny coincidence. I hardly know the man, and we had the longest conversation we'd ever had. He asked how you were, and I told him about the accident, your near miss, it was uppermost in my mind, sweetie, how nearly you came to not being here — you should have seen his face. White as a sheet.' Agnes stared at her. 'He's sweet, isn't he?' Athena was saying. 'Terribly upset, he was, to think you'd nearly died. What is it? Have I said something wrong? Are you all right, sweetie? Oh, no, look, now you're crying, I always do this. Has it got worse? I mean, between you two?'

Agnes bit back the tears. 'It's — it's like what you said about Nic. In a way. He's not there. I can't rely on him any more. Seeing this Mary again, it's brought on some kind of crisis for him. He was in love with her mother, years ago. She told me about it. And Patrick says that he can't talk to me about it because I represent the person he wants to be.'

'What does Patrick mean?'

'He was guessing, but I think he's right. Patrick said that I've only ever known Julius as a priest. When Julius and I first met, in France, he'd taken his big decision to relinquish his other life and finish his training. It's as if he relies on me to reflect that self back to him. And now, you see, it doesn't work any more. As Patrick said, the cracks are showing in that version of himself.'

'It doesn't mean he doesn't love you.' Athena spoke quietly.

'No,' Agnes agreed, after a moment. 'But you see, all these years he's been the perfect priest, serene and resolved ... and deep down there's been some other kind of Julius, some parallel Julius who's never stopped loving this woman who was Mary's mother. At least, that's what I've come to conclude. And I'm the last person he can talk to about it. It just makes me feel . . . it just makes me feel lonely — ' She burst into tears. 'He's my best friend, Athena. After you, of course.'

'Before me.' Athena spoke quietly. 'He rescued you. That gives him first place.' She handed her a tissue.

Agnes looked up at her. She dabbed at her face. Athena passed her her glass, and she took a large gulp of wine. 'Maybe . . . ' Agnes said, 'maybe I have to relinquish him.'

'Why? Why should you?'

'Maybe I have to learn not to need him.'

Athena sipped her wine, frowning. 'I can't see why. Human relationships . . . I mean, they're about dependence, aren't they?'

'Do you need Nic?'

Athena picked up a bread roll and broke it in half. 'I think — it's ironic this, isn't it sweetie? — I think I'd just got to the point where I might learn how to need him. And then it turned out I was too late.' She buttered a piece of bread. 'You see? It's all a mess. You and me, and Julius and Nic: none of it makes sense. Perhaps you're right about Lent, perhaps we should give up the whole damn thing and go and live in a desert somewhere and eat locusts.'

Agnes picked up her glass, and swirled the wine around in it. She smiled. 'To giving things up,' she said. 'Only not yet.'

Athena laughed. 'Cheers. To relinquishing life's pleasures. But not for a while.' She sipped her wine. 'And when it comes to eating locusts, maybe not ever.'

* * *

It was late when Agnes got home. She poured herself a glass of water and sat at her desk. Sunday night, she thought. I ought to get some sleep. I'm doing the afternoon shift at the hostel tomorrow. And there's Tad. And Patrick . . .

Did he really want to give up? she wondered. Was he really prepared to leave all those questions unanswered?

The phone at her elbow rang, shattering the silence. She picked it up.

'Agnes, it's Mary. I'm sorry to phone so late.'

'Mary.'

'I couldn't think of who else to phone, I tried Patrick but he's out.' She sounded distressed.

'What is it?'

'I've been thinking about Liz, and you see

268

— I know this sounds mad, but I don't think it was an accident. I think it was deliberate. Liz was saying all these weird things, last week, before she — before it happened. She was scared, Agnes. She was really frightened. Of someone. Or something. What I mean is, I think whoever threw that rock knew it was her. I think they wanted her out of the way.'

Agnes took a deep breath. 'I think the same,' she said.

Mary's relief was audible. 'Oh. Thank God. I thought I was going mad.'

'No. Unless I am too.'

'Can we meet?'

'Sure.'

'Tomorrow? Morning? Tenish?'

'Yes.'

'I'll come to you.'

Agnes gave her the address, and Mary rang off.

Agnes sat by the phone. All those unanswered questions, she thought. Does any of it make sense, Lord? Is there really any order in any of it? Or is Athena right, and we're all only human, and so it's all just a mess?

A police car siren cut through the night, then faded away.

Is it misguided, she thought, to search for meaning? Should we just accept creation, whether it makes sense to us or not?

She thought of Julius, reassessing his life. She thought of Mary's blue eyes. She yawned, stood up, and went to brush her teeth.

⋆ ⋆ ⋆

She woke to a chill, grey dawn. She got up, dressed, and left in time for the eight o'clock mass at St Simeon's. The mass was led by someone she'd never seen before. There was no sign of Julius. She thought of staying behind to ask someone where he was, but in the end she hurried away, back to her flat.

Mary arrived at ten to ten. She looked pale and flustered. Agnes made them both some coffee.

'It's crazy,' Mary said, sitting down on the chair by the desk. She was straight-backed, her hands folded in her lap. 'I woke up this morning, and I thought, What on earth was I on about last night? We should just leave it to the police, I thought. And then I thought, No, I owe it to Liz, she was trying to tell me something, I'd be wrong to ignore it, even if it seems mad.'

'I've had similar thoughts.' Agnes found some biscuits and laid them out on a plate. 'So did Patrick, actually, he was the one who got me into all this, going on about stuff being wrong at Matthias's work.'

Mary grew even more pale. 'When did he say that?'

'Some days ago. He's been in to the office, he knows all those people, Judy and Allen and that lot. But now Tad is very upset, and Patrick can't help him, and he's still in shock about Matthias.'

'I know the feeling.' Mary spoke softly.

'I'm sorry.'

'It's OK. Last night, when I decided to phone you, I thought, Perhaps this is what grief does. Perhaps it makes you see things that aren't there.'

Agnes picked up a biscuit, looked at it, then put it down again. 'Perhaps it does. In which case, Patrick and Tad and you and — and me — we're all in grief. We're all thinking mad thoughts.'

'How's Julius?' Mary asked suddenly.

Agnes met her eyes. 'Not brilliant.'

'Perhaps it's my fault.' Mary fiddled with the sleeve of her jumper. 'If Patrick hadn't come back into his life, if I hadn't seen him at the funeral . . . '

Agnes shook her head. 'No. Whatever he's dwelling on in his mind, it's always been there. It never went away.'

'How do you know?'

'I just do. I — I know him very well.' Agnes sighed.

Mary sipped her coffee. 'So,' she said. 'How mad are we? And what are we going to do?'

Agnes smiled. 'Speaking personally, I'm no madder than usual. And this is what I think we should do. Firstly, I'm going to seek out Judy again, even if I have to spend another weird evening at her gym. Secondly, I'm going to try and talk to Allen. He was in dispute about the land with Matt's friend Lode, and he was also, apparently, expecting Matt to risk some money on his leisure centre.'

'He never told me — Matt, I mean.'

'I think Allen got it wrong. But we should still ask. And we should definitely visit Lode.'

'Yes, and Annelise, that's Liz's friend. She pointed out about the note that he was carrying, the one intended for me, that he must have expected to see someone who'd get the note to me — else why write it?'

Agnes listened, frowning. 'And there's Charles. Liz's memory of him.'

'Someone said he used to work with Matt.'

'Mmm.'

'And Annelise said Liz had a dream, or a flashback or something, it was during the night. She saw this Charles holding a gun.'

Agnes looked up. 'Yes. She told me.'

'She said it was like a gun, only kind of big, like a toy, she thought. Not a normal gun. But she only had that part of the flashback once, and she thought maybe it was a dream.'

'And now she can't tell us.'

Mary turned her face away, her lips working. She shook her head. 'I can't bear it,' she said.

They sat in silence, sipping their coffee. Agnes put down her mug. 'Are you sure you want to do this?' she asked.

Mary nodded. 'It's the only way I'm going to survive.'

Agnes's doorbell buzzed, and she picked up the intercom, then pressed the buzzer. She turned to Mary. 'It's Patrick.'

Patrick appeared at the door, dishevelled and breathless. 'Tad's gone,' he said. 'I knew he would. The hostel phoned this morning.'

'Vanished?'

'No. He left instructions, so that I wouldn't worry, he said. He's found some bloody arch near the river, near those warehouses off the Jamaica Road. He's taken his dog, and some blankets. He says it's the only way.' He stopped for breath.

'Come and sit down,' Agnes said.

Patrick flung himself into a chair. 'Hello,'

273

he said to Mary. 'Sorry to interrupt.'

'We'd just finished.' Mary smiled at him.

Agnes made some fresh coffee for them all. 'Shall we go and find him?'

'I've got to, Agnes. He'll be arrested, or sectioned or something, and then he'll be banged up in some kind of secure unit, and doped, and I'll never get him out again. It was all going so well . . . ' He ran his hands through his hair. 'And I feel so alone with it all! Last night, I found I was shouting at Matt. Shouting out loud, pacing my room, saying, Why did you have to fall off your bloody horse, you bastard . . . ' He broke into a weak laugh. 'It would be funny if it weren't so bloody tragic.' He took the coffee Agnes handed him and drank a large mouthful.

'I'm angry with him too.' Mary's voice was gentle. 'But I'm angrier with whoever killed him.'

Patrick raised his head and met her eyes. 'No,' he said, after a moment. 'I can't go down that path. I'm too tired.' He shook his head.

Mary leaned towards him and took his hand. 'I know I'm right, Patrick.' She gazed at him, her eyes bright with urgency. 'I have to know,' she said.

He held her gaze, and Agnes saw the hard

274

486lines of his face soften as he looked at her. 'Oh Mary . . . ' He sighed. 'Don't do this to me.'

She let go of his hand. 'Let's go and find Tad, shall we?'

15

Tad was where he'd said he'd be. He was sitting on a wooden crate, his dog beside him, and he seemed engrossed in drawing something. He looked up as they approached him, and smiled, then returned to his drawing.

'Tad?' Patrick crouched next to him. 'You can't stay here.'

'We're fine here, aren't we?' Tad turned to the dog for affirmation. The dog wagged his tail.

'How are you going to eat?'

'I'm signing on. The benefit office is only across the road up there.'

'Tad, they'll section you.'

'They can't. I've already had one row with them. They're not going to risk it.'

'When?' Patrick looked at his brother wearily. There was a chill mist, but Tad was only wearing a thin jacket.

'This morning. I told them I was no longer at the sheltered flats, but I'd still be signing on. They wanted me to fill in some form, but I told them I didn't need to. They're so stupid there.' He chewed his lip, glancing at Patrick.

'I walked out in the end.'

'Tad, you'll starve. Or be arrested.' Patrick stood up, rubbing his back. A barge chugged past, and in its wake they could hear the lapping of the waves.

Mary drew her coat around her against the damp air. 'What are you drawing?'

Tad turned the pad round to show her. Within a grid of neat straight lines he'd drawn a series of curves, numbered at intervals, like graphs.

'What is it?' Mary looked down at his work.

'I'm working something out,' he said. 'If you threw something . . . this, you see, this line here is the height you throw it from, and this one how far it travels. This curve is the speed of the car . . . and these numbers here, that's the distance you'd have to throw something for it to hit the car at this point here . . . ' He turned the page back and wrote down another number.

Mary glanced at Patrick. Patrick was watching his brother, his eyes shadowed with concern. 'Tad' — Patrick touched his shoulder — 'come back with us. Come to the flats.' Tad shook his head. Patrick let his arm fall at his side, defeated.

Agnes went to Tad. 'Look,' she said. She turned to a blank page in his drawing pad, took his pencil and wrote down the address of her hostel. 'If things get too much, just come there. No one will make you do anything. You can bring your dog,' she lied. 'We'll feed you. And him.'

Tad looked up at her, and smiled, then turned back to his numbers.

Patrick looked at Agnes, then at Mary. Mary took his hand. He glanced back at Tad, then they all three left together.

They walked back to the main road, and by silent consensus went into a café. They sat, breathing in the steamy warmth, mugs of tea in front of them.

'What shall we do?' Mary asked.

'We're going to visit Stewart Lode,' Agnes said. 'I'll phone him as soon as I get back. Karen'll have his number.'

'What shall we do about Tad?' Patrick said.

'What can you do? He's an adult.'

'He'll either die or get locked up.'

'You have to let him risk it.'

Patrick shook his head. 'It's not his risk. It's mine. If anything happens to him — '

Mary interrupted. 'Patrick, what was happening at Matthias's office? What was it that was going wrong?'

Patrick's eyes narrowed. 'You two, what is this, some kind of game? My sole surviving relative puts his life in danger and you two are fixated on investigating things like some kind of distraction from the truth.'

'No, not a distraction from the truth.' Mary held his gaze. 'A search towards the truth.'

Patrick shook his head. 'It's an escape,' he said.

'Do you think I wouldn't escape, if I could?' Mary's voice was level, but her eyes burned with feeling. 'I have to do this.'

Patrick stood up, strode to the back of the café and asked if they had a telephone. He reappeared a few minutes later. 'The police,' he said. 'At Ongar. I just spoke to the incident room. They've been questioning three youths. They'd been seen before, throwing stuff from bridges. Someone identified them. That's your truth.' He sat down. 'The truth is easy. You just pick up the phone. It's living with it that's difficult.'

Mary looked at Agnes.

'I'll phone you,' Agnes said to her. 'I'll tell you when the Brigadier agrees to see us.'

They finished their tea in awkward silence. As they were leaving, Mary turned to Patrick. 'Is that it, then?' she asked him. She touched his sleeve and he looked down at her hand. 'Are you just going to give up?'

He looked at her, holding her gaze. 'That Judy,' he said. 'From the office. She's invited me out to dinner.'

'Oh.'

'Should I go?'

'Depends what you want from her,' Mary said.

He smiled then, and for a second the weariness lifted from his face. He shook his head. 'I ask nothing from women these days.'

Mary was smiling too. She patted his arm. 'See you, then.'

He nodded. 'No doubt.' They watched him retreat from them down the street, then went their separate ways.

Back at her flat, Agnes phoned Karen. Then she dialled the number Karen had given her. A gruff male voice answered.

'Lode.'

'Hello. Um, I'm phoning because — '

'Speak up. Can't hear you.'

Agnes raised her voice. 'My name's Sister Agnes. I knew Matthias. Matthias Kavanagh.'

'Yes?'

'I was wondering whether I could come and talk to you.'

'Whatever for?'

'There are some details I'd like to clear up.'

'Sister. Nurse, are you?'

'No, nun.'

'Heavens. Is it about the hunt?'

'Sort of.'

'If you're going to come here and tell me how much old Reynard enjoys the sport, you can forget about it frankly, holy orders or no.'

Agnes smiled. 'I wouldn't dream of commenting about old Reynard.'

'Just as well. All right, then. Tomorrow suit you? I'm here most of the time these days. How about eleven? Do they let you out?'

'Eleven would be fine. There'll be two of us. Mary Wells and me.'

'Name rings a bell. Local, is she?'

'Yes.'

'Don't come hungry. Not well provisioned.'

'We'll stock up on the way.'

'Yes. Good. Tomorrow, then. Know where I am, do you?' He gave her the address and she jotted it down. 'Goodbye, then.'

'Goodbye.' Agnes hung up, then dialled Mary's number and left a message on her answering machine. She stared at the Brigadier's address in her notebook, then put on her coat and went out to do the afternoon shift at the hostel.

It was dark when she finished work. A thin sleety rain was falling, and she walked through the icy streets, her hands in her pockets. As she turned into Borough High Street she heard the bells of Julius's church ring for evensong. She stopped still, the rain sharp against her cheeks, then turned round and headed for St Simeon's.

Julius was standing by the altar. He glanced

up as she came into the church, and for a second their eyes met, before he turned away and busied himself with a candle. Agnes chose a seat at one side of the church, and knelt in prayer.

Afterwards she waited until the few members of the congregation had gone before going to the door. Julius was standing there.

'Julius?' She looked at him, scanning his face.

'Hello.'

'How are you?'

'Fine.'

'No, you're not.'

He smiled, a brief flicker of the old Julius. 'No,' he said, 'I'm not.'

'What can we do?'

He shook his head.

'I'm here,' Agnes said. 'I'm here if you need me.'

Julius looked up. 'But you're not. You've decided that Patrick's brother's death needs investigating. You're not here at all, you're following some other path.'

'Mary believes me.' I didn't mean to say that, Agnes thought.

He met her eyes. 'Mary?'

'We're — um — I mean — '

'You and Mary?'

Agnes felt engulfed in misery. 'Oh Julius, this is all wrong . . . '

'You said it.' He turned towards the altar where the candles were still burning.

'Julius — '

'I don't care what you do.'

'It's not about you.' Agnes tried not to shout.

'Good.' He took some steps up the aisle.

'Julius!' She watched him as he turned, reluctant. 'Julius, I don't need — I mean, if you're suffering — Trust me. I don't need you to be perfect. Not any more.'

He hesitated. She saw his expression soften for a moment, but he turned away from her and went to the altar, and began to blow out the candles one by one. Silently she left the church.

★   ★   ★

At ten-thirty the next morning, Agnes got off the train at the small suburban station. Mary was waiting at the exit, and led her to a battered old Fiat. They drove out of the station, and headed for the road towards Brentwood.

'What was he like on the phone?' Mary asked.

'A bluff old cove, I think you'd say.'

'Friendly?'

'Told me to eat before we came.'

'That's no good, I'm starving.'

The farm was unmarked, and they peered up the drive, unsure. At the end of the drive was a house. It had ivy climbing unevenly up one side, and the roof looked as if it had been patched over many years.

'Do you think this is it?' Agnes asked.

'It must be. There's no other farmhouse for miles around.'

They drove through the half-rotten gate, closing it behind them, and parked outside the house. Agnes rang the bell, and was greeted by a chorus of barking. Eventually the door was opened by a large, red-faced man. One arm seemed to be tangled in the sleeve of a tweed jacket. Two Sealyham terriers jumped at his feet.

'Picked up my brother's bloody jacket,' he said affably. 'Much too small. Got me arm stuck now.' He surveyed them. 'Can I help, young ladies?'

'I phoned you,' Agnes said, offering her hand. 'Sister Agnes.'

'Ah, nuns. Yes.' He tried to shake hands, but the jacket seemed to be in the way. 'Wonder if you might be so kind . . . much obliged.' He turned his back, and Agnes rescued him from the jacket. 'Half my size,

Mick was. Chalk and cheese.' He took the jacket and smoothed it out over his arm. 'Come in, come in. Just find something else to wear.'

He ushered them into a large living room, the dogs at his heels, then disappeared, reappearing some moments later wearing an old cable-knit sweater. The room had thick beams in the roof, and was painted in a dark cream which seemed to have acquired a musty sheen over the years. It was comfortably furnished with huge, chintz armchairs. He sat down, gesturing to them to do the same.

'So. Matthias.' He looked at Mary, narrowing his eyes. 'Do I know you, young lady? Not a nun, are you?'

'No, I'm not. We have — um — we have met. Once. With Matthias.'

'Thought so. Terrible business. Horseman myself, scars to show for it. But like that . . . ' He shook his head. 'It's the wife I feel sorry for.' Again he shot a glance at Mary, and doubt briefly crossed his face.

'We wanted to ask you about the hunt,' Agnes began.

'Ah, yes. Nothing against them, of course, not as people. Nicer lot you couldn't hope to meet. But they can't get the hang of me at all. Oh no. All these years, old Micky Lode farming this land just like our father did before us, keen huntsman, keeps a lovely couple of mares. And then old Mick passes on, and who should come along but his eccentric younger brother, ex-forces, don't you know, and blow me if he doesn't want to turn the whole thing on its head, change the crops, change the layout of the fields, and ban the hunt. It's a lot for them to take on, particularly the ones who knew my brother Mick.'

'When did you inherit?'

'Ooh, now, must have been . . . spring before last. Against my will, of course. Mick was the apple of our father's eye, good luck to him, I thought, buggered off to join the army, had the time of my life. But needs must, I'm the sole survivor, got a nephew who's interested but he's got to put a few years on him before he's ready for this little lot. So I found myself here, surrounded by ghosts, hearing Father's voice in my ears, telling me that they always sow the lower field before the rest, hearing him say, Do this, do that, and it was always the tone of voice, that creeping tone which told me that I was always in the wrong, that whatever I did, it couldn't hold up to Mick's standards. So after a few months, hitting the drink a bit, doctor tried to say I was depressed but don't hold with things like that. After a few months I thought, Blow it. To hell with them all. Father's dead now, can't touch me. So I've gone organic.' He roared with laughter. 'I know, just like nutty old Prince what's-'is-name. And that's what they can't stand round here. I've heard it all now. 'Oh, no, you'll never sell for what you spend on it.' 'You'll be digging the whole crop back into the soil.' They're full of their tales of people who've tried it and bankrupted the whole bloody business.' He laughed again. 'But it's shut old Father up, I can tell you. Haven't heard from him since. Must be sulking.' He looked at Agnes. 'If you can sulk, where he is. What d'you think?'

'I'm — um — I'm not sure.'

'Anyway,' Stewart went on, 'last hunting season, had them all down here, promised not to cross the fields but you can't stop them, can you? Once hounds are speaking, they're all off like the clappers. I'd just done some winter sowing, bloody bad idea it turned out, and it was a wet winter . . . lost the whole bloody crop. That was it, then. Threatened to shoot every fox I set eyes on if they crossed my land again.'

'I bet that was popular,' Mary said.

He laughed. 'Haven't heard the end of it either. 'Mick wouldn't have stood for it,' they tell me. 'What would your poor father have made of it?' Still, it gives them all something to gossip about. I've served in India, in Burma . . . too young for the war, I was, but I've made up for it. They don't frighten me, these people. It's like this blasted dispute about the ditch — stubborn, y'see, once I get the bit between m'teeth. Have to see right is done. And I have right on my side. That nice girl showed me all her father's notes. Elizabeth she was called; terrible business that she should have died the way she did, I only heard last night. These hooligans need whipping, or worse.'

'And Matthias helped too.'

'We helped each other.' He nodded. 'Decent sort of fellow, he was.' He looked at Mary. He reached across to a small table on which there was a spectacle case. He took out the glasses and put them on, and looked at her again. 'You were . . . ' He paused, troubled, then tried again. 'I don't wish to be rude, young lady, but weren't you . . . I do seem to recognise you. We — um — we met, once, didn't we? With him.' His red cheeks grew redder.

'Yes.' Mary sat, straight-backed, waiting.

He turned to Agnes. 'It's the wife I feel sorry for,' he repeated.

Agnes saw a hint of steel behind the vague affability. The expansive comfort of the room seemed to have narrowed.

'Matthias loved the hunt,' Lode said. 'Irish, you see,' he said. 'In the blood. He was whipper-in last year, came to see me. Tried to reach a deal: just the upper fields, just skirt the edge of my land, draw the cover over by the stream, no nearer. Reasonable chap. I nearly agreed. But then the others got involved, some chap called Charles Fielding. I knew him vaguely, lives over past the lane there.'

'Charles Fielding?' Agnes asked.

'Yes. Charles. Nasty piece of work. Came round one evening, threatened all sorts. I ended up saying that if I caught sight of him on my land I'd shoot him, let alone any poor old fox. Undid all Matthias's work. True diplomat, Matthias. But that wasn't all, you see. Next time I saw Matthias, mentioned I'd seen Charles — he said, Rum old show, Fielding didn't even ride, let alone hunt. So God knows what was in it for him. And it's a shame, turns out this Fielding man deals in clocks, he's got an eighteenth-century cabinet clock he's working on, I'd have liked to have a look at that. Not even local, y'see, Fielding. Bought up the old Caddy farm, up the lane there. Some time ago now. Made his money in the City. Should've stayed there, if you ask me. And his friends, that other chap, another City boy — '

'Allen.'

'That's the one. He rides, that one. Townies. Poncing about on livery horses, thinking they know what the country is. Telling me I should let them trample my crops. I might be mad as a fish trying to farm this way, but at least I was born to it. Matthias was different, you see. I know he wasn't from round here, but he fitted in. Lovely couple, him and Karen. Popular with people, trod carefully when they first arrived. And he was a country boy, through and through. Irish, maybe, but still country. And their boys. Nice lads.'

Agnes threw a glance at Mary. She was sitting stock still. She turned back to Stewart. 'So Matthias's accident . . . ?'

He shrugged. 'My brother always said that golf course was a bad idea. Only encourages them. He was right.' He seemed to have recovered his bluff good humour.

'This dispute about the ditches' — Agnes felt as if something was slipping away from her — 'is it anywhere near resolved?'

'It's getting there. Personally, I don't object to this building they want to put up, I just want my land back. If they'd settle about the boundary, they'd get their planning permission and I could wash my hands of the whole thing. But both of them, impossible to deal with.' He was gazing vaguely out of the window. 'Good God.' He got to his feet. 'Talk of the devil. It's that Gough fellow.'

He went out into the hall, the others following. Paul Gough came to the door, which was opened before he could ring the bell.

'Well?' Lode barked at him.

Gough was not a tall man, and standing at the bottom of the steps seemed to put him at a disadvantage. He had black hair, slicked down at the sides. 'Brigadier,' he began.

'I could have you for trespass,' Lode said.

'Peace deal.' He held out a long brown envelope at arm's length. 'A settlement. This has gone on long enough.' He forced a smile, showing yellowing teeth.

Lode took a step forward and allowed Gough to hand him the envelope. He peered at it. 'More legal nonsense, then?'

'Please read it.'

Lode studied him a moment, then nodded. 'I'll read it. Make no promises, mind you.'

Gough inclined his head in farewell and turned to go, striding off down the drive again, treading carefully to avoid the puddles.

Lode turned to his guests, who stood behind him in the doorway. 'Horrible little man,' he said. 'Incomer too. Made all his money selling plastic garden furniture.' He waved the envelope at them. 'Better get on.'

'Yes, we'd — um . . . ' Mary went to get her coat. The dogs had jumped to their feet, and now they followed at her heels as she came back to the door. 'Thank you very much, Brigadier.'

He eyed her closely. 'My pleasure, young lady.' He turned to Agnes, and shook her hand awkwardly. 'Sister,' he said. He clutched the letter in his other hand, clearly in a hurry to read it.

Outside the sun was at its highest point, and the air was crisp. Lode stood on the doorstep as they got into Mary's car, and remained standing there as they drove away down the drive, through the gate, out on to the road towards the station.

Mary heaved a sigh of relief. 'That was tough,' she said.

'He rumbled you, didn't he?'

'Though there was no need for him to be rude,' Mary said. 'I'm starving. Have you got time for lunch?'

'If you have. Shouldn't you go back to work?'

Mary shrugged. 'I've taken leave for a few days. I'm just using up some holiday I'm owed. I asked for compassionate leave, but they said it wasn't as if I'd been widowed or anything . . . ' Her eyes filled with tears. 'Ironic, isn't it?' She tried to smile.

★ ★ ★

They sat down to pasta and salad in a country pub just off the A12. Mary was pale, lost in thought. Eventually she said, 'I only met him once. Old Lode. But once was obviously once too much.'

'When was that?'

'Matthias and I were having lunch together. There's a village some way off, towards Chelmsford, a hotel, we used to go there.' She looked away, towards the window. She sighed. 'He came in. By chance. Although now I come to think of it, I wonder if it was. Greeted Matt like an old friend, stared at me.' She smiled. 'That was one of the things about me and Matthias, people just knew, to look at us, that there was something . . . Anyway, he sensed what was going on. Didn't approve.' She twirled some salad around on her fork. 'They had this conversation, and Matt was embarrassed about drawing me in.'

'What did they discuss?'

'It was very short. Matt got some papers out, and Lode signed them. It was something about money.'

'This land dispute?'

She shrugged. 'Maybe. But it's only just now, talking to him, that I've realised it couldn't possibly have been by chance that he came into that hotel when we were there, despite Matthias claiming it was just a funny coincidence.'

'But . . .'

'But what?'

'Nothing.' Agnes took a sip of water. 'Did Matt discuss it with you afterwards?'

'No. It can't have been important.' Mary looked up sharply. 'He told me everything.' She pushed her plate away from her. 'Do you mind if we go back via the stables? I told Annelise I'd meet her there about now.'

★　★　★

Agnes got into the passenger seat of Mary's car. Mary started the engine. 'Tread carefully with Annelise,' she said.

'What's she like?'

'They were an unlikely couple. Both local, but from different ends of the scale. Annelise goes around with Wez and all that lot. Liz rides and hunts and — I mean, she did.'

'Do you know Annelise well?'

'Not that well. Liz kept her private life separate from the stables. But I bumped into her in town yesterday, and she . . . she's as you can imagine really. Terrible.' Mary turned out of the pub car park on to the main road. 'Sometimes I wonder what happened to the world I used to know. I used to think it made sense, or at least mostly. Now it seems to be filled with terrible grief; everyone, not just me. It's like that massacre in Africa last week. Or that avalanche in Austria. And those Balkan villages, those refugees, tiny children, the ones on the news . . . And Annelise, you could see the same thing in her face. The walking wounded, all of us.' She accelerated on to the dual carriageway. 'And Karen,' she added.

'Yes. Karen.'

They drove back towards the stables. 'He had no business to judge me as some scarlet woman, old Lode. What does he know about it?' Mary's voice was sharp. 'How can he know how it was for Matthias and me?'

Agnes said nothing. A few minutes later they pulled into the stables.

16

The yard was deserted. On a hay bale sat a lone woman. She was tall and thin, dressed in black with straggly blonde hair. She stood up as the car approached and walked towards it.

'I'm glad you're here.' Annelise smiled a thin smile. 'I don't feel I belong.'

'We can go somewhere else if you like.'

Deborah appeared from the office, nodded at the women and went back inside.

Annelise shrugged.

'Shall we walk?' Agnes suggested.

Annelise looked at the bright sky. 'OK,' she said.

They took the track that led out of the stable yard towards the woods.

'This is Sister Agnes,' Mary said, to break the silence.

Annelise turned to her and nodded. 'Hi,' she said.

'I used to ride with Liz,' Agnes said. 'A bit.'

'Yeah.' Annelise walked along, her shoulders hunched.

'How've you been?' Mary asked her.

She was silent a moment. 'It would be OK if there was a funeral,' she said. 'If someone would actually tell me she's dead and this is how it is. But she's just lying in some fridge somewhere . . . ' Grief choked her words.

They walked on, their footsteps crunching the frozen ground. 'And the police,' Annelise said suddenly. 'They're questioning kids on some estate that overlooks the bridge. But they'll get nowhere. Liz wasn't frightened of kids on an estate. She was frightened of someone real. Someone who meant her harm.'

Mary glanced at Agnes. 'Who?'

'She was remembering more and more about her fall. She remembered that man, standing there. That one you know. Then she had that dream about him holding a funny kind of gun. And then . . . '

'What?'

'She'd remembered this other thing. The day before she — she died — she told me she remembered more about her fall. She said the path was blocked. Deliberately. Her horse was brought up short by an obstacle of some kind. She remembered logs, branches, dragged across the path. And then something happened, and she fell.'

Mary and Agnes slowed to a halt. 'But — ' Mary began.

'In that case — ' Agnes said.

'You see?' Annelise faced them. 'There's no

point the police questioning kids on the bridge. Someone planned it, I know they did.'

'But, Annelise' — Mary reached out her hand and touched her sleeve — 'why? Why would anyone want to kill Liz?'

Annelise began to cry. 'I don't know. I think it must be about this dispute about the ditch and the fence. Wez says if they try and build that leisure centre now, he's going to move into the trees on the site there to stop them. But then sometimes I think, maybe she was just in the wrong place at the wrong time. When Matthias died in the same place . . . I don't know. Perhaps it was meant for him.'

'A trial run?' Agnes was appalled at the thought, that someone might practise a murder on an innocent woman. 'Or a mistake?'

'Oh, I don't know.' Annelise wiped her eyes with a tissue. 'I just want it all to stop, I just want her back. None of it makes sense.'

They walked on in silence. The sun went behind a cloud. Once again Agnes found herself at the edge of the golf course, once again retracing the steps of Liz, and Matt. The silence deepened between the three women. Annelise stopped suddenly, bent down, and picked something up from the scrubby weeds at the side of the path. She opened her hand to reveal a golf ball.

'Another one,' she said. She handed it to Agnes. 'Everyone says they should put up a fence. It wouldn't have saved Liz though, would it?'

★　★　★

Mary dropped Agnes off at the station.

'What do you make of it?' Agnes gathered her bags together.

'I don't know. If it is connected to Matthias, and if she was killed deliberately, then — then Annelise is right. The police are asking the wrong questions. And the truth is there, in the stables, or in the village. But . . . '

'But if it's not — '

'Then we're back to where we were.'

'And the obstacles on the path?' Agnes fingered the golf ball in her hand before slipping it into her pocket.

Mary frowned. 'I don't know.' She sighed. 'I wish I'd spoken more to Liz before she died. These memories of guns and obstacles . . . they're so vague, aren't they? I mean, to stop a horse you'd have to drag some pretty big stuff across the path. Someone would have noticed. Even if whoever did it dragged it all away again afterwards . . . I think I should have a word with Deborah. I'll phone you.'

Agnes dozed on the train back to London. At Liverpool Street she stumbled sleepily from the train. It was nearly four o'clock.

★ ★ ★

'Sorry I'm late.' Agnes walked into the office of the hostel, flinging her coat across a chair.

'That's OK.' Helen smiled at her.

'How's it going?'

'OK. I've had another session with Xenos.'

'And?'

'Horses. It seems to be the only thing he has any connection with. He lights up when he sees that picture in the book.'

Agnes sat down at the spare desk.

'You look tired,' Helen said.

Agnes tried to smile at her. 'I'm OK. How are you?'

Helen nodded. 'Fine,' she said, but something about her lacked conviction.

There was a loud thumping at the front door. Helen got up from her desk. 'Oh no.'

'What on earth — ?'

The two women went out into the hallway. Daniel, the other worker, joined them. The thumping continued.

'Hello?' a male voice was shouting outside.

'She said I could come here. Agnes. Is she there?'

'It's Tad,' Agnes said. 'Oh dear.' She opened the door.

'You said — ' He stumbled into the hallway.

'Yes. I said.'

'Here's George too.' Tad's dog bounded up the steps and landed in a heap at Agnes's ankles, wagging his tail.

'But — ' Daniel started, but Agnes shot him a glance.

'It's OK,' Agnes said. 'This is my responsibility. This is Tad, everyone. This is Dan, and Sister Helen.'

'We're hungry,' Tad said.

They sat in the kitchen. George ate at great speed from a plate on the floor, into which Agnes had put most of a cold chicken from the fridge. Tad slurped tinned soup from a bowl, and broke off large hunks of bread roll which he stuffed into his mouth. 'They wouldn't listen, see,' he said to Agnes, between mouthfuls. 'At the social. I've been in there every day, twice a day. They wouldn't give me any money. Then I tried begging on the streets but someone came along, this bloke, he said it was his patch and I couldn't go there. Look.' He pointed at his jaw, which had a livid red bruise.

Agnes sat opposite him. She watched him eat, refilling his bowl. She made them some tea. 'Tad,' she said, handing him a mug, 'wouldn't it be better — '

'No.' He shook his head. 'I can't go back there. Not now. Now that Liz . . . '

'But — '

He held up his hand. 'No.'

Helen came in and poured herself some tea. She turned to Agnes. 'I know it's not the time . . . '

'What?'

'Xenos. He tried to speak. Just now.'

'What did he say?'

'I don't know. It wasn't English.'

'Xenos?' Tad looked up.

'Yes.' Agnes smiled at him. 'Come and meet him.'

They went into the lounge. Xenos was sitting, alone, his arms wrapped round his knees. He looked up anxiously as they came into the room, but kept his eyes on Helen.

'Hello,' Agnes said to him. 'This is Tad.'

'Hello.' Tad eyed him, then went and sat down on a chair, George at his heels. Xenos flinched, refusing to look at him.

Helen got out the picture book, but Xenos wouldn't hold it. After a few moments his gaze went to George, and George returned it, with a big trusting look. Xenos's face softened very slightly.

'He likes horses,' Helen said to Tad.

'So do I,' Tad said. 'I ride horses. One horse, my favourite. Sancho. Liz used to drive me — ' He blinked, turned away, and stared at the floor.

George wandered over to Xenos and sat at his feet. Slowly Xenos leaned over and patted his head, gingerly at first, then more robustly, making little affectionate noises. George wagged his tail.

Xenos looked at Tad. He picked up the book, found a page and showed it to Tad. Tad looked up. 'Dog,' he said, nodding. He pointed to George. 'Dog,' he said again.

Xenos nodded, then thumbed through the book to a new page which he showed to Tad. 'Horse,' Tad said. He looked at Xenos. 'Horse,' he said again, nodding.

'H — ' Xenos began. 'H — '

'Best animals in the whole of creation,' Tad said. He looked at Agnes. 'We can sleep here, can't we? Me and George? We've been so cold these nights.'

* * *

Agnes was sitting at her desk with a pile of papers the next morning when her door buzzer went.

'It's Patrick,' a voice said.

'Good,' she said, pressing the button to let him in.

'Why good?' He appeared on her landing, breathless from the stairs.

'Because,' she said, standing aside to let him into her flat, 'your brother has moved into my hostel, with dog, and seems determined to stay there.' Patrick smiled. 'It's not funny,' Agnes went on. 'He can't stay, he doesn't qualify, and he certainly can't have the dog there. They were both starving hungry too.'

'Any chance of a coffee?'

Agnes sighed and went to put the kettle on.

'I had dinner with Judy last night,' Patrick said.

'Don't change the subject.'

'But it was very interesting.'

'What was she after?'

Patrick laughed. 'Women,' he said.

'Not 'women' at all. It's just that if anyone knows what she wants and knows how to get it, it's Judy.'

'Yes,' Patrick said. 'Milk please, no sugar.'

Agnes shot him a glance. 'You're in a very good mood,' she said.

'It was a very nice dinner. Very enlightening.'

'Oh?' Agnes poured herself a coffee too and

sat back at her desk.

'Allen wants to marry her, did you know?'

'I told you that. You weren't listening, were you?'

'But she's not sure. She's kind of seeing Jed at the moment. She asked me what I thought.'

Agnes smiled.

'What's funny about that?'

'You wouldn't understand.'

'Wouldn't I?' Patrick looked humbled.

'Anyway, what did you say?'

'I said it wasn't up to me. I asked her about Allen, and about the land. She said he'd cheered up about all that, it's all back on, apparently. They've written to Lode, and he's accepted their terms, and now they can get planning permission after all.'

'And the money?'

'She seems to think he's got the money. I told her there was nothing there from Matt, but she said she'd got that wrong, he's raised the money from business people, contacts from the golf course, she thought, and his slimy friend Paul, as she put it.'

'Well, I went to visit Brigadier Lode,' Agnes said. 'With Mary.'

Patrick leaned back in his chair and rubbed his neck. 'Go on.'

'He confirmed about the ditches, and Liz

and Matt helping him. He might have told us more, only he worked out who Mary was in relation to Matthias, and decided to disapprove of her. And then we met Paul Gough, who was bringing an envelope for him. A peace deal, he said. It must be what Judy told you about.'

'Funny that it's all resolved now that Matt and Liz have gone.'

'Yes.' They glanced at each other. 'And then we met Annelise, Liz's friend,' Agnes said. 'And she said Liz had remembered seeing some kind of obstacles put in the way of her horse, just before she fell.'

'Deliberately? But then . . . '

'Yes. I know.'

'Bloody hell.'

They sat in silence, sipping their coffee.

'Hadn't we better tell the police?' Patrick asked.

'Mary's going to ask Deborah if anyone else noticed.'

'Someone doing that, they'd have been seen, wouldn't they?'

'That's what we thought.'

There was a screech of brakes in the street outside, followed by loud male shouting. Agnes went over to the window to look. The shouting subsided. 'So,' Agnes said, sitting down again. 'Judy. Whom should she marry?'

Patrick smiled. 'I'm not the person to ask. As I told her. But then the conversation got difficult after that.'

'In what way?'

'She got very curious about Matthias. She kept asking me about where he lived. Was he rich? What were his sons like? She even asked ... ' He frowned. 'She even asked whether he'd properly provided for Karen in terms of insurance, trust funds, that kind of thing.'

Agnes laughed.

'I said, the best that money could buy.' He smiled. 'She was charming, and kind of appealing. She gave me her phone number.'

Agnes met his gaze. 'Will you see her again?'

'To be honest ... ' Patrick almost smiled. 'Women, you see. They're never straightforward. All evening, I had this feeling of something being demanded of me, some need I just couldn't meet. Something unspoken, as if somehow I'd intuit what she was after, by sheer telepathy. I had a sense of disappointing her, but never knowing what it was I was supposed to do.'

'It's simple, Patrick.'

He looked at her, questioningly. 'Is it?'

'You men are supposed to know when a woman wants to go to bed with you.'

'Her?' Patrick fumbled with a sheaf of papers on the table in front of him. 'Me?'

Agnes laughed. 'Oh, Patrick.'

He looked at her. 'Well, thank God I never rumbled at the time. Heaven knows what might have happened.'

Agnes stood up to clear the mugs away. 'Who knows?' She glanced at him.

'No,' he said, avoiding her gaze. 'All I mean is, it would have been awkward. Saying no. It might have offended her.'

'Of course, Patrick.'

He looked up at her, his cheeks flushed. He shook his head. 'Women,' he said.

* * *

At midday Agnes went to mass at the community house. She glanced up from her prayers to see Helen creep in late. She looked anxious, and she scanned the pews for Agnes. For a second their eyes met.

'What is it?' Agnes joined her in the hall.

'Bloody Home Office. Official letter.' Helen was pink-faced and nervous. 'Xenos, I mean.'

'What did they say?'

'He can't stay. He now counts as an illegal immigrant, due to our failure to fill in the papers properly.'

'But how could we — ?'

308

'I know. I've been on the phone to them all morning, trying to find someone to talk to. How can we file papers when we don't even know his name? Colin's pessimistic, though Tad tried to jolly him along.'

'Tad?'

'Oh, yes, he was — um — very helpful. He wanted to make all the phone calls on our behalf, but we had to say no. He — um — he seems to like taking on authority.'

'Yes.' Agnes sighed.

'Still, Xenos likes him. He made another attempt to talk this morning, did I say?'

'That's good.'

'Yes.'

Sister Madeleine came down the stairs, nodded at them, and went into the kitchen.

'What shall we do?' Helen asked.

'I don't know. Unless he speaks . . . '

'They're threatening detention centres and stuff. It would be the worst thing for him.' Helen buttoned up her coat. 'I've got to go.' She went to the door. 'Tad said — Tad said he'd take him to the stables.'

'Tad? But . . . ' Agnes met Helen's eyes. 'In fact, that's a brilliant idea.'

'I thought so. Shall we do it at the weekend?'

'Yes. I'll warn Deborah.'

★ ★ ★

Back at her flat Agnes switched on her lamp against the darkness of the afternoon, and sat at her desk. The letter from France was sitting there, gathering dust. Above it, the clock was still keeping perfect time, the perfect brass spheres gliding elegantly round and round.

Legacies, Agnes thought. The past, sending messages to the present. Sending clocks and letters and houses . . . and dreams.

What am I going to do?

She watched the clock, and thought about the web that joined her still to her past, to her childhood, her parents. A web of property, memories, lawyers, wills, trust funds . . .

Trust funds.

She frowned at the clock. It was Patrick who'd said it. That Judy had asked about trust funds. It was strange, Agnes thought. It's not a general kind of question. It's really very specific.

She picked up the letter, put it down again. She got up and put on the kettle, in readiness for Louise. At four sharp her door buzzed, and a few moments later Louise appeared at the door.

'Tea?' Agnes showed her to a chair.

'Yes please.'

'How's your work?'

'Which work? The hospice or The Work?'

'Both.' Agnes smiled. 'They're the same thing, aren't they?'

'Yes. S'pose so.'

Agnes handed her a mug of tea and sat down opposite her. Silence settled in the room, like the chill twilight outside that frosted the window with condensation.

Louise fished in her bag and produced a sheaf of papers. 'I've written more reflections,' she said.

'Thank you.'

'They're not very good.'

'They don't have to be good. They have to be useful to you, that's all.'

Louise sighed. She sipped her tea in silence. 'The thing is, Sister ... ' She struggled to contain her feelings. 'He's dying.'

'Who?'

'Richard. After all I've done. The nurse told me yesterday, that's why I've written all that stuff, I couldn't sleep last night.' She turned anguished eyes to Agnes. 'Why? Why is he dying?'

'Well ... ' Agnes searched for the words. 'Surely ... ' She sighed. 'It is a hospice. People die.' Stuff happens, she almost added.

'But not him.'

'Why not him?'

Louise looked at her as if she was a fool. 'I

311

promised him. I promised myself. That's why.'

'But, Louise . . . '

'What?'

There was a defiance about her that made Agnes hesitate. She stirred her spoon around in her mug, then looked up at the novice. 'In the end, we're powerless, aren't we?'

Louise bit her lip. 'I told him . . . ' She fought back tears. 'I told his fiancée he'd live. They trusted me.' Agnes waited. 'I won't accept,' Louise went on, 'I won't accept that we're powerless. What does prayer mean, if it isn't a direct intercession? Prayer can change things, that's what I've always been taught.'

A distant church bell chimed the half-hour.

'I was sure, you see.' Louise picked up her mug, but put it down again. 'When God called me to this work, I knew I could make a difference.' Agnes waited. Louise looked up at her. 'He won't die, you see.'

'But if God wills that he should die . . . '

'How can he? Why doesn't he listen?'

'We don't know the will of God, that's all I meant.'

Louise shifted in her chair. 'That doesn't mean we can't do anything about it, does it? It's not right just to sit back and accept whatever happens, is it?'

'No.'

'So I have to pray. I have to believe that Richard will live, don't I? You must have things in your life that you fight for, things you know are right. God didn't put us here just to be passive, just to be . . . powerless. Did he?'

Agnes went over to the window and drew the curtains. 'I do have things like that in my life. You're right. But . . . ' She flicked the last half-inch of curtain shut. 'But to pin all your hopes on one person, one individual . . . '

Louise stood up. 'Read my notes. Then you'll understand.' She put on her coat and took her gloves out of her pocket. 'I've always known I should be a nun,' she said. 'I know it's what God wants of me.' She put on her gloves with a series of dainty movements. 'Richard will live,' she said, going to the door. 'Thank you for your time, Sister.'

When she'd gone Agnes sat at her desk with the pages of reflections. Louise's notes were written like a diary, each page headed with a date and sometimes a time.

Feb 5, 3:10 pm. This morning, Anne (she's one of the nurses) said I could talk to Graham. He's the one with throat cancer, he can't speak any more. I sat next to him for a while, but he didn't seem interested in me and I couldn't

313

think what to say to him. After a while I
went to help serve the coffee instead.
Later Anne said he was an atheist, he
used to say that if there was a God he
had a bloody weird sense of humour. So
I don't know why she sent me to talk to
him . . .

Agnes turned a few pages. Some words
caught her eye: *vision of Jesus*.

I remember in our church at home,
one girl said she'd had a vision of Jesus. I
remember thinking she didn't seem the
right kind of person. I know in the Bible
people had visions all the time, but that
was then, wasn't it? I mean, I know God
talks to us, or Jesus . . . Jesus talks to me
all the time, but not like that, not
— directly, like that. It's more that I
know that what I'm thinking has been
kind of sent by him . . . Perhaps that's all
she meant. Perhaps she was praying and
it all seemed a bit strong and that's all it
was. It was all very intense, those days,
once Peter had become our curate and
took over the youth group, I used to have
very intense prayer time, particularly in
church with all the others, when we'd all
raise our voices together . . . And Peter

was such a good preacher, we'd never seen so many people there on Sundays, and there were youth groups and Bible study . . . When I told him I wanted to be a nun he kissed me on the cheek . . .

Agnes turned another page.

. . . how dare she say he's dying? He doesn't look as if he's dying. I know he'll get better. For some of the patients, it's a kind of resolution, and then I know God is calling me to help them out of this world and into the next . . . but not him. He's got every reason to live. And he's so full of life. He's so lovely to sit with, to talk with. His fiancée said they'd even set the wedding day. She's called Sarah, she's really nice . . . It's like they're relying on me, somehow. I prayed for them again last night. I pray for him all the time . . .

Agnes sighed. She clipped the pages together and put them back on her desk. She sat, staring into space for a while, then went into her kitchen to see if there was anything to eat.

17

Athena placed a large bowl of salad on her kitchen table. 'I've smothered it in oil. After all this gym nonsense you've been indulging in, think of all those calories you've got to make up. And there's some really creamy Brie cheese, in case your cholesterol level has sunk dangerously low.'

Agnes laughed.

'So, how is it, the gym torture?' Athena passed her a bread roll.

'I haven't been back. I'm no longer useful to her. It's Patrick she's after.'

'The lovely Irishman?'

'She invited him for dinner the other night.'

'How forward of her.'

'I thought so too.'

'Terrible, when these women start trespassing . . . '

'Athena!'

'But I bet he prefers you.'

'It really isn't like that. Really. Don't laugh.'

'How many times have I heard you say that?'

'He may be lovely, but not in the way you mean. I'm a nun, Athena.'

'Yeah yeah.'

'Not 'yeah yeah' at all. I'm being really good these days. Aren't I? Anyway, I thought we'd both decided that inappropriate desire only causes trouble.'

Athena put her fork down. She sighed. 'Don't I just know it, sweetie. If I had known, last year, when I was . . . playing around . . . If I'd known it wasn't playing at all . . . It's never playing, is it? Well, perhaps when you're fifteen. But not for grown-ups.'

'No,' Agnes agreed.

'I really thought Nic had forgiven me. In fact, I think he had. I think he thought he had too. And then along comes this woman, and she really has some kind of pull for him . . . ' She shook her head. 'And here I am fighting for him. But the stupid thing is, last year, because of my own . . . my own lapse, it's like I threw away any weapon I could use. I'm fighting for him with empty guns and blunt swords.'

Agnes looked up at her. 'How poetic.'

Athena pushed a lettuce leaf around her plate. 'I asked him about her, the other night. I thought it was time we stopped pretending that nothing was happening.'

'And?'

'It's even worse than I thought. It turns out

317

he nearly married her, all those years ago, but then Steph, that's Ben's mother, the one he married in the end, she found she was pregnant. And he thought he'd better do the right thing. He was only young. And so he let Linda go. And she got together with someone — she's got kids, I think, although she's so thin you wouldn't know it — and now here she is. And I haven't got — '

'A leg to stand on?'

Athena laughed, in spite of herself. 'Why's that funny?'

'I don't know.' Agnes poured herself a glass of water. 'So what did he say about her? Her and him, I mean?'

Athena frowned. 'He swore it was nothing, just friendship. I didn't feel like arguing.' She went to the fridge, pulled out a bottle of chilled wine and frowned at it.

'I thought we weren't going to — ' Agnes began.

'You're right.' Athena put the bottle back in the fridge. They sat in silence, sipping water. 'It's so hard, isn't it?' Athena said suddenly. 'Being grown-up.'

Agnes nodded. 'I think that must be why I put it off so long.'

★   ★   ★

At home her answering machine flashed with urgency. It was Helen.

'Agnes, are you there? Can you phone me? It's about Tad — and Xenos. The police have visited us. I was hoping you'd be there. I'll try you at the house.'

Agnes dialled the hostel. 'Helen?'

'Oh, there you are. The police have gone now.' She sounded tired and harassed. 'They've given me loads of forms to fill in. It was terrible. Xenos took one look at them and I thought we'd lose him. And Tad got involved, which didn't help. How long is he staying here?'

'He's not supposed to be there. It's my fault, trying to help as usual, making everything worse. I'll talk to his brother.'

'Are you in tomorrow? They're bound to come back; we can't stall them any more.'

'Yes. First thing.'

'See you then.'

Agnes dialled Patrick. There was no answer. She sat and stared at the phone, then dialled Mary.

'Hello?'

'It's Agnes. I was wondering if you knew where Patrick was.'

'Me? Why should I know?'

'Dunno. Just desperation, really. His brother's at my order's hostel and it's not good, I need Patrick's help.'

'Sorry. He's probably drinking or gambling.'

'Yes. While you're on . . . '

'Yes?'

'I was wondering . . . only now isn't the time, probably . . . about Matthias . . . '

'What about him?'

'Do you know anything about a trust fund?'

There was silence at the other end of the line. Then Mary said, 'For me, you mean?'

'Well, only that . . . '

'He did leave me money, yes.'

Agnes searched for the right form of words. 'It hasn't been the cause of any . . . any trouble, then?'

'For whom? It's all really straightforward. It's basically a lump sum invested and I get the income for now. It's not a great deal. He said it would be like a pension, so I'd have the same rights as if we were . . . as if we were married.' Her voice tailed off.

'Right. I'm sorry, it's really none of my business.'

'Is it connected to — to his death?'

Agnes took a deep breath. 'Judy took Patrick out to dinner, and introduced the subject of trust funds. I thought it was a bit odd.'

'Stupid cow. How did she even know?'

'I'm not sure she did. From what Patrick said, she was fishing, I think.'

'No one knows. Apart from Patrick. And Karen.'

'Karen?'

'It was mentioned in the will.'

'Of course.'

'She has enough of her own.' Mary's voice seemed to fade.

'Yes.'

'I spoke to Deborah. About people blocking the bridle ways. She said they'd felled a lot of trees in the woods, after the storms, and there are logs about. They've been using them for jumps. But then I had a cup of tea with Annelise, and she said she'd ask Wez, 'cos he's always lurking around the woods looking for foxes to protect. I'll talk to you soon.'

'Shall we meet at the stables?'

'I'll be there Saturday, for Charlie's lesson.'

'So will I. See you then.'

As soon as she put the phone down, it rang. 'Agnes, it's Patrick. You wanted me?'

'How did you know?'

'I was asleep. I heard the phone, didn't get there in time. Had a hunch, that's all. What did you want?'

'Your brother. He's still at our hostel.'

'It was your idea.'

'He'd have starved otherwise. But he can't stay there for ever.'

'No.'

'Any ideas?'

'None at all.'

'Thanks.'

'Where my brother's concerned, I ran out of ideas about ten years ago.'

'I've been thinking about this Judy business. Did Matthias have some kind of other fund, a trust fund, pension, something like that, that she might be interested in?'

'I can't see why.'

'Mary's money?'

'She doesn't know about that. And it's pretty straightforward anyway.'

'Tad's money?'

'It's a small amount.'

'I think she was trying to find something out.'

'I thought she was after my body, according to you.'

'Hmmm. Would Karen know more than you about Matthias's money?'

'Doubt it. We can always ask her. I'm visiting her on Saturday, do you want to come along?'

'Yes. Please. Maybe in the afternoon. I'm at the stables in the morning. Helen had a plan to take Xenos there with Tad, there's quite a bond between them to do with horses. And George,' she added.

'So he's not all bad, then.'

'No.' Agnes sighed. 'It's just the police visited today, about Xenos, and Tad reacted quite badly.'

'He's bound to. Police, doctors, social services, they all bring out the worst in him. I'll think of something, Agnes. And I'll see you Saturday.'

★ ★ ★

The smell of bacon wafting from the hostel kitchen next morning brought Tad downstairs. He seemed pleased to see Agnes there.

'It was awful yesterday,' he said to her, flinging himself down at the table and grabbing a piece of toast. 'The police. We saw them off, me and Helen.'

'Did you?' Agnes concentrated on the frying pan.

'I told them he has rights, he does. Xenos.'

'That's just the problem. He's come off some plane, and he won't speak. He has no rights.'

'But where will they send him?'

'I've no idea. They might just put him in a detention centre.'

'It would kill him.' Tad layered margarine on to another piece of toast.

'They said you were here.' Helen came into the kitchen and poured herself some tea. 'Has Tad filled you in?'

'Only that you both saw the police off.'

Helen allowed herself a brief smile. 'Sort of.' She glanced over at Tad. 'It reassured Xenos, anyway. He can see we're on his side. I think he wasn't quite sure before.' She sat at the kitchen table. 'What are we going to do?'

Agnes looked at her. 'What can we do? What are they accusing him of?'

'Being here illegally. Which is certainly true. No one knows how he got here, how he got past the airport staff. No one knows anything. Except that, legally, he shouldn't be here.'

'But he's suffered!' Tad's knife clattered on the table. 'Where he's come from, he's suffered. You can see it in his eyes. That gives him the right to be here.'

'Morally, yes.' Helen got up and began to open cupboard doors. She pulled out a packet of cereal and poured some into a bowl. 'But not legally.'

'There shouldn't be a difference.' Tad took the plate of bacon that Agnes handed him and began to eat.

'I'm just worried,' Helen said, 'that when

we take him to the stables he'll try and run away.'

Tad laughed. 'That would be great. We could set him free.'

'Oh, Tad, if only it were that simple.' Helen threw him an affectionate glance.

Tad looked at his plate, subdued. 'He's got to go to the stables,' he said. 'It will help him.'

★　★　★

Agnes answered her door on Saturday morning to Helen, who had borrowed the community car and now had Tad and Xenos waiting outside.

'Come on, quick,' Helen said, as Agnes tried to finish her piece of toast. 'Xenos is paralysed with terror. If it wasn't for Tad he'd never have left the hostel.'

They went outside into the crisp morning air. As they left London and headed for Essex, the early cloud cleared and sunlight glanced off windows as they passed.

Deborah was waiting for them. 'Does he ride?' She indicated Xenos with a jerk of her head.

'We don't know,' Helen said.

'This is Helen,' Agnes said.

Deborah nodded to her. 'I've put him on

Misty, she's good as gold.'

They trooped up to the yard. Tad was greeting some of the stable girls as he went to find his horse. Xenos followed, looking from side to side. Helen nudged Agnes.

Xenos's face was illumined. He approached a stall, from where a chestnut mare whinnied at him. He put out a hand and stroked her nose, then leaned close to her and began to speak, a babble of delighted sound. He looked suddenly young.

'He's just a child,' Helen said to Agnes.

'Clever old Tad,' Agnes said.

Misty was led out of her stall, and Tad, now mounted, indicated to Xenos that he could ride her.

Xenos looked uncertainly at the reins. Tad held his up to demonstrate. Xenos picked up the reins as if he'd never touched such things before.

'Are you sure horses are his thing?' Deborah was standing beside Agnes, watching.

'It was Tad's idea,' Helen said.

Xenos suddenly grabbed a handful of mane and flung himself into the saddle, and grinned at Tad. He bunched up the reins in one hand. Deborah went over to him and put his hands in the right position. 'Like this,' she said.

He smiled at her. 'This,' he echoed.

'Michelle will take you over to the paddock,' Deborah said. One of the girls arrived on horseback and led them both across the stable yard to the paddock behind the school. Agnes and Helen followed on foot.

Michelle began to walk them round the paddock. Xenos was looking around. In the field next to them two young girls were putting up a series of fences. Xenos shouted to Tad, and pointed, and laughed. Then something must have happened, for his horse broke into a canter. Agnes watched him circling the paddock, round and round, the reins flapping in his hands.

'Is he all right?' Helen asked.

'He did that on purpose,' Agnes said. 'Even if he doesn't know what reins are for.'

The horse circled, collected and calm.

'He's laughing,' Helen said.

'Let's leave them to it,' Agnes said.

They wandered back up to the office.

'Everything all right?' Deborah asked.

'He's doing a collected canter without using his hands,' Agnes said.

Deborah gave her a funny look. 'Mary's here,' she said.

They trooped into the office. Helen went to get everyone coffee from the machine.

'Hi.' Mary looked up from the scruffy bench next to the calor-gas heater.

'Hello.' Agnes sat next to her.

'I do have some news. Wez said he saw Charles Fielding in the woods, one evening, quite late — '

'Dragging tree trunks around,' Deborah interjected.

'When?' Agnes asked.

'Wez said it was about a month ago,' Mary said.

'On his own?'

'He thought there was someone else there, he could see someone further off. Also, he said, they were huge logs, he couldn't imagine how someone as frail as Charles would manage on his own.'

Helen reappeared and handed out plastic cups to murmured thanks.

'He thought they were to stop the hunt sabs,' Mary said. 'Except Charles isn't a huntsman.'

'He could have told us before,' Deborah said.

'He wouldn't have known it was relevant, would he?' Mary said. 'Until Liz mentioned this thing about seeing her path blocked.'

'I just wish those bloody golfers would take some responsibility,' Deborah said. 'Two falls at the same place. Their fence is worse than useless. I had a word with Allen about it, he's so in with the golf club up there, I thought he might sort them out for me. But I don't think he was listening, too busy ushering his lady friend into that smart car of his to drive back to London.'

'Seeing as I don't know what you're on about' — Helen stood up — 'I'll see how Xenos is doing.' The office door rattled with a blast of cold air as she went outside.

Deborah sighed. 'If the golf club doesn't do anything, I'll take the whole blasted lot to court.' She laughed ruefully.

Outside there was shouting. Deborah put down her cup and ran to the window. They could see the stable girls running through the yard.

'That's all we need.' Deborah strode to the door, followed by Agnes and Mary.

'Natasha's fallen,' someone shouted as they came out into the yard. 'Pony field.' They raced to the field next to the paddock, where the two girls had been jumping. One was still on her horse, standing stock still. The other was sitting on the ground next to a fence, rubbing her head. Her pony was running amok, riderless. Michelle was trying to approach her, but she bucked and reared every time she came near. She gave up and went to Natasha, and helped her to her feet.

'Bloody Doris,' Deborah said. 'Completely unstable. Ever since her injury last year. Shouldn't be ridden.'

Tad came and stood next to Agnes, on foot now. 'We've finished,' he said. 'Don't know where Xenos is.'

'There he is,' Helen said.

Xenos was walking across the field towards the bucking horse.

'I'll sell her,' Deborah muttered, watching.

Xenos approached the horse, who cantered away from him. He approached again. He seemed to be speaking. She ran off. He continued to walk towards her, then away, his head at a slight angle rather than looking straight at her. She kept a watchful distance, but slowed down. Gradually the distance between them shortened, and next time he approached, she came towards him, so that as he turned away she was following him. He turned round slowly, smiled at her, said something. She slowed to a halt, her eyes on him. He grabbed her mane, got on to her back, and set off across the field at a smooth trot, circling her back towards the onlookers. He was laughing. As he neared the jumps, he pushed her into a canter, and she jumped each fence,

330

brightly and neatly, as if she'd meant to all along.

'Don't sell her,' Mary said to Deborah.

'I'll keep her,' Deborah said. 'But only if I can have him as well.'

18

Karen showed Agnes and Patrick into the lounge and went to put on the kettle. From somewhere in the house came the beeping of a computer game, and the occasional shout from one of the boys.

Patrick stood by the fireplace. He picked up a photo, put it down again. 'Did you see Mary, then?'

'Yes, she was there.' Agnes settled into an armchair. 'She said that Wez had seen Charles Fielding dragging logs across the path in the woods.'

Patrick turned round to look at her. 'She said — ?'

'Probably coincidence,' Agnes said, meeting his gaze.

Karen came into the room with a tray of tea things. 'And I hope you've got room in your car this time, Pat.' She turned to Agnes. 'He's been promising to take some of Matt's stuff away ever since the funeral. Haven't you?'

'Perhaps Agnes has got room,' Patrick said.

Agnes shook her head. 'Helen's gone back to London in the community car, with Tad and Xenos. I'm relying on you for a lift.' She smiled. 'And by the way, your brother was a star this morning. It was his idea to take Xenos horse-riding. And Xenos was just transformed. It was wonderful to watch.'

Patrick glanced at Karen. 'He has his strengths, Tad does. Very particular ones. I told you, Agnes, he makes miracles happen.'

Karen nodded. 'It's just everyday life that defeats him.'

'Yes. Like where he's going to live now I've exhausted all possible hostel alternatives.'

Karen poured the tea into white china cups. Patrick ambled over to the french window. 'Early crocuses,' he remarked.

'Yes, they're nice, aren't they?' Karen handed Agnes a cup. 'Must be the mild winter.' She sat down in the other armchair.

Patrick stayed by the window. 'How are the boys?' he said.

Karen was silent. She shook her head.

Patrick turned away at last from the window. 'Karen, was there something wrong at his work? Was he involved in something that worried him? I can't escape the thought, you see, that he was hiding something — something he wasn't telling me — ' He paused in the middle of the room, abruptly silent.

Karen sipped her tea, the cup shaking in

her fingers. She put the cup down. 'I thought the same things. Perhaps I should have known. Perhaps I should have seen the signs. I was so used to him, you see . . . ' She looked up at Patrick. 'I was used to his — his distance from us. That space between us, that allowed him to be . . . to be who he was. Perhaps it was more than space, perhaps it was an abyss, perhaps I didn't know him at all, perhaps she knew him better.' Her cheeks flushed pink, and she bit back tears.

'No,' Patrick said. 'You mustn't think that.'

'When he went to Ireland — when was it, January? Couple of months ago — on business, I was left here. I had the house to myself, at night, just me and the boys.' She turned to Agnes. 'He never usually stayed away at night. And it felt no different. Now I think perhaps I'd got used to his absence, perhaps we weren't a couple any more.'

'He needed you.' Patrick sat down next to her and put his hand on hers. 'He relied on you.'

'Why did he go to Ireland?' Agnes asked her.

'Oh, business. And a funeral, I think. A family thing, wasn't it, Pat?'

Patrick shrugged. 'I wouldn't know. Some distant relative, I believe it was. But there were so many of us. There's lots of the old ones, still dying off. Matt knew more of them than I did. Favoured youngest son,' he said, without resentment. He stood up. 'Shall we go and look at all these things you want taken away?'

Once more Agnes found herself standing on the threshold of Matthias's office. Karen picked her way through the piles of papers, past the stacked-up boxes, the odd bits of furniture. 'I'm relying on you, Pat,' she said. 'I can't begin to sort all this.'

Patrick followed her. He picked up a file, read the label, put it down again. 'I won't know what all this stuff is,' he said. 'Perhaps we should just junk it.'

'Perhaps.' Karen stopped by an old wooden cabinet. 'This, you must have this.'

'The gramophone?' He smiled. 'Yes. I'll take that.' He went over to it and opened the lid. 'It was my dad's,' he said to Agnes. He lifted out a chrome handle and fitted it into the back, and wound it round and round. 'There are some old seventy-eights some-where.'

'In the cupboard bit underneath. Matthias kept them there.'

Patrick crouched down and opened the little double doors. He smiled, lifting out a small stack of black discs still in their paper sleeves.

'He looked after them, Matthias did.' Karen watched him. 'There was one he used to play.'

'I know the one.' Patrick sifted through the records, chose one and placed it on the turntable. He lifted the needle across and the record started to spin, emitting a crackling sound. Suddenly the room was filled with a tremulous soprano voice singing a sentimental song in Italian.

Karen looked at Patrick and nodded. 'That one. How did you know?'

'It was Dad's favourite.' Patrick turned away, blinking. The woman's voice sighed with love and longing. Agnes was aware of fragments of memory surfacing, summoned by the scratchy tones. She remembered a cabinet like this that had sat in one corner of a room in the house in Provence. She remembered it silent, but perhaps her parents too had played music like this from time to time. She wondered what had happened to it, now her mother was gone.

The song came to an end. Agnes dabbed at her eyes with her fingertips. Patrick put the sound-box back on its stand, and the rhythmic scratching stopped. He put the record away. 'I'll take it back today, if you like. I'll put the back seats down in the car. It should fit.'

Karen nodded. She moved silently amongst the heaps of papers, as if to offer him the whole roomful.

'There won't be space for much else,' Patrick said.

Agnes looked at the piles, the boxes, the papers. She remembered Judy's probing questions. Some kind of fund. But not Mary's. Something else. Patrick was sifting through a pile of books, and Agnes looked at him, wondering how to ask. To ask what? That he take the whole lot away with him? So that they could search through it for — for something? Some clue. Something that would explain his death, Liz's death. Something that would explain everything.

In her mind she saw her mother's room in the nursing home in France, sparsely furnished, a few objects here and there bathed in white sunlight. It had been the work of a few hours to gather up the things she wanted and organise the disposal of the others.

She looked at Karen, who stood defeated in the middle of the room, surrounded on all sides by Matthias's things, testimony to a life lived. A life cut short. She looked at Patrick, willing him to understand. Patrick glanced up. 'I'll take some of this too, if you like.' He gestured vaguely to the boxes.

Karen seemed to breathe again. 'If you would.' She turned and went downstairs, leaving him to it.

★　★　★

They drove back to London as night fell. The gramophone was crammed into the back of Patrick's estate car, and various boxes and files were stuffed around it.

'I've no idea what I took,' Patrick said.

'We should look through it anyway,' Agnes said.

He glanced at her. 'You think so?'

'If what Judy said — I mean, if she was really trying to find out . . . '

'Find out what?'

Agnes sighed. 'I don't know.'

'Neither do I.'

They drove the rest of the way in silence.

★　★　★

' 'The Lord is my light, and my salvation; whom then shall I fear? The Lord is the strength of my life; of whom then shall I be afraid?' '

Agnes chanted the psalm with the other sisters. A thin grey dawn stole across the altar window of the chapel.

' ' . . . though my father and my mother forsake me, the Lord will sustain me.' '

In her mind Agnes saw the room drenched in sunlight, the papery skin of her mother's face. She felt tears well in her eyes.

Afterwards Helen came to find her in the kitchen. 'It's wonderful, Agnes. The change in him!' She seemed to be speaking very fast. 'Usually he cries out several times in the night, screaming sometimes. Last night he was so much quieter, maybe one or two nightmares, but no more than that.' She beamed at her.

'Xenos?'

'Clever old Tad.' Helen poured herself a mug of tea. 'They slept in the same room last night; Tad moved his mattress in with him. And there's flea-bitten old George, keeping watch by Xenos's bed.' She giggled. 'I just hope no one inspects us.'

'Have you seen Louise? She wasn't in chapel.'

Helen frowned. 'No. Come to think of it, not since yesterday morning.'

'I hope — ' Agnes was interrupted by Sister Madeleine, who put her head round the door.

'Agnes — or Helen — you're wanted on the phone. It's the hostel.'

Helen and Agnes looked at each other and then ran to the phone.

'Agnes — it's Daniel. The police are here. They won't go without him. He has to go to a detention centre. They're very apologetic, but I can't hold them off much longer.'

'We'll be right there.' Agnes hung up.

'Xenos? They've come for him?' Helen was ashen-faced.

They grabbed their coats and raced out into the street, Agnes hailing the first cab they saw. They piled into the cab.

'They won't get him.' Helen's face was set.

Agnes looked at her. 'I hope you're right.'

★   ★   ★

At the hostel there was chaos. George was barking in the hallway. Three police, two men and a woman, were standing outside the office. Daniel was in the office on the phone. Xenos was nowhere to be seen, and Tad was upstairs, shouting something incoherent, over and over again.

'I wish we wore habits,' Helen said as they walked into the maelstrom. 'It would give us an advantage.'

Daniel looked up from the phone. 'I've found a lawyer; he's on his way.'

'He'll have to join us later,' one of the policemen said.

'OK,' Helen said. 'Just give me a chance to

explain it to him, will you?' Her voice seemed to carry such authority that everyone turned to her. 'It'll be easier for you if he doesn't feel he needs to put up a fight. He's a very traumatised person. A child,' she added.

'You must understand,' the WPC said, 'we don't want to do this.'

'I know.' Helen spoke gently. George stopped barking. Tad's shouting had stopped too. 'I'll go and get him, shall I?'

Agnes watched her go upstairs. She seemed to be in charge. Everyone waited quietly in the hallway. A nun after my own heart, Agnes thought. Which is no recommendation at all. She smiled to herself. Julius would laugh, she thought. She felt suddenly lonely.

George whimpered, and then dashed up the stairs. The three police shifted on their feet.

'Would you like to sit down?' Daniel offered. One of the men took a chair in the office. The phone rang, breaking the silence. Daniel answered it.

'Yes? Sure. Yes, we have a bed tonight. One of our residents is' — he glanced at the police — 'just leaving.' He wrote down some notes. 'Sure. Bring her over. I'll be here.' He rang off, looked at Agnes. 'A fifteen-year-old runaway. Girl. Found soliciting in Paddington.'

341

Agnes nodded. From upstairs there came no sound at all.

'I wonder where . . . ' Daniel began.

'Yes. I wonder too.'

The policewoman looked at her watch. 'Shall we . . . ?'

'I'll go.' Agnes stood up. She went up the stairs. There was no sign of George. She opened Xenos's door. The room was empty. His few possessions had gone. 'Helen?' she called. There was no answer. 'Tad?' The only response was silence.

She went back down the stairs. 'They've . . . I'm afraid they've gone.'

The police jumped to their feet. 'Gone? Where?'

'I don't know.'

'There's another exit?'

'Only the back stairs.' Agnes tried to keep her face solemn. 'They lead into the garden.'

The police ran through the house, up the main stairs, down the back stairs, out into the garden. They reappeared, one of them talking into his radio, the others pulling out notebooks, asking questions, taking statements. They left, flushed and irritable.

Agnes and Daniel looked at each other. 'Where did they go?'

Agnes shrugged. 'I've no idea. Over the garden wall? There's no other way.'

Daniel grinned. 'Some nun,' he said.

Agnes laughed. 'Some nun, indeed,' she said.

* * *

At home there was already a message from Helen on her answering machine.

'We're at Julius's church. Thank goodness he was there. We're claiming sanctuary. Julius says he's not sure of the legality of sanctuary, but it'll have to do. Um — Tad and George seem to be claiming sanctuary too.'

Agnes smiled at the machine as the message clicked to an end. The phone rang and she answered it.

'Sweetie, it's me.'

'You sound terrible.'

'I am. Nic's been round, we had a huge row. Are you busy later?'

'Um . . . no. I don't think so.' Sunday evening, Agnes thought. I ought to go back for chapel.

'A quick drink?' Athena sounded desperate. 'I'll come to you.'

'A quick drink. The wine bar by Southwark tube?'

'See you there.'

* ★ *

Athena was sitting in a dim corner near the bar. Her hair looked lank, her face barely made-up.

'What happened?' Agnes sat down next to her.

'To think this is the man who wanted to live with me. All last year, do you remember? Banging on about us spending the rest of our lives together. You'd think he was an entirely different person now. He 'needs space'. Needs to 'think things through . . . doesn't mean I don't love you' . . . ' Athena drained her glass.

'I'll get you another.' Agnes stood up.

'Gin and tonic. Double. Treble, in fact.'

Agnes stood by the bar. She glanced back at her friend. Athena was turning a drinks mat over and over in her fingers, her face pinched with misery.

'Quadruple,' Agnes said, rejoining her with two large glasses.

'What?'

'Never mind. So?'

Athena shrugged. 'I don't know. I can't make him change his mind, can I? I mean, most of this is my fault. I didn't behave well last year.'

'No.'

Athena flashed her dark eyes at her. 'What do you mean, 'no'? You're supposed to be my friend.'

Agnes patted her hand. 'Sorry. I don't mean 'no'. I mean, you did what you had to do. Having an affair last year, it was just one of those things.'

'That's better.'

'And now he's doing what he has to do.'

Athena sighed heavily. 'Yes. What he has to do.' She sipped her drink. 'I've made my bed, or whatever the saying is.' She drank some more. 'I mean, how much space does the boy need? We don't even live together. All I did was ask if he'd seen her recently, and he goes and bursts into flames. 'We don't need to know every detail about each other's lives, I don't ask you about your life.' That's because he knows about mine. Nothing is hidden from him, now I'm behaving myself.'

'It's guilt.'

'Whose guilt?' Athena looked up from her drink.

'His. That's why he's cross. Because he is seeing her, obviously, and he's uneasy about it. So you asking him just makes him want to blame you.'

'Mmmm.'

'And,' Agnes went on, 'he's still cross about what you did last year.'

'He says he isn't.'

'He does counselling for a living, what do you expect?'

Athena managed a smile. They sipped their drinks. 'I'm really terribly fond of him,' Athena said. 'I have this funny feeling as if I've taken a wrong turning. Without realising. And now we're in this mess, when we should be having fun together, and being close, like we were. You know, sweetie, I've always felt safe with Nic. I've always felt that if I jumped, he'd catch me. But now . . . somewhere back there, we went the wrong way. Oh, I don't know, it's the gin talking.'

'Makes perfect sense to me.'

'You mean, it's just like Julius and you?'

Agnes nodded. 'I thought we were perfect, I suppose. Complete. I knew everything about him; he knew everything about me. And now it turns out there's this other Julius, this new one, or old one, harbouring this passion for a woman, these regrets . . . ' She raised her eyes to Athena. 'It's a Julius I've never known before. A stranger.'

Athena turned her glass round in her hands. 'We tell ourselves stories, sweetie. 'This is how things are,' we say to ourselves. 'This is how it begins, and then there's this bit, and later maybe there'll be that . . . ' And these days, poppet, I'm beginning to think that there's a kind of gap. A gap between what's really going on, and the story we tell ourselves about it. And sometimes it's a very small gap, barely noticeable really, so the story matches up. And sometimes we go completely off the plot altogether, like me and Nic, for example, so that how I thought we were, and what was really happening' — she shook her head — 'just couldn't have been more different. As it turns out.'

Agnes looked at her. She nodded.

'Do you think it's like that for Julius?' Athena asked her.

'Julius, you see . . . ' Agnes frowned. 'He's been living one story. And now Patrick has come along and reminded him of an entirely different one, a parallel one, with . . . with this woman that he loved. Still loves. He's been thrown into turmoil, Athena. He's — he's vanished from view.'

Athena drained her glass, then peered at it. 'Maybe reality always eludes us. Maybe a good approximation is the best we get. Maybe it's always a story.' She looked up at Agnes and laughed. 'Sweetie, it really is the gin talking.'

Agnes saw Athena into a taxi, and then walked back towards her flat. It was a cold, clear night, and the stars were bright beyond the city's haze. The steeple of St Simeon's rose up darkly against the sky. As she got closer, Agnes could see lights in the windows. She hesitated, then walked up the drive, her footsteps crunching loudly on the gravel. She went to the side door and knocked.

'Who is it?' She could hear Tad's voice and a growl from George.

'It's Sister Agnes.'

There was muttered conferring, and then the door was opened by Julius. 'Helen's not here. You've just missed her.'

'It wasn't Helen I came to see.'

'Xenos is fine, he's just settling down for the night. Helen's brought bedding and stuff. I must say I'm not convinced it'll work, but she's a determined young woman.'

'It was you I came to see.'

'Oh.'

Agnes looked at him. He looked tired, his face hollowed in shadow from the streetlight above. 'Can I come in?'

He hesitated slightly. 'Of course,' he said, and stepped aside to let her in.

The Lady chapel was bathed in candlelight. Xenos lay cocooned in a large sleeping bag. He smiled at her, and patted George, who lay at his side. Tad was sitting on a makeshift bed of his own, drawing furiously on a notepad.

'It was Helen's idea,' Agnes said to Julius.

'It's a respectable tradition,' Julius replied.

'Yes.' Agnes looked at him, but his gaze was on his two guests.

'They seem to have all they need,' he said.

Agnes wanted to grab hold of him, to turn his face towards her, to make him look at her. 'Julius?' she began.

He glanced at her.

'Julius, I can't go on like this.'

He looked away again.

'What happened? With Mary's mother? All those years ago?' Agnes felt as if she had just jumped off the top of a diving board. If I jump, he'll catch me . . . Athena's words, echoing in her mind.

At last he turned and looked at her. The warm light caught the side of his face. He seemed to struggle for words. 'I was so certain,' he said. 'All those years ago. The holy fire burning within me.' His gaze went to the smooth, cold flagstones at his feet. 'I made my decision. It was a harsh decision, harsh like steel out of that furnace. And . . . ' He raised his face to hers, and his eyes burned with anguish in the flickering candlelight. 'And I was wrong. Terribly, terribly wrong. I thought God would be my guide, I was so sure . . . but all I know of love, of life, I learned from her. All that I am is not of God, it is of her.' He turned away to hide his face. 'I love her still,' he murmured.

Agnes wanted to reach out to him, but there was something cold like glass between them.

He turned back to face her. 'I'm glad of this.' He gestured with his head to the scene in the Lady chapel. Xenos seemed to be settling to sleep. 'I doubt sanctuary has any legal status at all these days, but at least the publicity will help his cause. I can be busy with this.'

For a moment they stood, seeing in each other's gaze the same pain; each helpless in the face of their own loss. Julius lifted his arm towards her, then let it fall again. 'Well,' he said, 'lots to do. Barricade the doors, perhaps. Who knows.' He smiled briefly. 'I'd better lock the door behind you.'

In silence they went to the side door of the church, and Agnes found herself outside in the cold night air, hearing Julius turn the key on the other side of the door.

19

The dream was different. The same corridor, the same sand drifting across the terracotta floor, but this time she was searching for someone. At the far end, framed by the window, someone seemed to be standing, a tiny figure veiled by the drapes of white curtain. Julius, she tried to call out, and this woke her.

She wondered whether she'd called his name out loud.

She sat up. The day was grey, dull, cold. Her room was cold too. She got out of bed and pulled on layers of clothes. It was a deadening feeling, this sense of loss; beyond tears. She made some tea, just as the phone rang. It was Helen.

'The police are outside the church,' she said. She sounded cheerful.

'Where are you?'

'In a phone box. They're threatening to arrest Julius. I haven't seen him in such a good mood for ages.'

'Oh.'

'Are you all right?'

'Um, yes. Really. So, what's going to happen?'

'Don't know. At the moment there's two or three coppers. Very polite. Julius offered them tea, but one of them only drinks herbal stuff. Can you imagine?'

Agnes laughed.

'They've had a wonderful night, Xenos is transformed, he's using words now, not making much sense, but at least he's trying. Tad taught him to say bagel.'

'Julius and his breakfast habits,' Agnes sighed.

'I wanted to ask you what I should do.'

'Do?'

'Now, I mean. I'm due at the hostel at ten. Or should I stay here?'

Agnes thought for a moment. 'I'll do your hostel shift. You stay there. Anything could happen and Xenos trusts you.'

'OK.' Agnes could hear the relief in her voice. 'I'll keep in touch.'

'Sure.'

Agnes stood by her desk. She glanced out of the window. The city rooftops seemed hunched under the heavy sky. She found she still had the phone in her hand, and now she put it down.

Her doorbell buzzed. She went to the intercom, hoping it was Patrick.

'Sister? It's Louise. Can I come up?'

Louise, she thought. 'Of course,' she said.

Louise stumbled into Agnes's flat just as Agnes had replaced the cushions on her sofa bed. She looked terrible, with puffy eyes and blotchy skin.

'Louise?'

Louise stood still, blinking. 'It's Richard. He's dying.' Agnes helped her to a chair. 'I've been there all the time,' Louise went on. 'At the hospice. I meant to phone.'

'It's OK.' Agnes sat next to her and took her hand.

'Why?' Louise turned her red-rimmed eyes to Agnes. 'What is God thinking of? Not Richard . . . he looks so awful, he's barely awake. I'm so angry, Agnes. After all I've done . . . ' She burst into tears.

Agnes sat quietly, still holding her hand.

'I prayed all night, last night, and the night before. I haven't slept for days. I was so sure . . . What does God want of me?' She looked up at Agnes. 'What more does he want? This morning, the nurse who came on the shift, I told her, I said, It's not too late, he might be saved. And she shouted at me. She was angry with me. She said I was a silly girl.' Louise turned her bewildered, tear-stained face to Agnes. 'And then she went on about acceptance, about there being a time to die, and said something about me getting in the way.' She dashed tears from her eyes. 'Perhaps she envies my faith. I was so angry with her. In front of him as well, to talk like that, it's terrible, isn't it, and to go on about people being love-sick and getting in the way, so I left, I was so angry with her, I came here. But I can't stay long, I must be with him . . . '

Agnes had a flash of memory. The rasping breath in the bleached-out room. White pillows, white quilt. White flowers. And the struggle to breathe in, out . . . her mother's last breath. The spheres on the clock, spinning this way, that way. A time to die.

'I mustn't let him down, Agnes.' The bout of weeping had passed, and Louise sat, upright, staring ahead of her. 'They're relying on me.'

'But, Louise . . . ' Agnes began. But what? she wondered. 'Isn't it in God's hands?' she said.

Louise looked at her, her gaze clear now, direct. 'What is prayer for, then?'

Agnes tried to answer, fell silent.

Louise stood up. 'I must get back to him. If there's someone by the bed who believes . . . It must make a difference, don't you think? Even if he's asleep, he'll know I'm fighting for him, won't he?'

Agnes nodded, defeated.

Louise got up and walked to the door. Agnes heard her footsteps on the landing, firm and certain, receding confidently down the stairs.

It was nearly ten. Agnes found her coat and went out.

I'm too tired, she thought, wrapping her scarf around her face against the sharp wind. I'm too tired to preach a message of acceptance to Louise.

And perhaps she's right. Perhaps God does intervene in his creation, perhaps he does it all the time, miracles here and there and everywhere, and it takes people like Louise to see it, and I'm just being dense and stupid and faithless ... Perhaps God daily raises cancer patients from the verge of death, like Lazarus, and Louise's faith will be proved right.

But I don't ask for proof, Agnes thought, waiting by the bus stop. Like Pascal, taking his chances. That's my faith. A gambler's faith. I don't ask for signs of God's order.

In her mind it was as if she heard a whistling, two golf balls flashing through the air, one after the other, landing in the bushes. Two horses rearing, their riders falling.

The bus came, and Agnes stepped gratefully into the crowd.

At the hostel there was more news. 'The refugee people have got us a barrister,' Daniel said, looking up from his desk as Agnes arrived, late and breathless. 'They're arguing about sanctuary with the Home Office. At least it gives us time. The press are outside the church now as well. We're short-staffed today, I'm glad you're here.'

'I'm glad to have something to do,' she replied. She went into the kitchen and made some coffee. She sat at the formica table. Out of the window she could see a cat balancing on a garden fence. The cloud was lifting, and a thin shaft of sunlight burst into yellow across a window box of daffodils.

There are no guarantees, she thought. But where does that leave Louise? What is prayer for?

She stood up and went over to the window. Into your hands, O Lord, I commend my spirit. Does that mean I shouldn't get angry with you when a young man lies dying tragically young in a hospice?

It's right that we feel, she thought. It's right that we feel pain, or sorrow, or joy.

The sunlight bathed the room in gold. Who are we to turn away from this? she thought. Who are we to deny the joy of life? If your universe includes this, this beauty, this light, this cup of coffee, then who am I to turn away from it?

Your universe gave Mary to Matthias. Should he have turned away? And was Julius wrong, then, to turn away from the woman he loved, as he thinks now that he was, even though he was doing your will?

She watched a squirrel ripple across the garden fences.

And Nic, turning towards Linda. And Athena, weighing up her life with him.

And me. With that house, those corridors, those overgrown gardens that I once loved, that I would love again . . .

Seven years, she thought. It's long enough, seven years. To have been in this order, renewing my vows from time to time, constantly postponing the final decision. Sister Christiane is right.

An image came to her, of green paint peeling on the old wooden shutters, in the clear Provençal sun.

What are you offering me, Lord? A house? A choice? A test?

There are no certainties. There are no deals to be made with God. That's not what prayer is. Louise is wrong. And that nurse who was angry with her, she was only trying to make her see . . .

Daniel put his head round the door. 'Phone call for you,' he said.

'Agnes, it's Patrick.'

'Hello.'

'Where's Tad?'

'Still at Julius's church. For now.'

'Right. Yes. Good. The thing is, you see, I've found — I've been looking at some of Matthias's stuff and I think I've found . . . '

'What?'

'Can you come round? Now?'

'I'm working.'

'This evening, then? Will you be hungry? There might be something here we can eat.' He sounded unsure.

'I'll pass a supermarket. Where do you live?'

'Um, oh yes. Got a pen?' He gave her the address. 'When can you be here?'

She looked at her watch. 'About six?'

'Good. I'll be here.' He rang off.

She stared at the phone. Yes, she thought. Feeling nothing is not an option. Doing nothing is not an option. She got out her notebook and found Stewart Lode's number and dialled it. Eventually the phone was answered.

'Lode.'

'Hello, um, Brigadier. It's Sister Agnes.'

'Ah. Yes. You.'

'I was wondering, you see . . . '

'I've been wondering too, young lady. The world's going mad. I get an offer of a full settlement from Gough and his man. Just getting to grips with that, when Fielding

358

approaches me in the pub last night, wants to talk. About what? I asked him. The man, practically whispering, says he can't tell me now. Asks me, did I know Elizabeth, the one who died in that car accident? Well, yes, I say, not very well, her father knew my brother. Upshot of all this is I'm going to visit him to see that clock of his, just the kind I'm after. Vowed never to speak to him again, but best not bear grudges, eh?'

'When are you seeing him?'

'This evening.'

'Brigadier, could we — could I come and see you again?'

'If you must. With your friend?'

'Well, um . . . '

'Both of you. If you think I've got anything to tell you. Serious matters.'

'Yes,' Agnes agreed. 'Serious matters. Are you there tomorrow?'

'Yes. I'm always here. Not well provisioned, though.'

'I know. You warned us last time.'

There was a brief bark of laughter. 'Ah well. Ten o'clock?'

'Fine. Thank you.'

Agnes stared at the phone. She wondered what Charles wanted to tell Lode.

Daniel put his head round the door again. 'Have you finished with the phone?'

'Yes. Thanks.'

'There're two new residents. They've just arrived. Twin brothers, they claim, twelve years old, although one's six inches taller than the other and has the beginnings of a beard. Can you sort them out with food? I'm trying to track down their social worker.'

★　★　★

'Top Flat' the bell said. She pressed it. Nothing happened. Eventually the door opened and a young man with very short bleached hair came out of it, wheeling a bike. He nodded to her. She walked past him into the dim hallway, then up the stairs. At the top there was one door. She hammered on it. She could hear music, a soprano singing, which seemed to slow down, becoming tenor, then bass, then stopped. She knocked again. Patrick opened the door and stood staring at her.

'I rang the bell,' she said.

'I can't have heard it,' he said, stepping back to allow her in.

'I've brought various things to heat up,' she said, walking past him into what appeared to be a kitchen. 'Do you — um — do you have a cooker?'

He pointed. 'There.'

Agnes looked at the two tiny gas rings. 'Microwave?' she said, against hope.

He shook his head.

She brought out a packet and frowned at it. 'Do you think Chinese Savoury Selection is nice cold?'

He shook his head again.

She sighed. 'Never mind. I wasn't hungry.' She wished it was true.

'Would you like a drink?' He showed her into the living room, opened a can of beer and poured himself a large glass. 'Beer, maybe? Whisky?'

'Not for me thanks. Not this early.'

He walked across the room in an odd zig-zag, as if to dodge awkward corners of furniture. The walls were a faded cream, and there were old brown curtains drawn across the window. He switched on a lamp in one corner of the room, then crossed back to the gramophone and wound it up. The soprano burst into song again. The music seemed to draw him into a reverie.

Agnes watched him. 'Why did you phone me?' Her voice seemed harsh against the music.

He looked up at her. 'What? Oh, yes.' He lifted the pick-up arm and the music stopped. 'I found some papers in Matthias's stuff. Now where . . . ' He surveyed the room, then launched himself at a table in the corner and snatched up a file. 'This,' he said, gesturing to her to sit down. She sat on the sofa and he sat next to her. 'Look,' he said.

She took the papers. They were computer printouts of figures, sums of money in columns, under different headings. Some were circled in biro. 'I'm afraid you'll have to explain,' she said.

'It's a printout of Allen's e-mail account. Matt must have obtained it deliberately.'

'And?'

'It shows that Allen's been squirrelling money away at the Seattle office.'

'What money?'

'Whatever he can get his hands on, I think. Look, all this money's been sent electronically to a US account, over several weeks. It stopped here.' He pointed to a date at the top of a page.

Agnes peered at the date. 'A few days before Matt died.'

Patrick looked at her. 'Allen must have found out that Matt was on to him.'

'So the leisure centre . . . ?'

'My guess is that the building plan was stalled by the dispute. Allen was losing money on the land, and in desperation, he set up this scheme to make up the shortfall.'

'Until Matt found out.'

Patrick emptied the rest of the beer into his glass. 'Yes,' he said.

'But surely someone in the other office would notice?'

'Allen's very senior. There're very few people to check on him. It's the sort of thing that can go on for a long time before anyone finds out.' He flicked through the pages. 'It's all disguised, you see, under new policies, different customer accounts, reinsurance.'

'How do you know it's dodgy, then?' Agnes looked up at him.

'Because Matt's been through it and circled the stuff that isn't right. And also because I found another thing. Now where was it — a note. Here we are.' He handed her a note in scrawled handwriting. 'I found it in the same file,' he said.

Agnes took the note and read it. *Matthias: I'll win this one. I can't afford not to. I've got too much to lose. You can buy into it. You have a choice.*

She looked at Patrick. 'Buy into it?'

'The leisure centre. It explains why Judy thought Matt had money in it.'

'It reads like a threat.'

Patrick was gathering the papers back into the file. 'That's what I thought.'

'Are you sure it's Allen's handwriting?'

He nodded. 'I checked. There's various

memos and things in here, you can double-check if you like.'

'Why does it help Allen if Matt invests in it?'

'Because then he doesn't have to defraud the company.' Patrick looked at her. 'But there's nothing in the will to say that Matt had any money that wasn't tied up. Certainly there was nothing invested in Allen's business.' He scratched his head. 'He'd been going on about setting up a fund for Tad. He'd promised, recently, that Tad would be well off, that we'd be able to afford for him to be really independent, instead of these ill-suited places. But in the will, although he does what he can for Tad, it's not much.'

He stood up, and the file he was holding fell to the floor. A white card fell out. Agnes picked it up and scanned it.

' 'May she Rest in Peace'. It's a funeral invitation,' she said to Patrick. He took it, read it, handed it back. 'Who's Bridgid O'Connor?' she asked.

Patrick shrugged. 'I've no idea.'

'She was seventy-five, according to this.'

'Some relative, I suppose.'

'It's addressed to Matthias.' Agnes turned the card over in her hands. 'Did he go?'

'How would I know?'

'It's dated January.' Agnes looked up. 'That's when Karen said he went to Ireland.'

'Oh, yes.' Patrick seemed distracted. 'Yes, he went to that.'

'A relative?' Agnes stared at the name again.

Patrick smiled. 'You have to understand, when we were young, there were armies of spinster ladies who were only too keen to take an interest in us, in Pip Kavanagh's boys. He had bags of charm, our dad. Attracted spare aunties for us without even trying. Matt was better at staying in touch with them, that's all.'

Agnes put the funeral card with the other papers. 'Was it like Matt to take a risk on Allen's venture?'

'No,' Patrick said.

'But he was a gambler?'

'Not with money. With his safety. With pounding across the countryside on unstable mares. But not money.' A car alarm went off outside, and Patrick ambled over to the window and peered out absently. 'Matthias thought money was a protection,' he said, turning back to her. 'After Dad's death . . . Matt was so young, it affected him directly. He was determined to be rich. And safe. For all the fact that he was a gambler, like our dad, he wanted an insurance policy too. That's why it makes no sense him sinking money into anything risky. If you read his will, everything's taken care of.'

'Allen said, at the funeral — '

Patrick flashed her a glance of recognition. 'He said that Matt played for high stakes.'

'But Matt didn't risk his money.'

Patrick shook his head. 'Perhaps Allen didn't mean money.'

Agnes sat, staring at the swirls of the pattern on the carpet.

'You must be hungry,' Patrick said suddenly.

'Ravenous.'

'Sorry about the cooker. I kind of get by. The university has a canteen.'

'What shall we do?' she said.

Patrick had flung himself down in the other armchair. He looked up at her. 'I should go to the police, I suppose. When I'm sure.'

'How will you prove it?'

'Don't know. I think I'd better find some other pretext to be at the office.'

'Judy might help.'

Patrick frowned, pulling the sleeves of his jumper over his hands. 'There seems to be a price attached to that,' he said.

★　★　★

Agnes walked out into the cold night air. She headed for the tube, joining the bustle of Bishopsgate. She passed the wine bar, hesitated, turned and went in.

It was busy, as usual. She scanned the tables, looking for Judy, or Allen. There was a young man sitting on his own, and it took her a moment to realise it was Jed.

She went over to the table, and he looked up. For a moment he seemed not to see her, his gaze distant and preoccupied, then he smiled. 'Sister Agnes. I'm sorry, I was miles away.' He gestured to the seat next to him.

'Do you mind me interrupting?'

'I'd be glad of the company. Can I get you a drink?'

Agnes eyed his beer. 'One of those please. And — and something to eat. A sandwich, maybe?'

While he went to the bar Agnes glanced round the room. Young men leaned in groups having animated conversations punctuated with loud laughter. She wondered about Judy joining this world, wondered about the price she'd had to pay.

'Mozzarella OK?' Jed reappeared. 'They said they'd bring it over.'

'Thanks.' She took her beer and drank gratefully.

'A long day?' Jed watched her.

'A bit, yes.'

'I've wanted to talk to you,' he said, colouring slightly under his blond fringe.

'Oh?'

'Yes. Since Judy said you were a nun.'

'Oh.'

He sipped his drink. Agnes waited. After a while he said, 'Do you think — I mean — do you think it's a good thing in life, to hand everything over to someone?'

She looked at him, at his open face, his symmetrical features, his neat, straight nose. 'It depends who they are,' she said.

'I mean, with you people, right, it's God, isn't it? Or Jesus? Or the Mother Superior?'

'Well . . . ' Agnes paused. 'God, ultimately. I suppose.'

'But what I mean is, it is a handing over, isn't it?' There was an urgency in his eyes as he waited for her answer.

'Yes.'

'You have to surrender something, your will as an individual, for the common good?'

'Yes.' Agnes wondered where this was leading.

'And does it work? Does it make you a better person?' His grey eyes had a deep intensity about them as he held her gaze.

She smiled at him, but he didn't return her

smile. She hesitated, then said, 'I think that's the idea.'

'But does it?' His voice seemed loud. 'Does it work?'

'It depends on the person.' Agnes picked up her beer and concentrated on drinking it. 'The structure of the religious life can be immensely helpful if you're the right person for it. If you're the wrong person . . . ' She thought of Louise, and wondered how she was.

'If you're the wrong person?' Jed was waiting for her to speak again, his eyes still fixed on her.

'If you're the wrong person, then no amount of spiritual guidance is going to help. In fact, it's just going to make you more miserable.' They were interrupted by the waitress arriving with her sandwich. Agnes bit into it hungrily.

'And how can you tell — if you're the right person, I mean?'

Agnes finished her mouthful. 'What is this about, Jed?'

He looked away then. His eyes seemed veiled, their urgency gone. 'I might go to California,' he said. 'To join — to join a group . . . ' He sighed. 'It's very difficult to explain, that's why I thought you'd under-stand.' He took a swig of beer. 'There's a runner there, a distance runner. He doesn't run so much now, he trains people. Doc Adamson, he's called. If you look at marathons around the world, if you look at the winners, they're his men. And women,' he added. 'They're achieving speeds that no one else has ever got. He's the best.' He looked up at her. 'I've been training, here, to get my speeds up. I e-mailed him last week. He's interested in me. I'm going to go and meet him.' His gaze flickered, uncertain.

'Is it what you want?'

'That's what I don't know. I mean, yes, it is what I want. But he asks a lot, and he gets a lot. That's how it works. He tells you what to eat, when to eat, when to sleep . . . you have to hand over everything to him, and he makes you your best self. He trains in the mountains, in altitude. If I join him, it's the end of everything else. It's like saying goodbye to your old self and becoming the self he makes you. That's why I thought maybe I should talk to you about it, 'cos you must have done the same thing in some way. You must have made that all or nothing decision.' His gaze was intense again, waiting for her answer.

Agnes finished her sandwich. All or nothing, she thought. 'Yes,' she began. 'But . . . ' But it wasn't a person, she thought.

It wasn't an individual. 'It's different with the order,' she said. 'You hand over to a structure.'

'But you still commit yourself.'

Agnes sighed. 'Yes. You're supposed to.'

'And you haven't?' He was concerned now, his gaze softer.

'It's difficult.'

'You see, with Doc it's all or nothing. That's what he said, on his e-mail. He doesn't take fainthearts. You have to want to be that self, the self that he can make you.'

Agnes poured the last of her beer into her glass. 'I'm not sure I can help. It's an individual path, isn't it? Even within my order, we're all different. Some are more sure than others.'

'Maybe.' He seemed unconvinced.

'And your work?' Agnes looked at him.

He coloured again. 'Between you and me — I'm trusting you with this — it may be time I left this job.'

'You mean,' Agnes said, taking a chance, 'that things aren't right at the Seattle office?'

He blinked at her. He looked down at his glass. After a moment, he said, 'I can't rightly say.'

'Is it Allen?'

'I can't betray a colleague,' he said.

'Let's just say,' Agnes said, choosing her

words, 'that you think you might be better off out of it?'

He nodded. 'Let's just say,' he repeated, 'that it seems like the right time to go.'

'And you'd leave the company?'

He nodded again. 'Doc asks everything.'

'And financially?'

He shrugged. 'I want to cut loose,' he said. 'Doc feeds you, clothes you.'

'Like an order, then. A vow of poverty.'

'It has an appeal.'

'And . . . And Judy?'

He stared at the table. 'That's my fault, I guess. I've allowed her to believe . . . to believe more than I . . . ' He looked up at her. 'I'm a coward. Like most men.'

'You'd better tell her.'

'Do you think she'll understand how much this means to me?'

Agnes looked at him. 'Yes,' she said.

'It's the end of a search. It's learning to belong where I am. Instead of all this.' He gestured around him with his arm. 'My mother cut my roots from under me when I was fourteen, and I've spent the rest of my life trying to find someplace to call home.'

'What happened?'

'Dad left. There were four of us kids.'

'In Minnesota?'

He nodded. 'I was the only boy. Mum sent me away to school, here in England, she worked all the hours to pay for it. The first vacation, when I went back, I'd been away a year, and they'd moved. The family had split up, the girls had gone to our aunt, our mother had sold our home, she was living with some guy, still working day and night, still paying for me.' He passed his hand across his face. 'I never went back after that. Sometimes I'd visit, but . . . ' He shook his head. He picked up his beer bottle and drained the dregs from it. 'I met Doc Adamson. Just once. I made the pilgrimage up to the mountains, a year and a half ago. I ended up telling him all this.'

'What did he say?'

'He said you have to learn not to look for what you're looking for. He said his runners train from a place of emptiness, a place where you ask nothing.' He looked up at Agnes. 'These days I have this image of myself. I see myself, running, alone in the wilderness, in the solitude.'

'You think that's what you want?'

He met her eyes. 'I know it's what I want. It's all I want.'

He stood up, reached for her coat, and helped her on with it. They went out into the street. The air was crisp, cut through with the white beams of headlights, the softer yellow haze of the streetlamps. They began to walk.

'I've got to work tonight,' he said.

They reached the office building, a huge edifice of quartz and glass reaching up to the sky. Through the smoky window Agnes could see the entrance hall: a fountain, floodlit, edged with palm trees, a modern, angular sculpture in hammered metal. Beyond that there was a lonely security man sitting at a marble desk that seemed to go on for ever.

'I'll walk you to the tube,' Jed said.

'No, it's fine, it's only over there.'

'Thanks for the talk.'

'I wish I could be more helpful.'

'You were. I know it's time to go. When Judy first introduced you, I — I envied you. You've made that choice, that commitment.'

'Well, I — '

'See?' He gestured to the building behind him. 'I've finished with it. And there's you, proving it's possible. I guess you even own nothing.'

'Well — at the moment, I own a house and several acres in Provence.'

He smiled. 'But you'll get rid of it, then?'

'You see, Jed, this decision you're about to make, it's ongoing. It's continuous. It's one you keep making, every day.'

He shook his head. 'Not me. Once I make up my mind, then it's done.'

'Then I should envy you.'

'No.' He laughed. 'Or then again, maybe.'

20

Once again, Mary and Agnes found themselves outside Brigadier Lode's sprawling and shabby house. It had been raining all night, and the morning was damp and grey. They stepped over mud puddles on the drive and rang the bell. Again, there was a chorus of barking.

Stewart opened the door and showed them in. He seemed preoccupied. 'Ah, yes, Sister. And — um — '

'Mary.'

'Yes. Mary.' He gave her a sideways glance, and opened the door of the living room. 'Coffee,' he said abruptly. 'Managed to do it properly this time. Think so, anyway.' He left them and disappeared into the kitchen. They sat down in the chintz armchairs. One of the dogs came to have a look at them, settling down warily in the doorway. In the silence, Agnes and Mary looked at each other. Neither could think of anything to say.

Lode reappeared with a tray, a pot of coffee and three stained mugs. 'You pour,' he said, going back to the kitchen, returning with a bottle of milk and a bag of sugar. Agnes had poured the coffee into the mugs, and he added milk to each one. 'Ah — spoon. Sugar, anyone?' They shook their heads. 'No spoon. Ah well.' He tipped an approximate measure, which seemed rather large, into one of the mugs and stirred it with his finger, then sat down in the largest armchair.

'So?' He smiled at them both, waiting.

'I gather . . . ' Mary began. 'I gather Charles Fielding is behaving oddly.'

Lode leaned forward in his chair. 'D'you know, found I quite liked the fellow after all. Showed me a clock, hope to reach a deal with him on it. Just the thing I'm after. Eighteenth-century, cabinet, y'know, grandfather clock. Very ornate, pictorial, shows God setting the universe in motion. God as clockmaker,' he chuckled. 'Got all manner of things stashed away, has old Fielding. Not just clocks. Armour, he's got. Worth a bob or two, told him to check he's properly insured. Obviously said the wrong thing, got a bit short with me then.'

'He used to work in insurance,' Agnes said.

'Yes.'

'With Allen.'

'That's right. Said that the City spat him out. Those were his words. Changed the subject then, had a look at his gun collection.'

'Guns?'

'Fine old things. No need to look so worried, couldn't fire them if you wanted to. Need powder, all sorts, complicated business. He had some miniatures, he showed me. Tiny things. Cannon as well, reckons they came from a model ship. About this size . . . Pretty things, in silver, all carved.' He stirred his finger around in his coffee again.

Agnes sipped her coffee, which tasted burnt and stale. 'Brigadier,' she began, 'we think that perhaps . . . ' She glanced at Mary.

Mary leaned across to him. 'Brigadier, don't you ever wonder how it is that both Matthias and Liz are now — I mean . . . ' She glanced at Agnes.

'We mean, it seems such a coincidence,' Agnes finished lamely.

Lode drank noisily from his mug, then put it down. 'Can't say I haven't had similar thoughts, young ladies. Particularly as, now Matt's gone, this land dispute's all settled. But then, it's settled in my favour. So that doesn't give anyone reason to — to resort to killing him, though. Does it? We were good friends: I helped him, he helped me. Perhaps these City people really will stop at nothing. But you know, I'm an army man, done my time with guns and targets — golf balls and horses, not a sensible way to go about it, not

378

sensible at all. I know young Elizabeth, she started thinking things weren't right. She'd had an accident, fell off her horse. She came round here to warn him, day or two before he died, he'd brought something of the old lady's for me to sign, she was in a right old state, said they'd stop at nothing. But in the end, did she mean — did she mean nothing short of murder?' He shook his head. 'Doubt it, myself. Doubt it.'

'What old lady?' Agnes asked.

'What?'

'You said, 'something of the old lady's'.'

Stewart seemed to colour slightly, then he stood up, nudging the table as he did so, so that Mary had to reach forward to steady it. 'No. No old lady.'

' 'To sign'?' Agnes persisted.

'No, the land. That's what we were signing. Legal things. Young lady, I meant, Liz, she had to sign affidavits, about the ditch and the fence.' He laughed. 'I'll tell you what, and it's a damned nuisance, all this boundary dispute has brought Father back. Can't shut him up about ditches and fences and whose land starts and ends where. Come on, I'll show you out.'

★　★　★

379

' 'Old lady',' Agnes repeated as they bumped down the drive in Mary's car. 'Do you know of an old lady?'

Mary shook her head, negotiating a large mud rut in the gravel.

'What would Matthias have asked him to sign that was to do with an old lady?'

'Don't you think you misheard?'

'You're sure you know nothing about it?'

'Positive. Matthias told me everything.' Mary braked suddenly.

'What is it?'

'I've just realised. What did Lode say about Fielding? That the City spat him out?' She put her hand over her mouth. 'It was Matt. I'm so stupid, Agnes, not to realise till now.'

'What do you mean?'

'Matt found out that someone in his company was being negligent. I never knew who it was. But it was Matt, you see, who reported him. And he had to leave.'

'But how do you know — ?'

'I just do. Or, at least, I'm going to find out. Come on.' Mary put the car back into gear and drove fast down the drive, back towards the village.

'Where are we going?'

'To Fielding's house. I think I know the way. It's the old Caddy farm, isn't it?'

'But what will we say?'

'I'll think of something. Like, did you kill the only man I ever loved?'

'But you can't — '

'Well, maybe not.' Mary's face was pale, her lips set. 'It's left at the pub, I think.'

'Mary?'

'Yes?'

'In January, Matthias went to Ireland.'

'Yes.'

'To a funeral.'

'Was it? I thought it was something about business in Dublin. I didn't take in the details.'

'You don't know anything about it?'

Mary shook her head.

'And the name Bridgid O'Connor, does that mean anything?'

Mary frowned, then shook her head again. 'Who's she?'

'It was her funeral. An old lady.'

The car came to a halt at the crossroads. 'He told me everything,' Mary said. 'If it had been important, I'd have known.'

Agnes sat in silent acquiescence.

'Does Karen know about her? Or Patrick?' Mary asked, revving the engine as her car tackled the narrow lane.

'No. They haven't heard of her.'

'He told me everything, you see,' Mary

381

repeated. 'I did say left by the pub, didn't I?'

* * *

Charles's house was set back from the road behind ornate iron gates. It was a wide, elegant two-storey building, painted pristine white. They stood on the polished steps and looked at each other, then rang the bell. A dog barked in the distance. After a while they heard dragging footsteps, and the door opened.

'Mr Charles Fielding?' Mary said.

He eyed them suspiciously, then nodded.

'I'm — I'm a friend of Matthias's,' Mary said. 'And this is Sister Agnes.'

There was a tension in his posture as he stood on the doorstep, and his face was pale. 'And what can I do for you?'

Mary swallowed. 'We need to know . . . ' She glanced at Agnes.

'We've just been visiting Brigadier Lode,' Agnes said.

'And?'

Mary spoke boldly. 'We think things weren't right. Between you and Matthias.'

'If it's about me leaving the company,' he said, his voice uneven, 'he should never have revealed anything. He promised — '

'That you'd all stick to the story of early retirement?' Agnes said quickly.

'For the sake of my reputation,' Charles said.

'And didn't he?'

He tried to smile. Agnes noticed how pale he seemed, his skin sallow, his features strained. 'Word got out,' he said. The hallway behind him seemed to be littered with furniture, and paintings hung side by side on the walls. A clock chimed the quarter hour, echoed by another a moment later.

He looked at them both. His face seemed chalk white, and Agnes realised he was very unwell. He leaned heavily on the door frame. 'Look, why have you come? Who's sent you?'

'No one.' Mary faced him. 'We've heard rumours . . . odd things . . . '

Charles seemed short of breath when he next spoke. 'Yes. Odd things.' He shook his head. 'Felt the whole village against me. It's been very bad for me, knocked my health back a bit,' he said.

'Why did you block the bridle path by the golf course?'

Charles was ashen-faced. His hand went to his chest, and Agnes saw his fingers were trembling as they clutched the expensive linen of his shirt.

'Why were you there, when Liz fell off her

horse?' Mary went on. Agnes glanced at her, trying to warn her not to go too far.

'That's ridiculous.' Charles tried to raise his voice, but he had no breath.

Agnes nudged Mary's arm, as if to go, but Mary's gaze was fixed on Charles. 'I loved him,' she said to Charles. 'He was my life. And now he's gone. And neither he nor I can rest in peace until we know . . . until I know what happened. And it seems to me, Mr Fielding, that you know. That you know what happened. You know why Matthias's horse stopped short on that path by the golf course, and you know how it was that someone made sure that Matthias fell and didn't get up again.' She had tears in her eyes and her hands were tight fists against her sides.

This time Agnes took hold of Mary's arm.

Charles spoke through clenched teeth, and two tiny pink dots had appeared on his cheeks. 'Go now,' he managed to say. 'Get out . . . set the dogs on you.'

Mary faced him. She seemed about to speak, but then turned and allowed Agnes to lead her down the steps and back to the car. They heard the front door slam loudly behind them.

Mary started the engine and revved it fast, then screeched down the drive. She pulled over to the side of the road, stopped the car and burst into tears. 'What are we going to do?' she said, through sobs, her hands over her face.

'Go to the police?' Agnes spoke quietly, staring out of the windscreen, thinking hard.

'And tell them what?'

'What we know. It's quite incriminating.'

'Of Charles, yes. But not of Allen.' Mary found a handkerchief and wiped her face.

Agnes sighed. 'Allen's leisure centre is going ahead. Though possibly on dishonest funding.'

Mary shook her head. 'No, Allen was in on it too. They were at school together, him and Fielding. It's obvious that Charles and Allen decided to kill Matthias and Liz.'

'But is it? How obvious?' Agnes watched the clouds gathering on the horizon. She was aware of a thought, nagging at the edges of her mind.

'We should challenge Allen.'

'And what's he going to say?'

Mary was silent. 'Let's ask Patrick. Let's ask him what to do next.'

'OK.' Agnes put her hand on Mary's arm as they pulled up in the station car park.

'We can't do nothing, Agnes. It's simply not an option.'

Agnes met her eyes. 'No. You're right. I'll phone you.'

It rained, heavily, on the train journey back to London. Agnes watched the lines of raindrops making watery webs against the glass. Interrelated stories, she thought. Matt was connected with Karen, with his family, with Mary, with Lode, with Fielding; with the City. With Ireland.

She watched the darkening clouds. Again, that thought, just out of reach.

She arrived at the community house for midday chapel, and was greeted in the hallway by Helen.

'Can you meet Tad this afternoon?' she asked.

'Why?'

'He wants to see Patrick. He's still at the church with Xenos, but he's got some idea about needing money for the legal fees, and he thinks Patrick will help. I thought maybe you could take him along, it might be easier for them both. You can come back to the church with me after this.'

They took up their places in chapel, Agnes slightly behind the novices and younger nuns. There was a gap where Louise should have been.

' ' . . . Jesus said, 'I came into this world for judgement, so that those who do not see may see, and those who do see may become blind . . . ' ' '

386

' . . . *so that those who do not see may see* . . . '

' ' . . . Some of the Pharisees said to him, 'Surely we are not blind, are we?' Jesus said to them, 'If you were blind, you would not have sin. But now that you say, 'We see,' your sin remains.' ' '

' . . . *now that you say, 'We see* . . . ' '

She thought of Fielding standing on his doorstep, challenged by Mary.

We chose to see randomness and chaos, Lord. Instead of seeing order. Your order, O Lord, she thought.

' . . . *I came into this world* . . . *so that those who do not see may see, and those who do see may become blind* . . . '

Agnes blinked against the watery sunlight that suddenly filled the altar window. She was aware of an uneasy feeling rising within her, in spite of the gentle murmur of the liturgy. She was aware that what she was feeling was plain, cold fear.

21

At four Agnes and Helen rang the bell at the side door of St Simeon's and Julius let them in. Julius immediately engaged Helen in a conversation about food supplies.

' . . . he seems to live on milk,' Agnes heard him saying as she walked up the staircase ahead of them. Ridiculous, she told herself, hearing Julius laugh at some remark of Helen's. Ridiculous to be jealous of her.

In the Lady chapel, Xenos was sitting quietly, leafing through a pile of magazines. Tad was pacing the aisle of the church, and when he saw Agnes he came over to her.

'It's the only answer, you see.' He started to pace again, leading Agnes with him, his gaze fixed on the floor. 'Colin, our lawyer, says it might take weeks. I said my brother had money. And there's Matthias's money, he said he'd look after me, if anything happened, Matt promised I'd be looked after, that's what he said.' He raised his eyes to hers, then looked down at the ground again. 'I must ask Patrick. Helen phoned him, she said you'd take me there.' He glanced across at Xenos.

'But I don't like to leave him.'

'We won't be long,' Agnes said, glad to leave the church. 'Do you have a coat?'

They went to say goodbye to Xenos, who started to his feet when he saw that Tad was leaving. Tad thrust George into his arms, in wordless promise of his return. Xenos sat down again, clutching the dog to him, his gaze fixed on Tad and Agnes as they went out to the vestry. At the door, Julius stared at his shoes, murmuring goodbye.

They went out into the street, Tad struggling into an old anorak. 'Will we take a bus? What number will it be?'

They waited at the stop. A number seventeen passed, followed by a number thirty-five. 'They make the same,' Tad remarked. 'Three plus five . . . Is this ours?'

They got on the bus, crossing the river to the City, getting off at Liverpool Street. This time Patrick heard the bell and let them in. He too seemed agitated, but tried to appear calm in front of Tad.

'It's the money, you see,' Tad began. 'For Xenos. They want to send him away. I won't let them.' He went over to the window. 'It might be a lot, even with that thing you get . . . ' He fiddled with the curtains.

Patrick glanced at Agnes. 'Mary just phoned,' he said.

'Did Matt leave me money?' Tad turned abruptly from the window. 'Xenos can have that.'

Patrick looked at his brother. He frowned. 'Not exactly. There will be, once we've sorted it out, there will be money for you. A trust . . . income.'

'But now?'

Patrick struggled for the words. Agnes imagined that the executors would be unlikely to entrust a lump sum to Tad.

'There'll be something, yes,' Patrick said lamely. 'Are you hungry? I've got some bread and things, somewhere.'

Agnes left them together and wandered into the kitchen. She assembled a loaf and some cheese and tomatoes on a large plate. When she came back, Tad was saying, 'But Matt said, he said there'd be money. He said he'd make sure I was looked after. He promised.'

'And you will be,' Patrick said.

Agnes cut some slices of bread and handed them round. Tad ate hungrily. From time to time he looked up. He noticed the gramophone and frowned at it. Between mouthfuls, his gaze kept returning to it. 'Dad had that,' he said at last, waving a crust of bread towards it.

'Yes,' Patrick said.

Tad shook his head. 'Never liked it,' he said.

They finished eating. Patrick stood up and addressed Agnes. 'I can probably find some money for Xenos.'

'You don't have to — ' Agnes began.

'Matt's money,' Tad interrupted.

'No, not Matt's money. It's still tied up. But I'll lend you some.'

'Your money?' Tad asked him.

'If it keeps him in the country, yes. I suppose so.'

Agnes looked around the shabby flat. She didn't think Patrick could be that well off, particularly given his gambling habits.

'Thanks.' Tad stood up, ready to go.

'I just want a word with Agnes,' Patrick said. He left the room and Agnes followed him. They stood in the hallway like conspirators. 'Charles Fielding,' Patrick said. 'Mary told me. I went across to the office to see Allen. Wasn't there.'

'What can we say to him, though?'

'Did you kill my brother? Because he wouldn't let you build this blasted centre? Or because he found out you were embezzling company funds?'

They were interrupted by music, as the gramophone in the next room seemed to spark into life and the strains of the soprano's song filled the flat. Patrick looked up, smiling. There was a loud scraping noise and the singing stopped. The smile died on Patrick's face. 'Tad?' He raced into the living room.

Tad was standing, white-faced, in the middle of the room. 'I never liked it,' he said. His voice was level but his lips were working, and he kept glancing at the gramophone.

Patrick opened the lid and took out the record. He held it towards the window. 'You've scratched it.'

'I didn't mean . . . '

'You shouldn't have done that.'

'I didn't like it. It frightens me.'

'It was Dad's.'

'I know.' Tad flashed Patrick a look of defiance.

The two men faced each other. Then Patrick shrugged. 'Oh well. No harm done,' he said. It seemed to cost him some effort.

Tad relaxed too. He turned to Agnes. 'Can we go now?'

'We'd better,' Agnes said to Patrick. 'Are you in later? I'll phone you.'

'I'm going to the university now. I'll be back this evening.'

Agnes nodded, and shepherded Tad out of the flat and down the stairs.

'Number thirty-five bus,' Tad said.

'That's right.'

'Or number twenty-six.'

'No, not twenty-six.'

'But they make the same. Two plus six . . . Three plus five.'

'Doesn't mean they go the same route.'

Tad looked up, puzzled. He shook his head. They waited at the bus stop. 'He was cross, wasn't he? Pat?'

'Why don't you like that record?'

Tad bit his lip, looking out at the traffic.

'Is it about your dad?'

Tad eyed her briefly, then returned to his study of the traffic. 'Look,' he said. 'Number two-four-two. Makes eight too.'

'Yes,' Agnes said. 'Here's our bus.'

They sat next to each other, and Tad looked out of the window. 'There was a woman,' he said, still looking outwards. 'I was little.'

Agnes stared at him.

'They played it,' he said.

'That music?'

'They played it,' he repeated. His voice was a monotone, and his eyes were fixed on the passing buildings. 'Dad and her. I got cross. I remember. Screaming. On the way home he bought me sweets. Toffees. They had raisins in.'

'Who was she?'

He was silent as the bus approached Tower

Bridge and the view opened out to the river. 'Maybe sultanas,' he said. 'Look at that boat.' He pointed out of the window.

Agnes followed his gaze. An old ship, with masts and rigging, was making its graceful way upstream.

'She wasn't my mother, you see,' Tad said.

Agnes turned to him, trying to hide the urgency in her voice. 'Tad, what was her name?'

He shook his head.

'Was her name Bridgid?'

He looked at her then, a glance sharp with recognition. He nodded. 'Bridgid,' he repeated. 'Bridgid O'Connor.' He frowned. 'Maybe they were raisins after all,' he said.

★ ★ ★

At home, Agnes dialled Patrick's number. She heard the clock of Julius's church chime seven.

He must be back, she thought, listening to the ringing. At last the phone was picked up.

'Patrick?'

'I've just got in.'

'I must talk to you. It's really urgent.'

'I need a drink.'

'The wine bar, then, at Bishopsgate. Half an hour.'

'Bridgid O'Connor,' Patrick repeated. 'Never heard of her.'

'Tad met her. When he was little. Your father played that music with her.' Patrick looked at her across the rim of his beer glass. 'And Matthias went to her funeral,' Agnes added.

Patrick sipped his beer slowly.

'And,' Agnes went on, 'Matthias told no one. Not Karen, not Mary. The only person he told seems to be Brigadier Lode.'

'Lode?' Patrick's voice was loud with surprise.

'He let slip something about him and Matthias signing papers for an old lady. Covered it up at once.'

'Why Lode?'

'I've no idea.'

'But . . . ' Patrick frowned and drank some more. 'Lode,' he said at last, shaking his head. 'So, what sense do you make of it, then?'

'I think your father had a mistress. I think he must have protected her financially in some way, and so someone had to know, to deal with it after his — after his death.'

'Matthias,' Patrick said. 'Dad always said Matt was his father's son. Matthias, you see. The twelfth apostle, to replace Judas. He was chosen by lot.'

'So, he told Matt.'

'And there was money, then. After her death.'

'And Allen was after it.'

Patrick scratched his head. 'Maybe Matt was going to set up a fund for Tad. Which would explain those odd promises, about Tad being provided for. It wasn't like Matt to make empty promises.'

'But it's not there now.'

Patrick met her eyes. 'No,' he said. 'There's no extra money in the estate. Just what was in his will. But you see' — he fiddled with a tuft of hair — 'she only died in January, didn't she? Maybe they haven't had probate yet. Maybe the money's not yet been released.'

'It explains Allen's note. Suggesting he come in on the leisure centre.'

Patrick looked up. 'Why would he know about Bridgid O'Connor?'

'He doesn't have to know about her, does he? He just has to know that Matt has some new source of money, some fund to find a home for.'

'Why would Matt have mentioned it to him?'

Agnes shrugged. 'Perhaps Allen asked him for money. He was desperate, wasn't he? You can tell by the tone of that note.'

Patrick drained his glass. 'It might explain it. Except that — except that our pa died in poverty. Our ma worked her fingers to the bone, trying to keep us after he went. There was no money in Ireland then. Not for the Irish, anyway. The idea that this lady somehow passed a fortune to Matt, some amount that Allen decided to fight over . . . '

Agnes turned her glass around in her hands. 'So,' she said after a while. 'What are we left with?'

'We know Lode knows something of Matt's affairs that no one else knows. We know that Matthias, Lode and Liz were all on the same side in this land dispute. We know that Fielding has admitted to blocking the bridle path by the golf course.'

'And that it's preying on his conscience,' Agnes added.

Patrick looked up from his glass and laughed. 'Oh, Sister, how sure you are,' he said. 'I'd be envious of your moral certainty if I thought it got you anywhere.'

'He's an ill man,' Agnes protested.

'His sins returning to haunt him,' Patrick smiled.

'Don't mock.'

'If it was true, Allen would be about to keel over as well.'

'Maybe he is.'

Patrick laughed again. 'Allen will live to ninety. The devil looks after his own,' he said. He glanced across the room. 'Oh — now, see, I've summoned him. He really is some kind of sprite. There he is.'

At the same moment, Allen seemed to see them. Agnes saw him hesitate, before he smiled a warm smile and came towards them.

'Well well well.' Allen's voice boomed across the table. 'Mind if I join you?'

'Not at all.' Patrick moved up on the bench to make room.

'Another drink, everyone? More of the same?' He launched himself off towards the bar again.

'Well well well,' Patrick muttered. Agnes laughed. 'Shall we challenge him now?' Patrick asked her.

'Anything could happen.' Agnes watched Allen waiting by the bar, feeling increasingly uneasy as he turned back towards their table.

'So, how's things?' Allen distributed drinks between them.

'How are you?' Patrick countered. 'How's business?'

'Booming, dear boy. The safer the world, the more people fear the future. More private pension funds, more assets for us. In fact' — he laughed, turning to Agnes — 'you and I, we're in the same game, aren't we? Offering people insurance policies against their death. It's just yours deals with the hereafter.'

Agnes allowed her smile to fade. 'It's not a deal,' she said.

'Of course it is. And you people, you can't lose, can you? Because by the time your customers have popped their clogs and gone into the void, it's too late.'

'Too late for what?'

He laughed again. 'What I mean is, my punters expect a return on their money. But your punter is six feet under before they find that your lot have defrauded them.'

'How true that is,' Agnes said, quietly.

Patrick glanced at her. 'I take it you don't believe in an afterlife, then?' he said to Allen.

Allen laughed. 'None at all. Why should there be?'

'In that case' — Agnes kept her tone light — 'my punters can't possibly know they've been defrauded. They can't know anything at all, being non-existent. Whereas your punters, should anything go wrong with their money, know all too well. So at least I'm not doing any harm, am I?'

'Ho, ho, *touché*,' Allen said. He studied her for a moment, and Agnes looked away.

'Don't you believe anything at all?' Patrick asked him.

'What, religion? It's all just chemical

reactions in the brain,' Allen replied. 'Every-one knows that.'

Patrick laughed, loudly, but Allen didn't seem to notice.

'Religious experience,' Allen went on. 'They've done tests, haven't they? On people like you,' he said, turning to Agnes. 'Your brains are just wired differently; they light up in different places. Neurals or something. They'll make a drug for it soon.'

'A faith drug?' Agnes asked. 'How very helpful.'

'A cure, I meant.' He laughed.

Agnes watched him as he gulped his lager.

'So you don't believe . . . ' Patrick spoke carefully. 'You don't believe that if people do something wrong in this life — really wrong — their actions come back to them in some way?'

'If only things were so easy. I can think of one or two people who ought to see their actions come back to haunt them.'

'Who?' Agnes felt Patrick's attention quicken next to her.

'Perfidious wenches,' Allen said. 'And their paramours.'

Agnes smiled, gently, deliberately. 'You can't mean Judy, surely?'

'She's a cow,' Allen said. 'I thought she was class, and here she is, a two-timing bitch like the worst kind of bimbo.'

'I'm sorry to hear that.' Agnes glanced at Patrick, who hid a smile behind his glass.

'Running off with golden boy,' Allen said, between gulps of beer. 'They reckon they're going to the States, you know? Good riddance, I say, he's welcome to her. She'll dump him when someone richer comes along.'

'She mentioned ranches to me,' Agnes said.

Allen looked at her. 'Ranches?'

'Horses, staff, you know.' Agnes watched him.

Allen's features tightened. His mouth was a thin line. 'If he thinks the Seattle office can make him rich . . . He's backing a loser, you see. I'd have made her richer than her wildest dreams.'

'Would you?' Agnes asked him.

'Oh yes. My plans are big. Ranches indeed. Horses. She can barely ride, silly cow. She'd have had an empire of her own if she'd stayed with me.'

'Oh well.' Patrick broke his silence. 'I'm so glad your business ventures are doing so well.'

There was a brief silence. 'Another drink?' Patrick said, eyeing Allen.

Allen watched Patrick go to the bar. He was quiet, turning his empty glass around in his hands. 'I should have known,' he said. 'I

401

should've seen the warning signs. Faithless bitch.'

'I thought you didn't rate faith anyway.'

'What?' He looked up, confused. 'Oh, that. That's different. Religion. That's not the same as being — being true to yourself.'

'Oh. Right.' Agnes nodded sympathetically.

Patrick returned with their drinks.

Allen sighed. 'He's my boy, you see. I brought him into the company, knew he'd go far. I know ambition when I see it.' He started on his next pint. 'And then he nicks my bird. You don't do that, see.'

'Maybe it won't last,' Agnes said carefully.

'Maybe it won't.'

'Ranches or no, maybe she'll come back to London.'

Allen sighed. 'Maybe,' he said. 'But if I'm honest . . . if I'm honest, that's it for me. I've seen through her.' He drank some more.

'And how is the leisure centre?' Patrick asked lightly.

Allen smiled. 'We'll show them.'

'I gather the land dispute is settled now.'

Allen's eyes narrowed. 'Yes,' he said, watching Patrick. 'We decided to bow out gracefully. Worked out a way of positioning the tennis courts without the extra field. To be honest, we were fed up with having local opinion against us. Me and Gough painted as the villains of the piece, when there we are bringing employment and facilities to the area.'

'There've been rumours.' Agnes spoke quietly.

He flashed her a look. 'Yes,' he said.

'Of bridle paths being blocked. On purpose.'

He was still watching her.

'By the golf course,' she added.

'You play golf, don't you, Allen?' Patrick said, vaguely.

Allen put down his glass, looking from one to the other. 'Is this poor old Fielding who's been talking?'

'Yes,' Agnes said. 'Poor old Fielding. He does seem to be suffering, don't you think? Almost as if his past actions have come back to haunt him.'

Now she watched him. He was biting his lip, and he dropped his gaze from hers and stared fixedly at the table. He sighed. 'Poor Charles. I've told him to go back to the quack. It's his heart, it runs in the family, but they have drugs for it these days, don't they?' He stood up. 'Another drink?' He'd regained his easy affability.

Patrick glanced at Agnes. 'We should get going.'

'Well, if you're sure. I'll come with you.'

Allen pulled his coat on and led the way from the bar. The cold night glittered with light, from the streetlamps, the windows of the office blocks, the floodlights of building sites. 'Well.' He waved his arm. 'Nice talking to you.'

'You too.' Patrick gestured in the other direction. 'We're — um — going this way.'

'Sure . . . See you.' Allen waved again and set off along the main road towards Moorgate. They watched him go.

'What do you make of that?' Patrick turned to Agnes.

'We didn't ask him about the money transfers.'

'No. I didn't want to make it obvious.'

They set off along the street, turning off towards Patrick's flat. 'Agnes?' He took her arm. 'We are right, aren't we? We are right to say that Matthias and Liz were killed on purpose? I've been thinking about this, about our reasons to believe that there was some kind of order in it all, not just chaos. For me it's all about Dad, and for you it's all about Julius. And so then I thought, Perhaps we're wrong, just following this because of our own stuff . . . '

Agnes was silent. They left the lights and bustle of the City behind them, turning down a dimly lit winding street behind Spitalfields.

404

A voice from a doorway asked them for money, and there was a chink of metal as Patrick handed over some coins.

'And all that money swishing about in Allen's office,' Patrick said, suddenly. 'One minute I'm trying to persuade my brother that he can't live underneath an arch on a mud bank, and the next I'm looking at seven-figure numbers rolling by under my nose, surrounded by people who earn enough in a day to keep my brother for a year . . . Now where did I put my keys?' He stopped, fishing in his pockets. 'That's why I'm here,' he said. He pulled out a small packet of sugar labelled with a café's logo, and stared at it. 'With you, I mean. Following this trail of yours that started with Matt's death.' He put the sugar carefully back in his pocket. 'That's why I'm here with you instead of being safely tucked away in my flat.'

'Is it my fault?'

He felt in another pocket and there was a jingle of metal. 'Ah, here they are. No, it's not your fault. It's my father's fault. The reason I decided to join you in your unlikely beliefs about Matt's death is that no one in our family can afford to leave anything to chance again. Or what's left of our family, anyway. Damn, those are my office keys.' He stuffed them back in his pocket and continued to fumble among his layers of clothes. 'You see, Matthias always said he knew what Dad intended to do, before he did it. Matt felt it very badly, Dad's death, and he was only a child. He felt he was to blame. He felt he could have prevented it, could have warned someone. They were close, you see, Dad confided in him, although he was only a kid. Which explains this Bridgid business. And now there's Tad, reliving the whole damn thing; it's the randomness of it that he can't bear. He saw Dad's death, running towards the car, shouting . . . ' His words tailed off, and he stood, staring unseeing into the distance. 'I have to rescue him,' he said, his gaze returning to Agnes. 'I have to bring order back into his life.' He put his hand in his coat pocket and drew out a set of keys. He looked at them in surprise. 'Here they are.'

'Patrick.' Agnes took hold of his arm again. 'Julius — do you think he did the wrong thing?'

'Becoming a priest, you mean?'

'Leaving her.'

Patrick stared into the distance. 'At the time, I thought he was mad. You should have seen them together. In her presence he was just — lit up. Alive. It did you good to see it. And those brothers, in the seminary . . . terrible people, some of them. They'd have

406

worked on him, you see, telling him that women are the work of the devil . . . ' His gaze returned to her. 'But Julius is strong, isn't he? He has that inner voice. I think he had it then. What can we know about someone else's life? Their regrets? Maybe he did the wrong thing, maybe not.'

'What was her name?'

'Catriona.'

'Patrick?'

He looked down at her.

'Mary has the same colour eyes as him.' The words came out in a rush.

'Agnes — I can't — don't ask me — '

'He won't talk to me. I can't bear it.' Tears pricked her eyes.

Patrick sighed. 'No one knows. Catriona met a man called Jack. Mary was born — after the wedding. Respectably, if you see what I mean. No one else knew about Julius. He'd gone to France. We all — we all chose to forget.' He looked away, focusing on some long-ago time. 'No one knows,' he said.

She turned her face up to him. 'I can't ask him.'

Patrick met her eyes. 'No,' he agreed. 'And would Mary thank you if you did?'

Agnes held his gaze for a moment, then shook her head.

'Well, then,' Patrick said. He bent and

kissed her on the cheek. 'It's been an interesting evening.'

'It certainly has. What do we do next?'

'I think we talk to Lode. I need to ask him about this Bridgid woman, for a start. And maybe we should go back to Charles too. I'll talk to Mary.'

'We'll speak — tomorrow?'

'Tomorrow,' he agreed. She squeezed his arm, and headed back to the station. It felt late. She checked in her pocket for some change, and decided to afford a taxi.

She hurried up to her flat, and stood, in her coat, in the darkness of the room. Her intercom buzzed loudly. She blinked at it, went over to it and answered it.

'Hello?'

'It's Judy. I've got to talk to you. Can I come up?'

22

Judy looked around her at the sparse simplicity of Agnes's tiny flat. She stood in the middle of the room, ill at ease in spite of her poise and elegance, her long grey coat and high-heeled shoes.

'Do sit down,' Agnes offered, and Judy perched on the edge of the chair at Agnes's desk.

Agnes switched on lights. 'A drink? Wine? Whisky?'

Judy shook her head.

'So?' Agnes tried. 'What's happened?'

'It's Jed. I think he fully intends not going to the Seattle office with me after all. And he won't tell me straight out. And I don't want to go there on my own. And it's all bloody Allen's fault.'

'Allen?'

'Yes. Jed won't let on 'cos these boys are so loyal to each other, aren't they, but I'm sure Allen's screwed things up for the Seattle project. And I need to see Patrick.'

'Patrick?'

She nodded. 'I think Patrick ended up with the papers that actually prove what Allen's doing. 'Cos Allen's all chipper now, about the leisure centre, when two weeks ago it had all stalled, and it had no money. I checked Allen's e-mail, he told me his password once, and there's money going from his funds to Seattle, and it all looks a bit odd. All I know is, Jed said he didn't want to involve himself in something that wasn't — wasn't clean, as he put it. And that's all he'd say.'

'Hmmm.' Agnes listened sympathetically.

'It's not fair.' Judy smoothed the folds of her coat on her knees. 'I thought Jed was too good to be true.'

'And what about this trust fund?' Agnes kept her voice light. 'The one you were asking about?'

Judy looked up. She bit her lip, frowning, 'Oh,' she said, 'that was just silly old Allen, trying to get me to find something out. From Patrick.'

'And did you?'

She shook her head. 'These boys with their secrets. I give up, you know.'

The phone rang and Agnes snatched it up. 'It's Julius.'

Agnes sat down in surprise. 'Julius?'

He said something inaudible.

'I can hardly hear you.' Agnes struggled to make out his voice above some kind of uproar in the background.

410

'Police outside . . . threatening to storm the church . . . phoned you to marshal support. And Patrick for Tad . . . terrible state, as you can imagine — '

'I'll be right there.'

'Tell Patrick.' Julius was shouting.

'Yes. OK.' She shouted back. The line went dead.

She dialled Patrick's number. Judy sat quietly, watching her. As usual, he took ages to answer. His voice sounded sleepy. 'Hello?'

'Me again,' Agnes said. 'The police. They're gathering outside Julius's church. Tad's there. And Xenos, of course.'

Patrick made a groaning noise. 'I was afraid of this. I'll see you there, I suppose.'

He hung up. Agnes grabbed her coat and keys. 'Come on,' she said to Judy, 'if you want to see Patrick.'

They ran down the stairs and set out through the darkness of the streets.

'Where — I mean, what's — ' Judy struggled to keep up.

'You don't have to come,' Agnes shouted over her shoulder. 'They're evicting an illegal immigrant from the church.'

A drizzle had started, and Judy pulled her fur collar around her face. She seemed to have decided to stay with Agnes.

They reached the church. Two large white

police vans were parked on the drive, and several officers were poised by the main doorway. Agnes grabbed Judy's arm, skirted the fence and ran to the side door. Two policemen were standing there awkwardly, dwarfed by the overgrown rhododendrons. One of them called out to them.

'We have to warn you, ladies — if you go in there, you'll be placing yourselves in danger of arrest.'

'Yeah, yeah,' a voice said wearily from the darkness by the door, and Agnes realised it was Patrick.

'I've had the same warning,' Patrick said as Agnes went up to him. 'Helen's going to let us in,' Patrick whispered. He noticed Judy and grinned at her.

The door opened a crack, and Agnes saw Helen peering out. She let them in, and bolted the door behind them. They stood in the darkness of the vestry.

'What's going on?' Judy sounded petulant.

'Ssshhh.' Patrick didn't move.

'I hope this isn't dangerous — ' she began again.

'Where's Julius?' Agnes interrupted her.

'He's up there,' Helen said. 'He's trying to keep Xenos calm. He went into a very weird state as soon as he saw the police.'

'It's the worst thing that could happen.'

412

'We've called our lawyer. He's on his way.'
'And Tad?'
Helen sighed.
Agnes heard shouting, a man's voice, increasingly loud. Patrick led the way up the stairs into the church.
'... They can't do this!' they heard. Tad was pacing the church, his arms flapping at his sides. Patrick went to him.
'Look, what is this?' Judy stood in the church, her hands on her hips. Agnes half expected her to stamp her foot.
'You wanted to see Patrick,' Agnes said.
'I've always stayed on the right side of the law before,' Judy said.
'In that case, I should leave now.' It was Julius, who'd been standing so quietly they hadn't seen him. He smiled at Judy.
Xenos was crouched on his sleeping bag, rocking backwards and forwards, his eyes staring ahead of him. Helen went to him and took his hand, but he seemed not to see her.
Patrick had calmed Tad down but now there was renewed noise as the police started shouting outside the door.
'Ignatius, you'll either have to let them in or they'll break down the door,' Patrick said.
Helen stood up. 'I think we should open the door. It'll be less traumatic for Xenos.'
She and Julius went to the door. A few

413

seconds later the church filled with police. Colin was with them, and Helen went to him. Julius was arguing with a uniformed officer who seemed to be in charge.

Then, somehow, it was over. Xenos was dragged away. He'd covered his face with his hands, and was making an odd moaning noise. Tad was fighting the officers who held him, until he too was overpowered and bundled into the van outside. Helen and their lawyer jumped into his car, ready to follow the police vans. With a screech of wheels, the police left.

A heavy silence fell. Julius surveyed his church, rubbing his arm. The chairs at the back were overturned. The bookstall was lying on its side, and books and leaflets were strewn across the flagstones. Xenos's sleeping bag was draped where it had landed, across the back pews. Agnes went over to it and gathered it up.

'It could be worse,' Julius said. 'In the old days they used to set fire to churches.'

Patrick began to gather up the books. 'What will they do to them?' He spoke softly, almost to himself. 'No sooner does Tad find something of value than it's taken from him.'

'They'll let him go, won't they?' Julius stooped to help him.

Patrick sighed. 'It won't be the first time

he's been in police cells. It just depends whether he can control his temper.'

'And Xenos?' Agnes picked up a chair.

Patrick and Julius looked up. No one spoke. For a moment, there was silence.

Judy was cowering in one corner, curled into a pew. Now she uncurled herself and came over to them. 'Well,' she said, dusting down her coat. 'If I'd known that calling on Agnes would embroil me in a situation like that, nearly getting arrested for God's sake . . . Downright dangerous, if you ask me.'

Agnes looked at her. Her hair hung in a perfect bob against her face; her lipstick was immaculate.

'Dear me,' Julius said. 'Calling on Agnes is always a dangerous thing to do. Didn't anyone warn you?'

Patrick laughed.

Judy pouted. 'And it was only because I wanted to talk to you,' she said to him.

'I was a trifle busy,' Patrick replied, still smiling.

'Well, you're not now.'

Patrick looked at Julius. Julius smiled at him. 'If they come back for anyone, it'll only be me.'

'You really want to talk now?' Patrick looked at Judy uncertainly.

She nodded. 'There must be a bar somewhere?'

'Patrick knows them all,' Julius said.

Patrick hesitated, then left with Judy. The church door was wide open and Julius closed it and locked it behind them.

Agnes sat down.

'You look terrible,' Julius said.

'Thanks.' She looked up at him. He smiled, briefly, a flash of the old Julius in his blue eyes, then looked away. 'What'll become of him?' Agnes said. She touched Xenos's sleeping bag.

Julius watched her. He sighed, then bent to pick up a book, and in the hunch of the movement he looked suddenly old. Agnes wanted to go to him, to hold him in her arms. He straightened up and looked at her. 'Tea?' he said.

They settled down in his office. He switched on the bar fire and his desk lamp, and went to put on the kettle. Agnes sat in one of his shabby red velvet chairs. She was aware that her hands were shaking, and she held one out to look at it. 'Adrenalin,' she said.

In silence Julius warmed the pot, spooned out tea leaves, arranged mugs. 'It's like your Louise,' he said suddenly. 'Being certain. That's how I was. Knowing what God wanted

416

of me. Being so sure of the holy fire . . . Did I get the milk out? Oh, yes, there it is.' He poured two mugs of tea and handed her one, then sat down opposite her. 'And I was wrong, you see. Terribly, terribly wrong.' His face was shadowed by the light from the anglepoise.

A car passed by, a low rumble in the dead silence of the night. Julius spoke again. 'Mary said her mother — ' He struggled, biting his lip. 'She said her mother never forgot me. And, you see, I never forgot her.'

Agnes held her mug between her hands, glad of its warmth.

'I can see now' — Julius stared at his hands in his lap — 'that I was wrong. The only woman I ever loved — and I was so sure, so certain of God's will . . . '

She wanted to reach out to him, but he seemed not to see her. 'I prayed,' he went on, 'and my prayers were answered, and what I didn't realise then was that the Lord was giving me a choice. I thought it was all about obedience. I was surrounded by men who saw it that way, and who believed that spurning women was the path of righteousness . . . And what was in fact a choice, I saw as an order. A divine command. And I was so clear, so fired up with my spiritual certainties, that I wrote to her . . . ' He rested his face in his hands. 'I was wrong,' he said suddenly, taking his hands from his face. 'All my spiritual fire, all my certainties, they were as nothing to her love. Seeing Mary again . . . ' His voice broke. 'Mary was being kind to me. She knows how her mother suffered. Because of . . . because of me.'

Julius sat silently, his face shadowed by the low light from his desk lamp. After a while he said, 'When I met you, in France . . . that was why. They sent me away.'

'To get over it?'

Julius stared at his hands again; now they lay flat on the desk.

'But when I met you you were so serene.'

He shook his head.

'You were like a rock for me then,' she said.

'It's just that you were in such terrible anguish, you couldn't see beyond it.'

'And there you were, suffering too. And we never even talked about it.'

'There was nothing to say.'

Agnes got up and went to the window. 'What will you do?' she said.

'What can I do?' His voice was flat. 'I'm an old man, full of regret. She is my truth,' he said.

'But God is your truth too.'

'God is love, Agnes. All I learned about God, I learned from her.'

418

Agnes stared out into the darkness. 'But doesn't God's love transcend human love?'

'I used to think that. But now I think it's the other way round. It's only through being able to love, through this great gift of human love that we can glimpse what the Creation might be. When I saw Mary at Matt's funeral, it was as if my whole world shifted on its axis.' His hand went to the crucifix at his neck, turning it on its chain. 'And as for — for us, I owe you an apology,' he said.

She shook her head, blinking back tears.

'You were the last person I could speak to,' he went on. 'Every time I looked at you, I saw someone who — who believed in me. Every time I looked at you, I saw how I'd betrayed you. You of all people . . . ' His voice shook.

Agnes sat down again. After a while she said, 'Julius, I'm an orphan now. I'm old enough. I don't need you to be something that you're not. I've seen you in pain; I've seen you turning away from me. I don't ever want us to — to go through that again.'

He leaned towards her and took her hand. The blackness of the window was softening with the dawn.

'Mary has your eyes,' Agnes said.

He looked at her. 'Mary has a father,' he said. 'Jack. Catriona's — husband.'

The image of Mary hung in the air between

them. They both fell silent, as the first birdsong punctured the night outside.

★ ★ ★

It was some time later when Agnes arrived home, yawning, in the fresh new light of the day. The streets were still deserted. Someone was slouched cold and stiff in the doorway. As she approached she could see it was a woman. She saw Agnes and got to her feet. It was Louise. She looked terrible, her face pinched with cold, her eyes red-rimmed. She stumbled towards Agnes.

'He died,' she said. 'Richard . . . ' She burst into tears, and Agnes put her arm around her and led her upstairs into the warmth of her flat. Louise sat motionless on the chair by her desk. Agnes went yawning into her kitchen, wondering how many more cups of tea she was going to have to drink before she could go to bed. She put on the kettle, wondering how Patrick had fared with Judy; wondering what Judy wanted to see him about. The kettle came to the boil. A thought flashed through her mind, an image of Xenos's sleeping bag, draped across the pews.

She put on a fan-heater and placed it next to Louise, and handed her a mug of tea.

She pulled up a chair next to her. 'When?' she said.

Louise looked confused. 'I came from the hospice,' she said. 'I sat with him . . . afterwards . . . ' She raised anguished eyes to Agnes. 'I've never seen anyone I know dead before.' She picked up her mug of tea and looked at it. 'And then Sarah asked me to go. She wanted to be alone with him. It was yesterday sometime, evening. It was dark. I left then, and I came here and sat on your doorstep. I thought you'd be here.'

'I'm sorry,' Agnes said, but Louise didn't seem to hear her.

'Sarah was cross with me,' Louise said. 'She said I should leave them in peace.' She looked at Agnes. 'I know why she was cross. Because I let them down. I promised . . . I promised him . . . I prayed, Agnes, all these nights I've stayed up praying, I asked God to save him . . . I thought he would.' Her voice faltered, but her eyes were dry. Agnes saw the colour return to her cheeks as she sipped her tea. 'How can you have faith?' she began. 'How can you if this is what happens? How can anyone . . . I saw it in Sarah's eyes, when she looked at me, it was as if I'd betrayed him — betrayed them both.' She shook her head.

In the silence, Agnes could hear only the quiet tick of her mother's clock. She spoke

421

quietly. 'Sometimes, maybe, all that's left is to accept.' An image came to her of Julius, sitting at his desk in the soft grey light of the dawn.

'No,' Louise said. 'What sort of faith is that? All this Lent, I've hardly slept, I've eaten as little as possible, I've been really good — and I've offered it all to God. And for what? For God to take him away from me?'

'Perhaps there's a lesson — '

Louise was angry now. 'When I told Peter, our curate, that I wanted to be a nun, he was so pleased. He said I was doing the right thing, I was doing what God wanted. He even kissed me. And so I told my parents. My dad was cross — I was glad he was cross, he's never understood anything about my life, anything at all . . . And my mum said it was up to me, but that's just because she was too busy with the twins, they're ten years younger than me . . . ' She drank some more tea. 'And I came here. And I met Richard, and I knew then that God was working within me . . . And it turns out it's all been for nothing. I thought God would prove my dad wrong, but now it's Dad who's right, and that's what I can't bear . . . '

'What did he say, your father?'

'He said I'd soon find out that there's no point relying on God.'

'You can still prove him wrong,' Agnes said.

'How?'

'By believing. By having faith. By letting Richard go.'

'Why should I? What sort of God is that, that asks me to accept that Richard should have died?' She gave a sob. 'I still can't believe it, Agnes. And Sarah said such a horrible thing, I know she was upset, but even so, to suggest that I was being selfish in crying for him . . . She said she wanted him to die in peace. And I just thought, I must love him more than she does, 'cos I was the one who was trying to keep him alive, wasn't I, Agnes, and she just seemed to get to this point where she was prepared to let him go . . . ' She raised her eyes to Agnes. 'She said, if I believed in Heaven, then I shouldn't mind him going there.'

Agnes looked at her, unable to think of anything to say.

'And she isn't even a Christian,' Louise went on. 'Or anything. So it's a strange thing for her to say, isn't it? I don't think she likes me very much.'

Agnes stood up and rested her hand on Louise's shoulder. 'You should get some rest,' she said. 'I'll see you at the house, later.'

'I can't face the house,' Louise said.

'Stay in your room.'

'I can't face chapel.'

'You don't have to go to chapel.'

'Jesus says that he'll answer our prayers, that God loves us as a father. Well, he's wrong, isn't he? That's why I can't go to chapel any more.'

'I'll let them know you're unwell. Keep to your room, get some sleep. I'll see you soon. Here, here's the money for a taxi.'

Louise took the money. She stood up, docile, and allowed Agnes to show her out.

It was a sunny morning. Agnes yawned, undressed, got into bed and fell into a deep sleep.

Some time later the phone rang. She reached out an arm and picked it up.

'Agnes, it's Mary.'

Agnes wondered what day it was. She blinked at the sun that still poured through her windows.

'Something's happened,' Mary said. 'It's very odd. Charles. Charles Fielding. He's dead.'

23

Stewart Lode was pacing up and down in his living room. 'Can't make sense of it at all,' he said. 'Said he wanted to see me, phoned me yesterday. I thought at first it was about the clock, but it was late at night . . . ' He glanced at Agnes, who was sitting, yawning, in one of his chintz armchairs. She'd had two hours' sleep between seeing Louise out and Mary phoning, and it felt like it. 'D'you think that girl can manage in my kitchen?'

As if in answer, Mary reappeared with a tray of coffee things. 'Stewart, do sit down, for heaven's sake,' she said.

'Can't make sense of it at all,' he said again, turning away from the window and pacing again.

'You've had a shock,' Mary said. She poured him some coffee. Gently she took his arm and helped him into a chair, and handed him the mug.

'Found him, y'see,' he said to Agnes. 'Went over there, couldn't get in. No answer, dogs going berserk indoors, looked through the window. There he was, collapsed in a chair. Broke the door down. Had the ambulance there, police, whole crowd of them.'

'They reckon it was a huge heart attack,' Mary said.

'They can reckon what they like.' Stewart stirred some sugar into his cup. 'The man phones me up, last night, bit of a state, can I come over? He's got something to tell me, can't say it over the phone. And then he's dead. They can tell me it's a heart attack, but we've had bricks thrown at that poor girl, and golf balls and all sorts . . . If you ask me, these townies coming here and trying to buy our land and change our rules, it turns things upside down, it does. Lets out all sorts of forces, makes people behave in extreme ways . . .'

'Have you talked to Patrick?' Agnes asked Mary.

'He's on his way, I phoned him too. He said he'd talked to Judy.'

'Would it be all right if I used your phone?' Agnes asked him.

She went out into the hall and dialled the order's main house. She was relieved to be put through to Madeleine.

'What is going on?' Madeleine's voice had its customary calm.

'I don't know where to start. You heard about the eviction?'

'Yes. Helen's phoned. Tad's been charged

426

with affray or something, Xenos is suicidal, Helen's still at the police station. And Louise came back here this morning, monosyllabic, said she was ill. No one's seen her since, she's in her room.'

'Two novices, one's in total crisis, the other's in the nick. I can't see they'll make me novice mistress again, can you?'

Madeleine laughed. 'And where are you?'

'Essex. Someone's been found dead. It's all rather complicated . . . '

'It always is. Still, at least Julius is talking to us all again. I imagine you're responsible for that as well.'

Agnes smiled. 'I'll speak to you soon.'

As she put the phone down, Patrick appeared at Stewart's door. Agnes let him in. 'You look as tired as I feel,' she said to him.

He took her hands in his. 'Has the world gone mad?'

'It seems so,' she said.

He went through to the lounge. Mary greeted him, and he hugged her briefly.

'Another one,' Stewart said to him. 'Fielding chap.'

'So I heard.'

'A heart attack,' Mary said. 'They think.'

Stewart made a harrumphing noise.

Patrick flung himself wearily into a chair. 'I gather he wanted to tell you something.'

Lode sat down next to him. 'Aye.' He nodded. 'I'll never know now.'

Patrick looked at Mary, then at Agnes. 'We're no further on, are we?' He sighed.

'What did Judy want?' Agnes asked. 'Last night, when she insisted on braving an eviction at Julius's church, just to talk to you?'

'She wanted Matt's papers. The ones that prove that Allen was sending money into a private account via Seattle.' He passed his hand across his brow. 'She holds him responsible for her losing Jed, I think.'

'Revenge, then?'

'Maybe. And maybe a sense of fair play too. She's quite a moral person. Keen on marriage, for example.'

Agnes caught Mary's eye. Despite their exhaustion, they both smiled.

'So,' Agnes said. 'It wasn't just the papers, then, that she was after.'

Patrick met her gaze wearily. 'No. Probably not. You women talk in code. I don't know what it was I was expected to do, but she's arranged to come round to my flat to get the papers.'

'No, not your flat.' Agnes smiled. 'If she sets eyes on your flat, that's the end of your chances.'

'All the better then.' Patrick smiled back.

'Oh, and she was still going on about a trust fund. In fact' — he turned to Lode — 'for some reason, she thought that you'd know about it.'

Stewart coloured slightly, and stared at the floor. 'Me?' His voice was gruff. 'Can't think why.'

'What's that?' Agnes pointed to an antique silver object lying on the table by the window.

'What?' Stewart looked up. 'Oh, that. Found it on Fielding, last night. He had it on his lap. Thought — thought it must have been meant for me, as I'd shown an interest in it. Wasn't thinking straight, now I come to think of it, finding him dead like that . . . Anyway, brought it home.'

'What is it?' Agnes went and picked it up. It was about a foot long, tarnished, ornately decorated.

'Miniature. Cannon. Early nineteenth century, he thought it was.'

'Does it work?'

Lode shook his head. 'It might have done once — '

'This trust fund,' Patrick interrupted. 'This money of Matt's that everyone's going on about . . . '

Lode was silent.

'Why didn't he tell me?' Patrick asked. 'If

there's extra money? And why isn't it in the will — ?'

Mary interrupted. She addressed Lode. 'That time, in the hotel, when you found us — '

'Coincidence.' Lode stood up.

'You were both signing something.' Mary was staring at Lode now.

'What is this about, Stewart?' Patrick got to his feet.

Lode was standing by the window, leaning on the table there. 'It's being taken care of.' He clearly found it an effort to keep his voice level. 'It's for Tad.'

Patrick was almost shouting. 'Stewart, none of this makes sense. I'm the executor, there's already a fund for Tad, not a great deal, but I'm supposed to be in charge of it. Surely I should know if there's more money!'

'He didn't expect to die so soon.' Lode spoke quietly. He took out his handkerchief and mopped his face.

'You have it?' Patrick stared, incredulous, at Lode.

Stewart didn't answer. It was Agnes who broke the silence. 'I don't think it's fair to cross-examine Stewart. Not when we have a murder weapon sitting on the table there.'

They all looked at her, then at the table. Then at the cannon where it lay on the table.

'He was holding it.' Lode was staring at it, transfixed. 'He said he had something to tell me . . . '

'How big are the cannon balls it would fire?' Agnes was aware of her heart thumping much too fast.

'Well,' Lode said, 'assuming it worked, about this size, I suppose.' The colour drained from his face. 'About the size of — golf balls.'

Patrick was standing by the window. He turned, illuminated by the afternoon sun. 'So, you block the path. The horse stops. You fire — that — at it. At close range. It works. So, next time, you fire it at — at the rider. At the part of the skull, just above the ear. You leave the golf ball as it lands.'

'Terrible noise,' Lode said. 'Firing something of that density. You'd be heard.'

'They were shooting, though, weren't they?' Mary said. 'Nick Caddy, he'd rented out the old hunting lodge, hadn't he? He'd opened up the grouse wood for tourists last month.'

'You're right.' Lode went to pick the cannon up, but stopped himself. 'Guns going off at all hours. Frightened the dogs.'

'And then . . . ' Patrick was talking as if to himself. 'And then when you're frightened that Liz is going to let on, because she's seen you, holding — '

'It must have been that,' Mary said, pointing to the cannon. 'She remembered him holding something.'

'You follow her route back to London. Deserted minor road . . . and you check out the bridges . . . ' Patrick sat down in a chair and passed his hand across his face.

'It's still leaving an awful lot to chance,' Lode said.

'That's just the point,' Patrick said tiredly. 'That's exactly the point.'

'And Charles?' Mary was sitting next to Patrick.

They all looked at each other. 'Charles,' Lode said.

They sat in silence. After a while Patrick said, 'Even if we tell the police . . . '

'No.' Lode was emphatic. 'Don't you see? Because Charles is dead. If we go to the police now, they'll think it's over. And the local bobby'll have us down as gibbering idiots if we try and say that Fielding's death is suspicious.'

Patrick frowned, then nodded in agreement.

'So, you mean' — Mary was staring at the cannon on the table — 'we still need to get — '

'The whole story,' Lode said.

Agnes felt suddenly exhausted. She was

aware of random images flashing across her mind, almost as if she was dreaming; of the corridor, again. Of the golf course, the trees, the bridle way. And a funeral . . . a graveyard, the gaping earth.

'Well . . . ' Patrick stood up.

'Do you want a lift back to London?' Agnes asked Patrick.

He nodded. 'Thanks. Back to Tad in trouble with the law again.' He sighed. 'And I've got a departmental meeting at four.'

'We might just do it.' Agnes picked up her coat and went out to the car. She waved to Mary as Patrick joined her and they set off down the bumpy drive.

'Are we absolutely mad?' Patrick asked as they joined the main road heading for the M25. 'We think Liz really saw Charles standing on the bridle path, holding a miniature cannon which could fire golf balls at close range?'

'No. We know she did. She told us she did.'

Patrick turned to stare out of the window, blinking against the pink light; the sun was low in the sky. 'And,' he said, after a while, 'Judy really thinks there's some other money somewhere. And Lode wasn't telling me all he knew.'

'No,' Agnes agreed.

'Jed clearly isn't interested in her.' Patrick

yawned. 'Even I can tell that.'

Agnes joined the motorway and pulled out into the middle lane.

'Do you know what seems very odd to me?' Patrick said suddenly. 'Always has done. That note to Mary that they found on him. Who did he think was going to pass that to her? I mean, why carry a note like that, unless you were meeting someone who knew her. And you see, in that community, no one knew about him and Mary. Only Liz — or maybe Liz's friends too, those anti-hunt people. There are very few people he'd be able to entrust with a note for Mary.'

'He might have thought they wouldn't read it.'

'In a village like that? He'd know better than that.' Patrick yawned again. 'So, what do we think?'

'We know that Liz saw Charles on the path where she fell,' Agnes said. 'Holding that cannon thing.'

'We know that Charles had a grudge against Matt. We know he possessed a weapon that seems to fit in entirely with the way Matt died.' Patrick glanced at her. 'And Liz?'

'He was at the stables, when she recognised him. He'd need her out of the way.'

'So he tracks her route home, and throws a

434

rock from a bridge.' He gazed out of the window, frowning. 'And then he dies,' Patrick said. 'Of remorse.'

'I thought you didn't share my moral certainties.'

'Just this once, perhaps.' He smiled.

Agnes frowned. 'Does it really explain Liz's death? The idea of Charles creeping across road bridges, waiting for her car . . . '

Patrick sighed. 'Perhaps that actually was just chance. Maybe it was nothing to do with anything.'

The traffic was thickening as they reached the outskirts of London. Agnes was aware of her mind wandering. She thought of Liz, driving home that night. Something about this reminded her of Deborah, prodding Allen in the chest, asking him to talk to the golf club about their fence.

Liz, she thought. Driving home. Why should that remind her of Deborah? She remembered Deborah saying that Allen had been too busy trying to help Judy into his flash new car to listen to any suggestions about the golf club fence.

'Liz,' Agnes said, trying to concentrate her mind. 'A mistake. Just one of those things. In which case,' she added, 'it's all over.'

He stared out of the window. 'Yes,' he said. 'All over. End of story.'

But no, Agnes thought. Not the end of the story at all. Allen drove back with Judy that evening. The evening that Liz died.

She pulled into the left-hand lane, slowing behind a lorry. Again, a thought stirred at the edge of her vision, like the sun which glanced off the corner of her mirror in a dazzle of pink as they headed south.

She dropped Patrick off and finally parked the car outside her block of flats. She let herself in and listened to the messages on her answering machine.

'Hi, it's Helen. The bad news is they're sending Xenos to a detention centre. The good news is we may be a step forward with his asylum claim, thanks to the Refugee Information people. But of course, he's silent again, which doesn't help. Tad has calmed down now. They might bail him. Can you ask Patrick to get in touch?'

'Hello, it's Madeleine. Louise has taken to her room and won't come out. How many meals does she miss before we worry?'

'Sweetie, it's me. Everything's terrible. I've parcelled up all my clothes for you, even the red suit, if it fits you, I'm sure it will. I'm only wearing black from now on. The colour's gone out of my world . . . ' There was a loud sniffing, then the message ended.

She dialled Athena's number, yawning.

'Hello? Oh, sweetie, how wonderful of you to phone. Are you hungry?'

'Well, yes, actually,' Agnes admitted, wondering what had happened to lunch. 'Are you all right?'

'No. Not at all all right. Couldn't be worse. How about that new place? Half an hour?'

'Fine.'

Agnes showered and changed her clothes. All the time she was aware of a truth, just beyond the confines of her mind. She still had an image of a funeral in her mind, of the earth opening, a body being laid to rest. In Provence? she wondered. Or was it Matt's funeral, with everyone gathered around his grave, all those intertwining stories, interlocking destinies. And one of them held the key to Matt's death.

★ ★ ★

Athena was already settled behind a bottle of white wine and a large basket of bread when Agnes arrived. 'Couldn't wait, I'm afraid,' she said through a mouthful of bread. 'Misery. Makes me eat.'

Agnes sat down opposite her and poured herself some wine. 'So, what's happened?'

'It's all awful with Nic. He's gone. I think. Haven't seen him or heard from him for days, can't get hold of him. That's it. I s'pose. Can't bear it, actually. I need him, sweetie, that's the truth of it. I — I love him. And now it's too late.' She sipped some wine. 'And you look awful too.'

'I've hardly slept in days. Xenos was evicted from Julius's church, and they've locked him up now, despite the medical evidence, and someone's been found dead, a bloke called Charles who was connected with Allen, and there was some kind of gun with him, which is the one that Liz remembered, we think, which means that it's pretty certain that he caused Liz's accident, and Matt's death, because he had a grudge against him too — and maybe he killed Liz, although that seems altogether weirder . . . But anyway, all of this means that Patrick and I were right to believe that none of these deaths was accidental . . . and if Charles's death is suspicious too, then it looks as if there's someone else involved, which means that all this time we've been up against someone who's capable of murdering — to get what they want — and who's sufficiently clever to plan a series of accidents so that they get away with it . . . And Julius said — at least he and I have had a talk at last, although he's in crisis — he thinks he did the wrong thing to leave Mary's mother all those years ago . . . '

Athena sighed. 'Even Julius.'

'I know.'

'We've always relied on him.'

Agnes nodded. 'That's why he couldn't talk to me before. Because he thought I needed him to be perfect.'

Athena shook her head. 'That even Julius should turn out to be just like the rest of us . . . '

'It's a shock, isn't it?'

Athena picked up her glass of mineral water.

'It's him having a child I find really difficult,' Agnes said. 'If he did.'

'Ooops!' Athena grabbed a paper napkin and dabbed at her clothes which were dripping with water.

'You all right?'

'No. I've soaked my jumper, and now you're telling me that this Mary is really — '

'I'm not sure. Julius said she had a father, a man called Jack, but there was something about the way he said it . . . and the way they are together . . . '

Athena pulled at her clothes, which still clung damply to her. 'I've slipped into a parallel universe, sweetie. That must be it. Everything looks the same but all the people are played by someone else. It's the only explanation. There's you being all sensible, for once. And me too. See? We've been jumbled up, and we're all behaving out of character.'

Agnes smiled. 'That must be it.'

'And even Nic, wherever he is . . . ' Her eyes filled with tears. 'He could at least tell me, couldn't he, sweetie — he's the one going on about honesty, and now he's just run off with this woman and can't even be bothered to return my calls. I don't think I've ever cared so much about anyone in my life. It's typical, it's typical of me, that just when I get to the point in my life when I decide I want to be with him, it's too late.'

'Are you cross with him?'

'I was. And then I was cross with her, moving in on him like that.' She poured some more wine. 'But really, it's my fault. All this. I'm the one to blame.'

The waitress appeared and took their order.

'What are you going to do?' Agnes picked at a piece of bread.

'What can I do? Run away? Take up your house in Provence, go and be reclusive and lie in the sun? Mind you, it's not a bad idea, you could do the same.'

'I'm needed here.' Again that thought, tugging at the edge of her mind. 'Patrick . . . ' she began. 'Patrick needs me.'

'Oh, sweetie, gorgeous Irishmen — perhaps some things haven't changed after all.'

'No.' Agnes shook her head. 'Not that. There's someone out there who killed his brother. Because of a grudge. Or because Matt was trying to stop them — ' There it was, out of the corner of her eye, the golf course. Two men, standing near the trees, conferring. Conspiring to do something terribly wrong.

Of course, she thought. That funeral. That earlier, Irish funeral.

'Sorry, sweetie, did you say funeral?'

Bridgid O'Connor's funeral. The final link, broken at last.

'Sweetie, you're muttering.'

'Sorry.'

'What is going to happen to your house?'

Agnes blinked, sipped some wine. 'I don't know.'

'Will you sell it?'

'The thing is, Athena, I've been thinking about it. I just can't bring myself to sell it. But then keeping it — it's a kind of failure. It's a postponement of my commitment, it's clinging to some kind of alternative, some kind of bolt-hole.'

'But surely it's better to do things slowly — not to burn your boats. Look at Julius. It was all or nothing for him, wasn't it, and look at the crisis he's in now. You can be so sure of something, and then twenty, thirty years later, it can turn out to be the wrong thing.'

Agnes met her eyes. 'But how do we know?'

Athena sighed. 'Oh, sweetie, that's the question, isn't it? Here we all are, floundering around, trying to make the best of things, do the right thing . . . ' She poured the rest of the bottle into their glasses. 'In the end, we're all just taking our chances, aren't we?'

★ ★ ★

Much later, Agnes lit her candles and knelt in prayer. Taking our chances, she thought. A game of chance.

Even Julius. Gambling on his future. And losing.

That's what Louise doesn't understand, she thought. Faith is about taking a leap. You can win or lose. There is no deal with God.

The image of the golf course flashed through her mind again, the two figures, deep in conversation.

She closed her eyes, thinking about Matt, out riding on the bridle way, the path blocked, his horse rearing. Matthias, the new apostle, chosen by lot. Taking his own risks. Carrying his note, to Mary.

She opened her eyes. The note. Patrick was right.

We've all been so stupid. When it's all in the note.

Her mother's clock ticked slowly in the silence. It was late. She yawned, stood up, blew out her candle. Tomorrow, she thought. Tomorrow, it would be time.

24

She'd set her alarm early. The first thing to do, she thought, reaching out an arm to switch it off, was to phone Stewart. And Deborah. And Mary. And Karen. And Judy.

She sat up. The chill morning light barely filtered through her curtains. She pulled on her dressing gown, made some tea, sat down at her desk, and picked up the phone receiver.

An hour later she was driving out to Essex.

Thank God Judy had answered her phone, she thought. She'd been surprised, but compliant.

She knows it's worth a lot to her, Agnes thought. Almost as much as it is to Allen.

★   ★   ★

Stewart Lode was standing on his doorstep looking out for her. She parked outside the house, next to his muddy jeep. Wordlessly, they went inside. Once again he showed her into the living room. They both sat down.

'It's still early,' he said.

A thin sun, still low in the sky, struggled through the clouds.

'Yes,' Agnes said.

Stewart looked at his watch. 'Do you think they'll tell that American boy?'

'Jed? Only if Judy still wants to marry him,' Agnes said.

Again, he looked at his watch. 'Did you tell Patrick?'

'Mary said she'd phone him.'

Lode nodded. They sat for a while. Lode tapped his foot on the floor. 'Come on,' he said. 'We might as well get going.'

They went out to the drive and climbed into his car. He revved the engine and accelerated down the drive, bumping over the potholes.

★　★　★

It was busy at the stables. Groups of young women called to each other across the yard, carrying tack and brushes and buckets of feed.

Deborah was waiting for them. 'They phoned,' she said. 'Both of them. Made out they needed an extra lesson. I hope it didn't show in my voice,' she added. 'If I'd known . . . and that other man, the one who died . . . ' She shook her head, lost for words.

'We should stay out of sight,' Lode said. He turned to Deborah. 'Perhaps the back of your office?' She went to unlock the door for him.

'I'll wait in the car,' Agnes said.

She sat in the passenger seat of Lode's jeep. She could hear the shouts of the stable girls, the whinnying of horses, the clip-clop of hooves. She looked out to the yard, and beyond the yard to the woods. The trees stopped abruptly where the golf course started. She could see figures on the course, just one or two here and there, tiny outlines against the expanse of green.

And there it was, again. The lone figure against the sky, skirting the edge of the course, heading for the fields. Gathering speed.

She watched the figure disappearing behind the trees, reappearing further along — turning — turning round, following the edge of the bridle way. Agnes tracked the path the figure was taking. If I go that way, she thought, I can take the path through the woods.

She jumped out of the car and shut the door silently. She left the stables and set off down the bridle path into the woods at a brisk walk. Amongst the trees she broke into a run, feeling the dewy air against her face, the soft ground at her feet. She caught sight of the lone jogger, nearer now. At the edge of the fields she left the shelter of the trees. She was walking now, keeping to the edge of the woods.

The sun had given up the struggle and disappeared behind thick cloud. Our paths will cross on that corner, she thought, as she caught sight of a clump of oaks. She set off along the flat edge of the field towards it.

Just before she reached the trees, the lone jogger appeared from behind their branches, running at an even, rhythmic pace.

'Jed,' she called.

He stopped, startled. He saw her. 'I thought you'd be with the others,' he said. 'I hear something's happened with that friend of Allen's — Jude said — ' He stopped, catching his breath.

'Yes.'

He settled into a walk and she fell in beside him. They headed towards the edge of the golf course.

'I gather you're leaving,' she said conversationally.

'Yes,' he said. 'Soon. Very soon.'

'You must be glad.'

'It's the best decision,' he said.

There was a whistling noise, and a golf ball flew into the trees behind them.

'They should put up a fence,' Agnes said.

'Yes,' he agreed.

'Could cause an accident,' Agnes said.

He nodded in agreement.

'When you went to that funeral,' Agnes said, 'with Matt . . . '

He looked at her then, but said nothing.

She kept walking. 'Did you know who that lady was?'

'He needed someone he could trust,' Jed said. 'No one else knew about Bridgid. He couldn't tell his family, he'd promised his father to keep it secret.'

'And he could trust you,' Agnes said.

He nodded. 'Yes,' he said. 'He could trust me.'

'To the extent of confiding in you about the money that his father had kept on one side for her?'

'Yes. Apparently he was devoted to her.'

'It was a shame when Matt died, then. For you, I mean.'

'A tragic death,' Jed agreed.

'Because you'd already promised that money, hadn't you? To your man in America.'

Jed's pace slowed. 'It's not about money.'

'You don't get wisdom like his for free, surely?'

'If I'm good enough, then I can belong. That's why I've trained for so long . . . '

'And sent several thousand dollars over to California in the last month or so.' She knew she was guessing.

448

'Doc agreed I was good enough.' Jed's voice was raised, his pace was uneven.

'Matt never meant you to keep that money — '

'It was Allen,' Jed interrupted. 'Allen was sending all that money over to Seattle. That's why I had to get out.'

'Matt intended that money to be for his brother.' Agnes's voice was level. 'He agreed with your plan to invest it, temporarily, to grow it a bit — he trusted you. Didn't he?'

Jed was silent.

'And he got Lode to act as co-signatory, so he didn't have to tell anyone else about where the money had come from. So he didn't have to betray his father's secrets. He trusted you,' she repeated.

'I tried to explain to him . . . ' Jed's voice faltered.

'And you used Allen as cover,' Agnes went on. 'Poor, silly old Allen, who believed your story about going in together on his leisure centre, who knew that Matt had come into some money but didn't question where it had come from. So he gladly agreed to send money to the Seattle office when he thought it was safe to do so.'

'Doc believes in me,' Jed said, weakly.

'Doc also has access to your bank account in Seattle, I imagine,' Agnes said.

Jed stopped short and faced her. His expression was tense. 'I have to — don't you see? There was no other way.' He was blocking her path. Then, abruptly, he set off again. Agnes sensed his tension, his nervousness as she walked beside him.

'I liked Matt,' Jed said suddenly. 'In Ireland . . . we had a great time. We got on well. I didn't want us to fall out.'

'Convenient, then, wasn't it, his accident? Just when he was about to challenge you about the fund, about where it had gone. He never found out it had gone to the States. To your training guru.'

Jed stopped. He laughed. 'Are you suggesting . . . Surely you can't be suggesting — an accident like that? You're crazy.'

'Crazy,' Agnes agreed. 'As a method of killing someone. Aiming a golf ball at a horse, at speed . . . '

Jed resumed his slow walking pace. 'For a moment I thought you were implying that I'd . . . '

'That you'd what?'

He shook his head. The sky was leaden, heavy with cloud.

'I mean, if you'd wanted to kill him,' Agnes went on, 'it would be quite a clever thing to do, wouldn't it? Make it look like an accident, factor in as much improbability as possible.

450

So that everyone's common sense tells them it had to be an accident. Because it's a crazy way to attempt a murder. So you make it look like a golf ball struck a horse and its rider falls, dying of freak head injuries. And you throw a rock at a car, having done all the maths. I realised,' Agnes went on, watching him, 'I remembered that the night Liz died you'd arrived at the stables with Judy. You'd offered her a lift and Allen was cross. But then, later, Deborah mentioned that Allen had driven Judy home. Which left you, I realised. To go home alone.' Agnes stopped. Jed looked at her. His eyes were hard like flint.

'All the maths,' Agnes said. 'The trajectories of rocks from bridges . . . or the likelihood of making a golf ball cross a path on which you knew someone was riding at a particular time — particularly if you've got your friend to block the path and you've borrowed a special gun for firing golf balls.'

'You're crazy,' he said. 'Fancy thinking up all that.'

'But that's just the point. We all think it's crazy. That's what probability is. That's what it's all about. The likelihood, the chances of things happening. Our common sense tells us one thing, but the maths tells us something different.'

They walked in silence. The air was cold between them.

'I thought you might understand,' he said suddenly. 'This is the only thing I want. The only thing I believe in. And Matt was about to take it away. Doc can't afford passengers, you see. Once you sign up, he keeps you. He feeds you. It costs.' He spoke fast, staring at the ground.

Agnes kept her pace next to him. 'It's a shame about Charles,' she said.

'Yes,' he agreed, distracted.

'Heart attack,' Agnes said, speaking carefully.

Jed looked at her. 'If you're thinking . . . ' He stopped. 'You think I . . . ' He shook his head. 'No, really. That was just chance. Just when I thought he'd tell someone, when his conscience got the better of him . . . and he dies. Natural causes.' He turned away from her, and they began to walk back towards the woods. 'Natural causes,' he repeated. 'Maybe you don't believe me. But I'm lucky, see. Things go my way.' His face lightened with a smile, steely like the sunless sky.

'You asked Matt to meet you, that morning?'

'I told him that I wanted to discuss the fund. He rode out to meet me.'

'He was carrying a note that he thought

you'd convey for him.'

Jed turned to her. 'Was he?'

'He never got to give it to you. Did he?'

Jed was silent.

'That grudge,' Agnes went on, 'the one Charles held against Matt, it must have gone back a long way.'

'Yes. I wasn't sure how much to let him in on the plan, but he was willing.'

'To the extent that it was Charles who suggested the gun.'

'He had a whole collection up there. Weird. And we didn't want to leave anything to chance. But I was the better shot. When we tried it out, he got the horse.'

'Liz's horse.'

'She happened to be passing.'

'And then she started to remember.'

'I heard her, that night. You were talking to Jude, at the stables. She recognised Charles.'

'You were there too?'

'I was training, out in these fields, I'd just come back. You didn't see me.'

Agnes remembered the shadow of movement behind the lights of the stable yard. 'So it was you,' she said, trying to keep up with Jed's striding pace.

'I realised I had even more to lose. She had to go too. Some days later, I followed her back. She took that B road towards the A12. I got ahead of her. There were a couple of bridges. And very little traffic. It was luck, again. I'm just a lucky kind of guy.'

'Not when you were a child, though.'

He stopped short. The sky was darkening. Thunder clouds menaced the distant trees. 'Now I'm lucky,' he said, in a voice level with restraint. 'I've left all that behind me. I've got what I want.'

'Yes,' Agnes said.

He seemed to relax, and resumed his even walking pace. 'Everything I want,' he said.

'An end to exile,' Agnes agreed.

'Odysseus can go home,' he said, and even smiled. 'I knew you'd understand. It's about having faith,' he said, animated now. 'Believing in yourself. That's what Doc does. He allows you to be your best self, he allows you to believe that you can do it. I have to go there. There's nothing left for me but that. You can see that, can't you? I knew you'd understand.' He stopped and turned to her, pink-cheeked. He looked very young.

Agnes hesitated, facing him. 'And if I was to say — if I was to say that your faith is the opposite of mine? Because for me, it's between me and God — '

'I don't need God.' His voice was loud. 'Look!' He stood before her, tall, blond, muscular. 'Look at me. This is what I'm

454

working with, this body, these muscles, as near perfection as I can get it, with Doc's help. It's not between me and God, it's between Doc and this.' He stood, shoulders squared, his feet apart, now blocking her path. 'This is my best self,' he said. 'Nothing can stop me.'

'Jed . . . ' She spoke gently. 'Jed. You've killed. You've killed two people. If that's your best self — '

'I had to.'

'How can your self be just your body?'

'You don't know Doc. He works with all of you. It's mental, emotional, spiritual. When you go through that barrier, when you're up there, alone, covering distances you never thought you'd cover . . . if your God is anywhere, then he's there.' He turned and, surprisingly, took hold of her hands. 'We live in faithless times,' he said. 'Please trust me. Please understand.'

Agnes felt her hands in his grip. 'Matthias is dead,' she said. 'And Liz.'

'And my plane leaves this afternoon. That's the bit that no one knows.'

'They'll stop you.'

'I could kill you. Now.'

Agnes felt his hands tighten hard over hers. 'What good would that do?'

'Who else have you told?'

'No one.'

'More fool you, then. If that's the truth.'

'It is,' Agnes said. She tried to wrest her hands from his, but his grip was strong. 'It won't work, Jed.' She faced him, her eyes staring into his grey, empty gaze. 'Two accidents, no one will know. But how will you kill me?' She saw him blink. 'Three bodies? It won't be an accident any more.' He lowered his gaze, staring at the ground. She felt his grip loosen. 'It'll be the end of your luck.'

He dropped her hands. 'You've told no one else?'

'No.' She wished it wasn't true.

'You could phone the airport.'

'I might — '

'I'll be gone.' He checked his watch. 'I'll be on that plane.' He'd begun to run before she realised what he was doing, calling back to her, his words frozen in the chill of the air. 'You're too late,' he shouted over his shoulder. 'My luck holds.'

Some instinct made her pursue him, but she'd taken only a few paces before she realised how futile it was. She slowed to a halt, and watched him as he sped away from her, a streak of colour receding against the metallic grey of the sky.

She stood in the field.

I must phone the airport, she thought.

456

Heathrow. She turned and began to run towards the stables, away from the direction he'd taken, imagining him in his car by now, racing to catch the next flight out.

She arrived, panting, at the stables, rushed into the office and picked up the phone, too breathless to answer questions from Deborah, from Mary, who was waiting in the stable yard, or from Allen, who began to stride angrily towards the office but was restrained by Patrick.

It was Judy who got to her first, coming into the office behind her. 'What did he say?'

Agnes waved away her questions, writing down the number from directory enquiries, dialling the airport.

'What did Jed say? Is he going today? Bastard.'

Agnes hung on the line, listening to the ringing, half hearing what Judy was saying.

'Bastard,' she repeated. 'Running off like that. And Allen accused of all sorts. I should choose my men more carefully.'

Agnes was still hanging on.

'Still,' Judy said. 'He won't get far.'

Agnes wondered why the main airport number took so long to answer.

'There'll be police everywhere,' Judy said to no one in particular.

'Hello?' Agnes stamped her foot in

frustration as the phone was answered by an electronic voice who gave her a series of options.

'I thought he could at least speak to me,' Judy was saying. 'He could at least tell me, honestly, that it was over. And then I found the ticket booking on his e-mail account. And the date. And I thought, How do you stop a flight? How do you stop someone getting on their plane? It would have to be a big story. A big, big story.'

'Hello?' Agnes tried again. She was told to hold for an operator.

'So I told them he was a murderer. I told them the flight number and everything. They assured me they'd catch him at the airport.'

Agnes dropped the phone receiver. She turned and stared at Judy. The phone swung in mid-air, beeping faintly as it awaited her response. 'You did what?'

'I phoned the police. I said that he was responsible for murdering Matt, that it wasn't an accident at all, and that he was about to make his getaway on a flight to LA this afternoon.'

'But ... ' Agnes felt suddenly dizzy, perhaps from running across the field. 'How did you know?'

'Know what?' Judy was still smiling.

'That he killed Matt?'

458

Judy laughed. 'Oh, no, of course he didn't. I just made it up to get the police there. I thought I'd make him miss his flight, the bastard, as he's trying to run away from me. They'll let him go once they realise it's not true.'

'But it is true.'

'What's true?'

'Judy, he killed Matt. He just told me. Now. In the field — ' She broke off as Judy's eyes rolled in her head and she collapsed in a heap on the floor of the office.

Outside, Allen was shouting at Patrick. 'Where is this Lode man, then? Calling me here on some pretext, offering me some kind of concession for my tennis courts — quite unnecessary of course — ' He broke off as Lode walked across the yard, accompanied by two police officers. Agnes watched from the window as one of them spoke to Allen. Angrily he shrugged, and followed them to a waiting car, which sped out of the yard on to the main road, into the distance.

Judy opened her eyes from her position on the floor. 'Had Allen really been defrauding the company, then?'

'Yes,' Agnes said.

'And Charles told you?'

'No. We worked it out, Patrick and me.'

Judy sat up, patting her hair. 'So saying that

459

Charles had grassed . . . '

'Was a fib,' Agnes said. 'To get you all here. Mostly, to get Jed here. We thought he'd be around, if there was any whisper of Charles having talked. What Charles did manage to say, before he died, was that he and Jed had used a particularly nasty murder weapon.'

'Charles told you that?'

'Not precisely. He was holding it, hoping to show Stewart. He died before he could explain. We had to work that out too.'

'You have been busy.' Judy got out a make-up mirror and peered into it. She smoothed her hair some more. 'It's Jed that's the real shock. I mean, I know I've made some pretty duff choices when it comes to men, but a murderer? I'm really losing my grip, I can't help thinking.'

The phone rang, echoing across the yard. Deborah ran in and answered it. 'Yes? Yes. OK. Sure. Thanks.' She hung up. 'That was the police. They've arrested Jed. He was on his way to the airport.'

Agnes looked at Judy.

Judy looked at Agnes. 'Shame, really. He was quite sweet.'

25

Agnes made yet another pot of tea and carried it through to the living room. They were all draped, exhausted, around Stewart's chintz armchairs.

'But . . . ' Mary was saying, then fell silent again.

Patrick leaned forward to put his cup down. 'It goes back to that funeral. Bridgid's death. It must have given Jed ideas.'

'Always knew Allen was a bad lot. But that American boy . . . ' Stewart took the teapot from Agnes and put it down on the table. 'I was taken in, like the others. I'd met him, in the past, with Matt. He was the only other person who knew about the old lady's money.'

Patrick looked at him. 'What did you have to do with it?'

Stewart glanced at Agnes. 'Matt made me a trustee of Bridgid's money, after her death, when it became the fund for Tad. Agnes here guessed, didn't you?' He turned back to Patrick. 'He needed someone separate from the family; he'd promised your father never to tell anyone about it. He'd helped me with this

461

tiresome ditch malarkey, it was only natural that I should return the favour. And I was an outsider, y'know, not an intimate. Matt thought I'd do. Shows how wrong you can be. When that boy came here with the documents and convinced me the money was his, I saw no reason to argue. And I couldn't ask anyone without revealing the truth about your father's life.'

'And Jed went to the funeral with Matt?' Patrick turned his cup round in his hands.

'I remembered him talking about a business trip to Dublin,' Agnes said. 'And then he went on to say how he'd envied Matt going home, and I realised he must have gone to the village too.'

'Why did Matt invite him?'

'They were friends.'

Patrick frowned. 'I remember. He'd sometimes be there for Sunday lunch . . . And Charles, though.' He shook his head.

'Matt was responsible for Charles leaving the company. They kept it quiet. It was malpractice, bad advice. It was hushed up, early retirement . . . but Charles was angry about it.' Agnes sipped her tea. 'Very angry.'

'Smouldering away for years,' Mary said.

'Until Jed came along.' Patrick scratched his chin. 'And needed an accomplice . . . '

Mary looked up from her cup. 'But was it Charles? Or Jed?'

'I think Charles was quite keen on it all, to start with. The gun idea was obviously Charles's suggestion. And I think the trial run with Liz was Charles's idea too. But when Matt died, he was on his way to meet Jed. Just Jed.'

'And Liz?' Mary was pale.

Agnes shook her head. 'That was Jed too. On his own. He drove ahead of her along the B road. He told me.'

'He must have moved fast to get up to the bridge, even so,' Patrick said.

'Moving fast was what Jed was all about.' Agnes almost smiled at him.

Silence settled on the room. An image seemed to hover between them, of Jed, standing on a bridge in the dark, a rock in his hands, waiting for a car to pass beneath . . .

'It would explain poor old Fielding's remorse.' Lode's voice broke in. 'Maybe he only wanted to give old Matthias a fright, and give one of his treasures a bit of an outing at the same time. Found he'd got talked into something a lot more serious . . . heard about young Elizabeth . . . obviously, all a bit too much for him.'

'So . . . ' Mary hesitated. 'When Charles died . . . '

'It really was a heart attack,' Agnes replied. 'Jed said it was luck.'

'But why call Stewart over that night?' Mary shook her head. 'And why was he holding the cannon?'

'Wanted to confess, I s'pose,' Stewart said. 'As I say, all got too much for him.'

'Why tell you, though?' Mary persisted.

'Because I'd do, p'raps. He had few enough friends, after all. Couldn't trust anyone with it, either.'

'Remember how you spoke to him?' Agnes asked Mary. 'Remember the way you accused him?'

'I didn't expect . . . I didn't mean it to . . . ' Mary stared at her feet.

'His conscience. Guilt, coming back to haunt him in the shape of the grim reaper.' Patrick smiled. 'Agnes's view of the universe remains intact, then. Morality restored.'

'Hardly.' Agnes met his gaze. 'Jed nearly got away with it.'

'If he hadn't scorned Judy, he'd be on that plane.' Patrick was still amused. 'Of all people, that daffy girl . . . '

'She's not so daffy,' Mary said.

'She's probably at her desk now, looking perfectly groomed as ever,' Agnes said.

Patrick turned to her. 'And in what way was I right about Mary's note?'

464

Agnes looked at Mary, then back to Patrick. 'I realised it was for Karen,' she said. She studied the carpet at her feet. 'Matt was expecting to meet someone who'd be able to pass on a message to Karen that he was hunting after all.' She raised her eyes again. Mary was staring at her. 'I — um — I phoned Karen, this morning, to check. She said they always had this system on meet days, so she'd know when to expect him.'

'A — a note?' Mary was pale.

'It was easier than trying to find a phone.'

'But he says . . . ' Mary's voice faltered. 'He says he misses . . . It says, *I miss you . . .* ' She wound her fingers together in her lap.

Agnes didn't look at her. 'Karen said it was a kind of joke they had.'

There was a small silence. 'Why Jed?' Patrick broke in loudly. 'Why would Matt think he'd give the note to Jed?'

'Jed said he'd asked Matt to meet him. To discuss the fund. I suppose he and Charles didn't want to leave it to chance that Matt might pass that way when they'd set everything up. With Liz it was different. For Matt, they needed certainties. And I suppose Matt thought Jed would pass the note to Karen so that he could join the hunt later on.'

465

'Matt never said he was meeting anyone that morning.' Patrick frowned.

'How could he?' Agnes turned to him. 'It was about Bridgid's money, he couldn't tell anyone. He pretended his horse needed some work instead.'

Silence settled on the room again, while Mary put her hand to an inside pocket and drew out the note. 'But . . . ' She spoke quietly. 'This . . . ' She turned it over in her hand.

'Did he usually bother with notes? For you?' Agnes asked.

Mary raised her eyes reluctantly. She shook her head. 'No. We had no need. If he said he was going to be there, then he was. Liz told me she'd heard they'd found a note on the body, and I just assumed . . . ' She stared at it for a while, then folded it up and put it back in her pocket.

Once again it was Patrick who broke the silence. 'The strangest thing of all is knowing we were right. We were right to see an order in things. Weren't we, Agnes?'

'I suppose so.' Agnes looked at him. 'Except — except, the universe hasn't changed, has it? Accidents still happen. Random things still come to pass. Your next winning streak will still come to an end sometime. Won't it?'

Patrick laughed. 'But so will my next losing streak.'

'So, whether you win or lose' — this time Agnes did smile at him — 'it's still a game of chance.'

★ ★ ★

Some time later they said their goodbyes to Stewart. At the door, Mary took Agnes's hand. 'I have to talk to you,' she said in a low voice. They watched Patrick get into Agnes's car.

'Julius,' Agnes said.

Mary nodded. 'I don't know what to do.'

'Seeing you again,' Agnes said. 'It's — it's turned his world upside down. It's not your fault.'

'They loved each other very much,' Mary said.

Patrick was making faces at them from the car.

Mary ignored him. 'Should I see him? Or will I make it worse?'

'It depends . . . ' Agnes took a deep breath. 'It depends what your relationship is with him.'

Mary met her eyes. 'I'd — I'd like to see him. I think . . . I think I will. You don't mind, do you?'

Agnes stared at her feet on the muddy gravel of the drive. 'I don't own him,' she said. 'Though once I thought I did.'

★ ★ ★

Patrick was mostly silent on the drive home. The dull cloud of the morning had given way to heavy rain, and Patrick stared at the windscreen wipers as they beat time against the glass. As they reached the outer edges of London he turned to Agnes.

'Maybe I'll give up gambling,' he said. He yawned. 'There's no need to look at me like that.'

'I don't believe you, that's all.'

'I'm not addicted, you know.'

'No, I know you're not. But how else will you make sense of it all?'

'Of all what?'

'Of the universe.' Agnes smiled as she turned on to the slip road for the M25. 'Your Godless universe.'

'Did I say it was Godless?'

'That's why you gamble. You took God out of your cosmos, and replaced divine will with chance. You're too clever to be an agnostic, you see. You have to see some kind of pattern, and without God you need to find a different one.'

'Thank you for that, Sister.' He yawned again. 'But you're wrong about the clever. I gamble because I'm stupid.'

'Either way, I can't see you giving it up.'

'Can't afford it, really. I've got Tad to think of.'

They fell silent again, listening to the rumble of the tyres on the wet road, the swish of passing cars. The tower blocks of the London outskirts seemed to cower under thunder clouds.

'Talking of Tad,' Agnes said, breaking the silence. 'That money. Matt's money. That Lode signed over to Jed. Do we get it back?'

'It's probably spent by now. The new-age training guru on the beach in Santa Monica, he's probably spent it all on burgers by now.'

'There must be a legal way — '

'I'm not taking on American lawyers. However broke I am.' He shook his head. 'No, Tad and I will just keep on muddling through, as ever. We'll manage. We get by.' They were skirting the Thames in the shadow of Canary Wharf. 'You can drop me off here, I'll take the tube.'

She pulled over to the edge of the road. He leaned over and kissed her cheek. 'Thanks,' he said. 'Thanks for believing.'

'It's my job,' she said, and he laughed.

She watched him amble across the road and disappear into the underground.

★ ★ ★

Her flat had a silence about it, as if she hadn't been there for weeks. She switched on heat and light and flung herself on to her bed. She didn't mean to sleep, but was woken an hour later when the phone rang.

'Hello.' Helen sounded surprised. 'I thought I'd get your machine.'

'Where are you?'

'Back at the house. I wasn't charged. Even without the habit, being a religious can be quite an advantage.'

'What's happening?'

'Tad's out on bail. He's supposed to be staying at Patrick's, but Patrick's been out for days, and I think Tad's back sleeping by the river. Xenos is . . .'

'What?'

'It's awful, Agnes. He's been put in this detention centre, it's like prison. There's no doubt it's just made him think he's back where he was; he won't look at me, he's — he's catatonic, terrified . . . We're at our wits' end, me and Colin, and Madeleine, and Julius. We're trying everything. The refugee people are helping us appeal on medical

470

grounds, but we don't know what to put on the form. If only he'd speak . . . '

'And you? How are you?'

There was a tiny silence. 'OK.'

'How are you really?'

'Agnes . . . the problem is, this has really challenged me.'

'In what way?'

Again, Helen hesitated. 'I don't believe God can mean this to happen. I don't know what he's trying to tell us, if this is how he does it. When I look at Xenos, at the expression in his eyes . . . you can see he has no hope, and you know that somewhere out there are the men who've destroyed him. And yet those people, those evil people, are still part of God's creation. And I think, What does he think he's doing? Like, did he just wind up his creation all those centuries ago and leave it to run, and then bugger off and do something more interesting? Because if this is the best he can do, it's pretty poor, really, isn't it? And I know that Jesus is supposed to be the example of God sharing in our suffering, and Sister Michaela, you know, our provincial novice mistress, she said I could reflect on all this in Holy Week as that's what it's about, the suffering to end all suffering — but I can't see it. I mentioned it to Julius, about looking in Xenos's eyes and just seeing the defeat of God . . . '

'What did he say?'

'He said the important thing with the Xenoses of this world was not to turn away, whatever you see reflected in their eyes. That sort of helped.'

'Mmm.'

'And he said not to worry about God, as God could look after himself.'

Agnes sighed. 'Why is that man always right?'

For the first time, Helen laughed. 'I'd better go, I've got to ring our lawyer and see if we've got anywhere. I'll see you in chapel tomorrow.' Agnes heard her falter, then she said, 'I just keep thinking, I love my work here, but I could just as easily do this kind of work as a secular person, couldn't I?'

'I can't answer that one. Except to say . . . '

'To say what?'

'That — that we all take our chances.'

'That's funny.'

'What?'

'Julius said that too.'

★   ★   ★

' 'Behold the handmaid of the Lord . . . let it be to me according to your word . . . ' '

Agnes glanced along the pews towards

472

Helen, who was staring resolutely straight ahead. The early sun threw shards of light across the altar. There was no sign of Louise.

' 'The Holy Spirit will come upon you . . . therefore the child to be born will be holy and will be called the Son of God . . . ' '

Two novices. One absent, one here but thinking of leaving.

Could I have done things any differently? Agnes wondered. Could I have encouraged them, offered them certainties, promised them eternal life if only they would stay? Only, she thought, if I believed all that myself.

' 'Let it be to me according to your word . . . ' ' Agnes repeated the liturgy, the words of acceptance uttered by the Virgin Mary all those centuries ago, when being told she would carry the child of God. Acceptance, Agnes thought. Is that what keeps me here?

Behold the handmaid of the Lord.

Mary, Mother of God. She made her own decision, Agnes thought. As a free human being, she decided to say yes. Helen and Louise have the right to do the same.

There's nothing I can do.

Afterwards, she sought out Louise, who was in her room.

'Can I come in?'

473

The door was opened wide enough to let her in, and closed again behind her. Louise looked terrible, her eyes shadowed with dark rings, her skin papery.

'I've been waiting to talk to you,' she said, sitting on her bed.

'I'm sorry.' Agnes sat on the one small chair.

'I've been praying, I've been asking God for a sign that I should stay.' She shook her head. 'Nothing's happened.'

Agnes picked up a pen that lay on the desk. She felt its weight in her hand, expensive, gold and shining.

'Peter, our curate, he gave me that,' Louise said.

'What sort of signs do you think the Lord might send?' Agnes asked gently.

'I don't know. It's just, up till now, everything's felt right. When I decided to be a nun, and when I told my family . . . I didn't expect them to understand anyway . . . And Peter — See, he even had the pen inscribed to me, 'Best wishes, Peter' — I knew he was pleased that God had called me . . . And working with' — her voice trembled — 'Richard . . . And now it's all gone wrong, it doesn't feel right at all, and God's gone silent . . . ' She stared at the neat square of carpet at her feet.

Agnes chose her words carefully. 'Surely you can't expect God to make his will known in an obvious way?'

'He sent an angel to the Virgin, didn't he?'

'That was a special occasion,' she said, but Louise didn't even smile.

'I just think, after all I've done, after all I've believed, and I've prayed and prayed, and . . . ' Her voice became shrill. 'I can't go home to them now, it'll just prove them right after all; they never understood, and if I go back it'll just confirm what they always thought, and my brother will laugh and say it was only because I was in love with Peter, but I wasn't, Agnes, really I wasn't . . . '

She looked young and vulnerable, sitting on her bed with her legs straight out in front of her.

'No,' Agnes said. 'Of course you weren't.'

'What shall I do?'

Agnes was silent. Louise's eyes were on hers, waiting. 'There are no simple answers,' Agnes heard herself say.

'It's like that stupid wager, that Frenchman saying you just have to bet on it, like buying a lottery ticket or something.' Louise pouted, tearful.

'It is like that,' Agnes began. 'It's about asking for nothing from God, and then seeing what happens.'

Louise stared at her, frowning. 'Asking for nothing?'

Agnes nodded.

'Don't you ask him for anything?'

Agnes frowned as she considered this.

'But then, what keeps you here?' Louise's voice was raised.

Agnes thought of sunlit orchards, red tiled roofs, sun-baked green shutters. The landscapes of her childhood. 'I'm not sure,' she said.

'I made a decision,' Louise said. 'And now it feels wrong. So now I have to make another decision. I just don't yet know what it is. And if God isn't going to help me, I'll just have to do it on my own.'

★　★　★

'Oh, Julius . . . ' Agnes sighed, leaning her head on her hands. 'Why do they always give me these jobs for which I'm so singularly ill suited? She's bound to leave, and Helen's not sure either. I've just set them a very bad example . . . Don't laugh at me.'

'I wasn't. Have some cake.'

'Cake?' Agnes lifted her head from her hands.

'You can't move for exquisite pâtisseries round here these days. Either that or

American coffee bars. And to think it used to be warehouses, and strange dimly lit pubs which only their regulars ever went to.'

Agnes accepted a slice of sugared pastry with almonds on top. 'At least you managed to give some words of encouragement to Helen.'

'Me?' Julius's mouth was dusted with sugar. He looked so surprised that Agnes laughed. 'All I did was mumble something about the whole thing being a gamble, I can hardly think that was helpful. And now who's laughing?'

'You look so funny.'

'At least I was honest, I suppose.' Julius returned to his cake.

'Look at us, eh?' Agnes picked an almond from the top of her cake.

'Like an old married couple.'

'Thank goodness.' She looked at him. He returned her look with his own clear blue gaze. She felt tears prick her eyes.

'It's not over yet,' he said quietly. Outside the sunlight was fading with the day.

'No.'

'There's your house in France. And there's . . . ' He fell silent, picking up crumbs from his cake on his fingertips.

'What are you going to do?'

'What can I do? I'm a priest. My ideas have

changed. I'm still a priest. I love her. I was a fool. If God sent an angel now to try and reassure me that his love is greater than all others, I'd — I don't know what I'd do. Punch him on the nose, I expect.'

Outside birds twittered in the gathering dusk. 'Louise is waiting for a sign,' Agnes said.

'She can have the angel, then.'

'I think that's what it would take to make her stay.'

'I suppose anything's possible. Like Tad and his miracles.'

'Charles Fielding — that man in Essex — he had a clock which showed God winding up the universe.'

'The clockmaker God.' Julius nodded. 'Winding the whole thing up and leaving it to run, perfectly, to perfect order. But you see, there's no room for miracles in that universe.'

'There may be,' Agnes argued. 'There might be things that seem strange to us but which are just part of his order that we don't understand.'

He smiled at her. 'I'd rather believe he's still capable of intervention. I suppose, in spite of everything, I'm with Tad on this one.'

'So God's moving stuff around without us noticing?'

Julius laughed. 'Something like that. By the

478

way, I meant to tell you, Xenos has been freed from that awful place. Helen phoned me at lunchtime. The appeal on medical grounds worked, at least for the moment. He's back at the hostel, on some kind of police conditions.'

'And Tad?'

'He's staying with Patrick. Who's enormously grateful to you, by the way.'

'I didn't do much.'

'You saw order in chaos. You saw human intention where everyone else saw randomness.'

'Don't tease me.'

'You saw the hand of God — '

'In a murder?'

Julius looked at her. He sighed. 'Nothing's simple, is it?'

26

Athena looked remarkably cheerful. She was wearing her red suit and lipstick to match. Her hair was newly cut, and framed her face with long black curls.

'It's just so weird how things turn out, sweetie. Shall we order more coffee? This is my breakfast, after all.' She waved to the waitress.

It was Saturday morning, bright and sunny, heralding spring.

'It's my breakfast too,' Agnes said, wondering whether to have another croissant. 'So?' She waited for Athena to pour some coffee from the cafetière. 'What happened?'

'He's back. Nic. It's all over with that woman. He's very sad about it, he says, it was a mistake, he's got to do some serious work about Him and about Us but everything's going to be wonderful.'

'But last time we spoke he'd practically run off with her.'

'She didn't want him.' Athena laughed. 'There I was, thinking he was a helpless pawn in her scheme to spend the rest of her life with him, and in fact she had another agenda altogether. There was some man in her life already and she wanted some kind of diversion. Reading between the lines, I think this man wasn't behaving and she'd decided to make him jealous, but, of course, you can't expect Nic to see the subtleties of it all, can you?' She sipped her coffee. 'Anyway, whatever her plan was, it obviously worked, because she's gone back to this other man, and she's very happy, and Nic is furious with her. He feels used, in a way he doesn't understand, poor love . . . '

'Who'd have thought?' Agnes took another croissant.

'See?' Athena smiled at her above the wide white circle of her coffee cup. 'It's what I said about stories. You always think you know what's going on, and then it turns out something different happens.'

Agnes laughed and poured some more coffee for herself.

'So,' Athena said. 'Here we are. Nic and me. Two old slappers, back together again.'

'And — and you're not angry with him?'

'I did try, but he's so crestfallen, poor lamb, and so sweet, and anyway, it was partly my fault. He won't hear of it, though, it's all his fault, he's got issues he's got to work through to be a better partner to me . . . ' She laughed merrily. 'They're so funny, aren't they? All he's got to do is buy me flowers and nice dinners and lots of presents, but they just don't realise, do they? So instead he's planning to join some men's workshop or go and drum in the woods or something. I don't mind, as long as he's happy again. And it's just so nice — *so nice* to have him back. Who'd have thought, as you so rightly say.'

Agnes, smiling, buttered her croissant.

'And you and Julius?'

Agnes looked up. 'We're — we're OK, I think. He's still — there's still all this uncertainty. For him, I mean. About Mary.'

'And is she — ?'

Agnes shook her head. 'I can't tell. But he's not hiding from me any more.'

'Perhaps he's got issues to work through too.'

'I can't see him drumming in the woods, though, can you?'

They both laughed so loudly that people on nearby tables turned to look.

★ ★ ★

Back at her flat, later on that afternoon, she took the thick cream envelope out of its drawer and pulled out the letter: ... *a decision must be made, madame ... at your earliest convenience ... the disposal of the property* . . . She stared at the words in their elegant, legalistic French.

The disposal of the property. To cut myself off from the last thread of my past. No longer to belong to that house, to those orchards. To be stateless, homeless — pastless. Like Jed. Like Xenos.

Like a nun, she thought. To belong only to my order, now, in the present. And in the future. To make that leap into faith.

No wonder I have no answers for Helen and Louise. I have none for myself either.

The phone rang.

'Agnes, it's Patrick.'

'How nice to hear from you. How are you?'

'Fine. Helping the police — very time-consuming. They've taken away all Matt's papers. It's been difficult for Karen too, I've been spending some time with her.'

'And Tad?'

'He's gone. Again. And this time with Xenos. Took him for a walk from the hostel, last night. No one's seen them since.'

Agnes sighed. 'The shrine?'

'We think so. Will you come too?'

★ ★ ★

The church was dimly lit, and Agnes thought at first that she and Patrick were alone. Then,

483

as her eyes got used to the light, she saw two figures, silhouetted in the candle glow, hunched before the statue of the Virgin. They were talking in low voices. Agnes could distinguish Tad's cracked bass; the other voice, she realised, was soft and light, and must belong to Xenos.

She and Patrick looked at each other. They could hear the two voices murmuring. Xenos's voice was louder now, and seemed to be declaiming some long narrative. He was kneeling before the statue, his face turned up towards her, as if telling her some story. His face glistened in the candlelight, and Agnes realised he was crying. Tad was silent, listening, although the language was incomprehensible. He nodded from time to time. After a while Agnes heard the occasional word she understood, fragments of English in the stream of alien sound.

Silently she joined Patrick in the nearest pew. She put her hands in her pockets, and shivered. She wasn't sure how long they'd been sitting there when Xenos's voice began to quieten, the words more halting, and eventually he fell silent. He covered his head with his hands and wept. Tad went to him and held him, and the two men sat in an embrace, kneeling still in front of the statue.

Agnes and Patrick looked at each other.

The light in the windows had faded as the afternoon gave way to evening.

Silently, Agnes approached the two men, and not knowing what else to do, knelt in front of the statue. They looked up, startled, then saw it was her. The three knelt in silence. Outside the wind got up, rattling the windows.

After a while Tad shifted, then pointed at the statue. He smiled. 'Look — Our Lady . . . '

Agnes glanced up. The statue's face seemed to be wet with tears. Agnes stared at Tad.

'Xenos told her his story,' Tad said, as if this were enough.

Xenos got up and went to the statue, and touched the cold porcelain. His fingers came away wet. He stared at them, then touched them to his own face, his eyes wide in the dim light.

Agnes stood up. She went up to the statue. Drops of moisture glistened in the corners of the blank eyes and rolled down the sculpted cheeks. She reached out her fingertips. They were wet. Agnes stared at her hands, aware that her thoughts were confused, that she couldn't really make sense of what her eyes were telling her. She glanced back to the Virgin, and she realised she was fervently hoping to see her eyes dry and normal again.

They were still wet. Patrick had joined her at the altar, and he too was staring at the statue. He seemed amused.

Xenos once again touched the tears, which now seemed to be abating. He turned to Agnes, and for the first time Agnes saw him smile. He looked like a young boy, a child, instead of the haunted, aged victim that she'd seen for so long. He pointed at himself. 'Ümit,' he said. 'Name. Ümit.'

Tad looked back at the Virgin. Her face was dry again. He smiled at Agnes, his features alive in the warm light of the Lady chapel. The rest of the church was in darkness as they all made their way to the door.

★ ★ ★

'It's extraordinary.' Agnes sat in the hostel office with the phone tucked under her chin. 'You can't shut him up now. We've been talking since last night, with an interpreter and the refugee people, though it's not an easy story to hear . . . Yes, Tad's here at the hostel too. Can you tell Julius . . . Yes. Thanks. Oh, and Madeleine? Are you still there?' Agnes hesitated, wondering how to describe the events of last night. 'Um, nothing,' she said. 'I'll see you later.'

She hung up and went into the kitchen,

where Xenos and Tad were eating a large breakfast. Xenos was looking younger by the minute, and now he joked with Tad, and laughed when George the dog tried to beg for food. 'Dog,' he said, pointing. 'Ümit,' he said, pointing at himself again.

★ ★ ★

Julius put a mug of coffee down in front of Agnes, and then sat down opposite her. The noonday sun streamed through the leaded windows, making little rainbow patterns on Julius's desk. 'Typical of Our Lady,' he said, 'to choose you of all people.'

'What's wrong with me?'

Julius laughed. 'Go on, admit it. You were looking for secret taps, weren't you? Or you suspected Tad of setting up some water system when you weren't there?'

'It's just my faith has never depended on things like that.' Agnes shifted in her chair.

'And your fingers were really wet?'

'Look, I don't really believe it either.'

'But she was moved. By Xenos's story.'

'Ümit, he's called. He's Kurdish. His father was accused of being involved in some anti-government organisation,' Agnes began. 'The whole family were arrested; he had two elder brothers and a sister who was eight.'

487

She swallowed. 'They were held separately. He thinks he was there three months, he's not sure. He was beaten . . . electric things . . . ' She blinked against the tears that welled in her eyes. 'When he got out, he went home. His home had been burnt. He spent months looking for his family. He never found them. He walked to the airport, stowed away in the hold of a plane and ended up here. He can't remember much about the flight. The rest you know. He didn't even know what country this was.' She dashed at the tears that ran down her face. 'Once they hung him on a wall, with his arms tied behind him . . . and the soldiers sat at a table below him, all through the night, and they played cards.' She covered her face with her hands.

Julius sat quietly next to her. 'Is it any wonder the statue wept?' he said.

27

Some days later, they walked along the edge of the Thames, Agnes and Patrick and Julius. 'Look at this,' Julius said, waving his hand towards the shimmering glass of the new developments. 'Terrible.'

'Did you prefer it how it was?' Patrick laughed.

'Yes. I did. We have no past, now, those of us who've lived here for years. They've knocked it all down.'

'Wait till you see our village again, then.'

Agnes glanced at Julius. 'Are you really going?'

'Next week. Flight to Dublin, all booked. Mary organised it. Four tickets.'

'Four?'

'Patrick, Mary, me and you.'

'Me?'

'Of course.' He squeezed her hand.

'And how's Karen?' Agnes asked Patrick.

'Better. It was a terrible shock. She knew Jed quite well. Although she said yesterday she'd always thought there was something odd about him. As if he was hollow, she said. She's frightened he's going to claim that it was all Charles's idea, which will mean a lengthy trial.' He sighed. 'I just want him locked away now. In a way, I wish he'd caught the plane, so he could disappear up some Californian mountain and get eaten by a bear.'

'And Allen?'

Patrick laughed. 'Allen.' He shook his head. 'He's accepted all the charges against him, left the company, cheerfully declared himself bankrupt. He's washed his hands of the leisure centre. He'll lie low in some nice rented flat for a while and then resurface running some other scam. In fact, the States might be a good place to start. He can get eaten by a bear as well.'

'And how's Tad?'

'Better than I've seen him for months. For him, all this has worked. It turned out not to be about luck, Matt's death. It was something planned instead. An action, a fixed, human action. And the odd miracle, that always cheers him up, that does. Though I'm not sure I've recovered from it. That ugly old statue, all white and blue porcelain — I mean, really, you'd think if he's going to intervene in his creation he'd choose something more tasteful. It's all right for you, Ignatius,' he said as Julius laughed. 'It's just part of normal life for you.'

'Did you speak to Father Dominic about it?' Agnes asked Julius.

'Oh, yes. He was in the church later on, saw the drops of water on the floor.'

'But wasn't he amazed? I mean, to have — something like that — in his own church?'

'No, not really. He says she always chooses her moments carefully because she doesn't want the tabloids after her.'

★ ★ ★

That evening Agnes came out of Liverpool Street Station, crossed the road and went into the wine bar. Nothing had changed: the same light wood, airy spaces and noisy crowds. Athena was sitting in one corner and waved at her.

'Ghastly people, darling,' she said as Agnes joined her. 'Look at them. All that money. Wasted on them, sweetie. I hope this friend of yours we're meeting is nicer than that lot. Let me pour you some wine.'

Agnes took the glass and looked up to see Judy approaching their table.

'Hello,' she said to Agnes, and nodded at Athena. She seemed subdued, in a grey suit and a toned-down shade of lipstick. She and Athena eyed each other as she sat down.

'Athena, Judy. Judy, Athena.' Agnes waved

at them both vaguely.

Athena hadn't taken her eyes from Judy. She was staring, astonished. At last she found her voice. 'But — of all the people . . . Some kind of miracle . . . ' she said. Agnes and Judy stared back at her. 'That suit,' Athena managed to say at last. 'Where on earth did you get it? It's perfect, it's the one I've been looking for all winter, and you turn up here, a complete stranger, wearing it, and it looks so good on you, it really does . . . '

'Thank you.' Judy smiled.

'And now you're going to tell me it cost about what my flat is worth, from some fabulous shop in Bond Street.'

Judy leaned towards her. 'Ninety-five quid. Bargain, it was. I'll give you the address; they still had some in last time I passed.'

Athena beamed at her and raised her glass. 'I'm so glad Agnes introduced us,' she said.

Judy raised her glass back.

'I mean,' Athena went on, 'when I first heard about you, I wasn't too sure — all this money and unsuitable men. Mind you, who am I to talk, the history of my love life makes rather tacky reading, really.'

'I'm trying to change direction,' Judy agreed.

'It's so difficult, though, isn't it, with men? They're just so odd. Not like other people.

492

And then, I thought, with you going to the gym — '

'I've given that up,' Judy announced.

Agnes stared at her. 'The gym? But you're so — '

'No, it turns out it's really bad for you. Bad for the joints. We'll be a generation of arthritics, apparently. I've taken up yoga, a new kind, it's really calorie-burning, none of that cissy stuff, it's called astanga vinyasa. I've met the sweetest chap who introduced me. A journalist — you might have heard of him. Nick Madrid, he's called.'

'My boyfriend's called Nic,' Athena said. 'With a 'c'.'

'That's classy,' Judy said. 'Is he nice?'

'Yes.' Athena frowned. 'Yes, I'm beginning to think he is.'

★   ★   ★

Sunlight poured into the lounge at the community house, lightening the pale walls and soft green carpet. Helen sat opposite Agnes in an armchair, straight-backed and poised, draped in a cream linen dress.

'Well?' Agnes said.

Helen was silent, lost in thought. At last she said, 'I don't want to leave.' Agnes waited. 'What's been so strange is finding I'm less

493

sure. A year ago, I was full of certainty about this being my path. And now . . . now it seems full of obstacles and doubts . . . It's about Xenos, really. Ümit, I mean. It's amazing, how he can speak now. Some kind of miracle. Tad said it really was a miracle, something about the Virgin Mary weeping, but he seemed so matter-of-fact about it, I didn't know whether to believe him.'

Agnes looked at her, but said nothing. The sun shone through the branches of the horse chestnut tree outside, making flickering shadows on the wall.

'I keep thinking about him, about people like him, about the suffering in the world . . . and I know I should do something about it. But I don't know if this is the right way.'

'Does prayer help?'

Helen raised her eyes to Agnes's. 'Does it help you?'

'Sometimes.'

Outside in the street some children passed, shouting, kicking a ball.

'I just don't know what else I'd do.' Helen picked at a thread at her hem. 'I've come this far . . . It's just . . . ' She frowned. 'Is it good enough?' Again, her eyes met Agnes's. 'Is it good enough, to be here because I feel there's no going back, rather than because I feel positive about going forward?'

'It's good enough for most of us,' Agnes said.

Helen smiled. 'When I first joined the order, everyone else seemed so sure. All the sisters who'd been here for years, they all seemed as if they'd always known . . . and Louise. Louise being so sure. And these last few weeks, with all my doubts, you've given me hope, you know.'

'Me?'

'Yes. To know that someone can be full of doubt, and not sure why they're here, and yet, struggling with all that, still stay here.'

Agnes didn't say anything. It didn't feel like a compliment, but she supposed, perhaps, it was.

'Louise is leaving,' Helen said. 'Did you know?'

'Yes. We've talked. She was adamant.'

'Did you try and make her stay?'

Agnes wondered whether to bend the truth a little, decided not to. 'No,' she said. 'I didn't try and make her stay.'

Helen sighed. 'It's funny. She seemed so right at the beginning. But I think she was here because she was running away. She was trying to prove something to her family. Maybe you can only be here for its own sake, even if it all feels fragile and difficult and uncertain . . . '

Agnes looked at Helen, at the sun throwing feathery shadows across her face. 'Yes,' she said. 'I think perhaps you're right.'

★ ★ ★

That night she sat at her desk, re-reading Louise's letter to the provincial novice mistress. She recalled her conversation with Louise, sitting on the bed in Louise's tiny room. It had been brief.

'I have to go, Sister, you can see that.'

Agnes had been mostly silent, except to agree, at the end, that yes, perhaps Louise did have to go.

Now, she took out notepaper and a pen, and began to write a brief accompanying letter to Sister Michaela.

'I'm sorry to have to send you the enclosed . . . ' she wrote. She stared at the words, then screwed the paper up. Why should I be sorry? she thought. It's you, Lord, who've let her down. You should be writing this letter: *I'm sorry that I let her down. She thought I'd promised her a miracle. I'm afraid there are no guarantees. Signed, God.*

Agnes took a fresh sheet of paper and wrote a brief letter, outlining the nature of Louise's crisis and the conversation she'd had with her. She signed it, sealed it up with the

496

other and addressed it to the provincial office. She put it on the desk, next to another envelope, which was addressed to Sister Christiane, and which she hadn't yet sealed. Then she took out the letter from her mother's lawyers, and, picking up her pen, she composed an answer: *Messieurs, I shall be keeping the house for now. A friend will be renting it out . . .*

She remembered Judy's rapture at the idea. 'A real house? Red tiled roof? How many bedrooms? But that's fantastic. Don't you dare sell it. I'll buy it off you . . . Rent it off you, then. Yes, really, of course I'm serious. And your nice friend, Athena, she can come out and stay with me sometimes too. I've been looking for property in France for ages, but the Dordogne is so *passé*, isn't it? This is ideal. Just name your price.'

Agnes smiled at the idea of Athena and Judy in her mother's house. *I do not therefore need your services,* Agnes wrote, *in the disposal of the property, or at least not for the time being. I remain, messieurs, deeply indebted to you for the help you have given me with the rest of my mother's estate . . .*

A postponement, Agnes thought. She sealed the envelope to the lawyers, and then picked up the letter to Sister Christiane. She took it out of its envelope and re-read it.

Dear Christiane, Further to our recent discussion, I accept that next year, after seven years, it might well be appropriate to consider final vows, and I look forward to your guidance as to a suitable time to take them. Yours . . .

She replaced the letter in its envelope. She sealed the envelope, placed it carefully on her desk with her other correspondence, and turned out the light.

She sat in the darkness. No leap into faith, then, she thought. Not just yet. No big gamble. Just the steady, daily, endless acceptance that this is how it is. That this is how my story continues to unfold. And it took Helen, who's all those years younger than me, to say it. That it's fragile and difficult and uncertain, and yet you still stay anyway.

And I've managed to leave open the opportunity, she thought, getting ready for bed, to cavort on a beach in the south of France with Judy and Athena. Except they'd be eyeing up tasty geezers and I'd be left out.

★ ★ ★

That night the corridor was still flooded with sunlight, still wafting with white muslin, but there was no sand, and she reached the end of the corridor. This time there were two doors, no longer in shadow. She chose one and stood, her hand on the door handle, which was ornate and made of brass. She listened to the ticking of the clock, a soothing, gentle rhythm, counting time in the silence. There was no hurry.

As she began to turn the door handle, she woke up.

There is no hurry, she thought.

She glanced at the anniversary clock on the mantelpiece. It had stopped.

Damn, she thought, piling out of bed, wondering what the time was. A whole year since it was last wound. Typical that it should stop now, just when there's every reason to hurry. I'm supposed to catch a plane, and Julius is going to be here in a taxi to collect me and I won't be ready. So much for the perfect ordered universe of the clockmaker God.

Epilogue

The cemetery in the village was small and pretty. Some corners were well tended, with orderly graves, neatly engraved headstones, arrangements of fresh flowers. They walked slowly through the graveyard, the little group, Patrick, Agnes, Mary and Julius. Mary had taken Julius's arm and was leading them away from the straight paths, into an older part of the cemetery, where lichen clung to tombstones, crooked and weathered, where the paths were strewn with brambles.

'Here,' she said.

They stopped at a simple grave, its edges softened with moss. Agnes, standing at a distance, remembered the cemetery in her mother's village, the grave newly dug in the dusty Provençal earth. This was old, this grave, long closed.

Julius took a step forward, leaning heavily on Mary. He knelt at the side of the grave. Slowly he lifted one finger and traced the name, which stood out clearly. Catriona. He murmured the word.

Mary left him and came to join the others.